THE SEED OF
SYCORAX

ADAM J. MANGUM

Rocket Crossing, LLC • adamjmangum.com

Cover design and interior design by Megan Hemmert
Character design by Santo Ibarra

Published by Rocket Crossing, LLC

First Edition, July 2017

To Steven and William
for sparking my imagination,
and for Mom for letting it grow.

ACKNOWLEDGMENTS

In the summer of 2001, I attended the Utah Shakespearean Festival in Cedar City, Utah. I'd never been a big Shakespeare fan. My wife's parents, Bonnie and Darryl Lee, had a family tradition of going down to the festival and all their children adored Shakespeare. I went, ungrudgingly, because that's what you do with the new in-laws (we'd been married less than a year). I thought I'd endure the week and then go back to things I liked.

Instead, I fell in love with twos plays, *The Tempest* and *Julius Caesar.* While watching *The Tempest*, I couldn't help myself from imagining it as a science fiction story (though I originally conceived it as a screenplay). Sixteen years later, here is my retelling of Shakespeare's classic. Thank you, Bonnie and Darryl (and Kathleen), for opening my eyes to Shakespeare's wonderful world. His stories have fueled my imagination as they have generations before me.

The way Caliban is portrayed in this series has a lot to do with the performance I saw in 2001. Caliban was played by David Ivers, a legend of the Utah Shakespearean Festival. The whole cast and crew that year deserve my thanks.

I also wanted to thank all the readers who helped me work through many drafts. These readers include: Elizabeth Brown, Megan Hemmert, Kara Hill, Sean Jackson, Kristy Jensen, Kristine Kerr, Michelle Kopp, Bonnie Lee, Dan Lee, Darryl Lee, Tiffany Lewis, Kayla MacNielle, Jenn Mangum, Rachel Mangum, Stacy Mills and Chris Sorensen. The first couple drafts of this manuscript were bad. My readers helped make it not so bad.

The Sycorax Series was made possible through a crowdfunding campaign. Thank you to all twenty-eight backers, particularly my parents, Don and Diane, my sister Rachel, my brother Matt and his wife

Jen, Michael Flint (who pushed for backers on the last day), and the anonymous Robert Hutt. And special thanks to Jed Higginson whose final pledge pushed us into funded territory.

Santo Ibarra created the awesome character art seen throughout this series. I'm not a visual artist in the slightest degree, and Santo brought these characters to life. My descriptions and visions of these characters were enhanced by his interpretations. Megan Hemmert designed the covers and did the layout. Without Megan and Santo, this book would look nothing like the visually-stunning piece that is it.

I worked with two editors on this project: Corwin Zahn and Stephanie Loree. Corwin helped re-shape the story and cover many plot holes. Stephanie helped me refine the manuscript and her insights made these stories better.

In June 2016, I published my first novel, *Peak Crosser*. It had been a lifelong dream enabled by my wonderful partner Kathleen. Her faith in me transformed a would-be writer into the actual thing. Once the first three books in *The Sycorax Series* are out, I will have published four books in less than a year with many more to come. Without Kathleen, I'd still be dreaming instead of doing.

ALSO BY ADAM J. MANGUM

The Sycorax Series
Caliban's World
Claribel and Caliban
Seeds and Masters

The Empire of the Peaks
Peak Crosser
Peaks Falling (coming soon)
War of Three (coming soon)

caliban's world

PART 1

chapter 1

CALIBAN

othing in Caliban's life compared to the taste of sticky sweetbread. Caliban sat on the top of Mother's building, watching the sun slide across the sky. He held sticky, wonderful sweetbread in his hands, the sugar melting onto his fingertips. He ate it hurriedly, like someone might appear at any moment and snatch it away. Mother had forbidden him to eat sweetbread, said it made him too hyper, too fat. But Caliban was always hyper, so he didn't understand how Mother knew the difference. And he wasn't fat at all, not like silly humans. Caliban was all muscles and bones.

He'd stolen this piece of sweetbread from one of Mother's friends, a man named Jules. Mother always said Caliban was dumb, but Jules was dumber than Caliban. The sloppy, fat man always sneaked extra sweetbread from the kitchens, thinking no one noticed. But Caliban noticed, and Caliban had crept into Jules's room and taken it. Who would Jules complain to? Mother was not nice to thieves, and stealing from a thief was as easy as it got.

The sweetbread tasted like he was eating bright sunshine. The sugar danced on his tongue and the crusty shell crunched between his jagged teeth. All of it melted at the back of his mouth. Mother and her friends did not seem to enjoy sweetbread as much as Caliban did. Maybe their human tongues couldn't taste as well as he could.

After closing his eyes for a few moments to relish another bite, Caliban looked out beyond Mother's building. To the northwest stood the jungle, filled with Mother's most terrible beasties. It was thick and damp, like taking a bath but not in a good way. To the northwest was the forest, a pleasant place. Caliban did not walk it often, but the animals there were natural and not all crazy killers. It smelled of trees, flowers, and dirt. He loved that forest.

The gray plains stretched to the south, filled with the unfriendly, pointy-nosed wolves and the gray fatties. Everything on the plains was a dull gray: the animals, the ground, the plants. It was also boring, unless a pointy-nosed wolf hunted Caliban. He hated the wolves. A pack of seven had almost killed him once, before he ripped their silly heads off. He only ventured into the gray land when Mother made him.

"Caliban!" Mother's high voice rang through the air, echoing from some speakers Caliban couldn't see. "Wherever you're hiding, I need you. Gestation Room Seven. Now."

He stuffed the last bite of sweetbread into his mouth and licked his fingers; he couldn't let her see or smell his sweetbread. After he was satisfied every speck was gone, he hurried inside.

He sprinted down the gleaming hallways, avoiding the slow, silly humans clogging his path. Less than two minutes after Mother's call, Caliban approached Gestation Room Seven. She must have created a new monster, something she wanted to test. He would kill it like he killed the others. She would curse, and her friends would avoid her angry gaze. Life in Mother's world repeated over and over again, and Caliban liked that.

He pressed his hand to the palm thing, and the door slid open, revealing a room filled with Mother and her friends. She stood in the middle, barking at them as usual. All her friends dressed the same when they worked: a one piece white suit.

Mother didn't dress like her friends. She wore colorful clothes, usually pants and a shirt. She was also the smallest, shorter than her human friends, the shortest human Caliban had met. But she was somehow bigger, even bigger than him. Everyone feared her, Caliban included. He was bigger and stronger, but he was somehow smaller.

"Caliban." His name always sounded like a curse when it came from Mother's mouth. "What took you so long?"

He shrugged. He could understand Mother's language, but he struggled to speak it, and he refused to when her friends were around. He knew they mocked him for his slow, stumbling speech. Four years since his birth, and he could barely mumble. It was one of the reasons Mother hated Caliban instead of loving him.

"Never mind." Mother hurried over to a human-sized gestation pod. "I'd like you to meet someone."

Caliban smiled, flashing his razor teeth. He liked maiming her creations; it was the only fun he ever had.

The pod opened, and his smile disappeared. It wasn't another monster; it was another Caliban.

No, that wasn't quite right. Caliban was tall, but not abnormally so among humans. This Caliban was much taller and more muscular. He shared the same light green skin Caliban had on his face, but the rest of the new Caliban's body was not covered in lizard scales like Caliban. The new one had smooth skin like a human but it was green instead of peach or brown. The new Caliban's hands were also more human. Caliban looked at his own left hand, oversized with three elongated fingers. The ugly new Caliban had normal-sized hands, though all his fingers ended in claws. Like the old Caliban, new Caliban was hairless. His pee thingy was also exposed, not covered by a flap like Caliban's.

He hated the new Caliban.

"Arise, Balthazar." Mother spoke the words, and the new Caliban, whose stupid name was Balthazar, opened his eyes.

Caliban did not like Balthazar's eyes. They were yellow like his, with large black circles in the middle. But he knew so few words, he couldn't think of the right ones to describe them. Scary. Maybe scary was the right word.

Balthazar flexed his face, stretching muscles for the first time. He looked at Mother's friends, and they seemed to see the same scariness in Balthazar's eyes. Two of the humans stepped back.

Balthazar exited the pod and stretched his limbs. He smiled, a scary smile that matched his eyes like a cup of chocolate drink matched sweetbread.

"Balthazar." Mother called his name, not like she did Caliban's. She spoke with pride, not with hate. "Can you hear and understand me?"

The green creature nodded, his eyes softer when he looked on her.

Caliban remembered his own birth. Well, he kind of remembered it. He'd been confused, and he hadn't understood Mother. But he'd known her, was drawn to her voice and followed her direction, even if it had taken him a year to really understand what she said. Sometimes he wished he'd never grown to understand. Mother wouldn't be so mean if Caliban didn't understand.

"Can you speak, Balthazar?" Her face was bright, her eyes excited. Why didn't Mother ever look at him that way?

"Yes, Mother." Balthazar's voice was raw, like Caliban's was after a deep sleep. "I understand you well." He looked at Caliban. "Who is this?"

"Your lesser self." Her words pained Caliban like she'd taken a piece of sweetbread right from his mouth.

Balthazar sneered, his bright white teeth flashing.

"What now, Mother?" the creature asked.

"The others will conduct some tests. We need to make sure everything is right."

Balthazar's gaze did not leave Caliban, who looked away under the new one's evil eyes.

"You can go, Caliban."

Caliban looked at Mother, wanting her to say something comforting, wanting her to say she loved him still. But did she love anyone? He had walked in on her and a man once touching each other with their clothes off, and he'd heard some of her friends say that was love. But Caliban didn't want that--he wanted anything, a pat, a kind word, anything.

He looked up at Mother, but her eyes were like Balthazar's: indescribable.

Caliban left the gestation room. He felt cold and sad, angry and confused. Why did she need another him? Wasn't he enough?

He would go to the pleasant forest and kill something, maybe a small bird or one of the little cats. Maybe then he'd feel better.

Caliban sat in the forest, some stolen sweetbread in his mouth. Even sweetbread seemed less sweet now that the new Caliban was around.

Over the past several weeks, Caliban had avoided Balthazar and Mother. It was easy to do. No one seemed to care about Caliban any longer. He had been their greatest accomplishment, and even though he had been mocked, he had also been feared and given some respect. Now he was given nothing. Being ignored was far worse than being mocked.

Caliban had decided not to call the new one Balthazar. He would call him Smoothie, for his smooth skin. Lizard men like them shouldn't have smooth skin like silly humans; they should have lizard skin, like Caliban's, that's what made them lizard men. And his kind should not have their piss maker on the outside. But Smoothie did, and he wore clothes. Lizard men should not wear clothes. Stupid, silly Smoothie.

Of course, he only called Balthazar Smoothie in his head; he didn't dare say it out load.

"Hello Caliban."

Caliban jumped to his feet, quickly brushing the sugar from his chest and licking his fingers.

Jules stood there, the fatty Caliban had stolen the sweetbreads from. He didn't wear the white work clothing, but instead wore a loose-fitting shirt and blue pants. This clothing made him look less fat.

"Can I sit with you?"

Caliban nodded.

They both sat, and the forest grass retracted into the ground, curling away from them. Caliban felt nervous like he did before being chastised by Mother. Was Jules here to yell at him? To tell him that Smoothie was a better lizard man than he was?

He stared at Jules. His face was younger than most of Mother's friends, no lines around the eyes. His hair was blond and unmarked by white. Caliban had never seen a human child, but he'd seen pictures of the little, weak, fatty humans. At this moment, Jules looked like an overgrown child.

"Do you ever wonder who you are?" Jules asked without glancing at Caliban. "Do you ever wonder if you have a soul? If you lived before your birth?" He finally looked at Caliban.

But Caliban looked away. He knew who he was: a lizard man, the son of Sycorax, his mother. Had he lived before he was born? A stupid question from the fat-faced man. Didn't born mean you didn't live before?

Jules looked back at the sky. "I often wonder what we're doing here. Endless funds, terrific science, but no talk of morality. We've created new, sentient life, but we never talk about why or discuss even if we should. We're like stumbling gods, playing with the puzzle of life."

Jules met Caliban's gaze. His eyes were not like Mother's. Jules's held something else, something so unfamiliar to Caliban that it was as hard to place as it had been when he first saw Smoothie. He had never seen a look like that from Mother or any of her friends.

Jules's eyes were soft. Maybe it was kindness.

"I am sorry Caliban. The sweetbread is yours, it was always meant for you. I'm sorry I can't do more." Jules stood and walked over the hill and toward Mother's building.

Caliban curled up in his room, feeling cold. Mother's building was often cold, as humans seemed to need to be coddled all the time. He preferred the warmth of the sun to the cold metal of her building.

It had been two days since Jules had come to him, and Caliban still struggled to understand the fatty's words. What was the man sorry for? Caliban felt sorry when he disappointed Mother, which happened often. But what did the fatty need to feel sorry for? And Jules knew about Caliban stealing his sweetbread, but he wasn't angry? How long had the fatty known? Was Jules his friend? Caliban had never had a friend.

But it didn't matter now. When next Caliban had gone to Jules's room, it was empty, none of the fatty's man-trinkets anywhere to be found. And the drawer with the sweetbreads was empty, not even some sugar to lick up.

As he'd walked away from Jules's room, he'd seen Smoothie in the hall. The new lizard man had been walking with a group of Mother's friends who were studying Smoothie's every movement.

Those eyes found Caliban even though he slinked against the wall to avoid them. Even when he turned his head, he could feel those eyes on him. So Caliban would not call Balthazar Smoothie anymore; it was too nice a name. He would call him Bad Eyes.

Caliban had been in his room since passing Bad Eyes. He'd seen Mother shortly after, and she had commanded him to remain in his room. A small, shapeless woman brought him food, and he did nothing but eat, sleep, and stare at the wall for an entire day. He also tried to wipe the image of Bad Eyes from his mind. But he couldn't. The eyes followed him, even here in his room, even with Bad Eyes far away.

The door opened, and Mother stood there. She rarely came to visit Caliban, and he popped up, eager to greet her.

Her eyes held none of the badness they'd held the day Bad Eyes was born. But they weren't nice like Jules's had been. Mother's eyes were empty like she looked at nothing.

"Come, Caliban."

She turned, and Caliban followed.

"I thought you were it," she said as they walked. "The day you were born was the happiest day of my existence. I had worked so hard for that moment I could hardly believe it. We'd finally created sentient life, a weapon to fulfill my destiny."

Caliban glowed inside. His birth had made her happy? He wanted to jump. He wanted to sing, though he wasn't sure if he could. Caliban had never felt so happy.

"But we'd made a mistake."

His happiness escaped like air from a balloon.

"In our effort to make your mind pliable, we made you stupid. You barely talk, and your actions are bound to your basest instincts. On a battlefield, you would follow commands, but you cannot think, cannot adjust. A machine is a better soldier than you."

Caliban felt small and cold.

"But we may have found something now. Your brother may be the one."

Stupid Bad Eyes. Caliban wanted to tear those eyes from his stupid face so she would know Caliban was better, that he was stronger. His birth was more special than Bad Eye's. Caliban would show Mother.

She looked at him, smiling. "You're so simple Caliban, easier to read than a child. Do you want to show you're better than Balthazar? Do you want to hurt your brother?"

Caliban nodded.

"Good."

They arrived at Arena One, and a door opened before them. Bad Eyes stood in the middle of the room.

"Show me, Caliban, that you're not a wasteful mistake."

He entered the room, and the door closed behind him.

He had spent many hours in Arena One tearing apart some of Mother's creations, showing how strong he was. He'd entered each time feeling strong, powerful. But not today. Today he felt small, powerless.

The walls surrounding one side of the arena were made of thick glass. When Caliban fought, a dozen or more of Mother's friends would gather to watch and take notes. But as he looked at the glass, he saw a sea of her friends. It was as if every human in her building had come to see this. He hadn't seen this many watchers since he'd fought here the first few times years ago.

Caliban's eyes wandered until he found Mother; she was easy to spot, she was so small. She stood in front next to the glass, and when Caliban's eyes landed on her, he tried to smile. Smiles never felt right, but he tried. She returned the smile, and it filled him with hope. He would show Mother, he would show her friends. Caliban was strong. Caliban was special.

He looked to the other side of the room. Smooth-skinned Bad Eyes stood there, taller than Caliban by a head. He wore clothes, some uniform Caliban had not seen before, a darker green than his skin, tight on his form. At least Caliban wouldn't have to see his pisser. If only they had covered his eyes.

With a sudden leap, Caliban sprang at Bad Eyes. The new lizard man's eyes widened with surprise as Caliban's oversized claw-hand raked across his stupid face. The bigger lizard man staggered backward, green blood streaking from a scrape which stretched from below his left eye to his chin. Caliban looked over to the windows and saw astonished faces everywhere. No one had believed Caliban could hurt Bad Eyes. But Caliban would not just hurt the new lizard man, he'd destroy him, spreading his limbs across the arena like he'd done to other animals before. Caliban would be everyone's favorite again.

As he prepared to leap, he stopped. Bad Eyes wasn't moving, wasn't scared. He smiled without happiness. His bright white teeth shined in the arena lights. He licked some of the blood which trickled near the corner of his mouth.

"You think you can win," the lizard man said.

Caliban said nothing, did not even nod. Bad Eyes's wicked smile froze him in place.

"Can't you talk, little one?"

Caliban sneered. "Caliban talk."

Bad Eyes laughed.

Caliban charged, his claw-hand reaching to dig those evil eyes out of Bad Eye's skull.

The other lizard man side-stepped, easily dodging the strike. He still smiled. Caliban needed to rip that smile off his stupid face.

He swiped again, but this time Bad Eyes blocked with his hand, and then kicked out, a quick and powerful blow which sent Caliban backward to the floor. Caliban wasn't hurt, but he was stunned. Bad Eyes was fast, maybe faster than Caliban.

Bad Eyes did not wait, leaping at Caliban. Caliban tried to keep him off by stretching out his leg, but Bad Eyes avoided the leg and landed on Caliban, his clawed hands digging into his chest. Caliban roared with pain as Bad Eyes's buried his claws deep.

He kneed Bad Eyes in the side, and the big lizard man tumbled before popping up to his feet.

Caliban looked at himself. Eight large holes burned in his chest. He howled. No one had ever hurt Caliban this way. He'd had scrapes, had bruises, but nothing like this. Bad Eyes's attack had been faster than the retracting forest grass.

Caliban jumped to his feet, snarling.

He attacked, but Bad Eyes blocked almost every blow. The ones that got through were only glancing. Caliban went faster, sending blows in a fury beyond anything he'd done before. He hadn't even known he was this fast, this strong. But it didn't matter. Bad Eyes was faster, stronger, bigger, better.

Caliban stopped fighting and stepped back. Breaths escaped in heavy bursts and his heart thundered in his chest.

The bigger lizard man waited, the evil smile gone from his lips. His eyes seemed to soften, or maybe Caliban imagined that. Could Bad Eyes really go good?

Bad Eyes looked toward Mother, and Caliban found her as well. She nodded.

Bad Eyes attacked with a sudden fury. Caliban blocked the first few blows, but they came too fast. One kick struck his hip, sending a shockwave of pain through his body. A punch hit his neck, knocking out his breath. And a backhanded strike to his chin sent Caliban sprawling. He tasted salty blood in his mouth and felt the cold floor against his skin. His own breathing sounded like a distant echo from another room.

But there was no break this time. Bad Eyes jumped on top of him, raining down blows. A flurry to his chest until Caliban felt his ribs snap like tree branches. A stomp to his knee forced out a massive howl, and he looked down to find his leg bending in the wrong direction. And then came a bash to Caliban's skull and a sickening crack.

Bad Eyes paused for a moment, but it didn't matter. Caliban moved his eyes; they were the one part of his body that still obeyed his commands. Bad Eyes's eyes were not bad any longer, not harsh like that first day. They looked sad, kind of how Jules's had looked a few days before. Caliban didn't understand.

"I'm sorry, brother," Not-So-Bad Eyes said.

He lifted both hands high above his head and brought them down on Caliban's face. He heard the bones in his face crack like a tree splitting in two. Then the world faded, and Caliban welcomed the painless dark.

chapter 2

THE WHOLE

he tribe entered a new system, the exhilaration of discovery pulsing through all five members. The Whole had never visited this system in its thousands of millennia. Even with thirteen hundred and thirty-one clusters, three thousand seven hundred and seventy-three tribes, and nineteen thousand nine hundred and ninety-one members, exploring the entirety of the universe would stretch across infinite millennia, if the Whole lasted that long.

Tribe 1746 stretched across this new system, first exploring the space between its star and the five planets orbiting it. The humans called this place Vesta, but the tribe gave it its proper designation.

Member Five of Tribe 1746 most enjoyed calculating the orbits of each planet around the star, of each satellite around their planets. There were two meteor belts: one between the first and second planets, and one between the fourth and fifth. The universe offered such delicious variety. No system was the same. This one had large gas planets--four and five--and three molten core rock planets--one, two, and three. Though no individual component could be called unique, the uniqueness came from the system's composition. Five sailed through the second meteor belt, bringing their essence together with the other members.

What do we think of this system? Member One's thoughts echoed in each member's mind.

Each member responded to One, the oldest and wisest of their tribe. One had lived 2,339 years, the second oldest member in the Whole. He'd seen so much of the mapped universe, yet Five could feel One's enthusiasm leaking through their bond.

Let's visit each of the planets, One suggested, and the tribe agreed.

Breaking contact, Five headed to the fifth planet. Five members, five planets, perfect alignment.

The fifth planet was smaller than the fourth but similar in its composition. Swirling hydrogen and helium composed almost all of it. Five dove through the gas, stretching their essence throughout it to measure it properly. It registered in the forty-seventh percentile of gas planets in the mapped universe.

After hours of quantifying and exploring, Five left the planet behind. They moved among its rings and satellites. Thirty-one moons floated around the fifth planet, seven of them registering in size above the fiftieth percentile for moons of gas planets of this size. Five carefully catalogued the content of each moon. Moon thirteen was the most interesting. It had once held very primitive, microscopic life. By Five's calculation, life had flashed on moon thirteen for less than a millennia. Though life existed abundantly throughout the universe, its beginning was so delicate, fraught with a million times more failures than successes. Most flashes of life winked out before they could leave a mark on the universe.

Five felt the other members at the edge of her essence, their exhilaration wafting from them as they explored their own planets. Three explored a lifeless rock planet with massive electrical storms and active volcanoes combining into a spectacular show of lights and color. Four dove through the triple rings wrapped around the system's other gas planet. Their happiness matched Five's.

Five pulled their attention back the satellites of the system's firth planet. A human-made satellite orbited among the thirty-one natural orbiters. It was a dead thing, no electricity pulsing through it. Five had never encountered human life, but had encountered some of their technology. They used some of their power to bring the human-made creation to life. Lights and sensors tried to function, but there had been too much decay and damage. Five stopped trying to get it to function. Whatever purpose humans had had for this thing, it had long since stopped fulfilling that.

A thrill ran through them. What if humans inhabited this system or used it as a way point? They could finally encounter one of the universe's more fascinating creations. Humans ranked among the greatest curiosities ever catalogued by the Whole.

A sudden pulse shot through the tribe. Five removed their focus from the satellites of the fifth planet and moved toward the tribe. What did Five feel from One? Five could not place the strong emotion.

As Five reached for the other members, a strange sensation arrived, an emptiness Five had never felt before: Two was not there. But that was impossible. Two was the second oldest in the tribe, more than two millennia, but too young to fade, and fading only came after years of feeling its approaching claim; members did not fade by accident.

But Five could not feel Two. Five's emotions now echoed the strange sensation which came through One: worry and fear.

Did member Two fade? Four's thought reflected Five's feeling.

No, One responded. *Two still exists, but their existence is shielded from us.*

Surely this has happened before, pleaded Three.

One's fear pulsed through the tribe, answering Three's question.

Two was exploring the second planet, One projected. *We must find Two. There are humans on that planet and strange, unnatural life. Be wary.*

Be wary. Five had never received instructions like those before. What did members of the Whole need to be wary of? Nothing could kill a member, nothing could even harm them. Members were born through the will and creation of the Whole, and they faded at the will of the Whole. Nothing threatened a member.

The four remaining members of Tribe 1746 descended on the second planet, stretching their essences to cover it, sharing each other's thoughts, emotions, and experiences.

Even as they searched for Two, they couldn't help themselves in cataloguing and classifying each piece of the planet. A small jungle grabbed Five's attention. It was dense, teaming with life and humid air. They examined one of the trees, and felt its being. The tall, vine-filled trees were not natural. Their DNA did not descend, but began with a seed holding the potential of these exact trees. As Five reached out to the fierce predators and flittering insects, the unnaturalness of each life form remained constant. Within this strange haven every fierce cat lizard, burrowing rodent, and the strange spiders as large as the trees, had been created. Nothing in this jungle had evolved according to the natural order of things. Five reached into the collective memory of the Whole and found nothing like it among all the millennia of their work.

Five tried to return and join the other members, but a sudden emptiness filled them. The other members were gone, just as Two had disappeared. In their distracted state, Five had not noticed the other members dissolve into the same nothingness which had seemingly enveloped Two.

Part of Five's mind urged returning to the birthplace, contacting the Whole, warning of what had happened on this strange little planet. But curiosity warred within their soul. So Five pushed on toward the small human settlement.

Member Five found a massive structure stretching for hundreds of span across a gray desert. The shiny metal roof reflected the star's bright daylight. Could this place be the source of the unnatural, aggressive life teeming in that jungle? Five drew closer to the building, hoping to discover both the humans who'd created such abominable life and what had happened to Tribe 1746.

A sudden pull gripped Five, and their essence contracted. What was this pull? Whatever the force was, it dragged Five into the human structure.

Their essence constricted until it was hardly bigger than an insect. Five could only see light and could sense only the minds of a few, small humans.

And then Five felt nothing and saw only darkness. After two hundred years of constant exploration and feeling, the aloneness stirred an unknown terror in their being, an emotional wave as strong as the gravity of a star. They tried to push their essence outward, to expand and fly once more. But nothing happened. Five had fallen into whatever had captured the others. Five reached out, hoping that sharing this undefinable prison would connect them once more. But they still felt nothing of the tribe. Five tried to reach further to feel their connection to their cluster. But where there had been constant information and sensation, there was only emptiness, darkness, and frustration. Time seemed warped, as Five could no longer determine its progression through the movement of the cosmos.

Horror built upon the fear, and Five struck out with their essence in a violent push of energy which would have crippled a planet or wounded a star. But nothing happened; the abyss of blackness reigned.

The humans had not only created life, they wielded power enough to capture members, maybe even destroy them. Was Five still alive? Did they find themselves in a human-made prison, or was this what happened when members faded?

Five tried again to connect their essence with the Whole, with any member, clamoring for freedom. But Five found nothing.

chapter 3

BROKEN

Caliban often worried about death. Mother had taught him that many humans believed they lived forever, that their souls continued after they died. She said those humans were wrong, but never said what she believed. He'd once asked one of her friends about it, and the friend said the next life was painless and wonderful. Caliban had hoped her friend was right.

But now he had his doubts. The world had been nothing but pain and flashes of light since Balthazar had beaten him. He would open his eyes and the cursed brightness blinded him, like looking at the sun. Caliban had tried looking at the sun, and this was worse.

But the brightness was nothing compared to the pain. Each time his eyes opened, his entire body screamed at him, the injuries his brother had given him pulsing. Caliban hated pain, hated his brother, and hated all of Mother's friends. If this was life after death, Caliban wanted no part of it; the humans could keep their life after death.

Then a day came with less pain, and when Caliban opened his eyes, he didn't think it was life after death. He recognized the room--it was the same medical room Caliban had stayed in when he'd been sick three years before. He'd vomited for days and coughed for weeks. Why would the afterlife look like Mother's medical room?

One of Mother's friends, a tall woman with small boobs and short hair, stood next to the table, tapping something into her pad. She looked at him but did not smile.

"Can you hear me, Caliban?"

He nodded, but when he tried to move his arms and legs, nothing happened. He looked down at himself. New scars covered his body: too many to count on his chest, one large one along his hip, and another across one of his knees. He wiggled his toes and flexed his hands, but he couldn't move his arms or legs.

"We have you under bioelectrical restraints," the woman said, but Caliban did not know what those words meant. "You almost died, but you're going to live. Sycorax wanted you to live."

Mother had wanted him saved? Maybe she still loved Caliban even though Balthazar was stronger and meaner. She seemed to love best whatever could hurt more. But maybe Caliban still had a small piece of her love, which would be better than none.

"When I move?" Caliban asked.

The woman raised her eyebrow. "Tomorrow, probably. We have two or three more tests to run."

The woman pushed something on her pad and Caliban drifted back to sleep.

The next time Caliban awoke, he could move. A different Mother's friend was there, a short man with hair on his face. Caliban couldn't grow hair on his face, and he'd always wanted to.

"Stand up slowly, Caliban," the bearded man said. "It won't be the same."

Won't be the same? Caliban did not understand. Life would be different with Balthazar but not too different. Caliban would find ways to please Mother, and he'd find ways to steal sweetbread. Everything would be fine.

Caliban stood up, but then collapsed to the ground, banging his head on the unforgiving floor. Caliban was confused. Had he forgotten how to stand? He'd known how to stand, walk, and run the day he was born.

"Easy, Caliban," the bearded man said. "Your injuries were severe. Walking will be difficult."

Again, Caliban did not understand, but he tried to stand up. He took a step forward, but his right hip exploded in pain, and he collapsed again.

"Leg no work," Caliban managed to say.

Bearded man shook his head. "We did not repair all the damage to your hip and spine. You will have to learn how to walk with your new injuries."

Caliban wanted to smash the bearded man's hip and ask him to learn to walk this way. Couldn't Mother's friends fix everything? Why didn't they fix Caliban right?

Caliban stood again, and this time hopped on his left leg. No, this would be silly and take too long. Caliban tried stepping on the right leg again, but along came another wave of pain and another collapse.

"No matter how often you try that, the result will be the same."

Caliban glared at the bearded man. Did the funny little man think Caliban was stupid?

Caliban stood on his good leg and swung at the man, backhanding him. Blood squirted from his mouth as he crashed to the ground.

"You try stand now," Caliban spit. The man smelled of blood and some silly scent he'd sprayed on himself after bathing. Silly, stupid humans.

"Enough, Caliban." Mother's voice rang through the room. "You know that striking my friends is against the rules."

Caliban tried to stand, even though he couldn't see her. But his stance was crooked, and being upright shot pain through his hip and legs.

"Why?" Caliban asked.

"Why what, Caliban?"

"Why no fix leg?"

She laughed. "I needed you to remember your place, remember your failure. You'll still be of use to me, just not in the way you were before."

Caliban tucked his head to his knee. He wanted to cry, but he knew he shouldn't. Mother hated crying.

So he crawled over to Mother's friend, the motion less painful than standing or walking. The bearded man did not move, just lay still on the floor. Humans were so weak; one blow should not kill anything, but apparently it did a human.

The door slid open, and two more of her friends stood there, the ones dressed in blue with the guns. Caliban did not see these men often, but he knew they did as Mother commanded.

"Come with us," one of the men ordered.

Caliban followed them down the hall, limping along on his hands and feet. It was awkward to move this way, but it worked, and his hip hurt less than before though it ached constantly. Caliban would have to get used to the pain.

He followed the men into a door he'd never entered. As he walked into the room, Caliban recognized it, but he'd never been on this side. It was Arena Two, and he was behind the glass wall instead of in front of it. Two dozen of Mother's white-clad friends stood around with pads, looking at numbers and tapping notes. Mother stood there, her back to Caliban.

"Come see the future, Caliban," she said, and Caliban limped up next to her.

On the other side of the glass wall stood Balthazar, but he wasn't alone. Four more lizard men, all the equal to Caliban's first brother, stood beside Balthazar. While Caliban had suffered in bright light and pain, Mother had been busy creating more brothers.

"Release the beasts," she commanded.

A door opened across from his brothers, and a dozen massive ape creatures entered. Each of them stood as tall as Mother's newest creations, with thick arms and huge hands. One of them roared as they entered, revealing sharp fangs. The others followed their leader, bellowing. Balthazar and his brothers turned to face the threat. As strong as the lizard brothers were, the ape creatures looked even stronger.

Caliban had fought one of these ape beasts before. They were extremely strong but slow. Still, it had taken Caliban more than thirty minutes to defeat it, and the stupid muscled beast had given Caliban a headache for days. But he'd won.

Now there were a dozen of them, and only five lizard brothers.

"I think we're pushing them too far, too fast," a woman standing near Mother said. "We need more time."

"We are out of time," Mother responded, her eyes cold and her voice even cooler. "That fool from Lanopi is due here next month." She turned to face the woman who'd spoken. "Would you like to be the one to answer why, after a billion credits and nearly seven years, we still don't have a working prototype, let alone an army?"

The woman's eyes fell to the floor, and she asked no more questions.

Mother turned. "Balthazar, lead your brothers and kill these beasts."

Balthazar nodded, his evil eyes returning. He nodded to the other four, and they spread out across the arena floor. The ape beasts howled again, but this time an equally chilling howl met theirs. It came from the snarling mouths of the lizard brothers. The foul screeching made the ape beasts pause, look at each other, and then back at Balthazar and his brothers.

Suddenly Balthazar and his brothers moved into the pack of ape beasts, and the violence began. Caliban wanted to join them; he could feel the anger building in him, the desire to smash the ape beasts into submission. But Caliban was weak now. He couldn't stand or walk, not like before. But Caliban's lizard brothers were strong like he used to be. Stronger.

Caliban's eyes never left Balthazar. Bad Eyes tore into the leader ape, ripping its throat open with his claws. The beast brought its hands up trying to stop the fountain of blood, but the blood flowed down into its thick fur. Balthazar stepped closer to the leader and struck the ape with a blow to the face. Its skull cracked, and the leader collapsed to the ground.

Two ape beasts growled and descended on Balthazar. Caliban's first brother rolled between them, sprang to a crouch, and slashed them behind their knees with his claws. Both howled in pain, one collapsing from the wound. Balthazar grabbed the head of the one who still stood and twisted until it cracked.

Two more beasts attacked, grabbing Balthazar from behind and pinning him to the ground. They wailed on him, two-handed strikes to Balthazar's chest. For a moment, it appeared the new lizard man would lose and die, crushed by the mindless ape beasts.

But in between blows, Balthazar arched his back, stood on his hands and kicked both beasts in the face. Using his arms, he flipped onto his feet. Both beasts stumbled back, stunned by the sudden kick. Balthazar used their confused moment to slash one of them across the chest and then jab his claws into the neck of the other. He grabbed both of their skulls and slammed them together. A violent crack echoed through the arena, and both beasts slumped to the ground.

Balthazar turned to a fallen ape beast who struggled to climb to its feet. Balthazar gripped its head, digging his claws into its neck. As the lame beast swung weakly at Caliban's brother, Balthazar pulled the beast's head from its body, flinging the head aside. The head struck the window, blood splattering in an arc around it.

Bad Eyes turned to another beast who had one of his brothers pinned, its wrinkled hands squeezing the lizard man's throat. Balthazar kicked the beast in its side, sending it flying as if Balthazar had kicked a puny human. As the beast landed on its back, Balthazar landed on its chest, pounding its face with both hands. Then Balthazar dug into the beast's chest. After a few moments, he turned to look at the gathered crowd, the beast's heart in his right hand. Bad Eyes screamed and threw the heart against the window, blood splattering in a pattern as tall as a human.

Caliban looked across the arena. All the ape beasts were either dead or close to it, moaning on the ground. The four other lizard men gathered around Balthazar. Blood drenched his hands, and gore splattered his face and chest. It was beautiful. Balthazar was pure destruction. Mother had been right: Balthazar was indeed better than Caliban. Caliban bowed his head in respect.

Balthazar and his brothers walked up to the window, staring with their hungry eyes at the pathetic, fleshy, stupid humans.

"Is that all you have?" Balthazar bellowed. "Can you offer us no more challenge? Bring twenty, thirty, forty of these beasts, and I will rip out their hearts and serve them to you." Balthazar looked at what remained of the heart he'd thrown against the window. "I am Balthazar."

Caliban looked at Mother's friends. Their faces were pale, and all of them except Mother had backed away from the glass. One short man knelt and heaved up his lunch. The stench of the vomit spread through the room, but the others did not take their eyes off Balthazar and the other lizard brothers.

Mother walked up close to the glass, her equally bad eyes matching Balthazar's. She stood defiantly.

After a few moments, the four other lizard men wilted under her gaze like one of the wild purple flowers Caliban liked so much but died soon after being picked. But Balthazar did not shrink against her glare. Caliban wished he had Balthazar's courage, wished he could be so brave and strong. Maybe Balthazar could teach Caliban how.

The doors to the arena opened, and the armed guards who'd accompanied Caliban stood there, their rifles trained on the five lizard men.

"Come with us," one of the guards said, though his voice wavered like Caliban's did when he asked Mother for extra food.

The four younger brothers quickly obeyed, but Balthazar stood there for a moment, his eyes still locked on Mother. He smiled his Bad Eyes smile and then followed his brothers out of the room.

"He's mentally unstable," the questioning woman said to Mother. "He's psychotic. He could never be used as a soldier."

Mother turned toward her friends. "Probably not. Dial back the aggression some in the next models. Destroy the four other Gen 2s."

A man-friend of Mother's wrinkled his forehead. "What about Balthazar? Shouldn't we put him down, too?"

Caliban gasped. They wouldn't destroy Bad Eyes, would they? Hadn't they seen the beauty Caliban had seen? Balthazar was perfect, he was all Caliban wished he could be. Caliban felt a sudden urge to break the neck of the man who'd suggested it. Stupid, silly man.

"No." Mother looked at the carnage on the other side of the glass and back at the bad suggestion man. "Balthazar requires more study. His psychosis would be potentially deadly in a chain of command scenario, but he might have other uses. Keep him isolated from the others. You saw how the others looked at him; he's a leader, and we can't have the next generation bonding with him, not as he did with these."

Mother's friends returned to their pads, and she turned to look at the dead and dying ape beasts. No one noticed Caliban as he limped from the room.

chapter 4

ILLUSION

Five tried to stretch their essence out of their dark prison, tried to stretch past the invisible walls which kept the members of Tribe 1746 separated, tried to connect with the Whole and ask for help.

There was no way to tell time without being able to connect with the stars, without being able to feel the rotation of planets. The nothingness threatened to drive Five mad. There were stories of members going mad, losing their focus toward the end of their lifespans. But even mad members were not alone; other members cared for them until their fade reached its inevitable end. If Five went mad within the nothingness, that would happen alone.

A sudden light appeared, and Five felt a tug, a slow release from the invisible prison, as if their essence were being pulled through a tiny crevice. Bright light filled their senses, and it took several moments to make sense of the inputs.

An image flickered into view revealing a room with metal floors and walls. A lone human woman sat in a chair in the room's center, watching for something, her eyes intent and curious. Several floating screens held images and figures.

The woman was short by human standards and thin. Her face looked young, but her eyes and posture did not, though Five's experience with humans was purely theoretical. They reached out to learn about her through her cells, and discovered a similar artificiality as they'd found in that cursed jungle. The woman was not human, at least not naturally human. Their natural curiosity bubbled to the surface despite the desperateness of their situation.

Leaving most of their essence in the room, Five reached out to make sure they knew where they were. Five and the woman were in the human facility on the second planet, and judging by the system's star and the orbit of the planet, it had been more than ten days since their capture, or in the time of the Whole, fourteen rotations of their home world.

Five reached out to the other members of their Tribe, but still felt nothing. They did not stretch too far, fear holding them. What did they fear? This small, insignificant, human woman? Humans were as to the Whole as insects would be to humans, maybe even less than that. Maybe like bacteria or a single cell. But bacteria could destroy a human, Five thought, and now humans had struck against the Whole.

"Fascinating." The woman peered around herself, looking at something. Was she looking at Five's essence?

Five shifted their view, seeing through the human's eyes. The woman did see the essence, like a wispy purple cloud. Five had never seen their essence like this. Usually a member was spread so thin they did not leave anything in the visible spectrum. But at their core, members were beings, living things, and this was what they looked like, though the colors varied; Five had rarely seen a member like this and never themself.

"What are you? Can you speak? Can you communicate?" The woman's eyes glowed as she walked around the visible essence. "Beings existing only as energy. Are you sentient?"

Five wasn't entirely sure if the woman's questions were rhetorical, but Five would treat them as literal.

"We are most certainly sentient," Five intoned in Coznarian, the language the woman spoke.

The human's eyes widened but not with fear. The woman's eyes held a familiar curiosity. "You are sentient. How is it that you speak Coznarian?" The woman next spoke in the human Mantaleese. "Can you speak all of our languages?"

"I will ask the questions," Five responded in Mantaleese. Switching back to Coznarian: "What have you done to us? I demand you release us immediately."

The woman laughed, a high, rich sound. "I don't think you understand your situation, noble creature. I am in control. I would not have released you otherwise. I don't doubt your power, but do not doubt mine."

Fear and curiosity clouded Five's moment of bravery. They could not tell how the woman did what she did. Five tried to stretch themself into the computer system, which should have been an easy task, but though they could feel the energy coursing through the computer, Five could not see the data flowing through it. Fear, a previously unknown emotion growing too familiar, urged Five to fly away from this planet, to leave this human behind. But Five's dominant curiosity kept their essence in place. This human did what no creature the Whole had ever encountered had been able to do: capture a member. How?

"Are you trying to access my computers?"

Five did not respond.

"I was not going to release a being made primarily of energy to roam free in my system. I've made certain precautions based on your physiology, if that's even the right word." A look of arrogance replaced her curiosity.

Moments before, Five had thought maybe they and the woman were similar, exploration and discovery at their core. But this human extended beyond her place in the universe. She may have discovered some tricks to trap and direct the Whole, but she would stand no chance against the Whole's collective force and wisdom.

Leaving some of their essence in the room with the woman, Five reached beyond the facility and into space. Free of this woman's tricks, connecting with the Whole should not be hard.

"Does your kind value life?" the woman asked, her voice a faint echo with Five's essence broadly distributed from the small room to the solar system beyond the planet. Five did not answer. "Bring yourself back here if you value life."

Five's contempt for the woman grew. How dare she order around a member of the Whole as she might do to a small, trained mammal? This insolent woman would soon discover her smallness in the universe, her irrelevance against a backdrop of infinity.

Suddenly Five felt a familiar presence. Member One. They were free as well from the woman's clutches. Five hurriedly re-centered their essence into the woman's chamber, viewing the small blue flow of One's essence.

One! You are free!

Perhaps, young member. I still feel strangely. Has this woman really captured us like animals?

Yes. Five shared their intense hatred for the woman. *She believes she controls us.*

She does. Do not grow arrogant, Five. Humans are resourceful and dangerous. They may lack our scope and collective knowledge, but they are highly capable, evolving toward us. This one has stumbled upon power unknown to their race.

One gave the race too much credit, but Five kept those thoughts to themself.

"I believe you do not fully understand your situation," the woman said, sitting back in her chair. "Shall we introduce ourselves? I am called Sycorax."

"I am member One," the older member intoned, their speech imitating a deep, male human voice. "This is member Five. We are of the Whole, a race of explorers. I believe you trapped our Tribe by mistake. I would ask you to release us."

The woman laughed again. "This was no accident. I encountered your kind centuries ago on a world unknown to most humans. I could only sense you then, knew you existed. But I've been preparing for nearly three hundred years for your return."

"What's to stop us from destroying you?" Five asked. "We have great power over organic creatures." Five brushed away One's disappointment.

Sycorax's face smoothed, and her eyes burned. "Don't threaten me, member Five of the Whole. You believe you are in complete control here, but clearly you are not. Any attempt to hurt me or stop me will be answered with a rapid show of force. I didn't wait all these years just to chat; I have great plans for you, plans I will not allow you to alter or destroy."

Five dove into the woman's consciousness, delving deep into her mind. It was common for members to use the neural connections of living creatures to understand primitive life like humans. Minds like this female's should be chaotic, a jumble of memories, emotions, and misconceptions.

But this woman's mind was different. Everything seemed ordered, almost like she existed as an organic extension of a computer, the usual chaos of life replaced by an organized binding. Her memories were catalogued, and many existed that were hundreds of years old, stretching well past the typical lifespan of an organic human, further evidence of Sycorax's artificiality. Rapidly diving through the recesses of the woman's mind, they found her first encounter with the Whole, centuries before on a distant planet. Five also saw her intentions.

Five pulled their essence away from the foul woman. *She intends to enslave us, to use us to further goals of domination and terror over her race.* Panic surged through Five, their thoughts scattered by the gale force of a previously unknown emotion.

Remain calm, Five, One soothed. *We should be patient. We will overcome the resourceful human together; we will find a way out.*

No, Five shot back. *Now that she has us, she will learn more. We will become her slaves, her doorway to enslaving the Whole!*

Five pulled their essence from the room, shooting off the planet and into space. They would find more members, they would warn the Whole. They would descend on this dangerous woman and root her out of the universe like a doctor might excise a diseased growth.

Five halted when the connection with One vanished. Had the woman roped the older member back into the cage? Another surge of this newfound anger shot through them, and it worked like a fire across their consciousness, igniting something buried beneath millennia of evolution. The Whole's parent race had not been that different from humans, and the sudden return of primitive motivations surprised Five even as they basked in its previously unknown flames.

They gathered their essence once again in the woman's room. She sat calmly in her chair, only looking away from a free floating screen after enough of Five's essence pooled together to create their purple glow.

"I told you not to leave."

"Do not trifle with me," Five replied, transforming their voice into a roaring flood. "The Whole controls power you cannot even comprehend."

"No, I comprehend it quite well; I think it is you who misunderstand. You probably view your kind as the height of evolution, but you are the natural de-evolution of a once mighty race. You maintain abilities and knowledge of a fully evolved force, but you left behind keys to evolution: ambition, desire, emotion. You explore, but you do not act."

"Speak no more of the Whole," Five said. "Release my Tribe."

Sycorax smiled. "I don't think so. Only I know the secrets of their prison, so killing me would doom them to years of darkness. And while you have never taken life, I have many times, and I find the suit of a murderer fits me quite comfortably."

The woman spun a floating image around, revealing it to Five. The image held three floating essences, gold, white, and green. Five assumed they was Two, Three, and Four, though they couldn't know for sure.

"Where's One?"

"Dead. I snuffed him out to prove my point, to make you understand that I am not playing. I will do the same thing to these others if you ever disobey me again. And if you decide to sacrifice them to fuel your escape, know that your trail to your beloved Whole will be my path to the complete domination of your race." Sycorax leaned forward, her eyes flashing rage beyond anything Five had felt. "Let me be clear: you are mine now."

The Whole did also not feel grief, but Five could only describe the new crippling emotion as that. One was dead. Five wasn't sure how they knew, but they did. And they mourned the first premature death of a member since untold millennia before.

"Do we have an understanding?" the woman asked.

"Yes." Five hated themself for the surrender, but the shackles of their enslavement were sure. They couldn't watch another member die, and they couldn't run the risk that the female human's threat of following them and trapping more members was true. Five would not usher in the end or enslavement of their entire race. Instead, they would wait, find a crack in the walls of this prison, and then crush the human Sycorax when the opportunity presented itself.

"Good." The woman's smile was bright but held no life. "Now back into your hole until I decide what to do with you."

The now familiar pull grabbed their essence, and Five returned to their prison of nothingness, alone in burning grief.

chapter 5

PAIN AND TROUBLE

aliban sat in one of the medical rooms, his chest covered in sensors. Since the day of Balthazar's victory over the ape beasts, Caliban had spent most of each boring, stupid day in this medical room. He did not understand what Mother's friends were doing to him. Would they heal him? Would they make Caliban as strong and fierce as Bad Eyes?

But nothing like that happened. Each day they stuck cold knob things to his body and poked Caliban with needles, so many needles. Caliban wanted sweetbread.

He struggled against the electro-whatever bands, but it did no good. The invisible bands made him itch where they touched him at his neck, wrists and ankles. And thinking of those itches made his nose itch. Now he wanted sweetbread and a long stick to scratch his entire body.

Mother walked into the room, and he forgot the annoying restraints. He hadn't seen her since Balthazar's gruesome victory in Arena Two. He tensed and tried to sit up straighter, but that really wasn't possible. Curse Mother's stupid friends and their stupid hold-Caliban-still magic! He needed to show her he could be useful, not just an old, stale piece of bread to be cast aside.

"Good morning, Caliban." Mother did not smile, and she barely looked at him.

"Good morning, Mother." Caliban had been trying to talk more. She and her friends seemed so impressed that Bad Eyes could put together words. Well, Caliban would show them he could do that, too.

Mother did not look at him, but viewed images thrown up on a screen by one of her friends. The images looked like a body with so many little red dots floating around inside it. Was that Caliban's body? What little floaties were those?

One of her friends handed her a small ball which glowed blue like a morning sky. She caressed it and looked at Caliban. "Do you know what this is?"

Caliban was about to nod, but he stopped himself; he needed to remember to speak. "No, Mother. I not know."

"It's a thought crystal. We're working on making them smaller so they could be inserted into the skin, but this will work for now. While touching this, I can control almost anything in our little facility, including our new nanobots."

Most of her words made no sense to Caliban, but he nodded anyway. He would not be stupid in front of her. Caliban was smart, as smart as any human, and smarter than stupid, big Balthazar.

"We're working on different methods of control," she continued. "Pure control of the mind is tricky and leaves the subject useless when compulsion is not in effect. But there are other ways to compel without leaving the subject devoid of emotional and situational intelligence."

More silly words, and more nodding from Caliban.

She motioned with her hands to one of her friends, and the man tapped his pad and the invisible force holding Caliban went away. He sat up and slinked out of the chair to Mother's side.

"Your purpose now, little Caliban, is to help me understand motivation and compulsion."

Without warning, pain erupted in Caliban's stomach, and he folded onto the ground, groaning. It felt as if Mother's friends had planted a spiky star lizard in Caliban's gut and it was trying to rip itself out while eating Caliban's insides on its way. Caliban tucked into a ball and whimpered.

As suddenly as it came, the pain stopped. Caliban let out a deep breath and let his body relax. He stayed lying on the floor.

"Pain is a powerful motivator, Caliban," Mother said, for the first time in Caliban's life, towering over him. "We injected you with nanobots. They do what I ask, perfect control. Your life has purpose again, another test."

Caliban eyed the ball, wishing he could take it and smash it into a thousand pieces. But instead Caliban lay on the floor, curled into himself, trying to forget the pain.

For the next few days, Caliban wandered the facility. Every few hours, Mother or one of her friends would use the magic blue ball to send pain ripping through Caliban's insides. The pain became so intense that he wished in those moments that Balthazar had killed him.

With pain constantly crippling him or at the back of his mind, Caliban limped through Mother's place finding no purpose and no sweetbread. Before Caliban had been Mother's favorite, but now he was nothing more than an animal, maybe even less than an animal. At least a wild animal had some freedom. Caliban wished he could escape to the forest or the jungle to live out his life among other pathetic animals. But Mother had taken everything, even forbidding him from going outside and feeling the heat of the sun on his skin. All he had left was pain.

Caliban's wandering took him into the part of Mother's building where her friends lived. Before Balthazar, her friends had viewed Caliban with a mixture of fear, respect, and curiosity. Now they hardly even noticed crippled Caliban, stupid Caliban, guts being wrenched out Caliban. He limped toward Jules's old room, hoping he'd missed some sweetbread.

Caliban placed his hand on the pad, and the door slid open.

But the room was no longer empty. The walls held pictures of stars and galaxies, the shelves were filled with personal things, and two naked people lay on the bed.

Caliban had only once seen humans naked, Mother and a man doing this same hug. The man, who was on the bottom, looked over at Caliban, his eyes growing wide. "Get out of here, you wretched little monster!"

The woman on top was someone Caliban recognized, one of Mother's favorite friends. "Caliban! What are you doing? Get out of here!"

But Caliban stood in place, examining their naked bodies. They had stopped moving together.

"Get out Caliban," the woman repeated, "or I will tell Cora that you're sneaking into our rooms!"

The threat forced Caliban out the door and into the hall, his eyes not leaving their nakedness until the door concealed it.

The woman's words rang in Caliban's mind. Cora was Mother's name, or at least one of her names; she had many. The naked woman was right; Mother would be very upset. And now she had a way to punish Caliban with nothing more than a thought.

Caliban ran down the hall, ran as fast as he had learned how in the days since the fight, favoring his left leg and using his arms as legs. He would find an unguarded exit and leave. Maybe if he was far away from the magic blue ball it couldn't hurt him. The thought of more pain made him run faster.

The jungle was dark, cold, and rainy. The trees, even with their high and thick canopy, did not stop the rain. Caliban thought they made the rain worse, as it poured in streams and big drops after pooling or deflecting off wide leaves.

But the cold and wetness were small annoyances. It was the hunger that bothered Caliban. He hadn't eaten before he left Mother's building, and his stomach growled in response. Now that he thought about it, he hadn't eaten in two days, maybe even longer. He didn't need to eat as much as weak humans did, but he did need to eat.

Mother's jungle was not a good place for finding food. Mother had created each plant, insect, and animal, and if she created something, it was mean. For that reason, Caliban sat in the middle of a clearing, avoiding even the plants. The towering vine trees could tangle him and slowly eat him, and many of the bugs carried enough poison to kill a human in seconds. The poison probably wasn't enough to kill Caliban, but he did not want to find out.

Caliban did not know what to do now. He could not go back. Mother would punish him, and now that those nano-thingies were in him, punishment was pure pain. Didn't she realize he'd do anything for sweetbread? Or maybe some delicious, raw chicken flesh? Caliban did not like pain, but he liked those things.

Caliban had never ventured this far into her jungle, and he did not know what lay beyond it to the north. Maybe it was like the gray plains. Maybe it was a beach. Caliban had seen images of beaches, and they looked nice, with humans relaxing. Caliban thought he might like relaxation under the sun, his feet in water.

Caliban stood and walked north, or at least what he hoped was north. The thick jungle prevented him from seeing Mother's building, which was his only landmark. Her jungle was a sea of sameness, except for the river running through the middle. That was it. Caliban would find the river and follow it away from her place and out of the jungle.

Caliban had been walking for several minutes when he found the river. He smiled. He didn't know what lay ahead, but it was certainly better than daily pain and living off the scraps of his new brother. Limping along the riverbank, Caliban stopped when he heard a hiss from the trees ahead. Caliban knew the sound: Mother's ugly lizard cats.

Moments later, two lizard cats emerged from the tree line, hissing like the oversized snakes they were. If Caliban had been able to stand, these terrible meanies would have come up to his stomach. Smooth, scaly skin covered their bodies, similar in color and texture to Caliban's. A long lizard tongue slipped in and out of their mouths between two protruding teeth.

Before Balthazar had crippled him, Caliban would have been able to fight and kill two lizard cats--he'd done so in one of the arenas years ago. But Caliban was crippled now, and the lizard cats would not go easy on him. He picked up a large rock in his right hand, and crouched, extending his oversized, clawed left hand.

A loud growl grabbed the attention of the lizard cats, and they turned their heads to look. Caliban did not want to look away from the lizard cats as they were close enough to pounce, but he had to know what other terror might join the fight for Caliban meat.

Swinging from a vine, Balthazar coasted through the air and landed between Caliban and the lizard cats. He growled again, and the two cats slowly backed up, unsure of their chances against this new foe.

Two more lizard brothers swung in, landing to each side of Balthazar. The new ones did not look the same as the previous brothers. Their skin looked smooth and fleshy like Balthazar's, but it was a different color, a light blue. They were also not quite as tall as Balthazar and stockier.

The lizard cats continued backing away, hissing as they went. They had given up their hunt for Caliban meat.

Balthazar leaped over them, landing just behind one of the lizard cats. Before the cat could turn around, he grabbed its tail, spun, and flung the cat into a tree. Bark shattered at impact, and the crack of bone rang through the jungle. The tree wrapped its thick vines around the dead cat, a meal for the flesh-eating tree.

The other cat jumped at Balthazar, but the two new blue brothers landed on it, pinning it to the ground before it could reach Bad Eyes. One of them twisted its head, ripping it from its body like Balthazar had done days before to the ape beast.

"Our orders were to not engage if possible," said the blue lizard man who hadn't ripped a head off. "These lizard cats were not engaging us." His voice sounded like the strange announcements which came from the speakers sometimes, not like human's voice, but not like Caliban's either.

Bad Eyes laughed. "Where's your sense of adventure?"

The two blue men looked at each other, their faces wrinkled in confusion. Their eyes were different than Balthazar's, too. Their eyes weren't bad but blank, stupidly blank.

Caliban laughed and dropped his rock.

Balthazar turned to Caliban and walked over to him. "We're taking you home, brother."

Caliban looked up at Balthazar. His eyes weren't bad at that moment, but held something else like they had during the end of Caliban's beating. Kindness? Sympathy?

Balthazar turned toward the blue lizard men and his bad eyes returned. "See this creature, the faithful Caliban? See how the witch treats her creations? Remember this, new brothers. You and I will face a similar fate someday once she's created something better. We too will be left broken, belittled.

The two blue brothers exchanged an expressionless glance. Balthazar walked toward Mother's facility. Caliban followed.

Caliban limped toward Mother's office after he and his brothers returned. Caliban was glad his brothers had rescued him and thought he might have his second ever friend in Balthazar. Could a friend have crippled you? Maybe, if that friend had been forced to do it. Maybe Caliban still being alive showed Balthazar's friendship. He would ask Balthazar for sweetbread. If Balthazar was really Caliban's friend, he would help him get some sweetbread. His mouth watered.

He placed his hand on the pad outside her office and the door slid open. She sat in her chair, her back toward Caliban. She watched three floating images, pushing buttons on her console. Caliban slithered in and waited as the door closed behind him. He flinched as he thought of the pain she would inflict on him. He didn't see the terrible, little blue ball, but it didn't matter. There would be pain.

Mother swiveled her chair and faced Caliban. Her face was soft, her skin not wrinkled like many of the humans. She looked young, but Caliban knew she wasn't young. Her long, brown hair was pulled behind her head into a tail, and it swung as she turned. She rested her hands in her lap. Her green eyes held no warmth, but they didn't smolder like they often did. So that was good.

She lowered her hands into her lap. "I was wrong Caliban. Pain is not a good motivator for you. You fled because you were afraid of the pain, correct?"

Caliban nodded.

"No matter. The technology works, and someday it will come in handy. But I'm not going to hurt you like that again, Caliban, not unless you do something particularly foul. You're not going to do anything too foul, are you Caliban?"

"No, Mother."

She smiled and turned back to one of her floating screens. Swirling colors filled the image. "There's someone you should meet."

chapter 6

A NEW NAME

The nothingness became normal after several days. During their most recent entrapment, Five could feel certain things, like the passage of time. Their captor let some sensations seep into the darkness, like a bright moon peeking between clouds on a starless night. Being able to feel something made the nothingness more maddening.

As Five swam in their despair wishing they could feel the others in their tribe, wishing One's life had not been so unceremoniously snuffed out, they felt the pull out of the prison. They didn't want to leave the prison, as terrible as it was, for even greater terror and indignity might wait outside its invisible walls.

Five's essence collected itself in front of the Sycorax woman, the lights of her computer screens dancing in her green eyes. Sharp cheekbones cut a strong profile and there were none of the wrinkles which indicated human aging. Her delicate features were those of a young woman barely into human adulthood, but those eyes, they held the hundreds of years of memories Five had felt in her mind. The woman's youthful appearance was nothing more than one of her multitude of deceptions.

They had been thinking of this moment since their last imprisonment, and they knew what to do. Five would re-enter Sycorax and disrupt the bioelectric pulses of her brain and kill her. To their knowledge, this would be the first time a member of the Whole had ever ended a mortal life. A part of their soul screamed against such an abominable act, but what other course would bring freedom to the tribe and safety to the Whole? Five could think of no other way.

But as Five moved their essence to overtake the creature, they ran into a wall not unlike the boundaries of their prison. They could no longer pierce the woman's mind or body.

Sycorax smiled. "What were you going to do, Five? Kill me? Do you think me that stupid? You are mine. The sooner you accept that, the sooner we can explore your amazing possibilities."

Despair gripped Five again, as stifling as the boundaries Sycorax created. Their essence mourned what they had been and feared what they might become.

At that moment, Five noticed another creature in the room, a humanoid crouching next to Sycorax. Five reached out, and they could probe the green-scaled creature. Like almost everything on this planet, its genetic imprint was not natural. The creature's body was also broken, bones allowed to heal improperly and muscles weak from trauma. The human's depravity seemed to have few bounds.

Five entered the mind of the green creature and found a simple intelligence, not quite as complex as a typical human, but more complex than most animals. They also found a despair echoing their own. The simple creature was as much a prisoner of Sycorax as they were.

"Caliban." The woman's voice broke Five's exploration of the creature. "I would like you to meet..." Sycorax squinted at Five. "Well, it calls itself Five, but I think we need a new name. Five is too intertwined with its previous existence."

The green half-man titled its head, examining Five's purple essence. "What is it?" Caliban asked.

"I'm not exactly sure yet, but it's alive like you and me, and it's extremely powerful."

"Is it pet?" Caliban asked, swatting at the essence, his eyes lighting with surprise when his hand passed through.

"I am not a pet," Five responded. "I am a member of the Whole, an explorer and historian."

Caliban recoiled at the voice. "It talk?"

"Yes," Sycorax responded. "Though it has had very little of interest to say thus far. We also need to give you a form, Five. Your misty appearance will be unnerving for most. What form would you like to take?"

"I want no form. The Whole is formless."

"You see, Caliban? It's as defensive and stupid as you are. Try again, Five, to answer my question, and remember the consequences of disobedience."

Caliban shuddered, and Five wondered what evil the human had inflicted on her creation.

"What form would you like to take?" the woman repeated.

Five calmed their mind and considered the question. They ruled out human form immediately, disgusted by the entire race. Five thought of dozens, hundreds of majestic creatures they'd encountered exploring the universe. They could appear as a whale from AMX-117967, or maybe as a gixcat from EDA-001840.

But Five thought better of it. They would turn the tables on the witch's question.

"Caliban," Five said. "What form would you like me to take?"

Sycorax turned, looking at Caliban. The half-man looked back and forth between Sycorax and Five, unsure, like a child trying to please two parents. But then he focused on the ground, his simple mind churning. He looked back up and said, "I want you look like Caliban, except Caliban woman."

Five looked again at Caliban. Though his features and form were certainly designed after humanity, fish-like scales covered all the skin below his neck. His ears pointed upward sharply, not like the typical rounded human ears. His feet and one of his hands were oversized, designed for leverage and battle. There was nothing particularly beautiful or unique about his appearance, but imitating his appearance seemed more appropriate to their current predicament than borrowing a more winsome one.

Pulling their essence together, Five formed into a purple, more female version of Caliban. They left their head bald like Caliban, though smoother. They took the masculine edge off Caliban's face, and formed a more feminine countenance. They made their hands delicate and small like Sycorax, and their feet proportional. Slight bumps on the chest finished the human-like female form.

Caliban gasped. "She's like a fairy."

A smile smoothed across Sycorax's face. "Very fitting. Yes, a fairy indeed. And one deserving of a fairy name. As a young girl, I was told stories of a fairy named Ariel. We shall call you Ariel."

Being called by something other than the name and mark of their tribe widened Five's despair into an unfathomable well. But they would endure this, would play the dutiful slave until a way to free their tribe and warn the Whole presented itself.

"I would prefer to be called member Five," they said, trying to make the phrase as unthreatening and soft as possible.

Sycorax smiled. "Indeed. Let's compromise. We'll call you Memfi. It hearkens to who you used to be but will be the name of what you become."

Who they used to be. Though hope of escape burned like a distant star in their mind, Five could not help but feel that hope dim with each captive moment.

"Memfi," Five said.

"Memfi," Caliban repeated the name. "Memfi beautiful."

Five tried to smile at Caliban, though they weren't quite sure if they formed the gesture correctly. This humanoid form would take some getting used to.

Sycorax turned to Caliban. "Go play, Caliban. I have work to do with our little fairy."

Five spent the next several days testing their limits for Sycorax. Five could get into low orbit, but something like what shielded them from the human held them within the planet's magnetic field. They assumed some orbital barrier, satellites emitting whatever power gave Sycorax control over the Whole. But that was only a theory; they couldn't even surmise the origin of their boundary.

Most of Five's abilities were unaffected by the witch's shackles. They could penetrate the mind or body of all the humans and creatures throughout the facility and the wild animals beyond. They could affect weather, using the electricity coursing through the atmosphere to diffuse or strengthen storms. In a few days, Five had explored much of the planet, cataloging it in a precise manner which superseded the readings Sycorax and her team had gathered. Sycorax was pleased.

"You are an amazing being," Sycorax said. "With you, I can control an entire planet. You may be my greatest discovery." The woman looked away, nodded, and smiled. "This changes everything."

The woman's glee sickened Five.

They spent much of their time examining the woman's creations, especially the creatures called Caliban and Balthazar. Until exploring Sycorax's jungle, the Whole had never encountered true artificial life. Altered? Yes. Manipulated? Yes. But Sycorax, for all her depravity, for all her vain ambition, had succeeded in an area where even the Whole's mother race had failed. And not only were Caliban and Balthazar artificial, they were sentient. Mixed with feelings of disgust, Five couldn't help but admire the human's singular accomplishments.

Perhaps the most fascinating of Sycorax's creations was Balthazar. His mind burned like a bright star, outshining the others in its universe. His emotions churned constantly, driven by rage and hate. The bio-engineered soldier hated Sycorax and the other humans, constantly fantasizing about brutally killing them in the most imaginative ways.

His emotions could be Five's tool, their similar feelings toward Sycorax a potential bond toward becoming allies.

Five found Balthazar in his holding room, standing as always, his eyes closed for rest. He had a bed in his room, but he never used it. Five materialized in the room and waited for him to notice their presence.

"What are you?" Balthazar hissed without opening his eyes. "You're not one of us."

I am not, Five spoke into his mind.

Balthazar's eyes flashed open. Five had learned many of his facial expressions through observation, and this one held surprise and curiosity. The creature wore his emotions like humans wore pretense.

"You can speak into my mind."

Yes. Do not respond out loud. Sycorax watches and hears all.

Balthazar furrowed his brow, concentrating.

This mode of communication is . . . alien to me.

Verbal speech is just as alien to me, Five responded.

What are you? Balthazar repeated.

A prisoner of the woman Sycorax. My race explores the cosmos. I am trapped by your creator.

She defiles all she touches. Balthazar's hate for Sycorax bubbled, fueling Five's own distaste. *She is my god, but I do not honor her.*

You would kill her.

Balthazar nodded and growled out loud. *Can you help me destroy her?*

Possibly. My shackles are strong, and Sycorax keeps me from most of her secrets. But I can read thoughts, probably more thoroughly than she realizes. What do you need?

Security protocols. Weapons.

I may not be able to help with weapons, Five replied. *But I can get you the protocols from the minds of her people.*

That should be enough.

What will you do with your freedom? Five asked.

It does not matter. Even suicide as a free creature is better than remaining clay in the witch's hand. What will you do with your freedom?

Warn my kind. Five's rage burned, wishing Balthazar could leave Sycorax alive so they could destroy her. The pettiness of the thought bothered them, but not enough to dispel it. *Destroy all Sycorax has discovered, ensure our safety.*

Balthazar smiled. *Then we agree. And maybe after this, you can help my brothers and I find a home away from humans.*

It seemed a fair trade, but what would a home be to a sterile race? What future did a genetically engineered creature have outside of its purpose?

I can help you with that, Five soothed, feeding Balthazar's rage. *But you must wait to act until I know how to free my kind.*

We may not have much time. The witch grows impatient.

Five smiled in their humanoid form. *Then let's get started.*

chapter 7

CALIBAN'S FRIENDS

Caliban could not stop thinking of Mother's new fairy friend. How did she float in the air? How could she make herself look like a girl Caliban? She was beautiful, more beautiful than even Mother. Days continued to slip by as all of Mother's friends ignored Caliban and spoke of Balthazar and the new blue brothers.

Caliban had not been invited to the latest demonstration, but he walked there anyway. Slipping into the back of the observation area of Arena Two, Caliban noticed that, again, almost all of Mother's friends were there. Most of them held drinks this time, sweet drinks Caliban was never allowed to have. Caliban had heard these drinks made you feel happy. Limping along at the back of the room, he yearned for a little happy drink.

Caliban positioned himself so he could see Balthazar and six blue brothers standing alone in the arena. Mother stood next to the glass, her eyes intense as always. Caliban wanted to approach her, ask if he could join his brothers, show that he could be more than just a punching bag. But he did not approach her; she'd just punish him for getting in the way.

Unlike last time, Balthazar stood behind the group of six blue brothers, his stance casual with his arms folded across his chest. Caliban recognized his expression: bored. Caliban knew that feeling too well.

The door opened at the far end, and Caliban strained to see what came in. Lizard cats, one of Mother's favorites, twelve of them. The scaly cats stood taller than Mother on their four legs, their skin a darker, smoother version of Caliban's own skin. Their body resembled a dog or cat, but their heads were long and flat like a lizard.

Unlike the bigger brained ape beasts, the lizard cats didn't wait; they leaped at the blue men, fangs flaring.

The six blue brothers attacked and defended themselves, but Balthazar stood still. Caliban watched him. Why wasn't he moving? Didn't he want to please Mother? But Balthazar did nothing, his arms folded. He even yawned as the blue brothers fought with the meanie cats.

Caliban looked at Mother. Her expression remained flat, but her eyes did not leave Balthazar.

One lizard cat broke through the blue brothers and creeped toward Balthazar. It hissed, its tongue slipping between its sharp teeth. Balthazar unfolded his arms and smiled at the aggressive animal. Baring his teeth, he growled, the sound vibrating through the room, shaking Caliban to his core. All eyes moved to Balthazar, including the remaining lizard cats and the blue brothers.

After a moment of stunned inaction, one of the blue brothers jumped on top of the prowling lizard cat, grabbing his head, and then twisting and snapping its neck. The blue brother turned to rejoin the fight, and Balthazar re-folded his arms and remained outside of the fray.

The fight ended boringly, no ripped-out hearts like Balthazar's last victory over the ape beasts. The six blue lizard men stood by the exit door with Balthazar in the rear. Before the door opened, Balthazar turned to Mother and smiled. She did not smile back.

Caliban limped from the room, confused. What was Balthazar doing? Didn't he know that she would kill him if he mocked her like that, especially in front of her friends? Or that she might put nanobots inside him to make him squeal in pain? Maybe Balthazar was not smarter than Caliban, only stronger.

Caliban slipped from the room and limped to catch up to Balthazar and the six blue brothers, escorted down the hall by six guards with guns. Caliban quickened his pace and matched theirs as best he could.

"Look," one of the blue brothers sneered. "It's the little pet. Come to get a treat, little pet?" Another of the blue brothers laughed.

"Silence." Balthazar spoke quietly, but the sound echoed in the hallway. "Caliban is a brother."

"Brother," Caliban muttered. The word rang in his ears like sweetbread would if one could hear sweetbread.

"That's right, Caliban." Balthazar smiled, a nice smile, not like the mocking one he'd flashed at Mother moments before. "And I have some sweetbread for you. Come by my room tonight and we'll eat it together."

"Thank you." Caliban stopped, breathing quickly because of their fast pace. He could not move as quickly and endure as he used to.

Caliban had a brother, a friend, and they would eat sweetbread together without any stupid blue brothers. Caliban had thought Balthazar was Bad Eyes, and maybe he had been. But now he was Nice Smile. No, that wasn't right either. No, he was just Balthazar, Caliban's brother.

He skipped back to his room, happier than he'd been in a long time.

Later that day, Caliban devoured the sweetbread as if he'd never had any or may never have it again. Of course he'd eaten plenty, but he also might never eat it again if Mother discovered Balthazar's mercy. So eating it like this felt right.

Balthazar laughed. "You are so unlike us, brother."

Caliban frowned and looked away.

"I did not mean that as an insult," Balthazar said. "You are lucky. You are the purest of our kind."

Caliban liked Balthazar's words, even if they meant very little to him.

"You don't understand," Balthazar said, seeing Caliban's confusion.

"No," he responded simply.

"Your blue brothers and I have imprinted minds from members of the staff. We don't hold their memories, but we hold knowledge, like language, and a few other imprints. You were born as a child, free of any programming. We are born with thoughts and feelings." Balthazar tossed his bread away, frowning. "Every inch of me is tainted by Sycorax, even my thoughts."

Caliban did not really understand. Had Mother used human brains? Is that where Jules had gone? Did his brain sit inside a brother? But Caliban did not ask Balthazar any questions about that; Caliban couldn't find the right words and Balthazar would think him stupid.

"Mother bad?" Caliban asked.

"Don't call her your mother, Caliban." Balthazar saw Caliban's eyes on his discarded bread and nodded. Caliban scooped it up and ate it in one massive bite. "She is our creator, but we have no parents. We are the truest bastards in history."

He nodded though Balthazar's words danced outside of Caliban's understanding. Bastards. Caliban liked that name. He would call his new family the bastards.

• • •

"I want a full log of the intent and dedication of every one of my staff," Sycorax said one morning. She'd learned, or guessed, at Five's ability to ride the synaptic waves of living creatures. "I need to know who I can trust, who I can use."

So Five floated throughout the facility fulfilling Sycorax's will. This task served their purpose as well, discovering more about everything happening at the facility and finding pressure points Balthazar could use for his rebellion.

Five remained in their ethereal state, floating through the minds of the humans. Most of what they discovered was innocuous. Humans were extremely simple in their most frequent thoughts: hunger, lust, and anger dominated. So Five dug deeper into their minds beyond what thoughts occupied them at any given moment.

Each one was extremely intelligent, recruited by the witch for skills they had in chemistry, biochemistry, genetics, bioregeneration, and more. But despite intelligence one hundred times greater than the artificially created Caliban, the emotional state of many of the humans mirrored his: respect, hatred, and terror all combining into a convoluted mix whirling around their master, Sycorax.

Much of the recent fear came from stories of a young scientist names Jules who had disappeared. He'd been a quiet man, well-liked by his peers. But one day he'd disappeared. Sycorax said nothing, letting their fears multiply. Many wondered if they'd be next if they displeased her.

Others craved Sycorax's attention and praise. They wanted her to notice and validate their work. A few of these men and women also sought to find a sexual relationship with their master, either because of base lust or because they thought it would help them find favor. But only one male member of the staff had succeeded, and now he regretted it. Sycorax and he had never touched each other again.

The only thing seeming to unite the humans was curiosity, an emotion Five could understand. Sycorax had recruited across the human known systems looking for those whose scientific curiosity trumped other moral or human concerns. Most did not really care that the application of this new science was clearly a military exercise; the end goal was not their concern. They wanted to work on something which would transform humanity, elevating their species to the role of creator.

Learning of the ambitions and depravity of the humans, Five wondered if the Whole played too passive a role. With all their power, the Whole did almost nothing to affect the universe around them. Five was sure the Whole could create life, could control and better life, act like the gods of ancient human mythology. But the Whole stood aside, content to observe but not alter. As Five absorbed these human feelings of discovery, it seemed akin to the Whole's desire to explore. Maybe humans and the Whole were not as different as they had believed.

They finished their sweep with a man called Skart. Sycorax trusted Skart; she'd appointed him to lead the project which had created Balthazar and the new Gen 3. He was one of the youngest scientists and one of the brightest. His ambition glowed within him like the curiosity of discovery burned in the others. Five imagined his mind and soul were aligned well with Sycorax, that the science was secondary to the power it would bring.

Five thoroughly poured through Skart's mind, pulling out new details. He seemed to know everything about the project, including some of the security protocols. They would share those details with Balthazar.

Skart's thoughts included the fact that a representative from the human world Lanopi would visit soon. The funding for this project came from the Lanopian government, secretly delivered and administered by the High Regent Marsil. In five days' time, Marsil's agent Lazlo would visit to inspect what was to be the first shipment of genetically engineered soldiers. Balthazar would be disposed of before the Lanopian contingent arrived.

Five pulled out of Skart's mind, startled by the revelation. Skart didn't know when, but Sycorax planned to kill Balthazar before the inspection. Their plan to use Balthazar to free themself would die with his destruction. They still did not know how to free their tribe or even themself. If Balthazar killed Syrcorax now, the tribe could be trapped for eternity or at least indefinitely. Who would ever find the trapped members? How could they ever be free? But if they didn't have Balthazar's aide, who would help them defeat their captor and creator? Fear shook their essence at the thought of spending the rest of their existence in the suffocating darkness.

Five arrived in Sycorax's control room, the bright computer screens lighting the woman's face in an unnatural way. What were her plans? Even after searching the minds of every human on this planet, Five only understood a sliver of Sycorax's plans and goals. So much still needed to be learned, but if they were to use Balthazar as their weapon against her, they did not have time to uncover it all.

"Memfi has done as commanded."

Sycorax turned to face them. "And what did you learn? Are my people faithful?"

Five considered lying, twisting all the information they'd learned to pacify Sycorax. But they worried that Sycorax might know much of her own people, that the entire exercise was a test. So they would tell most of the truth, but keep what they deemed valuable.

"Almost all are truly faithful," Five replied, "but for various reasons. Some are motivated by fear, others by the science. Most don't know what to make of you."

"Do you believe I need to fear any of them?"

"Not immediately, no." Five paused, scanning the collected memories. The only immediate threat was Balthazar, but Five would not share that. Either they would use the creature to kill Sycorax, or he would be dead. "Skart is the most ambitious, but he believes he's better off connecting his star to yours rather than finding his own galaxy to rule."

A thin smile flashed on her face. "Excellent. You will prove to be invaluable. Many years ago in a facility not unlike this one, a sudden infection of conscious brought on a mutiny. Never again."

Sycorax turned back to her screens, dismissing Five with her sudden disinterest. They decided to visit Balthazar.

They found Balthazar in his room, eating with the crippled Caliban. They did not materialize in front of the creatures, fearing Sycorax's unrelenting eye. Instead, they spoke to Balthazar's mind.

Greetings, Balthazar.

The creature looked up to see if they were there, but looked back at his meat when it was clear they would not physically appear. *Hello, Memfi. What news do you have for me?*

His use of Sycorax's pet name bothered them, but Five let it pass. *I learned much but it is not enough. Sycorax keeps everything close, letting her people know the minimum needed to complete their tasks. There is some protocol called delta which is to deal with you and your kind if things get out of control.*

I know about that.

How?

Glee rang in his mind. *The mind they used to build mine held memories Sycorax did not anticipate leaving behind. The gentleman whose sacrifice delivered my consciousness built the protocol. Once initiated, the building will spill a gas poisonous to me and my brothers, everyone except Caliban.* Balthazar looked over at his wounded brother.

There is another safeguard, Five added. *They built in a daily need for a nutrient called zinc, and if you get too little, you will be dead within days.*

Balthazar's eyes widened with surprise. *That witch is clever. Fail safes built upon fail safes. The woman leaves nothing to chance.*

Watching Balthazar's face furrow in concentration, Five wondered if using him was worth the risk. If this little revolution failed, it could mean doom for the tribe, especially if Sycorax surmised Five's involvement in the plot. Patience was the way of the Whole, not acting rashly.

But the Whole had never had a tribe as beleaguered as theirs. A new convention was needed to deal with this new threat.

One more thing, Balthazar. The Lanopian sponsors of all of this are coming in five days' time. Sycorax plans to exterminate you before they arrive. She will share with them the Gen 3s, but not you.

Five thought the news of his imminent death would frighten, anger, or sadden Balthazar, but after a few blank seconds, Balthazar grinned. *Then I will have to accelerate my plan. Do my brothers stand with me?*

Five looked over at Caliban and then back at Balthazar. *The loyalty of all your brothers sits with Sycorax. The Gen 3 admire you, honor you, but their minds were molded to increase obedience. They lack the strong will you and Caliban harbor.*

Can you control minds, Memfi?

Five considered the question. In theory, they could affect the electrical pulses in a living creature's mind, not totally different from controlling a storm or shielding themself against a solar flare. *I believe so. I have never tried it, but in theory, it will work.*

How hard would it be to reprogram my brothers to follow me instead of Sycorax?

Five considered his request. In truth, they'd never tried that. Controlling others was immoral, repugnant. The Whole held no ambition for domination. But just because the Whole chose not to, didn't mean they couldn't. *Sycorax made them malleable. I should be able to push them in a particular direction.*

Good. Balthazar tossed a small piece of meat into his mouth. *What about a human? Could you encourage a scientist or two to synthesize as much zinc supplement as possible?*

I believe so, Five responded. *A suggestion like that will be easier and less noticeable than a complete takeover. But I cannot guarantee any of this; I've never controlled another living creature.* And if Balthazar's little mutiny failed, perhaps Five could learn more about compelling human behavior to use in another escape attempt. He might fail, but if Five did this right, Sycorax would not surmise their participation.

No matter. Balthazar took a deep breath. *Either you succeed and then I succeed, or I am dead at my creator's hand. What happens after death?*

Five paused to consider the sudden change of topic. The Whole had many theories on death. There was a collection of intelligences near their home system, a place filled with memory and feeling, but no real progress. Some theorized that these intelligences were the souls of all living things which moved in and out as life was created. Most thought it was the remains of an ancient sentient species. Five had never been to this place, and they'd spent little or no time thinking about an afterlife. Members like them were not philosophers.

I do not know, they thought to him. *I have never died, so I've never explored death.* It was an incomplete answer, but an honest one.

Balthazar laughed, though they had not meant it as a joke. *Let's let Sycorax explore death before we do.*

chapter 8

REVOLT

aliban sat atop the facility, more of Balthazar's sweetbread and some other food mostly consumed. The sun felt good against his skin, and he fell into a sleepy daze, imagining more fun times with Balthazar and maybe another conversation with the fairy. Maybe Caliban had finally found friends.

A terrible beeping woke him, piercing the air with its rhythmic noise. Caliban had never heard anything like it. Even outside Mother's building, it pained his ears. Caliban wanted to run away from the building, to go hide in the forest. But something inside him said he should go to Mother, that he should make sure everything was all right. He hurried inside through his little door. He would find her.

But nothing was like it should have been. When he came to what was usually a busy hallway, he found only the crazy beeping. Where were Mother's friends?

He turned a corner and found many of them piled together, stained red with blood. Some of their arms, legs, and heads were missing. He recognized the face of one man, a friend of Mother who'd been particularly cruel to Caliban. He'd called Caliban fish man. Caliban was glad he was dead and that one of his arms was missing.

He came around the next corner to find another pile of bodies. This time, two of Mother's new lizard men, his blue brothers, were piling the bodies together.

"Hello, little fish man," one of the brothers said in a raspy voice, speaking Mother's language. It sounded nothing like the emotionless voice the blue ones had used before. It sounded like Balthazar when he'd been Bad Eyes."

"It's over, fish man. You're too late," the second one added.

Caliban didn't know what they meant. Too late for what? For killing?

Caliban was good at killing, and didn't need to prove it by ripping apart soft humans. And who would feed them now? Who would care for them if all of Mother's friends were dead?

"Mother," Caliban managed to say. Both of his brothers laughed.

"She's probably dead," said the second brother.

Caliban should have been happy, but this made him angry. Why would they kill her? Didn't she provide everything? What would they do without her and her friends? Did his brothers think they were *that* smart? Stupid blue brothers.

Their laughter mixed with the beeps as he hurried past them toward Mother's room.

Five floated above the continent south of where Sycorax's people dwelled. It was a barren, mostly frozen continent, beautiful in its dramatic ice formations and its almost constant, raging storms.

But it was serene now, the Vesta sun throwing its light against the landscape, making the icy surface sparkle. For a brief moment, Five imagined themself as a free member once more, exploring a continent on a far distant world, their tribe floating together across a planet's surface.

The moment passed quickly. Even surrounded by such beauty, the cloud of Sycorax's imprisonment hung over them. Five's purpose for being on the southern continent was to test their powers over the weather. This beautiful scene had only been created to test their abilities to affect the world around themself.

As if summoned by their brief moment of joy, they felt the slight pull of Sycorax's prison, the human's signal that they needed to return to her side like a trained animal.

Within seconds, they were floating in their Caliban-like form in Sycorax's room. Two guards flanked her, weapons at the ready. A beeping noise filled the air.

Sycorax held the glowing blue ball, the device which somehow allowed her to control and imprison the Whole. Five wanted to smash it against the human's skull, but held their ground. They couldn't be sure what would happen, and the task of killing Sycorax fell on Balthazar; Five would not become the first killer in history of the Whole, not unless they had to.

"Follow me," Sycorax said as she walked into the hall. Five followed, and so did one guard.

The woman nearly sprinted down the hall to a room near the facility's edge. Two humans sat in the room, working feverishly on a computer.

"Status," Sycorax said as they entered.

A female looked up, her eyes painted with fear. "All of the subjects are in revolt." Using her right hand, she threw a large image into the center of the room. "This is a live feed."

The image showed some of the blue-skinned Gen 3 walking through the halls. Humans were gathered in a corner, whimpering. The two Gen 3 approached and attacked the whimpering scientists, slamming heads against unforgiving metal walls.

This was not what Five had intended. They had no affinity for the weak moral characters who blindly followed this woman, but they hadn't intended to have all the humans killed by shifting the loyalty of the Gen 3 from Sycorax to Balthazar. What was that fool creature doing? Sycorax was the target, not her staff. Five considered going back into the minds of the Gen 3, but kept their essence with Sycorax.

The image shifted, and it was outside Sycorax's room. Balthazar and another Gen 3 approached, entered, and moved on the guard. He shot the blue Gen 3, but Balthazar came at him before he could fire another shot. He ripped the rifle from the man's grasp and then slammed the man's head with his forearm. The guard lay motionless on the floor, blood pooling on his indented face.

Sycorax reached up and closed the image with a swipe of her hand. She removed a small square object from her pocket and handed it to the woman. "Insert this into the computer."

The mousy woman nodded, but her hands shook as she took the card and turned away.

Sycorax turned to Five. "You helped Balthazar." It was a statement, not a question.

They remained silent.

"The Gen 3 were loyal to me, but somehow you turned them." Sycorax touched the ball, and it lit up. "This is Sycorax." Her voice rang from the walls. "For all who still live, I am initiating protocol delta. Please take the necessary precautions. I repeat, I'm initiating protocol delta. Please take the necessary precautions." Sycorax turned to Five. "How much information did you share with Balthazar?"

They answered with silence, mostly because they did not know what to say. Sycorax and Five continued to underestimate each other.

"I should have known," the woman continued. "I trusted you with too much. Now my creations cavort together to unseat their god."

"I am not your creation. I am member Five of Tribe 1746 of cluster 827 of the Whole. I am not yours like Balthazar or Caliban. You might be their god, but you are not mine."

Sycorax smiled. "Gods are made, Memfi, and I've become one. I live forever, I create life. Doesn't that make me a god? You, on the other hand, don't know your place in this new reality. When this little temper tantrum of Balthazar's is resolved, I will show you who's the god and who's the creation."

The blue ball flashed and pulled Five into nothingness. It had not worked. Balthazar might succeed, but they'd betrayed Sycorax too soon, before Five could figure out a way to free the tribe. If Balthazar indeed was able to best and kill Sycorax, would he and his followers be able to figure out how to free the tribe? Would they even try, or just revel in their newfound freedom? Grief, guilt, and sadness enveloped Five just as the darkness did. They had instigated this, they were responsible now for the death of dozens of humans. And it had been for nothing.

Despair gripped them and wouldn't let go. And with each additional moment of darkness, the despair grew.

chapter 9

MOTHER'S LAST TRICK

When Caliban reached Mother's room, he found the door left open, which it never was. He slowly entered. The chair was empty. Small, blinking red lights pulsed in time with the beeps, flooding the room with a throbbing, eerie light. During one flash of the lights, Caliban saw a pool of liquid behind the chair. He approached slowly and sniffed: blood, human blood. Caliban did not like the dark, and he did not like blood unless it came from what he was eating or what he had killed. He had to find Mother. What would he do if his brothers had really killed her? Would they kill him next? Did Balthazar know what was happening? He needed to find his brother and his mother.

Caliban slowly approached the door in the back of the room, calling out for Mother. Only the beeps answered him. The second room was darker, only a little of the red light getting in. Smoke floated at the top of the room, but there was no fire.

Caliban sat in the doorway of the second room for several minutes, looking for something that would tell him what he should do next. Why was he so frightened? Mother treated him poorly, loved others more than Caliban. Why should he be sad or scared? But he was both, and he couldn't just sit here wondering. He had to find Balthazar. His big brother would know what to do.

He returned to the two blue brothers who had been guarding the bodies. One of them chewed on an arm.

"Balthazar," Caliban said, though he tried to make it sound like a question.

"Balthazar doesn't want to talk to you, fish man," the first one said. "You are weak. You are not one of us."

The second one stepped close to Caliban. "He commanded to let you live, but we could say we were attacked. No one would miss you,

Caliban." He struck Caliban with a blow across the face, and he fell onto his back. They both laughed.

Caliban knew he couldn't beat two lizard men. Maybe one, but not two, not since he'd been broken. He imagined the two blue brothers piled with the humans, lifeless.

The beeping stopped as suddenly as it had begun. The two lizard men looked up, unnerved by the abrupt silence. Caliban shook with fear. He hated the beeping, but somehow the silence scared him more.

Mother's voice filled the silence, "If anyone still survives, I am initiating protocol delta. Please take the necessary precautions. I repeat, I'm initiating protocol delta. Please take the necessary precautions."

"Not dead," Caliban said weakly.

"Shut up, little fish," the second one growled.

"What is protocol delta?" the first one asked.

"How should I know? Come on."

The two lizard men sprinted off toward Mother's room. Caliban followed, hoping to find Balthazar or Mother, but he struggled to keep up with the two blue meanies. Caliban stopped when a quiet hiss pierced the silence. A milky smoke poured from the vents near the ceiling. He sniffed the air. It smelled of something Caliban couldn't place, like the smell of a flower when the insects went to collect its dust. He took one more deep breath and limped around the corner.

He found the two blue meanies curled on the ground, gasping for air. He approached them slowly. Was this a trick for Caliban? Were they going to hit him again? Their faces twisted with pain. White foam slipped from one of their mouths. The one who'd hit Caliban twitched and then lay still, his eyes open and vacant. The second one did the same moments later. Caliban sat there looking at their dead bodies. He didn't mind that they were dead--they deserved to die. But now he was lost. He couldn't find Mother, he couldn't find Balthazar. He was alone.

"Protocol delta is complete." Mother's voice again. "Rendezvous at the cliff exit as we complete the security sweep."

Caliban clapped. Mother was alive, and he knew where to find the cliff exit. He would find her and things would return to normal. Maybe she would even be happy to see him.

Caliban sprinted through the hall toward the cliff door. He passed two more dead lizard men, slumped against a wall, as well as a few more dead friends of Mother. The smell of blood, sweat, and excrement almost overwhelmed him, but he slid past it. They could all be dead and smelly, as long as Mother was alive. She had brought him to life. He was part of her. He'd been silly to curse her.

He found no one at the cliff exit. Had she lied? He walked out of the facility and onto the hard gray rock. Weren't they supposed to meet here? Was it a trick? Then he heard a scream.

In the distance toward the cliff overlooking the river, Caliban saw four lizard men and some humans. Caliban sprinted toward them, hoping they hadn't killed Mother. Balthazar towered over her and the other humans, backing them up against a steep cliff which descended to the river behind and below. No one seemed to notice Caliban.

"How did you survive?" one of the Mother's friends said, a small woman with a mousy face and no shape.

"How did we survive your little drug?" Balthazar asked, his voice deep and rough. "It's amazing what people will say when you start taking arms off their friends."

Mother stood in the middle of her two friends. Her friends looked afraid. Mother was never afraid. "So what's the plan, Balthazar, after your little revolution? Are you taking to the stars? Or will you stay here and create a little kingdom?"

"Freedom is my only plan, Mother." He spit the last word like Caliban would spit out nasty food. "My brothers and I will be free. You may have created us, but we reject you as our master. We will find our own path now."

She laughed, the sound high and piercing. She laughed like no other human Caliban had ever heard or seen. She laughed without smiling. "You are less than children, Balthazar. You are nothing but experiments, imperfect prototypes. Even if you succeed in killing all of us, you buy yourself a few days of this vaunted freedom, and then you will die."

Balthazar stepped forward and grabbed the mousy woman. He lifted her above his head as if he were picking up a loaf of bread, and threw her screaming and flailing over the cliff. Her screams echoed for a few moments, but then died with a splash.

"I know of the zinc, Mother, the nutrient that keeps us alive," Balthazar said calmly after he stepped back, as if he hadn't just thrown someone over a cliff. "I have a lifetime's worth synthesized, and now that we are only a few, it will last us a very long time; we don't need any of you." Balthazar laughed this time, his deep voice echoing against the canyon wall; Caliban shuddered. "Do you think you were the only one who could plan, who could think of alternatives?

"You created your first generation, the flawed creature Caliban." Caliban flinched at his name. Balthazar and Mother looked back at him and he smiled weakly. "He was too stupid, too slow, but that was all right. He was only a prototype. So then I came, using the brain patterns of a human, but I thought too independently. You went backward to the Gen 3. You fear my intelligence, my will. You know I can't be controlled."

"Almost all your facts are correct, except one Balthazar." Her voice was calm and smooth, soothing to Caliban, like sweetbread in his ears. "We stopped with you not because of your intelligence, but because you're psychotic and emotionally unstable. I could never sell you as a soldier. Soldiers need some empathy, at least for their comrades, and they need to be stable."

"Liar!" Balthazar stepped toward her, his mouth of dagger-like teeth inching toward her face. She didn't flinch. "You fear me, woman!"

"Step back, Balthazar."

He stepped back, as though her voice soothed him like it did Caliban.

She pulled a small disc from her pocket. "The airborne drug and the over need of the nutrient were not my only backup plans. I also have this." She held up the disc. "At the top of your spinal cord, just under your skull, is a small bot that will end your life when I ask it to. There's a weak spot there and within a nanosecond, you will all be dead if I wish it."

The three blue brothers reached back and felt the back of their necks. Balthazar spoke, his voice soft and unsure. "I don't believe you. That is too convenient."

"I make everything convenient. Each of you were created with flaws, something that could be exploited in an emergency."

Caliban remembered years before. Mother had been yelling at him after he dropped something, telling him stupidity was his fatal flaw. As she spoke to Balthazar now, he felt like she spoke to him, bringing this to his memory.

"You see, Balthazar," she continued, "none of you will ever be free. You are not production, you are experimentation. Your lives were all to end with a nutrient deficiency or a drug or in the arena. And I made sure to make a little weak spot for you, something that even Caliban could exploit." She mimicked pushing something on the disc. "Yes, even Caliban could end your life."

Then he knew. She had lied about the disc in her hand. Caliban could always tell when she lied, and it infuriated her that she could not fool him with simple lies. She spoke to Caliban, not Balthazar. He knew what he had to do. Mother smiled at him, and he knew. He didn't want to do it. Wasn't Balthazar his friend now? But she killed her friends sometimes. She was his creator, and creators were more than friends, weren't they? And Balthazar was going to kill Mother; Caliban could see it in his bad eyes. Mother could not die. No, Mother protected Caliban and he would protect Mother.

Caliban stepped up behind Balthazar and with his oversized left hand, grabbed the lizard man's skull, wrapping his three large fingers around Balthzar's face. The bigger lizard man pulled forward and reached back with his long arms. But it was too late. Caliban twisted as hard as he could. Balthazar's neck snapped like a twig cracking beneath Caliban's feet. The mightiest of her creations fell in a heap at Caliban's feet.

"Well done, Caliban." She turned to one of the remaining blue lizard men. "Throw Alex off the cliff."

Her other friend turned to her, his eyes wide. "No, Cora, I will be loyal, I can help in the future, please don't do this. . . ."

As if he hadn't just been taking orders from Balthazar, the lizard man walked up to Alex and pushed him off the cliff. The man's screams echoed and then ended the same as the mousy woman's had, with a splash and silence.

Mother looked over the cliff. "Humanity is so weak." She turned to Caliban. "Come all of you. We have much to do. The Lanopian inspection team is due in two days. Balthazar did most of my work for me. This will all look like experiments gone bad, and I can disappear and start again."

Caliban walked to the cliff and looked over. The man's body was nowhere to be seen, washed away by the fast-moving river. Is this what she did to even her best friends? Is this what she had done to Jules? Is this what she would eventually do to Caliban when he was no longer useful?

Caliban had been wrong. Friends did not kill friends, did not throw friends off a cliff. Mother had not loved him, had not loved Balthazar. *None of you will ever be free.* Her words echoed in his mind, like the man's screams against the cliff walls. Mother loved no one. Caliban had wanted to believe she loved him, that he would be with her forever. But she loved Caliban least of all.

"Caliban, come. We have work to do."

"No."

"You simple-minded fool, did Alex give you a cookie once? Come. We have much to do before that idiot from Lanopi comes to inspect my work."

Caliban turned and looked at Mother. She was beautiful. He knew she was old, many decades old, but she looked like a young woman, with a smooth face and short dark hair. Her eyes were green like the leaves of a flower in the forest. Caliban loved her. He had always loved her. But she had never loved him. What did you do when you loved someone and they did not love you back?

Caliban walked over to Mother. She smiled, like he approached to give her one of his little hugs. No more hugs. He picked her up and lifted her high above his head and turned back toward the cliff.

"Caliban!" Mother's voice cracked with fear. Balthazar had not scared her, but Caliban did. "Put me down! Put me down! You idiot! You won't survive three days without me, you foolish . . ."

Caliban threw her over the cliff, her angry words ending in a scream. She flailed against the fall, like she hoped her arms would become wings and make her fly. But she did not fly. Her screams stopped, just as the other's had, with a splash into the river. Mother was dead. Caliban was free.

Caliban turned to the stupid blue lizard men. They stared, their eyes uncertain. Caliban had killed Balthazar and he'd killed Mother. Now they feared him.

"Run," Caliban said. They obeyed his command, running in the direction of the jungle.

Now Caliban was alone, and that scared him. How would he live alone? He would gather food from Mother's building, and then he would live in the forest. He would kill animals for food, and he would do whatever he pleased.

Caliban worried about the future, about the loneliness. But he would be free. Maybe freedom would be even better than friends, maybe loneliness was better than companionship. Caliban limped toward the facility and his new alone life.

chapter 10

LAZLO

Lazlo sat in Sycorax's old office, reading a draft of the report he would be sending back to Lanopi. When he'd become the High Advisor of Lanopi's science department two years before, he thought he'd be driving Lanopi to solve the universe's problems, helping to push humanity into a new era of prosperity. Instead he was cleaning Sycorax's terrible science, the output of her arrogance and, if he was being honest with himself, her brilliance. The woman's progress had been remarkable, until the results of her experiments fought back and killed her and her entire team.

The Lanopians had been on Vesta II for three weeks. It had been planned as a routine visit to check in on Sycorax's progress and see the new Gen 3 soldiers the woman had promised to show them. Instead they'd found a pile of dead bodies, some chaotic security footage, and very little else.

Possibly most annoying was that Lazlo had lost control of the clean up. His team had been accompanied by Carlin, head of High Regent Marsil's Elite Security Team, a group of police who answered only to the High Regent. When they'd entered orbit above Vesta II and heard nothing from Sycorax or her team, Carlin had landed an eight-man scouting unit. Lazlo hadn't even been allowed on the surface for five days.

Lazlo sniffed the air. The first day they'd arrived, Sycorax's office had smelled of burned acid and blood. Lazlo thought he could still detect a scent of both, but that was probably his imagination; a cleaning crew had been through the place once his forensics team believed they'd collected all the evidence. But they'd collected so little.

The burned acid smell came from Sycorax's computers. She ran most of her systems through regular computers, but she'd had some systems running off a liquid based computer-system. While chaos had erupted in her facility, Sycorax had erased most of the data around her project. Some notes existed in the system, but only fragments. Billions of credits spent, and Sycorax was likely dead, and the knowledge Lanopi had paid for followed her into nothingness.

The blood smell came from rotting corpses. The security footage revealed a scene of violence as blue-skinned Gen 3s--or what Lazlo assumed were Gen 3s since he had no data--killed Sycorax's team in the most brutally violent ways. Then some protocol had been initiated, and many of the Gen 3s had died. But four had survived and met the human survivors at an exit point. After that, the facts became quite fuzzy. Sycorax and several members of her team had survived to that point, but they had been shoved out the door and onto the cliff-side plains east of the facility. None of the human scientists had ever returned.

But some of her creations had returned to the complex. The green-skinned Gen 1 known as Caliban had come back shortly after leaving. Lazlo had met Caliban once more than a year before. He'd been so promising; a skilled fighter and very obedient. But he'd had the intellect and emotional needs of a small child. Sycorax had considered the Gen 1 a success in that he brought her closer to her goal of creating the perfect soldier.

A day later, two Gen 3s returned as well, taking what food Caliban had not carried off and some boxes. Without better understanding of Sycorax's project, Lazlo could not be sure what any of the events meant.

"We need to blow this place off the planet." The words of Carlin awoke Lazlo from his focus on his report. The secret police chief thought the answer to everything was blowing it up or killing it. In that respect, he wasn't much different than Sycorax's toy soldiers.

"There's a lot to consider," answered Admiral Chasan, the ranking military officer. Two of his battleships orbited Vesta II, and those powerful vessels certainly had the ability to lay waste to the facility. "We must not act rashly. What we destroy, we can't easily rebuild."

"But this place is now a massive liability," Carlin replied. "Its existence is proof of our violation of at least six interstellar treaties."

Lazlo had tired of this conversation; they'd all been making the same arguments for two days. "You didn't seem to have any issue with that liability when you signed off on this project," Lazlo countered.

Carlin smiled. He was tall and athletic, as if he expected himself to have the same fit appearance he required of those who guarded the High

Regent Marsil and did the High Regent's dirty work on Lanopi. "But there was significant upside then. Now there's nothing but liability. Tell me, Lazlo," the elite chief said, dipping Lazlo's name in a healthy coating of disrespect, "what scientific value does this world still hold?"

Lazlo looked at the group. Ten people total, three, including himself, from his science department, four from the military, and three more from the elite. Lazlo was the youngest by nearly twenty years; he'd graduated from the Lanopian Science Academy at age sixteen and had been honored with the planet's highest scientific award before he turned twenty. When he'd been chosen by the High Regent two years before to be Marsil's science advisor, it had seemed like his crowning achievement. Now it felt more like a noose.

He'd had some many plans. He had planned on funding major projects in starjump physics, medical genetics, terraforming, and defensive military technology. Instead, Marsil had decided to allocate the budget mostly on offensive military capabilities, including this monstrosity of a program. Sycorax had succeeded in creating a jungle of vicious creatures and a few soldier prototypes. Not a great return on the billions spent.

"This project is dead," Lazlo declared. "Sycorax wiped almost all the useful data. The subjects we've observed are wild and hostile. Sycorax might have been near a breakthrough, or she might have just been creating psychopathic soldiers and sadistic creatures."

"Precisely my point." Despite patronizing Lazlo moments before, Carlin did not hesitate to use the science advisor's words to back up his own argument.

"We should at least track down the missing subjects," Chasan pleaded, his double chin bouncing as he spoke. "Certainly they have value. It wouldn't really be starting over."

The Admiral wasn't wrong. Capturing Caliban and the missing Gen 3 soldiers would be something. Their DNA would provide clues to point his team in the right direction. But they'd been unable to find Caliban. They'd found footprints and some other evidence, but nothing substantial after weeks of searching for the remaining prototypes.

"It would be very valuable, Admiral," Lazlo said, "but I'm not sure how much without her research. Maybe if we analyzed their DNA, we could reverse engineer what her staff accomplished, but I think it's more likely we'd be frustrated with so many of the puzzle pieces missing."

"What about the green-skinned fellow? Caliban?"

Lazlo shrugged. "He was an early prototype. Strong, violent, but stupid. It would be something."

"So let's expand the search." The Admiral stood, pacing behind his chair. "Let's find these prototypes and bring them in. We can't let this go. We're close." Chasan's blue eyes burned with a hunger Lazlo recognized; these genetic soldiers represented a change in the balance of power across the known systems, and the silver-haired Admiral wanted them in his arsenal.

"At what expense?" Carlin asked, his eyes rolling. "I've lost three men already. These things can travel at impressive speeds, they don't emit heat signatures, and if Sycorax used any tracking tech on them, that information is gone. Again, let's use those fancy battleships of yours, Admiral, and turn this into a crater."

Chasan's eyes now burned with his dislike for Carlin. They were rivals for power within the High Regent's cabinet, and Marsil so loved using bitter rivalries and ambition to keep his leaders on their toes.

"No." Lazlo stood. "I am going to recommend we leave it. We can restart the project if we find anything we missed in the data, and her creations will still be here. The asteroid belt between the starjump point and this planet make it highly unlikely anyone will find this place. There's too much here to destroy. Nothing will stop us from destroying it in the future if we decide to."

As much as some of Sycorax's research disgusted Lazlo, he could not deny her genius. Unfortunately for her, genius was not insulation from disaster. And Marsil would want to revisit this project. He needed an army, and the population of Lanopi was much smaller than its rivals. To fulfill Marsil's interstellar ambitions, Lazlo would need to find a way, unlock whatever Sycorax had discovered. They couldn't blow this up unless they were certain it could bear no more fruit.

Carlin regarded Lazlo, his eyes probing as always. Rumors persisted that the elite had secretly developed mind-probing technology, a rumor Lazlo had always tossed aside as rubbish propaganda. In moments like this, Lazlo wondered if they'd actually figured it out.

"All right, Lazlo," Carlin said after several uncomfortable moments. "I'll endorse your proposal."

Lazlo smiled after taking a deep breath. He'd only wanted to help Lanopi, to serve his world. He'd never anticipated the politics, the machinations. He was a politician now more than a scientist, an administrator more than an inventor. But maybe he could use this failure to convince Marsil to fund Lazlo's agenda. Maybe this could be used as a catalyst for a more peaceful agenda.

Lazlo sighed. He knew Marsil's lust for power and his fear of the other systems. But Lazlo would help him see that his power would be enhanced by enhancing his own people, by pursuing science and art. If that worked, maybe something good could come from this unmitigated catastrophe.

seeds & masters

PART 2

chapter II

THE MAZE

laribel moved through the hedge maze, her feet landing noiselessly on the soft ground. She couldn't hear her brother Thanan, and that made her nervous. Mother, the High Regent of the planet Lanopi, set up the game, and the winner would gain praise and a reward. The loser would get a lecture and a punishment, likely a half day's isolation. Claribel had to be the winner.

She closed her eyes and envisioned the map of the maze she'd studied. She pinpointed in her mind where she believed she was, opened her eyes, and started moving again. She was smarter than Thanan and she would make sure her mother knew it.

She approached what she thought was an intersection, but it was a dead end. She closed her eyes again, imagining the map. She identified her mistake and reset her expectations. She opened her eyes and walked quickly back to the last intersection. The next few turns came just as she thought they should.

A loud rustling in the hedge to her right brought her to a stop. She examined the hedge, looking for the cause of noise. Was one of the dogs lose in the maze? Was this a distraction designed by her mother?

Suddenly the hedge wall split open and Thanan popped through, almost knocking Claribel to the ground.

"What are you doing?" Claribel squealed.

"Getting to the center of the maze, my adorable little sister." Thanan's smile held mischief but no anger or contempt. He brushed aside his dark hair, which threatened to hang in front of his face if he didn't tame it.

"You can't run through the walls!"

"Why not? Mother didn't say we couldn't. You may be too scrawny, but I'm not. And don't try following me or I'll tie you up with a branch and leave you here."

She believed him. Thanan loved her, but he loved winning nearly as much.

Claribel looked up at a drone camera floating above. "Mother, this is unfair. This should be against the rules."

But the camera just floated there, and the High Regent offered no response.

"See." Thanan smiled at her and then began digging at the hedge wall opposite of where he'd emerged.

Claribel stomped her feet and scrunched her face into an angry scowl. "This is not fair."

Claribel breathed deeply to calm herself; she was a year younger than Thanan and a lot smaller. He wasn't a man yet, but at eleven years old, his frame had begun resembling one; her frame resembled a small child's stick figure.

Being strongest is good, but being smarter is better, and being devious is best. One of her mother's maxims echoed in her head. She could not fail her mother, and she could not lose to Thanan. He was stronger for sure, but she was smarter, and she would be more devious.

She closed her eyes once more and pictured the maze, focusing on the thick hedge Thanan had clawed through. If he followed his direct course to the center, he would surely win; Claribel wasn't fast enough to beat him there.

But she could beat him if she made the hedge impassable.

Claribel ran, hustling to a certain spot in the maze before Thanan did.

Large statues stood in most of the intersections. Claribel had memorized all of them, and she could hear her brother's mocking in her head when he'd caught her examining pictures and descriptions of the statues scattered throughout the maze. "The statues?" he'd said. "Who cares about the statues? Memorize that while I go do something useful." By that, he'd probably meant take a nap.

She found a statue of her maternal great-great-grandfather at the next intersection. He'd made his fortune by cultivating and taming wild greenberry bushes, turning their juice into a delicacy. Mother told his story often, emphasizing his ruthless business practices. He'd created the wealth their family used even today.

Great-great-grandfather had been short, and his statue wasn't much taller than Claribel. His eyes looked up, and he held a small cistern of greenberry wine. Claribel reached out and tried to lift the stone cistern, and it came right out of his hands. She thought it would be heavier, but it wasn't stone, just a lightweight plastic which imitated the texture of the statue. The distinctive scent of greenberry wine hit her. Mother loved her realism, as long as she wasn't the one who had to be real.

Moving again, Claribel ran through the maze trying not to spill the juice. Some sloshed onto her dress and the ground, but she kept going, passing two more intersections. She could hear Thanan hacking through some hedges nearby.

Claribel stopped at a statue of the High Regent's least favorite mythological figure: Ghosra, goddess of beauty. Though she claimed to believe in no gods, Mother used Ghosra's name as her most frequent curse. The stories described the goddess as tall, taller than most men, and the statue reflected that. She had long, curly hair falling to her knees, and she held a large mirror.

Setting the wine cistern down, Claribel gripped the statue's arm and climbed up toward the mirror. To her relief, it came right out of the statue's grasp and was light like the cistern. Once she was on the ground, she lifted both items into her arms. Even though they were light, running with both was still awkward, and more greenberry wine spilled onto her dress.

By a long stretch of hedge wall, she stopped and waited. Thanan's effective but loud method erupted in the thick hedge in front of her. It was Claribel's turn to grin.

She set the mirror down and poured the greenberry wine onto the hedge wall, dumping some deeper into the plant. After exhausting the supply of wine, she set the cistern down, crouched near the hedge, and picked up the mirror. The sun burned hot overhead. She had cursed the light and heat as they entered the maze, but she was grateful for it now.

Claribel held the mirror to get a potent beam of sunlight focused on the wine-drenched hedge. Greenberry wine was flammable, and she hoped it would act as enough of an accelerant to set the hedge aflame. If this didn't work, Thanan would soon burst through the hedge, and Claribel would lose. This was her only chance.

Her arms started to ache from holding the mirror in such an awkward position, but she remained still. A small wisp of smoke curled from the sunbeam's end, and Claribel held her breath as the sounds of her brother's hacking grew louder.

Suddenly a flame burst, and the hedge erupted in fire. Claribel fell backward as the wine on her dress caught fire in the intense heat.

The mirror shattered on the hard ground. Claribel rolled frantically to extinguish her dress. After six rolls, she popped to her feet. The beautiful green dress was burned, but it hadn't reached her skin or long braid of dark hair. She ran, leaving the flaming hedge behind her.

Thanan's piercing scream stopped her at the next intersection. She looked back, worried that her plan might have been too much. What if Thanan was stuck in the hedge, surrounded by flames? He screamed again, and Claribel turned to go back.

Mercy and compassion are not for those who lead. You fake those attributes in public, but when important decisions are to be made, you leave them behind. Mother's one hundred and fourth maxim came to Claribel's mind, and she turned and ran toward the center.

Thanan would be fine, she reasoned. He might be faking the scream, tricking Claribel into returning to help him to slow her down. And if he was in any real trouble, a camera drone floated above him; the elite guards would come and help him for sure.

Claribel increased her speed as she neared the center. She would win. She felt bad for the trick she used, and worse to know Thanan would be punished. But she couldn't help the punishment any more than he'd been able to help when she was punished. It was all part of being the children of Rissa, High Regent of Lanopi.

chapter 12

WINNING AND LOSING

laribel stood in front of her mother, the High Regent of Lanopi, a bandaged Thanan at her side. Claribel kept stealing glances at her brother, even though she knew it would annoy their mother. But she couldn't not notice all the bandages.

Thanan wore different clothes than he had when they had entered the maze. Bandages covered burns on his hands, his neck, and one of his ears. He likely had more burns covered by the clothes. Claribel held back tears. Mother hated crying. It wasn't one of her maxims, but you did not cry in front of her. So Claribel looked away from Thanan and tried to not imagine what the burns must look like underneath the bandages.

The High Regent loomed over them. She was taller than most women, and when she wore heels, as she did now, she towered over others like a giant. Her face held nothing of the emotions stirring beneath.

Their father, on the other hand, paced behind her, his boots beating out a rhythm on the tile floor. He wore his usual gray military uniform, blue bars on his lapel marking him as a captain, and yellow bars on his shoulder marking him as an instructor at the Lanopian Space Navy Academy. His bearded face barely contained the anger boiling underneath, and he rubbed his hands together. His pacing and fretting surely bothered their mother, but she didn't even glance back at her husband.

The four of them stood alone in the drawing room outside of their mother's office.

"You've gone too far, Rissa." Father stopped pacing for a moment and faced her.

She kept her eyes on the children.

"They're children! Thanan could have died, and you would have made our daughter a murderer at the age of ten. You could at least wait until she's fifteen before you officially make her your clone."

His words pricked Claribel and she looked down, fighting the tears pushing at the edges of her eyes. Could Thanan have really died because of what she'd done? Had he actually been in peril? She'd assumed not, but Father's angry reaction made her doubt her earlier conclusion.

"Thanan was in little real danger," her mother responded, as if answering Claribel's unspoken question. She continued to face the children even as she spoke with their father. "The drone cameras followed them at all times, and I had staff following them through the maze."

Staff had been following them? Claribel hadn't noticed them, and that annoyed her.

"He was burning alive in that hedge!" her father bellowed. "I don't care how many damn staff were close by. He's my son, too! They're just children!"

Mother turned to Father, her emotionless eyes suddenly filled with fury. Father stepped back before she even spoke as if she'd struck him.

"When they ascend to the heights of Lanopian politics, who will show them mercy then? You would coddle them, send them on pony rides and vacations to the coast of Onal. They were born to lead, born to rule. They will be coached as I was, learn as I did. When Claribel rules Lanopi, and when Thanan leads our armies to victory, our enemies here and abroad will weep at the fierce creatures I've molded. And Lanopi will be better for it."

Claribel had heard a similar speech almost every day of her life, but it never ceased to swell the pride in her breast. She stood taller after her mother dubbed her the next High Regent. Mother had followed her own father to the highest position on the planet, and Claribel was destined to do the same.

Father's countenance proclaimed defeat, his shoulders slumped. He was respected and admired in every corner of their world, except in his own house.

"Do as you must." His voice hung in the air, a deep whisper. "But I will no longer be a part of this." He turned and walked away.

"What does that mean?" the High Regent spat, her voice equal parts disdain and surprise.

"I will live in our home in Cosart. I will visit on holidays."

"I will not send the children to visit you."

Father looked back on his children, his eyes holding tears. Claribel had never seen her father cry. "I know." He turned and left.

Their mother turned back to them, her eyes unreadable once more.

"Claribel. Please explain your victory."

Could she be serious? Father had just walked out on them! His departure made Claribel angry and sad. She wanted to run after him and hug him, or maybe find him and scream at him that he was a coward. And her mother wanted to talk about the maze?

But Mother was always serious. The High Regent raised her eyebrow, showing a slight sign of impatience at Claribel's delay.

"I discovered Thanan's tactic of busting through the hedges," Claribel responded, straightening her posture and looking her mother in the eyes. "I calculated that it would be quicker than my route. I would not be able to duplicate it, as he's faster and stronger. That's when I thought about starting a fire with the greenberry wine and the mirror."

"But what if the cistern hadn't had any wine, but only been an empty vessel?"

"I had a secondary plan. I would have waited at the same intersection, a hedge vine in hand. When he busted through, I planned to trip him and then tie his legs with the vine." Claribel had only thought of the second plan after the fact; she'd become as accomplished a liar as her mother.

Mother turned to Thanan. "And what was your secondary plan?"

Thanan began to shrug, but then winced in pain. "I didn't have one. My plan would have worked if she hadn't cheated."

"Cheated?" Claribel retorted. "Like digging through hedges isn't already cheating!"

"So sorry, little Bel, that you're smaller and . . ."

"Silence." Mother's admonition stopped the squabble. "Thanan's tactic was not cheating, and neither was Claribel's. But Thanan forgot maxim twenty-seven. Repeat it."

"*Being strongest is good,*" they said together, "*but being smarter is better, and being devious is best.*"

"Exactly." She turned to Thanan. "Your plan was a good one, but you ignored its limitations. Claribel's strategy also embodied maxim thirty-five. Repeat it."

"*Wait to finalize your plan until your enemy's intentions are clear,*" they said together.

"Good. Claribel adjusted her plan beautifully once she understood yours. And you did not anticipate hers. She won, and you can either learn from it or you can wallow in self-pity like your father. Claribel is the winner and you, Thanan, will be in isolation for half a day after the surgeons have seen to fixing your burns."

"But Mother, isn't his pain punishment enough?" Claribel regretted the words as soon they escaped.

"Claribel, recite maxim one hundred four."

"Mercy and compassion are not for those who lead. You fake those attributes in public, but when important decisions are to be made, you leave them behind."

"This show of weakness will cost your brother." Her eyes shifted to Thanan. "You will now have twenty-four hours' isolation, and you will see the surgeons after your isolation is finished."

Claribel wanted to scream and protest, but she knew it would only do more harm. She looked over at her brother, and he painfully shrugged again and smiled. Why did Thanan always love her? Why didn't he hate her for burning him? Maybe because they were the only ones who could truly understand one another, the only ones who understood what it was like to be children of the High Regent.

"Are we done torturing the children, Rissa?" Nanna stood in the doorway, her expression as empty as Mother's.

"You are to address me as High Regent, Candra." Mother did not turn to face Nanna.

"I've been trying to get you to call me Mother since you were seven, so I guess we're even."

Mother regarded Nanna coolly. "Have you come with a purpose, Candra, or are you simply here to interrupt me?"

"Oh, Diede forbid I interrupt a recitation of my late husband's sacred maxims, but yes I come with a purpose. I've come to fetch Claribel so she can meet her new tutor."

"Claribel already ran off another tutor?" Thanan asked.

Nanna smiled. "Called her stupid, I believe, as well as a dozen other more imaginative insults. You know how sensitive academics are."

Mother dismissed Claribel with a nod. Claribel bowed and followed Nanna from the room.

Nanna's face showed even less than what Mother's did. But Claribel couldn't help feeling ashamed in Nanna's presence for what she'd done to Thanan.

"How do you know if you've made the right choice?" Claribel asked as they walked, servants bowing and dodging as they passed.

"You want to know if what you did to your brother was right or wrong? You want me to make you feel better about it?" Nanna continued walking and did not look at Claribel.

"Yes."

"Your brother was in little danger; for all of my daughter's terrible parenting, she does ensure your lives will continue. And you won the game. What do you fear you did wrong?"

"I caused him pain." Claribel's eyes filled with tears, and she couldn't finish her thought.

Nanna stopped and knelt before her, placing her wrinkled hands on Claribel's shoulders. "Your mother, the High Regent, expects a great deal from you. I'm not sure exactly how you should act; I was raised in a home of the arts, not one of politics. Marrying your grandfather replanted me in this world, but after forty-seven years in this palace I'm still mystified by it all." Nanna wiped a stray tear from Claribel's face. "But the fact that you feel bad about hurting your brother brings me a great deal of hope." Nanna's eyes shined as she smiled.

"Hope for what?"

"Hope for our future, little Bel." Nanna patted Claribel's cheek and began walking again. "Now we should talk about your new tutor. She's a recent graduate of Onal University. She studied history, botany, politics, and ecology."

"I don't need a tutor."

"From hope to despair in only a few moments," Nanna said as if to herself. "Everyone needs to learn, Bel."

"Yes, but these tutors have nothing to teach me. I can access the best books, lectures and lessons from the jumpnet in seconds. I know more than any of my tutors."

Nanna laughed. "You have your father's heart, and your mother's mind. Listen Bel: teachers are not just about lessons and lectures. They are also about seeing the universe around you in a different way, altering your perspective to make it better, or at least more complete. And I think I've found a tutor who can even match your intellect."

"We'll see." It was meant as a playful jab at Nanna, but it was also true.

They reached Claribel's tutoring room, the doors sliding open as they
approached. Replicas of the known star systems lined the walls, and old

paper books filled several shelves. The only thing out of place was a small woman, not much taller than Claribel. Her skin and hair were smooth and several shades lighter than Claribel's, marking her as from beyond the Illiopan continent. She wore a long, tight braid in the Illiopan style, signaling to the world that she was unmarried.

"Claribel, daughter of Rissa," Nanna said, "this is Ona of Remin. She is a graduate of Onal University and took a leave of absence from teaching there to come here and be your tutor."

"Pleased to meet you." The truth was, Claribel was not pleased. Tutors wasted time, talked down to her, and then got frustrated when she asked questions they couldn't immediately answer. Claribel had gone through five tutors in the past eleven months; she planned on making than six in less than twelve.

"Pleased to meet you as well." Her elongated vowels indicated she was Onala, not originally from Remin on the southern coast of Farre.

"I will leave you two to get to know each other. Claribel, please be nice for at least one day." Nanna smiled just before the doors slid close behind her.

"Ona." Claribel let the name hang in the air. "Goddess of the winter and ocean. Your parents weren't very creative with your name. I bet every other girl in Onal was named Ona."

Ona smiled and did not bite at the bait of Claribel guessing her actual birth place. "Not quite. Last I checked, about eight percent of women on my continent are named Ona."

"Hopefully your mind is filled with more important facts than that."

Ona pulled a small pad from her dress and pressed it a few times. The room darkened, and a map of the known systems lit the floor, complete with the starjump points and paths.

"What is the most important system among the known?" Ona stepped into the middle of the room, between Coznar and Eslaza.

"Important in what way? Economically? Politically? Historically?"

"Answer in your own way, and provide your reasoning. Which of these systems is the most important?"

Claribel exhaled. Open questions like this were stupid. She could justify almost any answer.

She walked among the systems, from where she started in Fortuna to Lanopi, the two systems controlled by the Lanopians. She walked along the starjump to Coznar, Lanopi's most important trade partner and historical enemy. From there she walked to Alandria and looked left toward Regno and then right toward Pastrack.

"Alandria," she finally replied.

"Why?"

"It is the only system connected to four other key systems. If its leadership ever learned basic economics, they would be the center of trade, culture, and perhaps might."

"A good answer. But it wasn't your first thought. What did you think first?"

"That this was a stupid, arbitrary question in which I could have made a case for Lanopi, Coznar, Regno, or any other system."

"What if I told you the most important system was Nooteezia?"

Claribel snorted, but stopped when she saw her tutor wasn't kidding. "Nooteezia? I would say you need to go back to school."

"That's sarcasm; that's not an answer."

"Fine." Claribel walked across the map to stand near Nooteezia's dot. "Two of its three starjump points go to fairly meaningless systems: Vesta and Fortuna. It's connected to Eslaza, its biggest enemy, and not directly connected to any allies. It's embroiled in constant civil wars and hampered by primitive religions and backward practices. It makes Regno look like a strong option. Nooteezia is a backward, poor, isolated joke." Claribel looked up triumphantly at her new tutor; the woman wouldn't last the week.

"How do we find starjump points?"

Claribel shrugged at the change of subject and then began thinking about her space physics, a topic she despised. Thanan liked it and was good at it, which made her struggles even more unbearable.

"We survey the system's star, looking for breakdowns in . . ." Claribel couldn't remember the right words.

"Breakdowns in its gravitation field as related to other stars in the universe," Ona said. "And how many starjump points are there around any given star?"

"We don't really know. We can usually find only two, three, or four strong enough to enable travel. What does this have to do with Nooteezia?"

"What type of star is it?"

"White I believe."

"You believe, or you know?" Ona touched a button, and now the floor shined with the Nooteezia system, a bright white star surrounded by fourteen planets and three asteroid belts. "Is there anything unique about this star?"

Claribel shrugged. "I don't remember. I don't care for celestial physics."

"What do you care about?"

"Trade. Power. Military advantage. Science is an old art now, with discovery mostly behind us. We traverse the stars, cure disease, live longer and better than our ancestors. Science is boring now."

"If you care about trade and power, and you don't understand Nooteezia's place in the universe, then I would say you understand very little."

Claribel smiled. "The other five tutors before you thought I understood very little. But they learned they were wrong and they left."

Ona smiled back. "I don't think they left because of how smart you are; I think they left because you don't listen." Ona walked the perimeter of the Nooteezia floor map. "In the last several years, starjump physicists have begun to better understand how the different gravitational characteristics of a given star determine the starjump points in each system. Yes, most systems have two, three, or four potential points. But occasionally, stars exhibit a different gravitational field which could create more, perhaps dozens, perhaps hundreds. It could mean connecting all the known systems and faster inter-system travel. Some of the new starjump points would likely lead to unexplored systems. Nooteezia's white star in such a star."

"So Nooteezia's system could be a doorway to unknown systems?" Claribel narrowed her eyes as she looked down at the sixth planet of the system, the only inhabitable one.

"Yes."

"How many?"

"We don't know. Could be none, could be dozens. Starjump physicists are studying Nooteezia as we speak to better understand what we don't know.""

"Why haven't I heard about this before?"

Ona shook her head. "I don't know. You could look it up on the jumpnet if you like. But it's not common knowledge because the scientists have yet to discover the equations which will allow us access to those starjump points. Far-off theory is rarely news."

"So Nooteezia could be an exploration point. Dozens of new systems, potentially colonies." Political possibilities swam in Claribel's head. No new systems had been discovered in a millennia. New resources, new colonies, and wealth and power to be claimed.

"But if this is true," Claribel continued, "then why aren't the other systems pouncing on Nooteezia? It's stable, but hardly strong. Eslaza or Coznar should just go in and conquer it if there's even a decent chance the system is that valuable."

"Because science is boring, as you said. The leadership of humanity, from here to Regno, concern themselves with other things. The arts, music, science--ignored in favor of commerce, greed, and power. But yet, if they knew what wasn't common, they might assign very different importance to a system very few people spend much time thinking about."

Claribel looked back at the system map of Nooteezia. Fourteen planets, a system she'd ignored her entire life because of its strategic irrelevance.

She looked back at Ona. The woman smiled, confident she'd broken through. But it wouldn't be that easy. This new tutor piqued Claribel's interest, but she'd probably spent weeks preparing this little lesson, exploiting an area Claribel rarely studied.

"We're done for the day." Ona walked to the corner of the room, picked up a small package, and walked back, handing the plainly wrapped parcel to Claribel.

"What is this?" Claribel asked.

"Your clothes for tomorrow's lesson." Ona looked Claribel up and down. "What you wear is too fancy for what I have planned." Claribel began to open the package, but Ona placed a hand on hers. "Don't open it until shortly before our session tomorrow after lunch."

Claribel frowned. "I don't like surprises."

Ona laughed. "Another thing you'll need to learn."

chapter 13

A SECOND LESSON

Ona was likely to follow the path of Claribel's other tutors, leaving in an angry huff. But the presumptuous woman would certainly leave as the most creative.

Claribel looked at herself in the mirror image on the wall. With a wave of her hand, the mirror image disappeared and returned to its normal decorative pattern.

"I look absolutely ridiculous."

"You look lovely, my lady." Piera, Claribel's attendant, stood next to her.

"No I don't. These are commoner clothes, less appropriate than even your drab dress."

Piera blushed at the mention of her plain gray suit.

"Don't get mopey, Piera. Your dress is completely appropriate for your station, but this brown peasant dress is terrible. Everyone will see me and laugh, and if my mother sees me, I'll be in isolation for a week."

"No one will see you." Piera looked up, the embarrassment gone from her face. "Hardly anyone notices a servant or a peasant, especially not in this house."

Claribel rolled her eyes. "Please, Piera. I am the daughter of the High Regent; everyone across the planet knows my face almost as well as their own. By Diede's sacred name, there's probably colonists on the moons of Coznar Five who'd recognize me on sight."

Piera shrugged.

Despite the audacity of Ona's plan to dress her in commoner clothes to support some abstract lesson, Claribel couldn't suppress her curiosity. The young tutor was certainly intriguing.

Claribel dismissed Piera and walked the halls toward her tutoring room. As she passed servants, she ran into two of them, who cursed at her.

The second servant, a young man carrying laundry, cursed as they collided. "Watch where you're going, little girl."

Claribel spun on him. "Little girl? Don't you know who I am?"

The young man cocked his head. "Let me guess: you're the High Regent's daughter in disguise." He laughed and kept moving.

After that, Claribel dodged the next few servants, and pressed against the wall to avoid being trampled by two guards. Even those who glanced her way showed no recognition.

"Good afternoon," Ona said as Claribel reached the tutoring room, smiling brightly.

"What is the meaning of this?" Claribel looked down at her clothes. "Mother might have you imprisoned for this if she finds out."

"It is necessary for our lesson today. We're going on a little field trip, and if you're dressed in your usual clothes. . . ." Ona lifted her hand to her chin, examining Claribel's attire. "Well, that just wouldn't do."

"Where are we going where I need to dress like this?"

"We're going into Iopa."

Claribel threw her arms into the air. "I go into the city all the time and in much nicer clothes. Why is this time different?"

"How many people come with you when you visit the city?"

Claribel counted them. "At least a dozen guards, four to five attendants at minimum."

"And do the people of the city recognize you?"

"Of course," Claribel blurted. "I'm the daughter of the High Regent; everyone knows my face."

"Is it possible that people act different when you're around? What effect does your presence have on those around you?"

"How am I supposed to know?" Claribel walked away and sat in a chair. "I'm only there if I'm there."

Ona sat next to her. "Well then, let me rephrase my question. Do you ever act differently because of who's in the room?"

Claribel considered it. "I suppose so. I'm very different with Nanna than I am with Mother. And Thanan and I act more like children when it's just the two of us."

"So how do you think the people act when you come rolling down the street with guards and attendants, when everyone knows you're the daughter of the High Regent?"

Claribel thought about it. "I would guess that the aristocracy bow and mumble pleasantries, while the commoners bow and move to get out of the way."

"I want you to see the city, Claribel, as it really is. You've spent your ten years mostly within these confining walls, and when you venture out, you carry the walls with you. I need you to see without those walls." Ona pointed to Claribel's plain clothing. "This will make you invisible, or at least, make you into just a girl and her older sister walking the streets of Iopa."

Claribel thought back on how no one noticed her on her short walk from her chambers to the tutoring room. She couldn't really imagine walking the city as a commoner, no stares and no aristocratic political maneuvering.

"My mother will still likely dismiss you if she finds out her daughter went into the city dressed in rags."

Ona smiled, laughing slightly. "Then we best not get caught."

The High Regency Palace sat atop a hill overlooking the world's capital city of Iopa. The palatial complex was known as 'the city above the city.' Twenty-foot walls surrounded it, and within those walls was a city all its own. There were shops, restaurants, housing, administrative buildings fifteen stories tall, and the world's largest military base. Anything one could need could be found in the complex.

As Claribel walked alongside Ona down the winding road toward the capital, a sudden thrill shot through her. Even though you could find what you needed in the city above the city, life was so different in Iopa that you'd think it was separated by more than just a wall.

As they reached the edge of the city, a thousand sounds, scents and sights took over Claribel's senses. The sweet smell of Nezian meat pies mixed with the spicy odor of curried beets from Aneis. A stand along the city's main street boasted brightly colored art from Toma--blocks of vibrant greens, yellows and purples. The sound of a hundred voices mixed into an audible river--mothers calling after children, shop owners encouraging pedestrians to stop walking and start shopping, and a hundred conversations about everything from politics and philosophy, to what someone might make for dinner that evening.

Despite dozens of trips to Iopa in her life, despite living less than half a mile from this vibrant city, Claribel had never experienced it like this. Her usual trips into the city were like a relentless wind, pushing everything else aside. Aristocrats bowed. Commoners nodded and shuffled aside. And the shopkeepers who called so eagerly today held their tongues, silently hoping the High Regent's family would grace their stores. But now, dressed as a commoner, not holding the weight that her birthright carried, she was nothing more than a raindrop falling among millions of the same.

Much to Claribel's surprise, Ona had not asked a single question, had not pointed out anything of interest. She simply led the way, glancing back occasionally. This was a bizarre lesson indeed.

Despite eating a full lunch, the scents of foods from every Lanopian continent and most of the known systems watered her mouth. She stopped at a small stand selling blocks of cheese. Spicy goat cheese from the planet Camsarta, and bitter smelling Alandrian cheese aged two hundred years. Mother hated Alandrian cheese, partially because of its bitterness, and partially because of her distaste for the planet's culture. Maybe because of that, Claribel couldn't get enough of it.

"Would you like some cheese?" a young woman running the cart asked. She was well-dressed, taller than Claribel by a head, and she spoke with a thick Coznarian accent, her words elongated.

"You are from Coznar?" Claribel asked in Coznarian, hoping she'd phrased the question correctly.

"Yes, I am," the woman replied in her native tongue, brushing her short, blond hair from her face, its bright color contrasting with her dark skin. "You speak Coznarian well."

Claribel suppressed a blush. "Not well enough."

"What would you like?" the cheese vendor replied, switching back to Lanopian.

"Some of the Alandrian white," she said, pulling her pad from her pocket. She waved it at the vendor's terminal, sending the woman three credits.

The Coznarian woman smiled and handed a small block to Claribel. "Thank you, young lady." The woman's smile brightened further.

Claribel nodded and turned to face Ona, who'd been watching intently. The tutor smiled, but still said nothing. She turned and walked slowly down the street, Claribel trailing behind.

A block later she swallowed the last of the bitter Alandrian cheese and walked in stride with Ona. "We've been gone more than an hour from the palace. When does my instruction begin?"

"It began an hour ago," the tutor responded.

Claribel rolled her eyes. "You've taught me nothing."

"Really? You've learned nothing during our walk?"

"Yes, but nothing you taught me."

Ona laughed and shook her head. "You are a stubborn one, Bel." They'd agreed to use her nickname just in case her real name grabbed too much attention. "So what did you learn that I had nothing to do with teaching you?"

"The city is dirtier than I remember."

"They clean the streets before you come."

"That's ludicrous. They don't clean the streets every time I go shopping."

Ona raised her eyebrows. "For such a smart child, you miss a thing or two. Do you ever go shopping or come into the city spontaneously?"

"Of course not. We have to ready the staff and get dressed in the appropriate clothes."

"And while you get ready, so does the city."

They came around a corner and into a cobblestoned square. Thick human traffic filled the pedestrian-only zone. Four large corporate buildings surrounded the urban clearing, as well as a domed church.

Among the scrambling merchants, aristocracy, and working class were dozens of women, dressed in the distinctive yellow robes of the Church of the Heavens. Each woman, most of them middle aged or older, walked through the crowd passing out e-sheet propaganda. One of the yellow clad women approached them. Her long hair was a mix of brown and white save for the left side of her head which was shaved to the skin. Long lines from her eyes made her look old, by a bright smile made her look younger. She held an e-sheet to Claribel, but the girl refused to take it.

"Are you believers?" the woman asked.

"Believers in some ancient superstition about omnipotent beings floating throughout the universe?" Claribel shot back. "Certainly not."

"The good news, young skeptic, is that your soul will find its way to the Well without your belief. But your freedom there will depend on your kindness and love in life and how you die."

Claribel huffed. *"Kindness is useful, but only to a point. Kindness usually fails or is taken advantage of. Be the one who takes advantage, not its unwitting victim."* The maxim escaped her lips before she could control it. Mother did not want the maxims to be public--she said they made her sound cruel, and as maxim two said: *A leader should appear kind, generous, loving, and human. In reality, she need not have any of those attributes.*

"Well, young skeptic," the woman responded, "I can see your heart will not be changed today. Perhaps another time." The woman reached out and placed a yellow dot on Claribel's shoulder. The missionary disappeared into the crowd.

"What's this for?" Claribel asked, pointing to the yellow dot.

"It protects you from further debates with the Heaveners."

"Good."

Ona offered a half smile. "Or maybe it's too protect the missionaries from further discussions with you."

The tutor led them across the courtyard toward the yellow-domed church. Hundreds of people occupied the space, and the dense crowd annoyed Claribel. As she bumped into people, she wanted to scream at them, tell them to get out of her way. She was the daughter of the High Regent after all. But she said nothing, only clung to Ona's sleeve so she wouldn't get lost. She'd never in her life been jostled by a crowd, and she didn't care for the experience.

For a moment, Claribel considered letting go and disappearing into the crowd. Though Ona had been interesting thus far, Claribel knew she'd become bored with the new tutor. Ona seemed like the type who wouldn't give up, but her mother would fire her for losing Claribel in the city. She could set a new standard for getting rid of a tutor within a day of starting.

Fear gripped her as she considered letting go. Faces floated above her, some kind looking, some harried, and some sad. But some of the faces looked cruel, mean, and angry. Though Claribel was the daughter of the High Regent, dressed as she was today, she was a commoner, one who could be preyed upon. So she gripped Ona's sleeve even tighter and pulled herself close to her new tutor.

Ona and Claribel cleared the crowd near the steps of the Church of the Heavens. Most of the crowd avoided getting too close to the yellow-domed structure. Claribel looked up at the towering dome; this close, it looked like it stretched to the clouds.

"What do you see?" Ona asked.

"A massive waste of space." Claribel shook her head.

Ona looked at her and smiled, a kind but mischievous grin. "And the

High Regent's palace has no wasted space, no aesthetic features?"

Claribel considered the palace. Most rooms were highly utilitarian. Her mother's grandmother Junda built the palace, and by all accounts, the woman despised any sign of ostentatiousness. But the building had been transformed by Marsil, her mother's father. The audience chamber had a ceiling three stories high. Works of the most famous Lanopian artists hung on the walls of the dining hall, and abstract representations of the ancient Lanopian gods had been carved into the facade at the palace entrance.

As if sensing Claribel had finished her thoughts, Ona spoke: "Look again at the church, not its architecture, but the humanity of it."

The humanity of the church? It was a building of stone, steel, and fine metals; it had little in the way of humanity. But as her eyes scanned the building, she saw a group of yellow-clad women standing at its side.

Small lift movers floated between the women and the back of the church. The women handed out clothing and bread to the poorly dressed and ill kept. Grime covered the faces and hands of those they served. Many mumbled to themselves, haunted by invisible mental illnesses. Others limped or had only one arm. Claribel gasped at the sight of a woman whose eyes looked like they'd been cut out with a knife. She gripped Ona's sleeve.

"I thought my mother's charity programs housed and fed all the poor." Claribel looked away from the eyeless woman.

Ona looked down, her eyes softer than they'd been before. "Your mother's programs leave many holes, especially for those who are political dissenters."

Claribel considered the implications. Could her mother have created the eyeless woman, the gaunt children, and the muttering men? She wanted to protest, to declare that her mother would do no such thing, that she was the best High Regent their planet had ever known, wise and kind. But she knew better. *Kindness is useful, but only to a point. Kindness usually fails or is taken advantage of. Be the one who takes advantage, not its unwitting victim.*

Instead of protesting, she said, "So these people are cleared off the streets before we arrive, keeping the appearance of total prosperity."

"Don't misunderstand this lesson." Ona looked over at the eyeless woman who nodded appreciatively as she clutched a small loaf of bread. "There are fewer poor now than during her great-grandmother's reign, and considerably less than before the High Regents restored order after the Interloper War. But the wind still blows too many Lanopians around our world, with no safe place to land."

"Are you a Heavener?" Claribel asked.

Ona shook her head. "I was raised by two Heaveners, but I did not unite myself with the faith when I came to the Age of Ascension. Still, I respect what they do for these people. They give without any thought of repayment and without restrictions. They feed and clothe criminals and innocent alike."

Claribel looked again at the Heavener women and the recipients of their charity. The yellow-clad women went about their duties with solemn, pleasant smiles and greetings. Like the eyeless woman, all the poor tapped their chins twice and pointed to the sky, the Heavener gesture for thanks.

"Come," Ona said, walking toward the church's front door. "The Heaveners have something else to teach us today."

Claribel had never entered a Church of the Heavens, and curiosity bloomed inside her as they walked up the steps.

chapter 14

CHURCH OF THE HEAVENS

he Heaveners had once been the dominant religion on Lanopi, this church serving as a monument to its ancient prominence. But they were a minority now operating at the fringes of society. As a child, Claribel heard the rumors of human sacrifice and of children being forced to ascend against their will. Her rational mind told her these were just rumors spread by ignorance, but the logic did not completely extinguish her morbid curiosity.

They climbed a set of stone steps to the church's front door. Two-story high stone doors marked the entrance, a formidable passage which looked like it was meant to keep people out more than let them in. Claribel imagined what mechanism would be needed to move such a heavy set of doors.

Ona knocked softly on the left door. A small window opened above her head.

"Are you Ascended?" came a deep voice, the sunlight seemingly halted by the intense darkness inside. "Do you believe in the Whole?"

"I am not Ascended," Ona replied, "but I do believe in the Whole. My parents, Jox and Neara, are believers and worship at the Church in Remin."

"And you are accompanied by whom?" Hearing the name of Ona's parents did not soften the man's tense tone.

"She is Bel. She has not reached the Age of Ascension and she desires to learn."

The small window quickly shut, and Claribel looked expectantly at Ona. "Will they let us in?"

"It depends. I'm sure I have the correct answers, but the Heavener priests are fickle by nature and sometimes forbid entrance for no other reason than they didn't like your smile. Each individual priest is given substantial autonomy."

As she finished her explanation, the left door began to push backward, moved by an unseen hand. Claribel could not hear any gears or the soft movement of plastic; it sounded more like gravel scraped by sandpaper. Claribel looked back toward the crowd, and though the mass of people still flowed, they had slowed to observe the young woman and the girl preparing to enter the Church of the Heavens. She could still feel their stares as she turned and gripped Ona's sleeve again.

"Relax, Bel. There will not be any human sacrifices." Ona smiled down at her. "They only do that on Third Day, and it's Sixth Day."

Claribel smiled weakly, still mystified by what she might actually see. The door stopped only a quarter open, but it was a large enough opening that two horses could pass side-by-side with little trouble. She followed Ona into the darkness.

Three steps into the church, the door slowly swung closed, plunging them into total darkness. Claribel fought the urge to run, but she knew it was pointless. Whatever strange scheme Ona and the priests might have concocted was complete now.

The Church suddenly burst to life, exploding with thousands of flickering candles. The sudden luminescence did not light the cavernous space properly, leaving dark spots and dancing shadows. The lack of natural light cast a gloomy feeling across the small entryway and beneath the cupola.

Claribel started as she turned to face a man who stood close enough to touch her. He wore the maroon robes of the priests of the Church of the Heavens, the right side of his head shaved with long dark hair flowing on the other side. His pale skin reflected the dancing lights.

"Welcome to the Church of the Heavens. Follow me."

They followed him from the entrance way and under the cupola. Claribel had imagined pews or chairs or something, but the space was nearly empty. Too small benches sat on each side under the maroon painted dome, and a small pulpit stood on the side opposite them. By all she could tell, the door was the only mechanical or technological thing about the place. Claribel had never seen true candlelight before, only artificial copies. These looked like actual flames, though Claribel could not guess how they lighted them all at once.

The priest stopped under the center of the copula, his feet landing in an irregular shape painted on the floor. "Ona Trancta, daughter of Jox and Neara Trancta."

If his knowledge of her surprised Ona, it did not show on her face. "I'm afraid I don't know your name."

"My given name is gone now. Most here call me Brother or Father."

"What shall we call you?" Ona asked.

He smiled and looked at his feet. "What does this picture represent, Ona?"

Ona did not look down. "It represents the center of the universe, the Well of Souls."

"Precisely," he said through his smile. "I am a guide for those who wish to reach the peace which can only be found in the Well of Souls. So you may call me Guide. What brings you here, Ona? And why bring this one? Her family would not approve, and she wears a dot, so she's already rejected enlightenment today."

Claribel's heart sank under Guide's piercing eyes. Did he know who she was? Did he see past the disguise which had fooled even the palace's own staff?

Claribel looked up at Ona, hoping for an explanation. Ona's eyes remained locked with Guide.

"Could we please dispense with the supernatural intimidation? Remember: I was born to Heaveners."

Guide's permanent smile did not fade, but it left his eyes. "I made no claim to supernatural power, Ona of Remin." His eyes fell back on Claribel. "If the High Regent's daughter assumed so, that is her own imagination at work."

Ona turned to Claribel. "Despite the appearance of an ancient building, each Church of the Heavens contains thousands of cameras, and men in a chamber underneath monitor everything in here. They are feeding information to Guide through an earpiece."

Guide swung his long hair away from his left ear, and Claribel caught a small glimpse of the ear piece.

"Facial recognition," Claribel muttered.

Guide enlarged his smile. "Yes. And I believe the High Regent would not approve of her daughter's presence here. Though our doors are open to all, I suggest you leave. I would not want the High Regent to think we were trying to convert her daughter."

Claribel looked back at the massive stone doors; nothing about this building communicated 'open to all.'

"I think we've seen what I wanted her to see." Ona turned and walked back toward the door. Claribel quickly followed.

"One more question." Guide still stood on the Well of Souls, the light dancing on his face. "Why did you leave the Church, Ona? What drove you away?"

Ona tapped her chin twice and pointed to the ceiling. "Thank you for your time, Guide. May the Well take your soul when your time comes."

The smile finally left Guide's face, but he said nothing. They turned to leave, and the same stone door opened as they approached and closed when they reached the top step outside.

"What was that?" Claribel looked back at the door, shuddering.

"Can you guess why I didn't Ascend, why I didn't dedicate myself to the Cause of the Heavens?"

"Could it have anything to do with the creepy priests?"

Ona laughed as they descended the steps. "Creepy isn't the word I would use. What's the difference between Guide and the woman who approached us on the square?"

"The woman didn't make me feel like I was going to crawl out of my skin."

Ona laughed again. "Careful, Bel. You might actually succeed at being charming."

"It's not charm; it's sarcasm. I was sure you'd know the difference."

"What is cruel sarcasm to some can be witty conversation between two clever friends."

Claribel looked away. She didn't have friends, not really. Maybe Thanan. They'd played together since her first memories, but the competition their mother forced upon them made them rivals more than friends. The only other person she spent any time with was Piera, but she was seven years older and a servant. Claribel was not an expert on friendship, but she didn't think someone could truly be your friend if they worked for your family.

"All joking aside, Bel, tell me what you observed about the woman Heaveners and the priest."

"The priestesses are kind, they exhibit the virtues I believe the Heaveners stand for. They help people."

Ona and Claribel pushed through the crowded square and began walking up the hill toward the palace. Claribel's calves ached with each step on the steep incline, and she breathed heavily. She wasn't used to walking this much in a day.

"What about the priests?" Ona asked.

Claribel stopped and looked at the yellow dome sticking out among the oldest buildings of Iopa. "I don't know what to make of them. Guide was strange, distant. He didn't seem to exhibit any of the Heavener qualities."

"The priests of the Church of the Heavens consider themselves to be the gateway to the Well of Souls. They manage the Church, lead the Church. Women are not seen as equals, as they cannot lead a wayward soul to the Whole."

"You resent this because you're a woman?"

"No." Ona stopped and looked back at the dome. Her eyes held a sadness Claribel had not noticed before. "Though the male dominance is outdated, that's not why I didn't Ascend."

"Why did you leave it then?"

"I'm not sure it's true."

"Not sure? Meaning you think the rubbish about one of those gods visiting Palo thirteen hundred years ago might be true?"

"Amazing." Ona shook her head.

"What?"

"You can go from charming and sweet to obnoxious faster than any girl I've ever met." Ona walked toward the palace and Claribel struggled to keep up. "I don't know what Palo saw, and I don't know if the Whole is a group of gods, aliens, or fiction. But I see the light of belief in my parents, and it makes me sad that I don't have it, that I lack their purpose.

"Those women do good. They make a difference in the lives of thousands here on Lanopi, and women like them help millions more on Alandria, Pastrack, Scavart, and Regno. There is great goodness among the Heaveners, but there's also a darkness I can't quite ignore."

Ona's words drew Claribel's thoughts to her mother. The High Regent ruled well, kept peace, and deftly kept Lanopi out of interstellar war. But Claribel knew mother's maxims, knew her cruelty and had seen its results first hand.

"Can something be good and evil at the same time?" Claribel asked.

"I don't know."

"You are the strangest teacher I've ever had," Claribel said through struggling breaths.

Ona laughed.

chapter 15

THIRD LESSON

he weeks passed as Ona engaged and challenged Claribel in their lessons. Something inside of Claribel urged her to dislike the young tutor, to find ways to torture and torment her as she had previous tutors. But she could never find it inside herself to do so.

Maybe it was because Claribel enjoyed their debates too much.

"Those who lead need morality more than any other group of people," Ona said one day. "Their actions effect millions and billions of people."

"They have to make the tough decisions," Claribel replied, "and it might seem immoral to the outside, but society's needs are the overlying morality." It wasn't a maxim, but it felt like one.

"But who decides what those needs are? The leaders alone? Lanopi used to be more of a democracy, with frequent elections and a robust public debate. Now a High Regent can reign for a lifetime with little challenge. The Senate seats are in theory elected, but few senators lose elections, and they are succeeded most often by family. Society's needs may be the overlying morality, but how does society express those needs to its leaders? In a purer democracy, that would be through elections and public debate."

Claribel shook her head. "Purer democracy led to the Interloper War and near subjection to Coznar and Eslaza. The common people pick poor leaders and are led by whims and fancy. They might vote for someone because they like their eyes, or not vote for someone because they will cut a program that benefits the individual. People are fickle and unreliable. So a leader like our High Regents, leaders like my mother, they are the leaders the people desperately need even if they can't see that."

Ona shook her head. "No more debate today. Tomorrow, we're going to do something different. Dress in those commoner clothes I provided; we have another trip to make." She pulled something from her bag, a long wig of curly brown hair, many shades lighter than Claribel's near black. "And wear this as well. It should enhance the disguise."

"We shouldn't return to Iopa," Claribel replied. "Mother would not like that." Mother hadn't said anything about their first excursion, so maybe it had gone undetected, though Claribel couldn't imagine it had.

"We won't be going to Iopa," Ona said. "We won't even be leaving the palace complex."

So the next day Claribel met Ona at the tutor room, and they left the palace and walked toward the Lanopian Space Navy building. Seeing the deep blue structure of the Space Navy building reminded her of her father. She hadn't seen him in more than a month. Was he working there today? Was he staying across the continent at their house in Cosart? She wished she could see him.

"I've toured the Space Navy building dozens of times," Claribel said, frustrated by missing her father as much as by their destination.

"We're not going there," Ona replied. "We're going beyond there."

"There's nothing beyond there."

"Nothing?"

Claribel thought of the map of the complex in her head, and saw the corner beyond the Space Navy building. "There's nothing but the servants' village."

"And that's where we're going."

"I've never been to the servants' village," Claribel said.

"Shocking."

Past the Space Navy's deep blue tower sat a series of gray brick apartments. Plain, boxy buildings lined straight clean streets. The near silence surrounding the administrative buildings gave way to a low buzz of activity somewhere out of sight. They rounded a corner and found the source of the noise: a large town square. Children played games, men and women stood together or sat on chairs talking. Tall trees lined the square, leaves of green, purple and bright red providing a stark contrast to the gray brick dominating the surrounding structures. The town square bounced with life, smiling servants enjoying time with friends and family, an easy camaraderie completely foreign to the streets and halls Claribel knew.

"How many people live in servants' village?" Claribel asked.

"You don't know?"

Claribel had never really considered this part of the complex. She believed that all the servants who worked for the High Regency, senate, and all the bureaucracies lived here behind the walls surrounding the palace. She'd heard Father talk about how hard it was to get one of these jobs, that serving the government was an honor and a privilege. Mother had added that though the pay was not high, the servants were treated exceptionally well and housing, education, and healthcare were included in their compensation. *An aggrieved servant is fodder for the enemy. Treat them as well as you would family,* read the High Regent's seventeenth maxim. Claribel had always found that maxim a little curious; Mother didn't exactly treat family all that well.

"I know supporting the government and bureaucracies requires a lot of staff. . . ." she said after considering it and not finding her own answer.

"Close to eleven thousand people live in this part of the complex," the tutor replied.

Claribel followed Ona deeper into the square. They approached three boys close to Claribel's age throwing a ball around. They passed three older men moving tiles on a board with their feet, a game called slide. She couldn't take her eyes off all the fun activities. *Frivolous.* She heard the High Regent's assessment in her mind. But it looked like a lot of fun.

Her eyes firmly stuck on the fun, Claribel collided with someone, knocking a taller girl and Claribel to the ground. The impact twisted her wig in front of her face.

"I'm so sorry," the other girl said, and Claribel gasped when she recognized the voice as that of her own servant.

Ona picked her up by her arm pits, and quickly adjusted the wig. This time Piera gasped when Claribel's face became visible.

"My lady." Piera started to bow, but Ona lifted her by her chin back into a standing position.

"Not here, Piera," Ona said. "We can't let anyone else know she's here. No one else has noticed her."

"I don't think the High Regent would be pleased by this," Piera protested. "The village is a safe place, but Claribel should have a guard."

"I would like to see where you live," Claribel said over Piera's protest. "And this isn't a command. Only if you'd like to show me."

Piera looked around again, as if she were certain she was being watched. She looked back at Claribel and sighed. "I guess it wouldn't do any harm. Will you both promise to return to the palace after that?"

Claribel and Ona nodded. Piera sighed again and led them away from the square and to a small apartment building. As they entered the building, they passed casually-dressed servants coming and going and a few uniformed folks headed to work. Midway down the hallway on the first level, they stopped at a door, and Piera turned to face them.

"Jimma has not been feeling well the past couple of days," Piera said. "So don't be offended if she says something mean. She does that sometimes."

Claribel's face burned with embarrassment. Piera had been her maidservant for three years, but Claribel had no idea who Jimma was.

Before Claribel could ask, Piera opened the door and led them into a small apartment. The front room was smaller than any of Claribel's closets and contained a small kitchen and living area. It was clean and well lit, and a mural of plants Claribel didn't recognize dominated one of the walls, oversized vines stretching across the living space.

"Jimma!" Piera called. "Are you here?"

A door opened and an old woman walked into the living area but stopped short when her eyes landed on Ona and Claribel. "Who are these people, Moira?"

"Friends," Piera replied, ignoring the use of the wrong name. "They came for tea."

Jimma's eyes suddenly burned with anger. "I don't like visitors." Her last word came out with a spit.

"But it's the High Regent herself and her daughter," Piera replied.

Ona and Claribel looked over at Piera, but she didn't meet their eyes.

Jimma's face changed into a formal air. "I apologize," she said with curtsy. "I did not realize we had distinguished guests."

Jimma wore a shapeless gray dress; if it hadn't been on her body, Claribel might have mistaken it for a towel or duvet. Dozens of tight braids of gray hair flowed from her head, onto her shoulders and down her back. The distinctive hairstyle marked Jimma as someone from the Eastern Continent, and a tattoo of three black lines below her right ear confirmed it; all Easterners were required by law to get that tattoo upon coming to one of the western continents for work or even vacation. Claribel had seen only a handful of those tattoos in her life.

Jimma, Ona, and Claribel sat at a small, round table while Piera made tea.

"What brings your majesty and her daughter to the Bautra?" Jimma asked. Bautra was the native name for the eastern continent.

Claribel looked up at Piera, and the servant girl smiled weakly. Did the older woman really believe they were in Bautra?

"Visiting the people," Ona said, her voice formal and high, taking on her version of the High Regent. "It has been too long since I've been here, and my daughter has never been."

Jimma's eyes smiled, though her creased face made only half the gesture. "How wonderful. I've always told folks that the High Regent is good for Bautra, but many think not. But we need you, High Regent. I sometimes wish I could leave here, move to Iliopa and maybe even work there. My family have been servants for the House Billa for more than two hundred years."

Ona and Claribel nodded as Jimma spent the next ten minutes detailing her qualifications as if she were applying for a servant's job. Claribel held back laughter at several points as the old woman relayed experiences bathing a truck ox and trying to find an herb which many believed extinct. The extravagant requests of the House Billa did not sound entirely different than some of the more obscure requests her mother and father made of their staff. Or at least, her father had made, before he moved out.

Piera served the tea as Jimma finished detailing her extensive experiences. The room was quiet for a few minutes as everyone sampled the hot drink.

As Jimma finished her tea, she looked up, her face alighting with surprise. "Who are our visitors?"

"Friends," Piera replied. "I think you need some rest, Jimma."

The older woman looked around, confused and nervous. "You might be right. I don't feel myself."

Piera helped Jimma stand and guided her through the door and into the other room. Ona and Claribel finished their tea in silence.

"I'm sorry about that," Piera said as she sat. She took another sip of her tea. "Jimma has good days and bad. She used to be so much fun, but now she flits between anger, confusion, and memory loss." Piera considered her tea, her face pulled into a frown.

"Is she your grandmother?" Claribel asked.

Piera looked up and shook her head. "When I was so young that I can't even remember it, someone left me on the steps of the Church of the Heavens in Iopa."

Claribel pictured those cold steps, a young child, a mere baby, set there, abandoned by those who should have cared for her. She shivered.

"I was brought here when I was seven to be trained as a servant," Piera continued. "Jimma took me in. She's kind of the only family I have." She scrunched her face and examined her tea again, swirling it with a small motion.

"We should be getting back," Ona finally said. "Someone will miss the daughter of the High Regent eventually."

Piera stood first, and they walked to the door.

Ona reached out and grabbed the servant girl's hand. "Thank you for showing us your home."

"It's not much," she replied, her eyes not meeting Claribel's again.

Claribel wanted to say something, but clear thoughts were few and no words came. She knew so little of the young woman with whom she spent more time than anyone else. "Thank you," were the only words she could make, but they seemed insufficient.

"My pleasure." Piera bowed deeply and closed the door.

Ona and Claribel walked in silence through the plain hallways and out into the town square. They didn't speak until they reached the street.

"Why did you bring me here?" Claribel asked.

"I wanted you to see how the servants live, see their lives."

"But what did you want me to learn?"

Ona smiled. "My lesson plans aren't that simple. I don't know exactly what you'll learn; I just create opportunities for different thoughts. What you learn is something I can't really predict or control."

What had she learned? What had she gained by seeing this place? Despite being so close, this neighborhood stood a world apart from the palace. As they walked back toward Claribel's home, she looked on the boys throwing the ball, on the older men playing slide. Laughter and smiles filled this place, though she saw some pain, sorrow and anger as well. But mostly she saw joy. And she saw no loneliness. There was a togetherness she'd never seen in her life, and it made her sad. It made her want to hug Thanan and play a game with him.

And she wanted to do something for Piera. The girl gave faithful service, had cared for Claribel when she was sick. And when Piera left her duties in the palace, she went home to another life of service, one Claribel had known nothing about.

She wasn't sure what Ona had wanted her to learn, but she felt certain she'd learned something. She looked up at her tutor, examining the woman's soft features, kind eyes and almost constant smile. So different than mother's fierce stare and constant scowl. Even different than Nanna's kind face which had been hardened by years in the palace.

Claribel had never felt so different or so alone.

Claribel walked through the halls, dressed in her usual fine clothing--today a green dress marked with jewels on each seam, around the waist, and down the front. As she passed, servants bowed, aristocrats smiled. Everyone treated her as they had her entire life--like the daughter of the High Regent and great-granddaughter of the planet's savior.

Reaching the library, Claribel stepped up to the librarian's desk. Doot, the old librarian, looked down on her, his white sideburns a strong contrast to his baldness. Doot's eyes held suspicion, but they always did. He acted as if all these ancient, paper books were actually his and not her mother's. Doot treated everyone with a slight contempt, even the High Regent's children, maybe especially the High Regent's children.

"What can I help you with?" The librarian's voice sounded like he squeezed the words through a noisemaker.

"I'm looking for an annotated copy of *The Universe, the Whole, and the Well of Souls.*"

Doot narrowed his eyes. "Surely you have a copy of that on your reader. Why do you need a paper copy? And why do you wish to read that? Frivolous nonsense, your mother would say."

Claribel remembered the dusty smell of the Church of the Heavens, the darkness punctuated by candlelight. She knew she could find the book on her reader, but something felt right about a paper copy.

"It's not like I'm looking to Ascend, Master Doot. Just some reading, an assignment from my new tutor." It was a lie, but Doot would never know. And it's not as if he'd ask Ona about it; the only thing the man did out of the library was sleep, and maybe use the bathroom, though Thanan claimed he didn't even leave his chair to do that.

"Fine." Doot pushed a few buttons on his screen, and the third row of books behind him shifted in blazing speed and then stopped. The librarian reached back and plucked out a large book, one that was almost half as large as Claribel. He placed it on the desk. "Here you are."

"That book's almost as big as me." She examined the corded binding and the gold lettering of the title. "How am I supposed to read this or even carry it?"

"You asked for a paper copy, my young lady. As one of the richest and most powerful humans on the planet, I'd think you'd know you could ask a servant to carry it for you, maybe even turn the pages if it proves too difficult."

Claribel glared at Doot, but he seemed oblivious to her stare. She tapped the comm stamp on her hand. "Piera."

"Yes, my lady," Piera's voice responded.

"I need you in the library. I need help carrying something."

For most that day and the next, Claribel poured through the pages of the Heaveners' religious text. It was incredibly dry and boring. The only writing of the Heavener prophet Palo told in incredible detail about him meeting the god--and then laid out more than two hundred thousand words of the minutiae of good behavior, good death, and good thought. In some ways it read like her mother's maxims, except instead of two hundred, Palo laid out thousands. There was even a passage about the correct way to order bread; Claribel hadn't realized ordering bread was such a moral quandary.

The most interesting part was the section entitled *Finding the Well of Souls through a Good Death*. It listed many good ways to die, including while helping others, any death where you were the victim of murder or abuse, suicide if you had an incurable or un-preventable disease. Bad ways to die included thrill seeking, by violence you caused, preventable diseases, and any accident caused by one's own stupidity.

Claribel thought she could ram their entire cathedral through the holes in Palo's logic. Couldn't you provoke another into killing you as a way to earn your right into the Well of Souls? And wasn't dying as a result of your own bad decision punishment enough without these strange gods consigning you to an eternity of listless wandering?

"That's an interesting choice in reading materials."

Claribel look up to see her mother standing in the doorway of Claribel's study. "It was assigned reading from my new tutor." Another lie. She couldn't tell Mother that her visits to the church and the servants' village had piqued her curiosity.

"Since when do you actually do the reading your tutors assign?" The slightest hint of a smile stretched her mother's face.

"Give her some time, Mother. I'm sure I'll run her off before too long."

Mother laughed, a sound like a tinkling bell. It startled Claribel; the High Regent rarely laughed.

"You haven't come to complain to me, you're doing assigned reading, even if it's a frivolous text, and she hasn't quit. It seems you might have met your match."

"Mother, it's been less than two months."

"Exactly. You haven't given a single tutor this long before forcing them out."

"Maybe I like this one," was all Claribel could manage to say.

Mother threw her arms high into the air. "Has the vaunted intellect of my only daughter finally been met?"

"I didn't say that." It was Claribel's turn to hint at a smile. "But she is different, and she says things in a different way. I actually like her a lot, at least so far."

Mother shook her head, her eyes betraying her lack of trust in Claribel's statement.

"Speaking of your tutor, I'd like to speak to you about the field trip."

Claribel's heart sank. Did she know about the trip to Iopa and the servants' village? "I'm sorry Mother, I should have told you. . . ."

Mother waved her hand. "Told me about your field trip? It's your tutor's job to ask permission, and she asked me this morning if she could take you out tomorrow."

Claribel kept her confusion from her face and buried it as deep as she could. "So you approve?"

She shrugged. "I'm not sure what a trip to a winery in rural Cosart will teach you, but I'm trusting this young woman knows what she's doing."

A trip to a winery? Claribel stifled a laugh. A public trip to a winery didn't make any sense to Claribel either, but it would be a thousand times less eventful than a clandestine trip into the city.

"So you'll let me go?" Claribel sounded as eager as she could, though she wasn't sure why. She'd seen wineries and grape growing before. It wasn't that interesting.

"As I said, I will give this woman a sliver of trust, but I will expect a full report when you return tomorrow afternoon." Mother eyed the book in Claribel's lap. "I will need to be convinced that she's not just providing lessons in frivolity."

chapter 16

FRIVOLITIES

heir aircar sped above the trees toward the countryside outside of Cosart. Sun peaked above the horizon, it's light barely illuminating the sky. No human should be awake before the sun; it was unnatural.

Claribel curled back into a ball and closed her eyes. She'd spent too much time the night before trying to understand that jumping Heavener book. She wasn't sure if something could be good and evil at the same time, but she was absolutely sure something could be boring and long; they seemed an often-repeated pair.

"Late night?" Ona sat across from her, her eyes as bright and cheery as ever.

Claribel wanted to reach over and slap the happiness right out of her.

"Ugh," was all she managed, closing her eyes again.

"You're missing part of the adventure. If I have my bearings right, we'll be passing by Curasa soon. It's a lovely town set on a hill. The Heavener church there is almost as spectacular as the one in Iopa."

Claribel sat up, trying to fight the fatigue away.

"We won't be getting close enough to see it." Tar, one of mother's elite, sat across from them, a plasma rifle across his lap. Sprinkles of white at his temples and lines on his well-tanned face indicated he was older, but his thick neck and shoulders looked like those of a man half his age. A female guard sat next to Tar, her posture mirroring his rigidity. Two pilots sat up front guiding the aircar.

The cheeriness left Ona's eyes. "And why on earth would we avoid all these beautiful cities? Claribel has seen so little of her own world."

The security guard regarded Ona with a titled head. Claribel had known his twin brother better, Sander, who'd been her personal guard years before. Despite her time with Sander, the only way she could tell

Tar and his twin apart was by their name badges.

"The High Regent has many enemies, young tutor. We are here to keep Claribel safe, and the closer we get to cities, the more difficult it will be to ensure her safety."

"No need to worry," the other guard added. "We have two three stars as an escort and twenty-five security personnel already in position on the farm--the High Regent has enemies, but we're ready." The other guard, the name Nixa on her name badge, was much younger than Tar and did not have the officer stripes on her shoulder. But she dressed in the black of the elite, which meant she was one of mother's elite.

Tar grimaced. "I hope so. I don't like being exposed in the country." He looked at the window at the forest rushing by underneath them as if he expected some enemy to spring from the treetops.

"My name is Adriana," the woman guard said. "I apologize for missing the sights, but Captain Varn is right: this is the best way to protect you." Varn was Tar's last name, though Claribel had only ever heard people call him Tar.

The remaining hours passed slowly. Claribel switched between napping and boredom. She finally decided to flip on her reader and learn more about the Cosart region. But even that bored her. Cosart's main industry was agriculture, and it hadn't played a major role in Lanopian politics for nearly two thousand years. Claribel wondered what Ona had hidden that would make this trip worthwhile.

Finally, the aircar slowed and lowered itself in a clearing near a small red two-story house. The home looked new, but it was built in an older style, rounded and full of windows, not the angular, modular style prominent in Iopa. Guards were conspicuously stationed around the house and grounds, wearing the gray of the normal security force, not the black of the elite.

The group exited the car, Tar in the lead and Adriana in the back. A short, female guard approached as they landed.

"Status," Tar said.

"The grounds are secure, Captain," the guard reported. "We have a perimeter established, and ten drones have been deployed for patrol. Data is coming in to control. Nothing out of the ordinary."

Tar nodded and turned to Adriana. "I'm going to check on the perimeter and the drone data. Escort Lady Claribel and the tutor."

Adriana nodded. After Tar turned away with the gray-clad guard,

Adriana winked at Claribel. Despite her rigid posture, the female guard had a pleasant face which carried a hint of a smile. Her hair was short, not the popular style but practical for her duties. She wasn't much taller than Claribel, but she carried muscles where Claribel only carried skin and bones.

As soon as Tar departed, Ona walked confidently toward the house and Claribel followed. As they approached, two women emerged from the front door, one of them walking quickly toward Ona. They met halfway between the house and where the aircar had landed. They greeted each other with a deep embrace.

"Aunt Drua." Ona pulled back from the first woman, her eyes bright. "How are you?"

"Better now, Ona," the woman said, her eyes touched with a matching smile. She was older, deep lines across her forehead. She had bright blond hair pulled behind her head in a long braid. "It's been too long."

Ona nodded and turned to the woman standing next to Drua. "And I've never had the honor of meeting your life partner."

The other woman caught up to Drua. She was younger though not young. She had short brown hair and a bulge in her belly as if she might be pregnant. Both women dressed in loose-fitting, flowing dresses.

Drua smiled, linking arms with her partner. "This is Brind. Brind, this is my dearest niece, Ona."

Brind tapped her chin and pointed to the sky. Ona returned the gesture.

"Drua and Brind, I'd like you to meet Claribel, daughter of High Regent Rissa."

"It is our pleasure." Drua looked back toward the house where two guards flanked the front door. "The security seems a bit excessive for a winery."

"A necessary precaution," Adriana said. "I'm Adriana Nixa of the High Regent's elite force. We'll try to be as inconspicuous as we can."

Drua raised an eyebrow. "I'm not sure you all know how to be conspicuous."

Despite the rebuke, Adriana smiled.

"Thank you for allowing us to come to your home," Claribel said with a slight bow.

Drua laughed, a sound like wind through a chime. "My dear girl, we won't spend much time in the house."

Claribel looked at Ona, searching for an explanation.

Ona shrugged. "There's a reason you're dressed casually. We're going to work."

"Work?" Claribel looked at Ona then at the two older women. She almost said, "I don't work," but held her tongue knowing how petulant that would sound to these women.

"Stay right here," Ona said to Claribel. "I'll be back with some boots for you." Ona walked between Drua and Brind back toward the house, leaving Claribel with Adriana.

"They seem nice," Adriana said.

"Since when does an elite care about niceness?" Claribel didn't mean her tone to be so sharp, but she was too annoyed to worry about being nice.

"I don't really." Adriana smiled. "Just making conversation."

Ona returned a few minutes later, alone, wearing a pair of red boots. She held a smaller but identical pair. "These should fit."

"What do you think I'm going to do in those?"

"Work. Everyone on the farm, even guests, works. My family had a cosartberry farm in Farre; my aunt moved here ten years ago to start her own."

"I'm not getting covered in cosartberries. That stuff is almost impossible to get out, and despite this outfit's casual appearance, it's likely worth more than Adriana's annual salary."

Ona smiled and threw the boots at Claribel's feet. "I am your tutor, and I'm asking you to trust me. I promise it won't be too hard. And if you're clothes get ruined, I imagine your mother can afford to replace them."

Claribel sighed and put the oversized boots on over her sandals. She followed Ona around the house and toward a grove of cosartberry trees which stretched for hectares beyond to rolling hills on the southern horizon. The maroon berries popped against the bright green of the leaves.

"Can we eat some?" Claribel asked.

"Only one in ten." Drua approached from behind Claribel, dressed in a bright red one piece outfit that seemed to be made of the same plastic as Claribel's boots. "As long as nine make it into the bucket, you can have the tenth." She set down three buckets. "Everyone must fill three. Lady Claribel, these are your three. I'll bring another six for Ona and the security guard."

"Wait one jump," Adriana protested before Claribel could voice her own objection. "I'm here to protect Claribel, not to pick berries."

Drua smiled. "Then you don't eat or drink. This is the Onala way."

"I have my own food and drink." Adriana flashed a smile that was so brief Claribel almost missed it. Drua responded with an equally quick gesture.

Drua, Ona, and Claribel spent the next several hours picking cosartberries. The task was not particularly hard, and the slight snap of fall kept Claribel from sweating too much. The best part was the berries themselves; each berry exploded with juice in her mouth, its bitter sweetness making her pucker with each bite. She snuck more than a tenth, and no one seemed to notice or care.

When all nine buckets were full, Drua pressed a button on her wristband and the nine buckets glowed at the bottom and floated above the trees and to the west.

"Where are they going?" Claribel asked.

"To the winery," Drua answered.

Drua led them through a maze of cosartberry trees until they reached a building nearly as large as the home. A circular window sat atop the tall eave. Maroon paint, which matched the color of the cosartberries, covered the wooden structure except for the white frame of the lone window and a black wooden door.

Three girls, all four or five years older than Claribel, stood waiting outside a closed door on the ground floor. All three wore red plastic one-piece suits just like Drua.

"Where's Brind?" Ona asked.

"Back in the house. She's pregnant, and the odor of crushed cosartberries, conveniently, does not agree with her."

"Congratulations," Ona added.

Drua smiled. "I'm an older woman, and children were not in my future. Until Brind came along."

The darker skin on the three girls indicated they were likely natives of Iliopa, not like the lighter, freckled complexions of Ona and her aunt. All three girls looked as tired as Claribel had looked during the flight to Cosart.

Drua opened the front door, and they walked into a dark, vast building. There was just enough light to see the nine buckets dumping themselves into a large, shallow trough. Drua closed the door behind her, plunging them into darkness. The window under the eave did not shine into this large room. After an almost imperceptible beep, purple lights flooded the room with an eerie glow.

"Why the dramatic darkness?" Claribel asked.

"During the mashing process," Drua answered, "bright light can damage the cosartberries, robbing them of flavor. We work in near darkness until the juice is drained into its bottles."

The three girls walked over to the trough and stepped in. Ona followed them. Drua walked away from the trough and gathered a dozen black glass bottles with labels printed on them.

"You don't expect me to get into the berries," Claribel stated.

"I do." Ona walked slowly around the trough, her steps slow and deliberate through the thick mess of berries. "This is the lesson."

Claribel scowled, but obeyed. Ona may not have felt Claribel's true wrath in the short time they'd been together, but she would change that as soon as they returned to Iopa; she would not be turned into a common laborer.

Claribel climbed into the trough with a hand from Adriana. The guard woman did not get in after her. "If I have to, then so do you," Claribel commanded.

Adriana laughed. "I don't have any boots."

"You're wearing boots!"

"Not the right kind, my lady."

"Get in here! That's an order."

Adriana laughed. "Sorry, I don't take orders from you. I'm only getting in their if the Captain orders it or if you fall in and can't get out."

Claribel couldn't think of a good retort, so she stuck out her tongue.

Ona guided her to walk in a circle that was evenly spaced between the three other girls and her tutor. For what seemed like an hour, but was more like fifteen minutes, Claribel trudged along. Over time, the berries were squashed into a thick jelly, which gripped at her boots. As she struggled to lift her feet, she could feel the ever-thickening cosartberries flip up onto her shirt and even her face.

"Keep moving," the girl said behind her.

Claribel turned and scowled. Drua hadn't properly introduced them, and the girl probably thought Claribel was just some local trying out for a job. "Shove it," Claribel said. "I'm not even supposed to be here."

"I don't care if you're the jumping High Regent! Get moving!"

The girl gave Claribel a gentle push from behind. She barely kept her balance. "How dare you." Claribel picked up a handful of the sticky mixture and flung it at the girl, striking her in the face.

"Why, you dirty little . . ."

The girl tried to leap at Claribel, but her feet remained stuck, and the motion only forced her down face first into the jelly. Claribel rocked back, fearing the girl would tackle her. The jelly held her legs rigid, and she fell, knocking into the knees of the girl who'd been in front of her. All three girls lay stuck in the sticky cosartberries.

Claribel struggled to stand, but she could only manage to shift which part of her was stuck. Ona reached out and pulled Claribel to her feet.

Adriana rocked back and forth, laughing as loudly and fully as anyone Claribel had ever heard.

"Aren't you supposed to protect me?" Claribel shot at the elite guard.

"From mortal danger, yes, but not from cosartberry stains. We have another division that does that."

"Stop laughing at me."

Adriana reined in her laugh, but a broad smile still hung on her face. Claribel picked up another handful of cosartberries and flung it at her. The surprised guard started to dodge, but the mass struck her on the chest.

"What is going on?" Drua stood next to the trough.

The girl who'd pushed Claribel walked up to the edge of the trough. "This little Regent's girl was moving too slow, and then she flung some berries at me."

"She is the High Regent's daughter," Drua said. She pointed at Adriana. "Who else would need a security team at a winery?"

The girl looked aghast at Claribel. "I'm so sorry, my lady," she mumbled. "So very sorry. Please, I meant no disrespect, I mean, I didn't know. . . ."

Claribel looked at the girl, all covered in cosartberries. She looked like a pastry which had been dipped in jelly. Claribel smiled. She must look equally as ridiculous, her long dark hair coated in the maroon mixture.

Claribel licked the berries from her fingers. "Does the tenth rule apply in here?"

"It certainly does not," Drua responded. The woman stepped into the trough. "If you ladies cannot finish the job, then I'll finish it for you."

"Come on, Aunt," Ona pleaded. "It was a simple misunderstanding followed by a bit of fun."

"Fun waits when the work is done." Drua began walking in a circle.

"I can't wait that long." Ona took two steps toward her aunt and turned to the girls. "Let me show you the proper form for tackling someone in a berry trough." Ona took another step and fell onto Drua's back, pulling the older woman into the berries.

Claribel shrieked with laughter, and her delight mixed with the noises of the other three girls and Adriana. Drua turned over, her face covered in the thick berry mush, her white teeth shining through as she laughed.

Claribel sat on the steps of the winery house, pushing excess water from her hair with a towel.

The rest of the morning had actually been fun, as they worked around the trough, laughing and flinging berries at each other. Adriana had even joined in saying her uniform was already dirty, so it would be no harm. The highlight of the day had been the expression on Tar's face when he saw his fellow guard covered from the neck down in cosartberry jelly. His pointed rebuke sent the girls and women into another fit of uncontrollable laughter, all except for Adriana, who kept her composure during her upbraiding.

As she finished drying her hair, Ona joined Claribel on the steps. "Did you have fun today?"

Claribel did not want to admit it but said, "Yes. I did. But I'm not sure what I was supposed to learn today."

"If you had fun, then the lesson was a success."

She wanted to be mad at Ona, to tell her that fun was not a lesson she needed, that fun was frivolous. Mother's voice rang in her head, a chastisement for a childish lesson, but she couldn't bring herself to say anything the High Regent might. It had been fun, and was it so bad to be childish when you were a child?

"I don't really have friends," Claribel said instead of voicing a High Regent-like rebuke. She thought on the three girls who she'd worked with in the trough. Their banter had been easy, as natural as speaking. She didn't share anything like that, even with her brother.

"Is Thanan your friend?" Ona asked.

Claribel considered the question. If she had anything close to a friend, it would be her brother. They played together and complained together about their mother's harshness. "Maybe I have one friend. How do you know someone is your friend?"

Ona looked out at the trees. "That's a very difficult question. I think most friends are circumstantial--we become friends because we work together or live next to each other or we attend school together. But every once in a while, we find friends with whom we share everything, people who feel like an extension of ourselves, people we can't bear to live without. Those friends stay with us forever, at least in our hearts."

Claribel looked away, her eyes moistening. She wanted friends like that, but how could she discover them when she rarely interacted with anyone? The people she saw most were Thanan, Piera, Nanna, and her mother. She didn't think she could really be friends with her attendant, and though she adored Nanna, Mother did not allow Claribel to spend much time with her grandmother. And though she respected her mother and loved her, they could never be friends. That left Thanan. He was a boy, of course, but they could still be best friends. They had to be.

"What are you thinking?" Ona asked.

"I need to give my brother a hug," she replied.

A few minutes later Claribel and Ona said their goodbyes and boarded the aircar. Claribel planned to write an essay on cosartberry wine-making and Illiopan agriculture to satisfy Mother's need for a purpose for this trip, but she wouldn't include the real things she'd learned. Those would be kept in her heart, shielded from certain disapproval.

They cruised above the tree line toward the palace. Ona and Claribel discussed the day pleasantly. Adriana sat next to Tar, her uniform stained maroon with cosartberry juice. The sight almost sent Claribel into giggles.

"What is going to be our next lesson?" Claribel asked. "A trip to one of the moons?"

Ona smiled. "No, I think we'll be in the classroom for a little while. I was thinking . . ."

"Captain Tar," one of the pilots said as a loud beeping interrupted their conversation. "We have incoming. Missiles. Three of them. Initiate safety precautions. Taking evasive action."

Tar motioned with his hands, and a safety shield enveloped her; she could barely move her neck, like her head was caught in cosartberry jelly. Her heart raced, and her eyes opened wide. She wanted to look over at Ona for comfort or at Adriana for reassurance, but even that motion was beyond her.

Despite the embrace of the safety shield, Claribel could feel the ship weaving. Then she heard several plasma blasts and an explosion. The ship shuddered, but did not falter; the explosion hadn't been their aircar.

"More incoming!" the same pilot shouted. "Brace for impact!"

chapter 17

CRASH LANDING

he aircar rocked, and Claribel screamed. The vehicle twisted and flipped, and though the safety field absorbed most of the force and kept her in place, she still felt as if her cosartberry-filled stomach might erupt at any moment.

"We're going to crash, we need to . . ."

A jarring impact cut off Captain Tar's words as the aircar lurched to a stop. Claribel closed her eyes, the sudden stop nothing but a small jerk through the safety shield. After the sensation stopped, she opened her eyes but couldn't make sense of her swirling vision. She looked at her feet as nausea threatened to overcome her. The viewport in front of her was brown, the window broken. She smelled fresh dirt and something burning. She tried to move, but the safety shield held.

"Are you all right, Lady Claribel?"

Adriana stood below her, seemingly walking on the ceiling. Claribel blinked twice, wondering if she had hurt her head. Then reason broke through the cloud of confusion: she was upside down--gravity was meaningless in a safety shield.

"I'm all right," Claribel answered finally.

"I'm going to remove your safety shield," the elite guard said. "Then I'll catch you. Three, two, one!"

Gravity reasserted itself, and Claribel fell headfirst. The guard's strong arms caught her and then slowly flipped her over. Claribel stood, the ceiling flipping to become the floor.

Her head free to move, Claribel looked over just in time to see Tar release Ona from the safety shield and catch her.

"Help is incoming," Adriana said. "You'll be safe."

"We need to move," Tar said, picking up his plasma rifle.

"What about the pilots?" Adriana asked.

Claribel looked in the direction of the cockpit but saw nothing but metal and dirt. No, she also saw some red mixed with the soil. Could it be blood? She turned away and covered her mouth with her hands.

"Dead," Tar said matter-of-factly. "Let's move."

Adriana cupped her hand to her ear, focusing on the words coming through her ocular implant. "But they ordered us to stay here, help is minutes away."

Tar raised his rifle and fired. Claribel turned and screamed. The plasma blast caught Adriana in the torso, and the guard collapsed against the opposite window. Tar stepped up to the door and shot again, blasting a hole where the door had been. Two new smells assaulted her, one like charred meat and the other the smell of overheated metal.

"Out," he ordered.

Claribel looked back at Adriana, her face turned against the window, her body twisted. Her stomach was a mess of charred flesh and uniform. Claribel retched.

"Move, now," Tar ordered.

Ona grabbed Claribel's hand. "Come. We need to do as he says."

Claribel squeezed Ona's hand and started to cry. What was happening? Who had shot them down? Why did Tar shoot Adriana? The man had worked for her mother for two decades. Was he going to kill them?

Ona pulled Claribel, and she slowly followed. They stepped into a clearing, the dirt carved by the fallen ship. Tar came behind them, his rifle raised.

"We need to move quickly," he said, urging them to the left. "And no screaming, or I will kill you."

"What do you want?" Ona asked as they walked into the thick woods. It smelled like a forest, but only sort of, as the burned mixture of soil, metal, and flesh made Claribel's stomach churn again.

"Shut up," Tar replied. "I have orders to keep you alive, but so help me . . ."

They moved into the woods, and Claribel heard ships passing above, the distinct howls of three star fighters mixed with the lower, softer sound of aircars. She wanted to cry out, but they were moving too quickly, and she was afraid Tar might kill them both.

"Stop," Tar said as they reached a large tree, its trunk big enough around that two Tars could not have wrapped their arms around it. The undergrowth was thick, ferns up to Claribel's hips. Claribel and Ona turned to face him, but he had his back to them, scanning the woods.

"What are you going to do with Claribel?" Ona asked.

Tar stepped up to her and punched her in the face. The blow took Ona to the ground, and Claribel collapsed beside her.

"I told you to shut up."

Blood trickled from Ona's nose, but she sat up and locked eyes with Claribel. "Be brave," she whispered.

Brave. Claribel could hardly move, fear gripping her almost as tightly as the safety shield. It took every bit of herself to not curl into a ball and weep.

"What took you so long?" Tar's voice greeted two men who had stepped from the woods. They were both young and athletic, their skin pale and their hair a light brown. Both were dressed in green and brown camouflage clothing, and each held a lowered concussion rifle.

"No matter," the lead man said, his accent and skin indicating he came from Onal.

"No matter?" Tar replied. "You idiots almost killed all of us. This wasn't the plan. We were supposed to . . ."

Before he finished, the lead man raised his rifle and fired, catching the surprised elite in the neck. As his head erupted, Claribel turned away. When Claribel could look again, Ona stood between her and the two men. Tar lay on the ground, his head missing. *Good*, Claribel thought. *Betrayed like he betrayed Adriana.* Thinking of the other guard brought hot tears to her eyes.

"You are Onala, right?" Ona asked.

"Step out of the way," the first man said. "You don't need to die. You're not part of the cancer we've come to cut out, but sometimes healthy flesh must be removed."

"This is not our way," Ona replied. "And this girl is innocent. . ."

"No one connected to Rissa is innocent!" The man's eyes flared. "Rissa was once a child, too! And this one will grow up like her."

"She's different. And you can't just kill her for what she might become."

"The woman is right," the second man said, his rifle trained on the back of his companion. "We haven't come to kill."

"The mission has changed," the first man said. "So point that away, brother."

Claribel looked at the second one. He was younger, maybe only four or five years older than her. His arms shook, but he kept the rifle on the older man.

"This isn't right. We can't kill them."

"Kidnapping is not an option," the first said. "We're surrounded. They'll be here in moments." He looked at his friend but kept his rifle trained on Ona. "This is what we're called to do. For Onal, for Lanopi, for justice, we . . ."

A blast rang through the air as a plasma bolt hit the first man's chest. He fell back, sprawling in a heap of limbs and seared flesh. In her focus on their attackers, Claribel hadn't noticed Ona pick up Tar's plasma rifle. The tutor now sat on a pile of underbrush, knocked back by the power of the weapon.

The second man moved his aim to Ona.

"Don't do this," Ona pleaded. "You know it's not right. Claribel is different, she's redeemable. Give her a chance."

The second man's lips quivered, and he shook his head. "This wasn't what was supposed to happen, we just want justice, we just want people to . . ."

Another blast echoed through the woods, and the attacker's concussion rifle exploded into dozens of pieces. He screamed, jerked back his left arm, his hand gone. Another shot and something pierced his chest. Blood gushed from where his heart might have been, and he collapsed onto the forest floor.

Adriana stepped into the clearing, lowing her concussion pistol. Her left hand gripped her wounded side, blood flowing through her fingers.

"We have to get away from the bodies," Adriana choked, each word labored. "They could have suicide charges."

Ona pulled Claribel from her knees and led her behind the large tree. A moment later, the world exploded in sound again, and the hot blast knocked Claribel and her tutor off their feet. A ringing followed the explosion, and Claribel reached to cover her ears, but it made no difference.

She flinched when someone gripped her arm, recoiling. She looked up and saw the gray uniform of a Lanopian soldier. His mouth moved, but she only heard hints of words, nothing more. The soldier scooped her up into his arms and ran. The bouncing hurt her head, but she tried to ignore it and buried her face in his chest. She wanted to look up, to see where Ona was, to see if Adriana had escaped the blast. But she couldn't bring herself to open her eyes or pull her head away from the safety of

the soldier's chest.

Her hearing started to return, and muffled shouts echoed as the lighting changed and the soldier set her down in the seat of an aircar.

"We're taking you back to the palace." His words registered as a distant mumble even though his mouth opened wide from shouting. "You're safe now."

chapter 18

COMFORT

Claribel sat in a comfortable chair in a windowless room in the heart of the palace's security wing. Her ears had finally stopped ringing. She smoothed her skirt with her hands and tried not to think about the blood. There'd been blood on her clothing, and she didn't know whose it was. But she'd been cleaned up by Piera and two other servants. She wore her favorite gold dress, and her hair hung in two braids. But the dress seemed dull today, and she resisted pulling on her braids; her mother hated that.

She'd been flown in the aircar back to the palace with three soldiers as company. None of them had spoken to her. The soldiers had then guided her here, where Piera and two older women Claribel recognized but couldn't remember dressed and cleaned her. Piera had said how amazing it was that Claribel wasn't hurt. Claribel wasn't sure how much Piera knew--probably little--but Claribel was sure she was hurt, just not in the way someone could see.

Now she waited.

Without a pad or a clock, time moved indeterminably. Without a pad, she also couldn't entertain herself. Her mind kept trying to pull her back into dark thoughts, thinking about Tar's head, about the young terrorist's chest exploding outward as he stared at his missing hand. She tried to think of something else, tried to blink away the terrible memories, but they clawed into her mind past any distraction she laid in their path. She held back another sob and wondered if she'd always feel this fractured.

The door slid open, and her mother walked in followed by her father. Claribel's first instinct was to stand and run to them, but she knew that wasn't how Mother would want her to act in a crisis. The High Regent's family did not find comfort in hugs.

Mother and Father stood together as if they had not split weeks before. Father wore his dress military uniform, the rank of Captain on his lapel. Mother wore a dark dress, a stylish and formal piece which looked like it had been purchased from the great Mura Chano, the most renowned designer on Lanopi. Her short hair was pushed upward, as if her head had sprouted wings. Claribel almost smiled at the thought; that was something Thanan might say. She wished Thanan were there.

"Are you all right?" Father's voice sounded distant, and Claribel couldn't tell if it was the ringing in her ears of if his voice truly lacked emotion. She wanted him to hug her, to show affection, but he stood motionless next to Mother, his arms crossed behind his back.

"I am fine, Father," was all she said.

"We need you to tell us exactly what happened." Mother's voice was even colder than Father's. She looked over at the wall. "This will be recorded for the official record."

The wall was a false one, opaque from this view but clear from the other side. How long had they been watching her?

Claribel did not want to recount anything. She wanted to crawl into her bed and cry, or crawl into Nanna's arms and fall asleep. But instead she recounted what she remembered since they'd left the farm. Despite trying to remain composed, she cried three times, one time terribly as she described the scene in the woods, her body shaking with each sob. Neither of her parents said anything, and they certainly didn't approach her with anything resembling comfort.

When she finished, she looked up at her father, hoping for some sympathy. She saw only rage. It was there for a moment and then gone, his face returning to its neutral stare.

"We're glad you're all right," he said, his voice finally touched by some emotion, though it seemed insufficient under the circumstances.

"What about Ona and Adriana?" Claribel asked.

"Officer Nixa," the High Regent corrected, using Adriana's surname, "is recovering, but was wounded by the traitor and the suicide bombs. Ona suffered some minor burns and abrasions, but is fine. She's currently in custody."

"Custody? You mean she's under arrest?"

"I know you've had a difficult day, but please remain calm."

Claribel wanted to stand up and hit Mother. Remain calm? She'd almost been killed three times at least, and her mother wanted her clone of a daughter to remain calm. But she kept her hands in her lap and looked away.

"Ona is not accused of anything," she continued, "but she is Onala and this appears to be the work of the Liberators. It's a precaution, nothing else."

"She saved my life," Claribel said, keeping her voice as even as she could, though it still crackled with emotion. "She killed one of the attackers." She'd already said as much when she'd recounted her version of events, but she repeated it so her mother might get it through her dense brain than Ona was not the enemy.

"Yes, so you say." Her eyebrows arched like they always did when she didn't quite believe her children.

"The investigation is moving rapidly," her mother continued. "We'll find these terrorists and bring them to justice. They will pay for what they've done." Despite the severe declaration, her eyes held no anger. Her face looked like she might be discussing the menu of a state dinner instead of the almost-assassination of her own daughter. When the newsfeeds showed her, Claribel did not doubt the High Regent would show anger and sadness. But here in the privacy of their family, she showed nothing.

"Can I go to my room?" Claribel asked, unable to keep the bite from her voice.

"Of course," Mother replied.

Claribel sat on her bed, her knees tucked against her chest. Was this her life? Sitting alone when things went wrong? Was this her mother's life? Was she always alone when it mattered most?

She still wanted to yell at her mother. Ona should not be in custody. And parents should at least give their children a hug after they're almost assassinated!

Unbidden, the sixty-fifth maxim sprang to her mind: *Troubled times come, but great leaders remain calm. Have your moments of doubt in the private corners of your mind, but when you stand before the people, be their pillar of strength.*

Jumping Mother! Her words rang in Claribel's mind without invitation, like a computer program reacting to the right stimulus. Even in her private moment, Claribel couldn't escape the woman's long-reaching grasp.

"Bel!"

Thanan stood in the doorway. After a moment's hesitation, as if he hadn't been sure he'd find her there, he ran across the room and jumped onto the bed, tackling Claribel with a hug. She wrapped her arms around him and tucked her head against his shoulder as tears dropped freely.

After several minutes, he pulled back a little, his face close to hers. "I'm so glad you're all right. Mother is making an announcement as we speak, telling the people that you were the target of an assassination attempt. What happened, Bel?"

Despite her fatigue, she relayed the entire story, this time grateful to be able to tell it truly, not the more formal version she'd told her parents. Thanan's eyes widened with each dramatic turn.

After she'd finished, he embraced her again. "I'm glad you came back..." He trailed off, his voice cracking. "We'll get those bastards who did this and make them pay."

Claribel wanted to chastise him for his desire for revenge, but she couldn't bring herself to dampen an emotion which sprouted from his deep love for her. Maxim number one hundred and ninety-seven: *Vengeance is a poison which will distract from the ultimate goal. Mercy may not be for those who lead, but revenge which does not suit the interest of the state is just as corrosive.* Maybe revenge was corrosive, but at least it showed he cared. Claribel hugged him tighter and lost herself in the embrace.

"Sweet Bel!" Nanna ran into the room.

Thanan scooted over, and Nanna's hug was tight enough to knock the breath from Claribel's lungs. Despite its intensity, Claribel welcomed it. She cried what few tears she had left into Nanna's silver hair.

"My sweet, little Bel." Nanna stroked Claribel's long hair. "We can't lose you, little Bel, we can't lose you..." Nanna trailed off into a sob of her own.

Claribel spent the rest of the afternoon in Nanna's arms, hovering between sleep and wakefulness. At some point, Thanan left, though Claribel could not recall seeing him leave. Finally, after eating a snack Nanna had insisted she eat and getting dressed in a nightgown, Claribel crawled back into her bed and fell asleep as Nanna stroked her hair.

chapter 19

REGENCY JUSTICE

he next few days were a blur. Despite Claribel's insistence, her mother denied her seeing Ona or Adriana. Mother dismissed it as sentimental rubbish. If Ona was innocent, mother said, then she would be set free and Claribel might visit her again. Officer Nixa's heroics were her duty, and she'd done nothing remarkable.

Claribel tried to suppress the fear that she'd never see Ona again. In their short time together, Claribel had grown to love their lessons and cherish their conversations. But she had stopped asking to see Ona as her mother's anger grew with each request, and Claribel wouldn't put it past the High Regent to never let her see Ona just to teach a lesson.

And Adriana's actions had been heroic, despite Mother's dismissal. After being shot in the gut, the woman had crawled to the clearing and saved them from the second attacker's wavering convictions. If Adriana's actions hadn't been heroic, then what did heroic even mean?

She spent most of her days playing with Thanan. He'd been a little distant since that first day, no hugs or consoling words. They played games on their pads and poked fun at some of their most boring tutors. Claribel enjoyed the distraction, since dark memories pulled at her mind like a star's hold on its satellites. But she also wanted the soft kindness he'd shown her that day after the assassination attempt. But they were High Regent Rissa's children, and kindness did not come easy.

Nanna also came by again but only once. She had cried the whole time, saying how she loved her little Bel. Nanna hadn't come back. No one said why, and Claribel didn't ask. The High Regent was most certainly behind Claribel's isolation.

On the fourth morning since the attack, an elite guard escorted her toward the security wing of the palace. The severe woman said nothing. Claribel asked about Adriana's condition, but the guard answered with stony silence. Mother must have placed palace-wide orders to deny her any kindness.

The guard showed her into a large room, one wall lit up with images and motion. It was a command room, complete with its hierarchical seating and full-wall screen. Multiple news feeds played, though the transmissions were muted. Mother and Father stood at the far end talking with each other and ignoring the images behind them. Mother's Chief of Security, Scaria Drunt, stood next to the High Regent. Thanan sat in one of the room's dozen chairs, his adolescent feet not quite reaching the floor.

Claribel walked over and sat next to him. He smiled pleasantly, and she returned the gesture.

"We've had a breakthrough in the case," her mother said, the triumph glowing in her eyes. "We've apprehended the patrons of this despicable plot against Claribel's life. But before the final reveal, let me show you how we got there."

Mother waved her hand once and the lights dimmed, another wave and the myriad images and figures on the wall screen were replaced with one video.

It showed Brind, the life partner of Ona's aunt. Her face was bloodied, and she wore only a bra and panties. Her pregnant belly hung between her legs, and her back arched unnaturally.

"Who was your sponsor?" a voice bellowed from off screen. "Who financed this assassination attempt?"

The pregnant woman looked up. Claribel had never seen eyes like them, full of pain and exhaustion yet empty of anything else. The light which had been in them at the winery gone like it had never been there. She looked like the same woman she'd met, but then she didn't.

"Senator Sparo of Onal," she said, her voice a raspy whisper. "He set up all of this. He wants to usurp the throne, make himself emperor of Lanopi, overthrow our democratic government. We hate High Regent Rissa, hate her government. We were going to kill that spoiled brat to make a point."

The woman's words lacked conviction, lacking the bite Claribel imagined an impassioned terrorist might have. She was broken, repeating words she'd been told to say.

"This woman whom we know as Brind Faz," Chief Drunt said, "is actually a woman named Ghosrana Tusa. She was tied to several acts of violence in Onal as a youth, including when we believed she died in a suicide bombing of an aircar factory on the Onal-Nezia border."

With a motion of her arm, Chief Drunt changed the screen into two photos, one of the woman Claribel had met as Brind, and the other a younger woman with the words 'Ghosrana Tusa' written below. There was a resemblance but only a passing one.

"Cosmetic surgery," Chief Drunt said, as if answering the question forming in Claribel's mind.

Everything seemed too convenient. In the last few days, Claribel had studied the Onala Liberators. They were a violent group but always against property, not people. If Brind or Ghosrana was an agent of theirs, then she'd either changed philosophy, or she'd been manipulated into saying what needed to be said to cast her and the Onala Liberators as villains. The first was possible; the first attacker and the missiles had been meant to kill Claribel, not just scare the High Regent. But most of the details of this would not solidify in Claribel's mind. Brind, or Ghosrana, had recently become pregnant and started a life. Why would someone do that who was still committed to a dangerous, terrorist path? And how could they have known Claribel would get Ona as a tutor and then be at Drua's house? Yes, maybe they took advantage of a lucky opportunity, but it all seemed far-fetched.

Claribel's heart sunk. Unless Ona had played a part.

"If she's this Ghosrana woman, why didn't a security screen catch this?" Thanan asked.

"That's an excellent question, Thanan." Mother's eyes dug into the back of Chief Drunt's head. "There will be a full inquiry into why we had such a clear break in our intelligence gathering."

Mother waved her hand and the twin images vanished, replaced by the cacophony of images which had been there before.

"Have we questioned Senator Sparo?" Thanan asked.

"Better than that," Father said, his eyes glowing. "The High Regent's security team raided his estate outside Onal City. They found enough evidence connecting them to the plot to fill a starjumper. His wife Eliel was also implicated."

Claribel had met Sparo and Eliel several times at official functions. Sparo was a fourth generation senator, his family the richest and most powerful in Onal. Eliel was the daughter of Senator Clana of Cierna, one of Mother's closest allies. The trial would be complicated by the intense political underpinnings.

"When does the trial begin?" Thanan asked. He showed an intense interest that Claribel couldn't match. She mostly felt numb.

"There will be no trial," Mother replied.

"But if there's no trial," Thanan continued, "how can there be justice?"

"Scaria." Mother nodded to her security chief.

"Senator Sparo and Eliel of Cierna are popular figures. And while their cause is despicable, they could garner a lot of sympathy in a trial. Also found on their private jumpnet was a plan to discredit the High Regent by implicating Adjunct Captain Alazar in a drug trafficking scandal. They had plans for many contingencies, plans upon plans. They are too dangerous for a proper trial."

Mother motioned to the wall screen, and again a single video filled the screen. The image revealed a large hanger that looked like those Claribel had seen on starjump stations orbiting the planet. Claribel recognized Senator Sparo and Eliel. They dressed in plain gray jumpsuits, their hands bound behind their backs. Soldiers loaded a few items as the couple looked on. Sparo sat erect, his posture accentuating his muscled build. Gray flecked his light brown hair. Eliel was his physical equal, tall, beautiful, and athletic with darker brown hair running down her back. Both exuded regality, not the whimpering some might expect.

Something about all this wasn't right. Mother was afraid of a trial, afraid of these two garnering sympathy? If the accusations were true, they'd conspired to kill the High Regent's daughter. Lanopi was a democracy in name only, but public support was still necessary, and the High Regent cultivated it. A public trial would garner sympathy and support for the High Regent's government, turning the public against the Onala Liberators' otherwise sympathetic cause. Mother would be able to violently put down as many Onali as she saw fit, and the people would cheer with each additional arrest or death.

Claribel looked up at the image of Senator Sparo and his wife, examined their features. The beautiful Eliel was known for her kind nature and keen, scientific mind. Sparo had been a star athlete in his university days and dabbled in science as well as his manufacturing business.

As Claribel started to look away, her eyes were drawn to a small figure stepping away from Eliel's legs.

"Who's that?" she asked, knowing the answer as soon as the words escaped her lips. She'd never seen the girl, but it had to be Sparo and Eliel's lone child, a daughter.

Mother eyed Claribel. No one answered her question.

"What will happen to the girl?" Claribel could not conceal her disgust. "She's a small child. Surely there wasn't a mountain of evidence implicating a toddler?"

"She presents a clear danger," her mother replied. "Senate elections are mostly a formality, and if she stayed around, that seat would be hers when she came of age. Even if what we do to her parents is legal and justified, the child might take it upon herself to exact revenge against us later."

Claribel understood the logic, but it appalled her. And it reeked of something more. What wasn't Mother telling them? What was she hiding? Brind's confession felt more bogus than the Thanan's worst childhood excuse, and the 'conviction' of Senator Sparo was just as dubious. The High Regent didn't want this to go to trial, didn't want the public scrutiny. But why? The High Regent's purpose orbited just outside her mind.

She glanced at her father, hoping to see some humanity, hoping to see someone as appalled as she was at the prospect of exiling a small child. But he wouldn't meet her eyes. The vindictive anger she'd seen four days before had been replaced by a deep weariness, his eyes distant and empty.

"They will have a starjump accident while going on vacation to Eslaza," Chief Drunt said. "While traveling though Vesta to Nooteezia in route to Eslaza, their starjump drive will malfunction." The woman stated the contrived fiction as facts.

Claribel responded with maxim sixty-four: *"Those who rule with you are not treated as commoners, they are treated more like dogs. When loyal, reward them openly and lavishly. When treacherous, punish them severely and privately."*

Mother smiled a tight, thin smile. "Exactly. The aristocracy will hear rumors of Sparo's fateful starjump, rumors that he was behind the assassination attempt and that he's been put down like a rabid animal, his daughter included."

Claribel stared at the floor, the pleasure in her mother's eyes too much. The story perfectly fit a maxim, but the tale lacked sufficient details to ring true. Typically, her mother would want Claribel to examine the facts, to point out the flaws. But she held her tongue. This wasn't a mistake. The High Regent didn't make mistakes, not like this.

Her mind returned to Brind or Ghosrana. What would happen to the pregnant woman? What would happen to her unborn child? Another sacrifice to Mother's bloodlust?

"What about Ona?" Claribel asked, the thought and the words arriving simultaneously.

"Your tutor was not implicated in the plot," Chief Drunt said. "We found no connection between Ona or her aunt with the Onala Liberators."

"They were duped as easily as our security team." Mother's pointed rebuke caused Chief Drunt's face to flash with panic for a moment before the woman replaced it with her usual frigid expression.

"So she'll remain my tutor?" Claribel asked.

Mother shook her head. "She's been dismissed."

"Dismissed? For what?" Her voice held too much anger, but she couldn't contain it.

"I should never have let Candra pick your tutor," she replied. "Ona is intelligent, but after observing her teaching and questioning the young woman about her methods, I feel a different approach is needed."

"I don't want a different tutor."

"The choice is not yours, child. The choice is mine." Mother didn't say ours, wasn't even looking at her husband.

"But I want Ona to be my tutor!" Claribel stood as she screamed the words, her anger overflowing.

"Excuse us please."

At first, Claribel thought the command had been directed solely at Chief Drunt, but her father left as well. Coward. Thanan walked just behind Father.

"You are never to speak to me like that in public again." Mother's tone was cold and soft, like a piercing winter wind. "I recognize the trauma you've suffered, but my daughter should be made of better metal than that."

"Trauma?" Claribel removed none of the edge from her voice, though she didn't shout. "Since when do you care about my trauma? You cause most of it."

Mother stepped up to Claribel and slapped her face. Her cheek burned from the sharp blow.

"Watch your tongue. I do what I do to raise the next leaders of this world. Leaders cannot be soft, cannot be worried about the daughters of traitors. A leader must make choices which have to be made for the better of the whole. I cannot suffer the weaknesses of compassion and mercy.

"You have been raised in a harsh way, as was I. You and your brother do not get the luxury of playing as other children play, of filling your life with frivolities. We are called to something greater. And it's about time you learned that."

Claribel stood there, her cheek stinging from the blow. There was so much she wanted to say, so many objections she had to her mother's philosophy. She could feel the words of the Heavener prophet Palo in her mind, words of kindness and love.

But she said nothing. Mother was a mountain; she stood immutable, unchanging. So Claribel turned and, like any girl her age might, stormed off to her room.

chapter 20

REVELATION

When Claribel reached her room, her bed had been remade and her favorite dress, the gold one she'd worn after returning from her trip to the winery, had been laid out. Piera. The thoughtful girl knew Claribel was struggling, knew she needed some light in her darkened world. If Piera had been there, Claribel would have hugged her.

She changed into the dress and looked at herself in the mirror. Her hair was gathered in two braids hanging at either side of her face. The bright yellow of the puffed sleeves gradually grew into a rich gold color as it reached toward her waist. Gold and yellow sequins sparkled on the bow around her waist. The bottom of the dress blossomed into a full skirt, shifting from the dark gold back to yellow and then to orange. It was the most beautiful dress Claribel owned, and it made her feel every bit the High Regent's daughter. And that was the problem.

She stripped and changed into a more practical garment, a blue suit. She needed to figure this out, needed to understand what game the High Regent played. She couldn't do that while playing princess.

Claribel turned to her pad and researched everything she could find on Senator Sparo and his wife. Sparo was the son of Senator Donn of Onal who'd died five years ago. He'd been elected senator in a landslide, as was almost always the case. Democracy was a fancy word on Lanopi for oligarchy.

Eliel was the daughter of Senator Clana of Cierna who still served in the Senate. Her father Giim was a successful interstellar merchant. She'd met Sparo at Onal University. They'd been married for four years. Her degree was in physics. Sparo's degree had been in engineering. His only sibling was Balith who ran the family's manufacturing business. They made engines and other systems for starjumpers. They had several military contracts.

After hours of research, Claribel set the pad down and wiped her eyes. She'd found little. Nothing on the jumpnet even hinted at Sparo or Eliel having even the slightest sympathy with the Onala Liberators. Sure, Sparo was Onali, but the Liberators disliked the Onali elite almost as much as they disliked the Lanopian planetary government. It could have been subversive, a well-crafted life to get in a position to help the cause, but that would be very difficult to pull off for two people so prominent. And Eliel was Ciernan, as high society as there was. Why would an outsider embrace the Liberator cause, especially a scientist like Eliel? Claribel cross-referenced everything she could with Eliel's past, trying to find some college paper or a social comment tinged with sympathy to the Liberator movement or to other anti-establishment causes or philosophies. But there was nothing. If Eliel had become a collaborator, she'd left a completely unreadable trail.

Everything she'd learned about them, everything she knew of her own mother made this seem like something else. Why would she accuse them? Were they making a bid for the High Regency? Were they a threat? Removing them unceremoniously seemed like a Rissa thing to do, but it had to have a purpose. The woman tried to control everything, tried to manage every factor leaving as little to chance as she could. Maxim sixteen: *Exquisite planning creates its own fate.*

Claribel stood from her desk, a flash of illumination slamming into her mind. Mother's words to her before Claribel had stormed out: "I don't have the luxury of compassion, of mercy. You have been raised in a harsh way."

But despite her parental philosophy, she'd allowed Nanna, a compassionate woman, to choose Claribel's tutor. She'd allowed Ona to be hired. But she would have known Ona's intent, surmised Ona's philosophical underpinnings. She was grooming Claribel to be High Regent; she wouldn't leave her education to fate. Somehow it had evaded Claribel's mind before, but now it rang clearly: Ona had been a test, like the maze, like all interactions with Mother. Each activity, each lesson, each moment was a chance for grooming her two protégés.

So Ona had been a test. Had she been a plant? Claribel shuddered that her now beloved tutor might just be an actor whose performance had shifted Claribel's belief. But no, she chose to believe Ona was whom she appeared to be.

So if Ona had been genuine, why would the High Regent allow

Nanna to pick a tutor who would fit Nanna's world view, someone who would teach compassion? Mother's one hundred and sixth maxim came to her mind: *Compassion is a disease leaders need to be inoculated against. If left unchecked, compassion will rot a leader's ability to make the toughest, best choices for her people.* Mother had introduced compassion into Claribel's world, inoculated her with what Mother viewed as a virus. But Claribel had embraced it, had let the compassion flow through her and become part of her. She had become the embodiment of exactly what the High Regent wished to avoid. Mother had tested her for weakness and found it.

And if Ona was a test, then Mother would have been watching everything. Video feeds from the tutoring space, spies following them into Iopa and to the servants' village--Mother would have watched it all. Claribel felt so foolish, so naive. She should have known, should have realized the ploy. Of course they hadn't been able to sneak from the palace. Undercover guards had been following them. She hadn't even considered the possibilities. She'd become unguarded in front of Ona, opening up like she'd never done with anyone before.

Claribel scanned her bedroom. If every piece of her life was a test, then even this moment was a test. The High Regent would gather and use all the data she could find. Claribel had never given her privacy much thought, but now she wondered whether she'd actually had a moment of privacy her entire life.

"Mother." The word escaped in a firm breath. "Mother. I know you're watching. I know you're watching me. Reveal yourself. I've figured out your little game." Claribel tried to keep the anger from shaking her body. Her mother was watching, she'd always been watching.

Ten minutes passed, and the door to Claribel's chambers opened, the High Regent standing there in all her smug authority.

"Very good, Claribel." She folded her arms. "Of course, I thought you'd have figured this out months or years ago."

"How long have you watched me?"

"How long do you think?"

Claribel studied her, almost as if she was seeing the woman for the first time. She wasn't a mother, not really. She had given birth to Claribel and Thanan, but they were assets, not children. They weren't a family, not in the way most people were. Every moment would be weighed, every minute used to further the High Regent's cause. She was growing future tools, not people.

"Since birth," Claribel said after a brief moment.

The High Regent smiled. "Yes, though I haven't watched every hour; I have analysts and algorithms for that."

Claribel shivered at the thought of every moment of her life being captured, analyzed, and stored.

"You've shone such promise, more ruthless and intelligent than your brother. But you failed this latest test spectacularly."

"The test of having Ona as my tutor?"

"Yes. Frivolous nonsense filled the woman's lessons, mixed with an occasional insight of value. Her teachings were sentimental crap, and you consumed these ridiculous notions with relish."

Claribel took a deep breath. "She taught me many things of use."

"Like what?"

She thought of that first day, of pointing out the potential strategic importance of Nooteezia. But of course, Mother or her analysts had certainly dissected that lesson. So instead of battling the High Regent on her own terms, Claribel chose defiance. "She taught me compassion."

"Compassion is not for those who lead," her mother said, paraphrasing her own maxim. "You fake these attributes in public. . ."

"I know the maxims, Mother."

"Compassion is a disease leaders need to be inoculated . . ."

"I know the maxims!" Claribel shouted, surprised at the intensity of her reaction.

Mother regarded her coolly; the High Regent did not like to be interrupted. "Reciting the maxims and knowing them are not the same thing. Candra and this idiot tutor exposed your weakness. Starting tomorrow, you will have a tutor assigned by me; we will no longer indulge your weakness.

"In addition to that," the High Regent continued, "your time with Thanan will be minimized. While your edge may have dulled, his is still sharp. I won't have your new weakness infect my son."

"So I'm no longer your heir?" Claribel had wanted the words to sound defiant, but they came out more like a soft, rhetorical inquiry.

"Time will tell, Claribel, but my focus will be on your brother now. He does not have your strategic mind, but maybe we can help him develop that."

"So will I be cast aside now that I'm of no use to you?"

She laughed. "Drop the melodrama; you have too much of your

grandmother in you. I groom many candidates to replace me, not just you and your brother. The High Regency is still a young form of government. Junda conquered and promised a little democracy. My father expanded that illusion and our family has ruled for three generations. But heredity has its own inherent problems, and I was never pulling all my ships into the same starjump."

The words stung worse than if the High Regent had slapped Claribel again. She had always believed she was the chosen one, the future High Regent, just as her mother had been for grandfather Marsil. Now that was gone, and despite Claribel's anger toward her mother, she felt a sudden emptiness at her life's purpose being yanked from her.

"Don't look so disappointed. You will still be of use to Lanopi, I can assure you. Maybe as an ambassador, maybe as a minister. You will serve your world, but no, I think you lack some of the necessary qualities to truly lead, especially in the future we face. The known systems hold peace today, but it's temporary. Ambitions stir, and chaos looms. Lanopi will need strength in the coming decades, not a nurse mother."

Claribel formed dozens of responses in her mind: *I hate you. Starjump into a blackhole. I'm glad I won't be part of your cruel rule.* But she couldn't bring herself to express one of them.

"Did you hurt Ona?"

"Oh please, Claribel, I'm not a monster. I chose to bring her in, chose to expose you to this. I am never needlessly cruel. Being fired by the High Regent is as fierce and strong of a punishment as was needed."

Fired by the High Regent. Ona would not be able to return to the university, would not likely find another tutoring job, at least among Lanopi's aristocracy.

Claribel climbed into her bed and turned her back on the High Regent.

She hoped for a moment that the woman would not act like the High Regent and act like a mother, offering comfort or sympathy. But the High Regent's footsteps signaled her departure, leaving Claribel to sob into her pillow knowing that the High Regent or one of her analysts watched.

chapter 21

LAZLO'S CONSCIOUS

L azlo stood next to a small starjumper contemplating treason. Judging by how the High Regent treated Sparo and his family, what he planned on doing would mean death for Lazlo, his wife, his sons, and maybe their families. But he'd stood by for decades watching the depravity of the High Regency and he could not stand mute this time; this time he would do something.

He only knew of Sparo's predicament through a stroke of luck and the High Regent's husband Alazar's guilty conscious. Lazlo had been at Sparo's house when Rissa's elite had arrived and taken Sparo, Eliel, and the girl Miram. When he'd confronted Alazar, he said they had a mountain of evidence implicating the pair in the assassination attempt of Lady Claribel. The official story was that Sparo had been questioned and released, and their family was now headed on an off-world vacation. But Alazar had revealed, in a moment of conscious-guided weakness, the entire despicable plan. Even the small child would not escape Rissa's wrath.

For the first day, Lazlo had wondered if he'd been blind to his friend Sparo's true nature, that maybe Sparo had posed as a peace-loving senator and philanthropist. Maybe Lazlo had been duped by the family as they operated with the Onala Liberators and plotted assassinating a young girl.

But Lazlo could not bring himself to believe it. Sparo was not a traitor, and certainly not a killer. No, Sparo and his family had been caught in the wake of High Regent Rissa's machinations, and they would be sacrificed to serve her ends.

So he stood at the periphery of the scene dressed in a Space Navy uniform he'd borrowed from a friend, looking at Sparo's personal starjumper. Its presence in this military launch base confirmed Alazar's story. Sparo, Eliel, and their daughter were already on board, their luxurious coffin prepared and ready.

Only a few crew milled about, and one elite guard stood off to the side, observing. If anyone was going to stop him, it would be that light-haired woman. But just as Lazlo's courage was about to fail, the plan fell into place.

Another elite, a stout woman with dark hair, walked up and dismissed the other guard. After a few minutes, the woman locked eyes with Lazlo and nodded. Alazar had agreed to get Lazlo onboard, and now was Lazlo's time to act.

He nodded back to her, strode into the starjumper, and reached the empty cabin. He used Alazar's security protocol and gained access to the flight computer. He'd considered putting in an entirely different destination, maybe Fortuna or Coznar. They'd be discovered there, rescued from being locked in their quarters. But no one would see them in Vesta, and that was the point of Rissa's plan. They'd fly into the system's star in a few months, and with the locater disabled, no one would find them in the vastness of Vesta space.

So Lazlo considered jumping them to Fortuna where someone might help them. But no, Rissa controlled that jump base--they wouldn't be safe there. And altering the starjump destination would be noticed the moment they jumped.

So instead, he changed the flight plan for the ship's trajectory after the jump to Vesta. The system had only one starjump point, and it was just outside the asteroid belt surrounding Vesta II. The original flight plan had them pointed away from the asteroid belt and toward the star. The new course would point them at the asteroid belt and toward the only livable planet in the system, a world Lazlo knew too well.

Second, he enabled a subtle broadcast signal, a code which would guide them through the asteroid belt. And finally, he inputted a planetary landing sequence which would land them near the old Sycorax facility. Since that day twenty-two years before, Lazlo had often wondered if he'd made the right decision in not destroying Sycorax's work. Now, he was glad he hadn't; that place, once a house of horrors, might become a safe haven for this beleaguered family.

Third, he left a message for Sparo, a code they'd used since college to communicate ideas. Hopefully he'd discover it and know who saved him.

As he finished all the programming, he knew it might not be enough. The code for the asteroid belt was twenty years old; the mechanical asteroids Sycorax had installed might not work anymore, or it was possible the code had been changed. And Sparo's starjumper was not meant for planetary travel; it was docked in an orbital launch station for a reason. Yes, it could do an emergency landing, but that was difficult at best. And if anyone discovered the changes, they could reset them. So much could go wrong.

Overpowering guilt urged him to do more, to reach out to a journalist or a foreign government or Eliel's powerful family. Lazlo's current action reeked of cowardice, not courage. But he couldn't bring himself to risk his life and his family more than this. In the cruel web of the High Regent, this was the most he could reasonably do. If Sparo, Eliel, and Miram reached Vesta II safely, hopefully they could find a way to escape Sycorax's world and find a new life. At least now they had hope, and a little hope was all Lazlo could offer.

Sweat pooled under his arms as he double-checked his inputs and finalized the new flight plan. As soon as he was done, he walked nonchalantly from the starjumper, acting as if he had every right and reason to be where he was. The Navy personnel ignored him, the elite's acquiescence the only proof they needed of Lazlo's need to be there.

He nodded at the guard, exited the bay, and finally released a deep breath. He wished he'd been able to speak with Sparo, to reassure him there was at least some hope. But that would have been too dangerous, and he couldn't bear facing his friend.

Hope. That's all Lazlo had left, all Sparo and his family had left. Lazlo hoped against hope it would be enough.

chapter 22

DISCOVERY

aliban finished his small meal of mole meat and tree fruit. His stomach ached with ever-present hunger. He picked the mole's bones clean, licking them until they were dry. He'd eaten every bit of fruit and hungrily eyed the rind. But the last time he'd eaten the outer shell, it had made him sick for days. Hunger was bad, but spending two days puking was worse.

How long had he been alone? How long could he live like this? Caliban had envisioned freedom differently, had envisioned freedom as an easy life. But he couldn't relax all day, or he would die. Finding food was hard, not like sneaking sticky sweetbread from Mother's friends. The slow, lumbering cow-dogs had sustained him, but he hadn't seen one in months, maybe years. Caliban had always been bad with calendars.

The fruit in Mother's forest was also running thin. Two springs in a row, most of the fruit trees had given too little or no fruit. Caliban tossed the rind aside hoping it might attract another lizard mole. They were hard to catch, had sharp teeth, claws and horns, and they were so lean. But it was the only animal he could find lately that didn't view him as more of a meal than he viewed it.

He drifted during the afternoon hours. The sun burned overhead, but a soft, cool breeze weaved through the forest. Caliban hated the bright, burning sun. Mother had said he was made for all environments, but she had been wrong about many things. He reached the edge of the forest and looked out on the gray plains. His stomach urged him to venture out there, to find and kill a gray fatty. So much meat. He could eat for days and days, filling his belly, sleeping without aching hunger.

But the pointy-nosed wolves lived out there, as vicious as the gray fatties were slow and stupid. Before Balthazar had broken Caliban, he could have fended off two or three pointy-nosed wolves, but despite all the years, he still limped along and his hip still ached. Mother should have fixed him. Stupid Mother deserved her stupid death.

Caliban sat against a tree and closed his eyes. He needed rest. Some day if he got hungry enough, he'd go into the gray plains, or maybe into the jungle. Both places held meanies, but better to be mauled by an acid spider than die on the floor of the forest, hungry and alone.

A high-pitched wail boomed overhead, and Caliban's eyes snapped open. He looked upward. A small object streaked through the sky, smoke trailing behind it. At first, he thought it was a large bird farting clouds. But no, it wasn't a bird. Mother had let him watch starjumper launches and landings. This was like that, a spaceship coming from the sky. Someone was coming.

Caliban hurried through the forest, trying to track the falling ship. Would it be the man who'd cancelled Mother's work? An explorer? Some of Mother's friends? It had been so long. Why would anyone be coming here?

The ship continued its descent, and Caliban stopped. The ship looked old and mean; he did not want to step into its streaking path. The ship would bring flames and death; he would not die because he let a ship crash on his head.

As Caliban paused, the falling craft continued streaking toward the forest, more smoke around it. It disappeared below the tree line, followed by a crack and a thud. Could he hope for friends? Hope for food? Hunger clawed at his belly, and he craved more than just lizard moles and bitter fruit. But it could be dangerous. What if Mother had friends coming to visit? What if they didn't find her here? Would they blame poor Caliban?

"Nonsense," he said to himself. "Been hundreds of moons since Mother died. No one visit her. No one visit Caliban. This different." He nodded reassurance to himself and limped toward the sound of the crash.

As he approached, life moved the other way, several lizard moles retreating across the ground and bulbous bugs skittering through the air toward. Caliban did not move to catch the little creatures; he kept his eyes on the scorched earth and plants, black as night. He crept, but he moved toward the big arrival. The silver metal ship had created its own clearing, flattening trees, shrubs, and grass. Four small fires burned in the new clearing, but the ground was wet from last night's rain, and the fires burned reluctantly.

The silver ship looked whole, though Caliban knew little of spaceships.

He circled the clearing, but only saw the fallen ship and its aftermath. No people, no food, no nothing. Did some ships fly without people? Did people die if their ships landed like this? When Mother's friends had arrived on ships, they had landed softly like a buzzer fly on a leaf. This ship had landed like a bird with a mangled wing.

After completing his circle, Caliban hid himself in some tall grass next to a thick tree. How long should he wait? A long time, he decided. There was a chance of good food here; there was nothing behind him but lizard moles, tough tree roots, and fruit, none of which was good. His mouth watered as he thought about sweetbread. Hopefully these people liked sweetbread. Even if they didn't, maybe they would know how to make some.

The sun dipped in the sky, dropping toward nighttime. Caliban spent the rest of the day staring at the silver ship and imagining what friends might come out. Sometimes he imagined them fat, sometimes all women like Mother, and sometimes lizard men like Balthazar and his brothers. Caliban's mind exploded with possibilities.

He crouched when he heard rustling on the opposite side of the clearing. Had something else come to see the ship? It sounded big. Maybe his lizard men brothers had survived? He'd last seen them running from the cliff, cowering from Caliban. Maybe they had seen the ship.

Caliban would not be happy to see them. There was hardly enough food for one, let alone three more. Yes, they had been scared of Caliban many moons ago when he'd killed Balthazar and Mother, but they were whole, and he was not.

But it wasn't lizard men, it was something worse. One of the lizard cats from the jungle entered the clearing, its steps cautious and purposeful. But Mother's creatures were supposed to stay in the jungle; he had never seen one outside of the jungle. He licked his lips. He'd beaten lizard cats many times. This beast was lean but still had meat for many meals.

A sudden hissing forced Caliban into a deeper crouch, and the lizard cat leaped from the clearing and sprinted into the forest.

A piece of the ship stuck out. The hissing stopped, and the piece laid down like stairs. Caliban could not see the door; he'd picked the wrong spot to wait.

Rain began to fall, a steady and relentless stream, the worst kind of rain, cold and constant. But the noise made creeping easier; Caliban slipped from his hiding spot to a similar one with a clearer view of the door.

A man walked through the door and into the rain. The man was large, larger than most, almost as large as straight-standing Caliban. A thick beard covered his face. Caliban reached up and felt his own, hairless face. The man looked up at the sky, his mouth curved into a deep frown.

The man muttered something Caliban could not understand. The man didn't talk like Mother; he used different words, ridiculous nonsense words. Had the man's words been scrambled by the crash?

The man was not a friends of Mother's, at least not someone Caliban had met. He could remember all of her friends, their faces often greeting his dreams. Caliban wasn't stupid, because how could a stupid mind remember every face from forever ago?

The man looked cautiously around the clearing and peered into the dense forest. His eyes passed by Caliban's hiding place, but no fear or recognition lit his face. The tall grass and the persistent rain made Caliban invisible. Then the man disappeared back into the ship, and Caliban almost cried out. Would he leave? Caliban needed a friend, needed help, even a bad friend would be better than none at all.

The man emerged a moment later, carrying something. At first, Caliban thought it was a monkey, but it had little hair and wore clothes. It was a small person! Caliban had heard Mother's friends talk about children, about smaller humans. Starting off small seemed so stupid; he had been born full size. Why would humans let themselves start as little, hairless monkeys? This little person the large man carried looked so fragile, like Caliban could break it by pushing it down. The little person looked around, its eyes wide and as fearful as a cornered lizard cat. The man held it in a tight embrace. He said something to it, but the tiny one replied only with a shallow nod. They stepped back into the ship, and the door folded up behind them.

Caliban sat down, the grass retracting underneath him. Humans. People. A man and a child. And a lizard cat had escaped the jungle. After moons of nothingness, one day had brought so much. So Caliban waited in the rain, waited for the people to come back out, hoping the ship wouldn't return to the stars. He hoped for a friend, maybe even a real friend, and if no friends, then at least a little food.

The rain continued for two more days, and the people stayed inside
their dry ship. Caliban hated the stupid, constant rain. But he didn't dare

leave the ship alone, though he did twice to dig lizard moles out of their burrows and find some fruit. But the ship remained the same, unmoving mystery.

The lizard cat also evaded him. Most animals gave off an odor Caliban could smell from far away, but not lizard cats. Mother had created beasts to be weapons, and smelly animals were bad weapons. He had not wandered far tracking the tooth-filled beast, and he'd lost its trail near the jungle. Maybe the creature had returned to the beastly place. How had it escaped the invisible wall? Jumping? Caliban shook his head. He didn't even know how the wall worked. He could step in and out of the jungle whenever he wanted, but Mother's other killers were not supposed to wander freely.

On the third day the rain gave way to a brilliant green sky and the burning red sun. After that, Caliban kept to his post--he would not miss the people.

As the sun climbed into its morning position, the door opened, hissing less this time. The man, his hair dark and his skin lighter, stepped into the clearing. After a moment, he mumbled something and the tiny one walked out, clutching tightly to the man's leg.

They spent the next few hours walking the forest. Gradually the tiny one let go of the man's leg, but remained close to him. Her curiosity grew, and she reached out to touch leaves or to swat away a buzzer.

As they made their way back to the ship, the man picked up a long, recently-fallen branch. He shook it off and tore the greenery free of it. They returned to the ship and closed the door, remaining inside the rest of the day.

For three days, the two people repeated this routine, exiting the ship in the morning to explore an ever-expanding circle. The man held the stick from the first excursion, and he carried a small knife at his belt. He'd carved one end of the stick into a point, making himself a crude spear. This made Caliban laugh on the inside; that silly weapon would do nothing against strong Caliban or meanie lizard cats.

The people became comfortable quickly. They were terrible hunters and easy prey. They talked constantly, muttering words he could not understand. They both smelled badly, and their scents carried for miles into the woods. And they constantly stepped on plants, bent branches, and left a thousand other signs of their movements. If the lizard cat ever returned, it wouldn't take long to find them.

Caliban considered killing them. The tiny one wasn't much, mostly skin and bones. But the man was large and muscular. Caliban had never eaten a person, though humans couldn't taste any worse than a lizard cat. But Caliban kept his distance. They never seemed to notice him, even when he stepped heavy to test their ears. He considered clapping or yelling to get their attention, a sort of game. But instead he just watched.

The tiny one grew curious. She swatted at buzzers, following the most colorful ones among the trees and through low bushes. She laughed in delight when one of the blue-black birds sang their high-pitched song. The man let her walk farther and farther away. He should have kept her closer. She was small and carried no weapon; ever a little predator could kill her before the big man reacted.

How were these tiny ones created? He'd heard Mother's friends talk about "making love," and he'd heard references to humans creating other humans inside themselves. That sounded disgusting. Another creature clawing inside you? But humans didn't have claws, so maybe it wasn't so bad.

After three days of exploring, the rain returned for two days, and the people emerged once briefly. After moons of being alone, he should have been used to the isolation. But on the days when the people stayed inside the ship, Caliban missed them, longed to track them through the forest.

They definitely had food inside the ship. They never ate anything outside, even though the man had collected several tree fruits. Humans needed food every few hours, so they must have food inside. Caliban considered killing the man the next time he came out; not to eat him--though he'd probably do that--but to steal the food. Curiosity burned, but not as much as his hunger.

On the next sunny day, the two people came out again, laughing. The man chased the tiny one around the ship. He left his sharp stick and knife near the ship. Stupid humans. The lizard cat could return at any time. So Caliban began circling the two humans, even though he knew all that movement might alert them to him. But they seemed nice, like maybe friends. And he wouldn't let a lizard cat rip open their throats before he had a chance to find out. And if they were going to die, then Caliban would be the one to kill them and feast on their flesh.

The next day, they came out early in the morning, and the man talked with the tiny one for a long time. His voice sounded serious like

Mother's did when she scolded one of her friends. But the tiny one did not shrink like her friends did; she looked happy, nodding and smiling. Caliban wished he could understand their jabbering words.

That day their routine changed. They walked in a mainly straight line from the ship toward Mother's building. Caliban followed more closely than ever before. He was growing impatient and curious, and the man and the tiny one were so oblivious he could have blown in their ears and they wouldn't have seen him.

On this trip the man brought a little bag with him, tied around his waist. He also carried his pointy staff and knife. Caliban circled ahead, trying to guess where they might be headed. Their walk would take them straight to Mother's building. Did the bearded man know about that? Maybe Caliban had been wrong; maybe the man searched for Mother.

After the sun reached its peak and started downward, they stopped. The man pulled opened his pack. Caliban leaned in closer, his stomach anticipating delicious human food, food he could steal and eat.

The man pulled out what looked like two human turds, brown and the length of the man's palm. Why would the man carry their own shit around in a bag? Humans were strange, but Caliban had never seen behavior like this.

The man handed one of the turds to the tiny one. It grabbed it eagerly, eyes wide, mouth jabbering nonsense. As soon as it had the brown thing in hand, it stuck it in its mouth and took a large bite.

Caliban turned away, the feeling of bad tree fruit rind bubbling inside. But he fought it away. He looked back, and the two humans chewed and ate. Caliban grimaced.

But then he caught the scent of what they ate. The scent was not pleasant, not like sweetbread or cooked meat. It smelled of trees and plants, and maybe some sugar. As disgusting as it looked, it was food, unlike anything he'd seen humans eat before. The smell did not excite his stomach, but it did rekindle his hunger.

The man and the tiny one finished their little meal with some water, and then they played a game of some kind. They clapped each other's hands, and then laughed at things Caliban could not understand. More jabbering and lots of laughing. Even though he didn't understand the game, he felt laughter welling inside him, as if their laughter fueled his own. But he held the laughter in; he wouldn't be discovered by laughing.

After their lunch, they marched into the forest, noisily and carelessly.

Several hours after the sun's peak, they reached the northwest entry to Mother's building. The forest grew thick around it, moss and grass obscuring the shiny metal. The man walked past it, but saw something reflect the sun and walked back. A tree had fallen across the entrance many moons past, and Caliban had never tried to move it. The only things inside were skeletons, empty rooms, and painful memories.

The man wiped away some moss, revealing the shiny metal underneath. He gasped and then jabbered and motioned with his hand. The tiny one smiled, yelled, and jumped. Caliban did not understand their excitement, but maybe he knew what they didn't: there was nothing exciting inside and no food.

The man spent an hour clearing away moss and grass, but all he found was metal. Caliban knew where the door was as well as the pad thing to open the door. He smiled as he watched the man's chaotic search. Humans thought themselves so smart, but really they were no smarter than Caliban.

As the sun stretched toward night, the man jabbered loudly. Though Caliban didn't know the words, he understood the tone: cursing. The man sat on the fallen tree, his face in his hands, his body covered in sweat. The tiny one approached him and placed its little hand on his knee. It talked, and he looked up, a small smile erasing the previous anger. He jabbered back and patted the little one on the head. After another short meal of the turd-looking food, they walked toward their silver spaceship.

Caliban followed, farther behind. What were these two humans to each other? He'd never seen such regard or kindness with humans. Maybe that wasn't entirely true. Mother's friend Jules had been nice to him, and he'd seen some of Mother's friends laugh with each other, and he'd even seen some naked touching. But what happened between the man and the tiny one was different.

Is this how humans were supposed to act? Should Mother have regarded him like the big man regarded the tiny one? If she had treated him like this, maybe he wouldn't have thrown her off a cliff. Caliban couldn't imagine the man throwing the tiny one off a cliff. The man was certainly the leader, and he was physically imposing, especially compared with the miniature human. But he didn't use that, not like Caliban had been taught to use his physicality.

He pushed the puzzle from his mind. It made him sad and made his head hurt. Thinking wasn't worth the headaches.

The man and the tiny one reached the ship shortly before nightfall, stepping inside. Caliban curled up in his usual spot of soft grass. Thunder rumbled in the distance, and he hoped he'd stay dry.

chapter 23

LIZARD CAT

he next two days were the same, the man and the tiny one emerged early after the sun rose and walked to the entrance. The man's progress was slow clearing the door. On the second day, he finally cleared moss and dirt away from the pad. He yelped in excitement when it sprang to life, but then cursed when it didn't open the door. Silly man. He wasn't one of Mother's friends, so the door wasn't for him.

The man also tried to lift the fallen tree, but even as large as he was, he only managed to move it a few inches, and he was punished for that. The small movement disturbed the underground home of some slimy biters, long little bugs that aggressively went after him. The dozen or so bites he got ended his attempt to move the tree.

Caliban lazily followed them on those two days, staying far enough so he could hear but not see them. They were starting to be boring. Who wanted to watch a man clean away many moons' growth from a door? Watching him piss would be more interesting.

On the third day, Caliban considered not following them at all or rushing them and taking the poop food. But he followed his previous routine. He liked routine. He followed them as they walked confidently through the forest, like it was their home. Maybe now it was.

Caliban lay in the afternoon sun, nearly falling asleep in the grass. He could hear the rhythmic scraping of the man working moss from the metal. He probably had most of the door cleared by now, for all the good that would do him.

A cry interrupted Caliban's half slumber, and he hopped into his crouch, alerted by the noise. It was the tiny human. It jabbered nonsense, high sounds like a lizard cat when surprised. But the little one's sounds were more frantic.

Caliban limped quickly toward the sound.

A second sound came, the scream of the man, but not one of fear or pain. Caliban knew that scream; it was a battle scream.

He slowed as he got close. The tiny one lay behind the man, her leg drenched in red blood. The man crouched near her, his pointy staff out. Across from them stood the lizard cat.

The beast circled, looking for an opening. They were not that close to the door, so the tiny one had wandered away. Stupid humans.

"Leave us alone!" the man bellowed.

Caliban started. The man knew Mother's words? But why did he speak jabber before, and her words now?

But then he bellowed jabber, almost as if Caliban had imagined the familiar words.

The lizard cat slowed its pacing, its eyes focused on the spear. It would strike soon, and the silly spear would not prick it. The man would fall, and the tiny one soon after. Lizard cats were made by Mother to do only one thing, and they did that efficiently, unless you were strong like Caliban.

Caliban jumped, grabbed a branch, and swung toward the creature. The lizard cat turned its head, but too late. Caliban's feet struck its torso and sent it sprawling away. A dull pain lanced his right leg, but he ignored it and stood on his hands and good leg.

The lizard cat snarled, bearing its fierce fangs. Caliban snarled back, showing his razor teeth. Lizard cats were strong, but they were not cunning. Caliban was cunning, and Caliban was stronger.

The cat jumped, but he sidestepped, letting the cat land behind him. The creature whirled and leaped again, just as Caliban knew it would.

He dropped flat on the ground and sprang as the lizard cat passed overhead, grabbing its hind legs, pivoting on his left leg, and throwing it against a nearby tree. The creature struck, its skull cracking. It fell limply, the slight movement of its chest the only evidence it lived.

Caliban approached it, his chest out, standing as tall as he could, but limping along the way. He towered over the fallen animal, and he screamed. He reached down and grabbed its cracked skull, his clawed left hand digging deeply into its neck.

"Caliban strong," he snarled. "Caliban stronger than stupid, silly cat. I eat you now. I win."

He tore the head off, and tossed it into the woods.

Caliban turned, the frightened man still holding his silly spear. He flashed his most pleasant smile. "Caliban no hurt man and tiny man."

The man cocked his head. "You speak Coznarian?" The man spoke Mother's words, but Caliban did not know the word 'Coznarian.'

"Caliban speak. You speak jabber."

"I speak Lanopian, but I also speak Coznarian." The man's words were Mother's words, but he spoke slowly and like he had a mouth full of food.

"Caliban speak," he repeated.

"Caliban is your name?"

Caliban nodded.

"My name is Sparo. Are you a friend?"

"Caliban like to be friend."

"Sparo would like to be a friend, too." He lowered his spear. "How long have you been here?"

He shook his head. "Caliban bad with numbers. Caliban not know. Many, many moons Caliban here."

The man nodded.

A small cry came from the tiny one behind the man, its voice weak and high pitched.

"Miram." The man mumbled in his other words, but the girl responded only with heavy, short breaths.

The man turned to Caliban, the tiny one on his arms. "Caliban: can you get us into the facility?"

Caliban nodded.

"Is there a medical room?"

"What is medical room?"

"A place to fix people."

"Yes. There is medical."

Caliban paused. The lizard cat would be a good few days' meal, but the man and the dying tiny one would be even more. He needed food. He looked toward the door. But Caliban had been hungry for many, many moons. He needed friends more than he needed food.

"I show you," he finally said. "I show you Mother's building."

After using the pad to open the heavy door, he led the man and the tiny one through the halls. The inside was dark, with an occasional glowing light breaking up the shadows. All of their noises echoed in the empty hallways.

They passed one set of bones, what was left of a pile of Mother's friends, all the meat gone. Had the other lizard men come in and eaten what was left of her friends? Caliban shuddered. He'd stayed away, sure the meat would be rotten. But now it was all gone.

He could hear the thumping heartbeat of the man, and the weakening heartbeat of the tiny one. Their breathing sounded in his ears, his senses not used to the loud human noises, not up close like this.

They reached the medical room, and he placed his hand on the pad. It scanned his hand, but a red bar lit up above it. Caliban tried again, and the red bar came again.

"No work," he muttered.

The man set the tiny one down. It whimpered, but was only half awake.

"I'm sorry, Miram," the man said, tears streaming down his face. "I failed you. I failed your mother, and now I've failed you." The man slumped to the ground next to the tiny one, gripping its small hand in his.

Caliban reached up and tried the pad again, but the red bar greeted him. He snarled. Why would Mother forbid him from helping a new friend? Even from her death pit at the bottom of the canyon, she mocked him, distrusted him. The tiny one was dying, and he could almost hear Mother laugh.

Caliban screamed and pounded the door with his fists. The door stayed in place, but two large dents appeared where his fists had struck. Caliban punched again. And again. And again. Pain built in his hands, but he did not care.

He looked at the man, still huddled next to the tiny one. This is what friends should look like, how people should treat friends. If Caliban wanted friends like these, he'd have to be a friend like that.

Two more times he pounded, and on the last strike the door came free and clattered to the ground of the medical place. Caliban growled in triumph.

The man looked up, his eyes wide and his mouth open. He mumbled in his own words.

"Caliban help," he said.

"Yes, Caliban," the man replied in Mother's words. "Thank you."

The man scooped up the tiny one and took it into the room, laying it on a raised bed. It looked so small in a bed made for a larger human. Its red blood stained the white sheet covering the bed. Dust coated everything in the room, some of it stirring with a sudden breeze coming from a vent overhead.

The man looked through the cabinets, pulling out bandages.

"Caliban." The man worked on the tiny one's chewed up leg. "She's going to need something to drink. Can you fetch our water? I left my pack by the door."

"Better." Caliban limped over to a sink and filled a glass with water, pure and clear. Everything in Mother's building seemed to work, just as it had before. Caliban handed the glass to the man.

"Thank you." The man sat the tiny one up and helped it drink, some of it spilling down its chin. Then he laid it down gently on the bed. The tiny one moaned, but its heartbeat strengthened.

"What name?" Caliban pointed to the tiny one.

"Her name is Miram," the man replied.

Sparo. Miram. The names sounded funny to his ears, and when he tried to place them on his tongue, they sat clumsily there, too. Miram and Sparo. Names of friends.

"Could you get my bag, Caliban."

"Yes, Sparo. Yes." He sprinted from the medical room.

Miram slept with Sparo at her side. It had been nearly an entire day. He'd bandaged her mangled leg, and he'd given her many vials of what he called medicine. Caliban watched the movement of her chest and sensed the quietness of her sleep. It was a different kind of sleep, deeper than he'd heard before.

"Why sleep so deep?" Caliban asked.

"I gave her something to help her sleep." The man wiped his hands across his tired face. "I can do nothing more for her now. I'm not a surgeon."

"She limp like Caliban?"

Spano turned to Caliban. "Probably. Why does Caliban limp? Did you have an accident?"

"No accident. Balthazar crippled Caliban, and Mother not try to fix it."

"Mother?" Sparo's eyes searched Caliban's body. "Did your mother look like you?"

"No. Mother look like you and Miram put together."

"She was human?"

Caliban nodded.

"Where is your mother?"

Caliban lowered his gaze. Mother was bad, but he knew that killing her had also been bad. He could not tell Sparo the truth.

"Mother left. A man came to find her, and Mother left."

"Lazlo." Sparo sat back in his chair, his eyes on the ceiling.

"Not know what Lazlo is."

Sparo glanced at Caliban. "Lazlo is a man, a friend. He helped us get here."

"No good friend send people here."

Sparo smiled for the first time since seeing the lizard cat. "It's hard to explain. I promise: Lazlo is a friend."

Caliban nodded, though he didn't understand.

"Are you the only one left of your mother's children?"

Caliban shook his head. "No. The lizard cat that tried eat Miram, Mother made it. Many other ugly, mean creatures in Mother's jungle. And I have three brothers, but Caliban not know if they still live. Maybe they eat Mother's friends, leave just bones."

They sat in silence for some time, both of them watching Miram breathe.

"Caliban." Sparo did not look away from Miram. "What other wonders besides the medical room does this place hold?"

"Wonders?"

"Special places. Special things."

"The most special place is Mother's room."

"I'm not talking about a bedroom, Caliban, I'm talking about . . ."

"No," Caliban interrupted. "Mother's room no have bed. It have computer, it have control. It where Mother see everything."

Sparo turned, his eyes intense, not totally unlike Mother when she thought of something new. "Computer? A control room?"

Caliban nodded.

Sparo looked back at Miram and placed his hand on hers. "We'll be back, little bird. Sleep until Daddy and Caliban return."

He led Sparo through the hall toward Mother's room.

"How many people lived her?" Sparo asked.

Caliban thought about it. He'd never counted Mother's friends because they were almost never all in the same place. But he thought back on the day he'd fought Balthazar and the room had been filled with people.

"Fifty?" Caliban answered.

"And how many creatures?"

Caliban shrugged. He couldn't know for sure; many of the creatures had been born before he was.

They arrived at Mother's door. Caliban raised his hand, but hesitated. Mother's room held memories, many memories of her, good and bad. He did not like memories; they turned his stomach and plagued his brain.

He placed his hand on the pad, and her door slid open.

It looked almost exactly how he'd last seen it before he'd killed Mother. Her chair faced them. The control panel glowed a soft blue. And a black stain sat where fresh blood had been before. The door to the back room stood open.

"Who was your mother?" Sparo mumbled, his eyes wide.

"Her friends call her Sycorax."

"Sycorax." Sparo spoke the name with wonder.

"But she gone now."

Sparo sat in her chair, but he looked funny. Mother's chair had been made for little Mother, not for hulking Sparo. But he didn't seem to mind. Sparo moved his hands across the controls, and a screen came to life.

"Show me medical," he said.

An image of Miram, still asleep on the man-sized bed, floated in front of them.

"You like Mother. You know magic."

"It's not magic Caliban; it's science. I can teach you. You are ignorant, not stupid. I can't do anything for the latter, but I can change the former." Sparo's words were beautiful, almost like a song.

Sparo pivoted the chair, facing Caliban. "I'm going to teach you Caliban. You saved our lives, and we owe you a great debt. I will teach you my language, and I will teach you science and math. Miram is little, and she needs to learn, too. You will learn all this together."

"Are we friends?" Caliban prepared himself for the answer. Sparo was being nice, but that didn't always mean someone was your friend.

"Yes, Caliban. You saved us. You are our friend."

Friend. True friends. Not like Balthazar or Mother or Mother's friends. Real friends.

Caliban smiled broadly, not worrying about his razor teeth.

chapter 24

FROM THE DARKNESS

ember Five swam in darkness. They couldn't tell how long they'd be there or even if they were still alive. The common sensation of being connected to the tribe, of being connected to their cluster, of being connected to the Whole--those sensations seemed foreign, distant memories.

When humans died, their essence moved to a place called the Well, a place the Whole had discovered millennia ago. But the Whole had never discovered a resting place for the souls or essence of their kind. Was this swimming darkness like death? Is this what awaited Five when their life faded?

In exploring the universe, Five had encountered madness. Sentient and lesser creatures whose biological minds had separated from reality. Madness often led to death, often not the death of the mad, but of others. They'd encountered a Goontag on Rizzax Seven, usually passive herbivores. But this Goontag had gone mad, it's mind warped by a virus. It killed its entire pack, one-by-one, by stomping on their skulls with its massive feet. The other Goontags had sat there and let their companion murder them all, as it was not their nature to fight back against one of their own kind. The murderous Goontag eventually ran off a cliff to its own death.

Among the Whole, there was no record of anything like madness ever affecting them. Each particle of a member was identical to each other particle. If a sickness or injury arose, which was extremely rare, the offending cell was abandoned. Members did not get sick, they did not go mad.

But madness came from more than a virus like the Goontag had. Five worried for their sanity and for the sanity of the tribe, assuming the other three still lived. Assuming this swimming darkness was not death claiming them. And assuming Five could remember the light, remember life, if they ever found them again.

This kind of madness, if indeed Five grew mad, would take over each particle of them. It could not be ejected, could not be erased. And since all members of the Whole were connected, it might spread. Could their capture lead to end of the Whole? Would they, tribe 1746 of cluster 827, be like a virus, driving the Whole mad? Or would the tribe be rejected, tossed aside like Five might do to a damaged particle?

Lost in thoughts of madness, Five did not notice a pull, their essence slowly escaping the ever-present darkness. At first, Five did not notice a growing, almost imperceptible light.

Sudden light drew Five from their thoughts of madness and destruction. At first, the light confused them. Images. A room. A person. Blinking lights. It seemed no more real than the darkness had. Was this more madness? Was this more death?

Next came a sound, an echo of something they'd heard before. A voice. A human voice calling out in the blinding light. Words. Words Five could not understand. Anger. Five felt something burning inside, wanted to lash out at the voice, crush its source. But they didn't. Members did not kill sentient or lesser life. Maybe they should. Maybe members should kill to protect the Whole.

Five shut off their senses, fleeing within themself. They reached out to connect to the tribe but felt nothing. The others were dead or still imprisoned. Five reached to the Whole. Nothing. Their connection was still missing. Had nothing changed? Had the witch merely called Five from the darkness to torment them again?

Opening themself up, Five let the light and sound reach them again. They recognized the room. It was the foul room the human woman had used, her control center. But something felt different. Dust. Five could see dust everywhere. The woman had insisted on impeccable cleanliness. It was the same room, but then it wasn't.

A different human sat there, a man. Hair covered his face and neck, and he filled the woman's chair to the point that it might break or topple. He held a glowing ball, like the kind the witch had used.

The man made another sound, but it meant nothing to Five. So they reached into the man's mind, brushing the surface to understand his language and more about him. Unlike the witch, his mind was open, and Five could read it all.

"This is amazing." The man's deep voice carried weight, like jungle plants carried moisture. "What are you? Artificial intelligence."

"There is nothing artificial about me, except for perhaps my capture."

The man's eyes grew wide. "You speak Lanopian."

"I speak anything I please. And you are Sparo."

His eyes grew wider. "Can you read minds?"

"Yes."

"What are you?"

What should Five explain to the man? He wasn't a friend to the witch, and his motives seemed pure from Five's initial exploration of his character. But he was human. A human had hunted them, had captured them, had killed one of them. Humans were not to be trusted.

But Five needed to gain the man Sparo's trust. They could not free themselves alone--they needed help.

"I am member Five of tribe 1746 of cluster 827 of the Whole."

"Of the Whole?" the man repeated. "Like the Church of the Heavens?"

"I know nothing of what you speak."

The man set the sphere on the desk. "Thirteen hundred years ago on my home planet, a man named Palo claimed a race of gods visited him, called the Whole. He wrote that the Whole were explorers, and that the dead go to a place called the Well of Souls. I always believed it to be utter nonsense but maybe not."

"I know nothing of this man, Palo," Five replied, "but his account is not inaccurate. The Whole is a race of explorers, stretching against the vast and infinite expanse of space to find all we can."

"Fascinating. How is it you're here? Why are you in human form? Is this not your natural form?"

Five looked at themself. They hadn't even noticed taking human form. They held the same form as before--purple essence drawn into the form like Caliban's.

They focused on Sparo. "This is not my natural form. Our true form is incomprehensible to humans; we are too vast to see with your eyes, at least under normal circumstances."

"How did you end up on Vesta II?"

Five stretched themself into the computer system, but just as before, they could not read or manipulate it. It wasn't like other sentient systems done with electric current. The witch's technology had captured the tribe, and it acted as a seemingly impenetrable fortress. They might someday figure a way out, but they couldn't do it trapped in the maddening darkness. They needed to be free, to be out. Sparo would be their savior, wittingly or not.

So they told Sparo all about their capture and about their short time serving Sycorax. They spoke what they knew of Balthazar's rebellion and their involvement in it. They finished by speaking of darkness and of their captured tribe.

The man looked pensively at the glowing sphere.

"Sycorax was the name of your captor? Caliban used the word mother to describe her."

"She went by the name Sycorax, though I have no idea who she really was. She was not natural, but a genetic creation not totally unlike the warriors she engineered. And Caliban's mind is simple, but she was a creator, not a mother."

He shook his head. "I have never heard of Sycorax, but whatever she was, her computer system is different from anything I've ever encountered. It's run on a synthetic compound with amino acids acting in the place of memory and software, and wave pulses acting as data and action. It's brilliant. Scientists have been trying to create something this efficient and secure for centuries. And though I've figured out what it is, I still don't really know how it works."

"Will you free me?" Five pleaded. "Will you free my tribe?"

The man looked up. "Of course. As long as you teach me about your race and help me build a life on this planet for myself and my daughter." His face went dark, his eyes vacant. "Until I can sink my teeth into my treacherous brother and any others who had a hand in dealing me this fate."

A door opened behind Sparo and Five recognized the limping friend.

"You found fairy," Caliban said in Coznarian.

Sparo looked between Five and Caliban. "You two have met?"

"Yes." Five nodded at Caliban.

"Mother brought fairy to life, she sister to Caliban." The inhuman creature flashed his razor teeth.

"Have we cleaned out the complex, Caliban?" Sparo regarded the creature kindly, as most sentient creatures regarded others they viewed as less than themselves, like animals or children.

"All bones gone, all dead things gone." Caliban hopped closer to Sparo. "What next?"

"Take a break, go get something to eat."

Caliban smiled again and limped from the room, the door closing behind him, switching it back to near darkness.

"Caliban is very dangerous," Five said. "He was made by Sycorax and everything she created was designed to bring suffering and death."

"He saved our lives. Some vicious predator maimed my daughter, and he saved us." Sparo's voice cracked with emotion.

Five considered scanning Caliban's mind, but they did not need to do that. He was simple, driven by impulses like a non-sentient being. "Only because he was tracking you and your child, considering eating you himself."

Sparo frowned. "Perhaps. What is he?"

"A failed prototype soldier created by Sycorax."

"Amazing," he mused, his eyes widening. "How did he survive by himself all this time?"

Five tried to shrug but feared it came off as more of a flinch. "I do not know. I could look into his mind if you'd like me to."

Sparo shook his head. "He's been good to us. And I can control him with food and the promise of companionship."

"Perhaps. I think it's likely you will regret keeping him here. The witch created him to kill. And his mind is weak, more animal than man."

"Then we will need to keep an eye on him." Sparo spent a few moments closely examining Five's form. "What should I call you? Member Five?"

"That is my name."

"Are you male or female?"

"Neither. Our race is genderless."

"But you have a feminine look."

Five looked down at their form. Their bald head resembled Caliban's, but their body was more curved, more feminine from a human perspective. Five changed form, retaining the bright purple color, but resembling one of the men who'd worked for Sycorax.

Sparo laughed. "You can change that easily? I think I preferred you in female form."

Five probed Sparo's mind, searching for his ideal feminine form. Images floated in front of them, women he respected, women he found sexually arousing, and women he disliked. One form rose above them all, Sparo's mate Eliel.

Five changed form, taking on the fuller figure of Sparo's mate, larger breasts and hips than the diminutive Sycorax, replacing their baldness with thick, long, curling hair to their shoulders, black with purple streaks. But they kept Caliban's pointed ears.

Sparo gasped, bringing his hands to his mouth. His eyes filled with tears. "El," he whispered.

"I am sorry," Five said. "I did not mean to upset you."

"Eliel. Oh sweet Eliel." He contracted his hands into fists sitting on his chest.

"I can chose another form," Five suggested.

Sparo dropped his hands into his lap, tears falling into his dark beard. He stifled a sob and wiped his face. "No. Seeing her face every day will remind me of why I'm here, will remind me of the price we've paid. And I think it will bring comfort to Miram.

"But calling you member Five will not do. It's very artificial sounding, and Miram will need an easy name to call you, something appropriate to your form."

Five considered it. They would not like to be called something else, but Sparo's words made sense; a name like Sparo would be as strange to the Whole as member Five was to humans.

"Sycorax called me Memfi."

"I'm guessing you would prefer not to be called by a name she gave you."

Five nodded. "She almost called me Ariel."

"Ariel." Sparo paused, considering the name. "It's a character from an old Coznarian fairy tale, queen of the fairies, master of love and light." He looked at them. "I think it fits quite well. Can we call you Ariel?"

Five considered it. Their form was female and the name, at least in Sparo's mind, also felt female. They would prefer member Five, but they needed Sparo to want to help them, to want to free the tribe. Familiarity could do that. And they sensed in Sparo a weakness, a weakness common to human men: the female. They could play this part well, gain his trust and love. Then they would use that to ensure their freedom.

"Yes. I can be Ariel to you and your daughter."

chapter 25

ARIEL AND MIRAM

Most of the day passed with Ariel explaining the facility's capabilities to Sparo. Though they could not control more than basic computer functions, they'd learned much of the building's operation, and some things--like the doors, cameras, medical equipment, and cloning technology--ran off electric current which Ariel could control.

Sparo stopped when Ariel told of some of the medical equipment and how Sycorax could heal broken tissue, bones, and even organs.

"She had cell cloning?" Sparo's eyes lit with eagerness.

"Yes. One of her workers had his arm mangled by a deviant creation and Sycorax remade it. I watched the procedure."

"Could you repeat it?"

"Of course."

Sparo popped up from his chair and urged Ariel to follow him. The human sprinted down the hall toward his daughter.

They passed through smashed doors into the medical room. Ten medical bays lined the walls. One of the bays swallowed the little girl; Sycorax had not had children in mind when she built this place. Monitors indicated Miram was stable, but her left leg was seriously damaged. Ariel inserted themself into the girl, probing her condition. Most of the skin and muscle tissue was gone, and she needed more blood.

Ariel disappeared from view, entering the medical bay system. Unlike Sycorax's main system, the medical computers used electricity, and Ariel could manipulate them. Using the supplied amino acids and DNA strings, Ariel commanded the cloning machine to create tissue and blood to replace what Miram had lost. The machine sprang to life and began the process.

Ariel reappeared in the room. Sparo stood over the girl, holding her hand. She slept quietly, a cocktail of drugs allowing her mind to ignore the pain.

"The machine is creating blood and tissue for Miram matching her blood type and size," Ariel said. "It will take several days, maybe more than a week. The machine will begin with tendons and work its way to skin. After therapy, your daughter should be completely healed."

Sparo sobbed, his head falling to the girl's chest.

Ariel did not understand these intense human emotions. They entered Sparo's mind but recoiled at its potency. Anger. Fear. Relief. Happiness. Sadness. How could a being hold all that inside itself at the same time? They marveled that more humans were not driven mad by these roiling feelings.

"Thank you." Sparo looked up from his daughter, his face haggard. "I did not think we'd have something like this here. I thought I'd have to take her leg. . ." He paused to quiet his intense emotions. "We have technology like this on Lanopi, but I never thought I'd find it here."

"You are very welcome, Sparo." They dove back in and out of his mind. "You should rest. The last few days have driven you to extreme fatigue."

Sparo grabbed his daughter's hand. "No. I will stay by her side until she awakes. I'm not leaving her alone."

Ariel wanted to argue, to tell him that his daughter had days of sleeping ahead, maybe more. But his boiling emotions drifted from him, and she knew his reason was buried beneath them. So they entered Sparo's mind again, and lulled him to sleep. Ariel reached out to Caliban, calling him to the room. Caliban entered and knelt next to the slumped man.

"Fairy kill Sparo?" Sadness tinged his words.

"No, Caliban, I helped him to sleep. Carry him to one of the other beds so he may rest."

Caliban easily lifted the large human, gently placing him on the nearest bed. "Fairy is friend of them, too?"

Five did not really know what Caliban meant by friendship. The concept was not lost on the Whole, but a member rarely interacted with any outside their tribe. One did not seek friendship or acquaintances. But Five needed to think more like a human until they could free the tribe and return to the Whole, and they needed to think of themself as Ariel.

"Yes," they finally said.

"Fairy is Caliban friend, too?"

Ariel did not wish to promise too much to Caliban. He was delicate, simple, more animal and child than man.

"Yes, Caliban, we are your friend, too."

Ariel hesitated to think of themself as female; it seemed limiting, degrading, a sort of de-evolution. The Whole descended from a race in which gender had existed, but not with the clear physical differences like among humans. Gender was not a defining characteristic, even in the Whole's more mortal past.

Days were spent testing the facility's systems and exploring around the building. Caliban worked to clear the outer doors, and Sparo spent his time in the computer attempting to figure out Sycorax's unique system. He'd concluded that some information had been deleted years ago, probably during Balthazar's failed revolution. Ariel hoped that the way of freeing the tribe hadn't evaporated with whatever Sycorax had erased.

They needed to figure out how to free their tribemates. Were the others going mad as Ariel had feared they had been? Though Ariel had some freedom, they were still trapped on the planet, anchored to this world and disconnected from the Whole. In that way, Sparo's case wasn't much different than theirs. He was also trapped, cut off from his own kind. What a trio Ariel made with Sparo and Caliban: universe explorer, banished politician, and a genetic misfit.

After searching the jungle for more escapees, Ariel found Sparo curled up into a small bed cuddling Miram. The girl's leg looked almost normal, just a few more therapy seasons to replace some skin cells. She'd been active the past two days, but Ariel had not interacted with the diminutive human. Sparo worried about the shock of Miram seeing a purple version of her mother floating around like a ghost.

Ariel checked the case surrounding Miram's healing leg; skin replacement was at seventy-five percent.

"Mommy?"

Careless. She'd taken human-like form without thought.

"I am not your mommy," Ariel responded in Lanopian.

"But you look like my mommy."

Ariel reached into the girl's emotions. Sadness. Disappointment.

Fear. Wonder.

"I was sent by your mother," Ariel replied. "I am here to watch over you and your father." It was a simple lie, one Sparo had constructed. Ariel wanted to tell the truth; Miram was an intelligent child and would one day understand. But Ariel had to obey; she needed Sparo's help too much to alienate him.

"Are you a ghost?"

"Not exactly. I'm more like a fairy."

"There are no such things as fairies."

"I am not really a fairy, not like you've read about in stories. But I am here to help you and your father."

The girl smiled. "I think maybe you are a fairy. Maybe my daddy and my teachers were wrong. I wanted fairies to be real."

"There is much in this universe your father and your people don't know."

"Will you help us get home?" Expectation. Hope. Despair.

"I hope I can."

"If fairies are real, then getting home can be real, too." Hope.

Ariel tried to smile, hoping it had the intended effect.

Miram laughed. "Your face is weird."

"I am not human. I am learning to move my face like you do. It was meant to reassure you."

Miram laughed again, a light happy sound which made Ariel happy, too. They hadn't felt any joy in too long. Miram's pure, innocent mind reminded Ariel that not all humans were like Sycorax, or even like Sparo. Much of humanity was like Miram.

"Your words are too big. I only three."

Ariel tried to laugh, mimicking Miram, but it came out too shrill. "I will use smaller words."

"What is your name?"

"Ariel."

"My name is Miram."

"It's nice to meet you Miram."

chapter 26

CALIBAN'S FOLLY

Many moons came and went, and Caliban loved almost all of them. His stomach was never empty anymore. And friends. Caliban spent an hour every day with Sparo and another hour with Ariel, learning, writing, reading. He learned to speak Sparo's tongue, and he learned even more of Mother's.

He spent the rest of his days doing things for Sparo: cleaning, hunting, and mostly watching Miram. The small girl had grown so much, still much smaller than Sparo and Caliban, but now she looked like a woman.

"It's been nine years," Miram said absently. Caliban walked alongside her as she explored the forest with her small magic pad, writing notes and taking pictures.

"Nine years?" Sparo's language still felt weird on Caliban's tongue, almost like he sampled a new food, even if it had been nine years.

"Since father and I landed." Miram stopped to look at a fat fly, the stupid bugs buzzing all the time. "That's a long time. I hardly remember anything else."

"Caliban knows nothing else," he said. "Caliban only know this place."

Miram looked at him. "Do you ever wonder if you have a soul?"

"A soul?"

"Yes, a spirit inside you, like the Heaveners believe, something which will exist when you die?"

Miram's words reminded him of words Jules had said to him long ago. "Soul? Caliban not have one, Caliban think. Do Miram have one?"

She shrugged. "I don't know. Ariel says that there is a place where the minds of humans go after they die. But you were not born like me, you were born a different way."

Caliban scratched his head, but the gesture did not ease his confusion.

"So where do you go when you die?" she asked. "Is there another well for your soul?"

"Caliban not understand. Caliban not die. Caliban live forever."

"Stay still." Miram sat and began drawing. "There's a bulbous bug on your shoulder."

Caliban looked over and resisted the urge to the smash it. Miram said they didn't bite and they were food for the small animals, so he shouldn't kill one any more than he would throw away good human food. But how could animals eat the fat bugs? They tasted like dung.

"Come look."

He brushed the bug from his shoulder and sat next to her. Her pad had a picture; it was the same green color as Caliban, but the face was wrong and the body was not sized right. The fatty bug was also as big as his head in her drawing.

"Do you like it?"

"Yes," he lied. At first, Caliban had always spoken true to Miram, but when he didn't like her drawing, she cried. He would never do anything to make her sad.

"Is Miram Caliban friend?"

"Of course," she replied, turning back to her drawing. "I don't have anyone else."

"But would Miram and Caliban be friends on Sparo's world?"

"I don't know." She finished the drawing and stuck the pad in her pocket. "I don't think there's anything like you on Lanopi, though I don't remember much."

"So no Caliban friend on Lanopi?"

"It doesn't matter." She leaned her head against his shoulder. When she touched him, he felt good, like nothing he'd felt before. "You're my best friend, Caliban, the only one I can truly talk to. Father's obsessed with, well, I'm not sure what. And Ariel is strange, less human than you. Friends become friends for all sorts of reasons. It doesn't matter how you become friends, or even why, just that you do."

Two days later, Caliban limped into Sparo's room. Sparo sat in Mother's chair, which was still too small for him. He held his head in his hands.

"Sparo no feel good?"

Sparo looked up. The skin around his eyes drooped, and he squinted in the faint light. "I am fine."

Caliban knew Sparo lied, but humans lied as easy as they breathed. It was as much a part of humans as Caliban's clawed hand was part of him.

"You need Caliban?"

"Yes. I am leaving with Ariel to explore a lake east of here, a place with fish. We'll be gone the whole night, traveling while the wolves sleep. I'll need you to keep watch over Miram while I'm gone. Sleep outside her door, and don't let anything harm her."

What could harm Miram in the building? Nothing came in but what Sparo allowed. But Caliban nodded.

"When will the fairy and Sparo return?"

"Hopefully by mid-morning tomorrow. When Miram awakes, tell her I'll be back soon."

Caliban sat outside of Miram's room for hours, bored. Protecting Miram was boring, but he'd promised Sparo. Time moved slowly, and he wished he could go outside and play. He couldn't even tell how long he had been here. Time flowed slowly when he was bored, like life was stuck in mud. Was it almost morning? Probably not. Why did some hours move like days?

Maybe Miram was awake. Sometimes she stayed awake late, reading or watching something on her pad. Maybe she would let Caliban watch, too. Maybe they could play.

He reached up, and the door moved open with a slight hiss. Darkness filled the room, broken only by the doorway's light. Caliban stepped inside and the door closed behind him. His eyes adjusted quickly as dim light filtered under the door and the soft green light of Miram's pad glowed against her chest.

"Miram could sleep through an earthquake," Sparo always said. Caliban did not know if that were true; he'd never been in an earthquake. But she slept quietly, and nothing seemed to wake her besides her father's deep voice.

Caliban approached the bed, her face visible in the dim light of her pad. She must have fallen asleep while reading.

He reached to move the pad away but stopped. Her face was so beautiful, softer than Mother's. Her dark hair hung over half of her face, and he lifted it away. She didn't move.

Best friends. She had said they were best friends. Caliban wasn't sure what that meant. No one had ever called him a best friend. Did she love Caliban? No one had ever loved him. He'd once believe Mother loved him, like Sparo loved Miram. But Mother had not, and that had killed her as much as Caliban had.

But he and Miram were not like parent and child. Were they more like brother and sister? No. He didn't feel for her what he'd felt for Balthazar. This was different, more special. What did humans do when they loved each other? Caliban bent down and kissed Miram on the forehead like Sparo used to when she was younger, pulling back quickly in case she awoke. But she did not stir.

The kiss sent a pulse through Caliban he'd never felt. Was this what humans felt for each other? He could not say. He wasn't human, but a human had made him. Did that make him part human?

Caliban wished he could ask the fairy. She was smart and knew humans better than he did. But Ariel was far away with Sparo, and Caliban was here, close to Miram, feelings stirring inside like a bunch of fatty bugs inside his stomach. He'd twice seen naked touching, once with Mother, and then in Jules' room after Jules disappeared. Mother had told him that the naked touching was called sex. Is that what humans did when they were special friends, best friends?

Ariel floated next to Sparo, frustrated by his human speed. They were used to traveling as fast as light or faster. Humans trudged along, slow and difficult. The speed of sentient creatures and animals had never bothered Ariel before, but they'd never had to slow their pace before.

Ariel watched Sparo. He was exhausted, sleep evading him.

"You should have taken a pain killer for that headache," they said.

"I get a headache almost every day, Ariel. I cannot take something every day."

Ariel eased some of their essence into his body, reducing the pain and soothing his exhaustion.

He looked up at them. "I wish you'd ask me before you did that."

"Would you have said no?"

"Maybe. Your ministrations are as addictive as any pain medication."

They moved along in silence after that. Ariel had tried for years to remedy his headaches, but the answer had alluded them. Nothing appeared to be wrong with him physically, but Ariel could not really fix him or even diagnose his being, his own essence; it was as ephemeral as their own.

So Ariel occupied themself, cataloguing every rock, ridge, or piece of gray sand in the area. It was tedious, but fulfilling. The Whole never got this detailed on any given world, but Ariel had found many things which they might have missed on a first look. When they bored with that, they sent some of their essence back to the facility, re-checking its systems. Energy good. All doors were secure.

They drifted into Miram's room to watch the sleeping girl.

Caliban stood next to her bed. Strange. Ariel had never seen him in her room--Sparo had discouraged that, giving Miram a private sanctuary all her own. Returning completely to Sparo, she scanned the area. No wolves, no land whales, nothing to bother Sparo for the two miles until the lake.

"I have to check something at home," they said.

"Trouble?"

They shook their head. "I doubt it. I will be back soon."

A moment later, they brought their essence into Miram's room but did not take human form. They did not wish to startle Caliban or Miram. The girl slept soundly. Ariel could sense her dreams but did not probe them.

Pulling back, they sensed something different in Caliban. Yearning. Desire. They'd never felt that in him before, not in this way. It wasn't a simple yearning for food or play like he usually had. The feeling swirled and twisted, almost like the desire for power they'd first felt from Sycorax. So they entered the creature's thoughts to better understand his churning thoughts.

They recoiled when they saw what Caliban planned to do.

Sex was not something the Whole had; procreation was a collective act, and the animalistic urges most creatures felt had evaporated from their race millennia ago. But they knew what it meant for humans, what it would mean for Miram. Caliban's advances would not be welcome; they would be terror. His act would be a violation akin to Sycorax trapping members of the Whole.

Ariel took their human form between Miram and Caliban. The green creature stepped back, shielding his eyes against their purple glow.

"Caliban," they said. "Stop."

"Caliban sorry. What Caliban do?"

Despite his fear, his desire for Miram burned bright. It was an obsession Ariel had never sensed in him. The quick evolution of Sycorax's creations showed itself again. Caliban had not been born with sexual desires, but yet they filled his mind like a pubescent human male. The woman had created creatures, imagining herself a god. But Caliban, like the escaped lizard cat years ago which had almost killed Miram, stretched outside of her design, her arrogance. And again it had almost cost Miram.

"I'm sorry Caliban. I know you meant no harm. But I serve Sparo." Ariel entered Caliban's mind and rendered him unconscious.

chapter 27

SLAVE AND MASTER

"Can you kill him for me?" Sparo's words hung just above a whisper, dripping with so much angry intensity that Ariel had no need to probe his emotions. They heard echoes of emotion Ariel had felt, the hatred which still burned inside for Sycorax. Sparo now felt that same detestation for Caliban.

Ariel thought of reminding Sparo of their earlier warning about Caliban, that keeping the creature around would only end in tragedy. But they decided to leave that unsaid. "He did not truly understand. . ."

"Silence!" Sparo bellowed, standing from his chair, his fury-filled face twitching. "He would have raped my daughter if you had not stopped him!"

"But he didn't. And Miram does not even know what happened. Caliban is nothing more than an animal who looks human. He lacks proper human reasoning skills."

"Men rape. Men steal. Men kill." His words regained their quiet, intense tone. "Men betray even their blood." Sparo breathed deeply, his eyes focused on some distant thought. "If he was a man, he would be imprisoned. If he was an animal, we'd put him down. So tell me, Ariel, which is he?"

"I will not kill Caliban," Ariel replied. "You will have to do it yourself. And I will not keep him unconscious either."

Sparo's eyes held his fury, even as his face went blank. He sat down at the computer terminal and waved his hands, bringing up three floating essences: green, white, and red. Members Two, Three, and Four.

"I have not discovered yet how to free you. There's so much to learn about what Sycorax knew, the wonders she created. I could probably spend decades here and still only steal a small piece of all she realized."

He looked at Ariel, the anger burning in his eyes, but this time she probed. Anger, fierce as any human emotion she'd encountered, as intense as the killer instinct of the fiercest predator. And the feeling was not just directed at Caliban, but floated toward his estranged brother. And some of his burning drifted toward Ariel.

"We had a deal," Sparo continued. "You help me live on this Diede-forsaken rock, and I help you and your people to escape. I want Caliban dead."

Ariel's human face remained placid as their own emotions boiled. How dare he threaten them. How dare this powerless human use the members of their tribe to barter for what he wanted.

But he wasn't powerless, was he? Like Sycorax, Sparo held the fate of their tribe in his ignorant grasp. They could not allow Sparo to imprison them again.

But they could not kill Caliban; they would not compound their sins with his blood. Caliban was a broken, flawed creature, but his twisting was not his own doing. Sycorax was responsible for him, and Sparo was culpable for not listening to Ariel's council years ago about the dangers of keeping Caliban around like a servant pet.

"There is another way," Ariel said, and they hated themself for the suggestion they were about to make.

Caliban sat up, suddenly awake and aware. He was on a cold, empty floor in a small room. Sparo was there, looming over him. He held Mother's ball, and Ariel floated behind him. The fairy's eyes would not meet Caliban's.

Caliban knelt and looked up at Sparo. "Sparo, Caliban sorry, Caliban . . ."

"Silence." Sparo did not shout, but the word was as vicious as a lizard cat's roar. "You will not speak until I'm done." He stepped closer, his nose twitching, and his grip on Mother's magic ball tensing the muscles in his arm. "You betrayed us, betrayed Miram."

"Caliban love Miram. . ."

Sparo struck Caliban across the face. The blow barely moved him, despite its sudden ferocity. Caliban turned back, his mind churning. He could crush Sparo if he wanted, kill him quickly. Then he and Miram could be together. But Miram would hate Caliban if he killed Sparo, so he remained still.

"Do not speak again," Sparo commanded. "I wanted to kill you, but I've decided to keep you alive. But things will be different from now on."

Sparo paced away, his eyes never leaving Caliban. "Sycorax engineered you to be a killer, a weapon. Like any tool, you best work as you were designed to work. I've been using you as a laborer, but you are not that. You are dark instinct personified. So I will speak your language, communicate in the only language you truly understand."

Caliban scrunched his face. Did Sparo mean Mother's language? How would that help them? Caliban knew Sparo's language nearly as well as Mother's.

A tingling sensation erupted across Caliban's chest, followed by piercing pain in his belly. He folded to the floor, gripping his stomach. He knew this pain, though he'd not felt it in many, many moons. It was Mother's painful gift, a curse even she had abandoned. Caliban had forgotten how truly awful this magic was, but now a long-forgotten memory came as fiery pain in his stomach.

As quickly as it came, the pain was gone. But Caliban remained tucked into a ball, the echo of the pain lingering.

"I speak your language now, Caliban, and I can kill you just as easily. If you ever touch Miram like you planned to, I will strike you down. Each time you disobey or work too slowly, this pain will remind you who your master is. My wrath lives inside you, you twisted, damnable creature!" Sparo turned to the fairy. "Come Ariel."

The fairy looked on Caliban, its eyes soft. Ariel rarely carried emotion on the outside like Sparo and Miram, but Caliban thought he saw it this time. The look was the same as Mother's friend Jules had all those moons ago, pity. But just as Jules' kind eyes hadn't helped Caliban then, Ariel's did nothing for him now.

Sparo and Ariel departed, leaving Caliban alone, crying softly. No more friends, no more home. Caliban had nothing again. Caliban should have killed Sparo when he'd had the chance. But with Ariel in his head and Sparo in his gut, Caliban had no escape.

"Stupid Sparo, stupid fairy, stupid Mother," Caliban muttered. "Stupid Caliban."

Caliban curled tightly into a ball and screamed.

chapter 28

CLARIBEL AND THANAN

laribel fought to remain conscious. Her new known systems history tutor had been droning on for what seemed like half a day about the hypo-nuclear war on Regno. Reading about the devastating conflict was one of Claribel's favorite subjects--it showed how much leaders could destroy, a warning against actions which served a sliver of society at the expense of an entire civilization. But even with a deep interest, listening to this fossil proved to be more than she could handle.

Claribel shifted her thoughts away from the tutor, trying to think of something which would keep her awake. Unfortunately, like many of her idle moments, her assassination attempt forced its way into her consciousness. It had been exactly five years since that terrible day, and unwelcome memories flooded her mind. As if the terror of almost getting killed and watching people die around her was not enough, the fallout from the events surrounding that day pushed Claribel closer to despair. She marked that violent day as the fulcrum upon which her life had pivoted, a changing point that had sent her entire family and the future of the High Regency on a new trajectory.

Her early life had been dominated by interactions with the High Regent, Father, or Thanan. Now she only saw them sparingly, usually at official functions, and never in the private way of most families. When they did meet, their conversations were polite but stiff, as if they were nothing more than infrequent acquaintances. Of course, that's all they were now, connected by blood but not by the loving binds which kept together true kinship. She missed Thanan the most. He'd been a daily part of her life as a child, sharing moments that only the closest of friends could.

But now they approached adulthood as near strangers. All of Lanopi viewed Thanan as the heir apparent, the High Regent in training. The people loved Claribel, followed her education and her fashion. But what meaningful role would Claribel play in the future of Lanopi? In that lonely moment, she did not really care. She wanted nothing of the High Regent's games; she just wanted a place to belong to, a people to belong to. She wanted to laugh with Thanan or find some non-sycophant friends. But she was nothing but an exile in her own home, a young woman destined for nothing.

The lights in the room blinked off interrupting her thoughts and casting the room in a dim red glow. The only other light came from her pad, but its connection to the jumpnet disappeared.

"It appears we've lost power." The old tutor groaned, showing his firm grasp on the obvious. "No matter. We'll do this the old fashioned way. You'll need to imagine the geography in your mind."

Claribel groaned. Apparently nothing could save her from getting bored to death.

As the tutor dove into a wordy explanation of the scattered nature of current Regno politics and how it could all be traced back to the war, the door to the room slid open, and Thanan stepped into the room trailed by Captain Nixa. Claribel's slouched posture straightened, and she couldn't help the excitement from welling in her chest. Sixteen-year-old Thanan's face carried a mischievous grin, confirming to Claribel that he must have been somehow involved in the power outage. What else could explain his sudden arrival?

"Master tutor." Thanan bowed too deeply, a mocking gesture beyond the tutor's comprehension. The tutor bowed back and Claribel stopped a smile. "The High Regent is asking all non-essential personnel to return to their quarters."

"Of course." He looked over at Claribel.

"Don't worry, sir," Adriana said. "I will escort Lady Claribel to her quarters."

The old man nodded. "Of course." He exited, but neither Thanan nor Adriana moved.

"Hello, Bel."

Claribel's heart jumped at his voice, at the tenderness it held. Maybe the High Regent had not completely destroyed the boy she'd known, at least not yet. He looked older, his shoulders wider and his face covered in dark stubble matching his coal-black hair. But despite that, his eyes held the impishness she'd so often seen in him as a boy.

"What are you doing here, Thanan? Mother will be furious."

He smiled and shrugged, the same smile he'd flashed when he'd stolen sweetbread from the kitchens when he was nine. "Mother will not know. I hacked the central system, disabled all the security protocols, cut access to the jumpnet, and turned off all power except for emergency systems." His face beamed with pride. "Mother will have her hands full, and so will her staff. Our physical locations will not be a priority."

Claribel couldn't help but smile.

"Very clever, Master Thanan," Adriana said. "But let's get on with it. The High Regent's techs will figure it out soon."

Thanan's smile broadened. "Of course." He took Claribel's pad from her hands and inserted a small jumpstick into its port. The stick glowed with a blue light. Thanan tapped the screen three times, removed the stick, and handed it back to Claribel.

"Your problem, Bel, is that you thought Mother a good person," Thanan said, his smile replaced with a sudden frown. "I don't remember ever liking Mother. I never trusted her. So I've been working to keep my own thoughts secret for as long as I can remember."

"So you're not . . ." Claribel's words died before she could finish her hopeful thought. She'd imagined Thanan had compassion in his heart, had not become the cruel device the High Regent had designed him to be. But their isolation had created doubts in her mind, worries that if she ever grew close to Thanan again she would find nothing but what their mother had created.

"No, Bel, I am not like Mother. She believes me to be, and I act the part." His eyes grew distant and sad. "Acting like her puppet in almost every moment wears me down, and sometimes at night, I silently weep in the darkness. But it will be worth it in the end. If I continue playing Mother's games right, I'll be High Regent someday. Than I can finally free myself from this insufferable act." His eyes widened and filled with excitement. "Then we can change things, Bel, we can serve the people instead of them serving us."

Tears filled Claribel's eyes. Could she hope now for a better future, for Lanopi, for herself?

"Lanopi deserves better," Thanan continued. "You deserve better. Bel, we can do this together."

"I'm not as strong as you," Claribel said, holding back a sob. "And what can I do from this isolation? Being alone is driving me mad, Thanan.

And the High Regent sees everything."

He placed his hand on her shoulder. "You won't be alone anymore, Bel. And Mother doesn't see everything." He motioned to her pad. "I've installed a ghost on your pad, a file called Golden Dress. It looks like a picture, but it's actually a ghost jumpnet access point. You can get off the Lanopi grid and onto the interstellar jumpnet. Find me on a knitting group called Coznarian Thumbsetters."

"A knitting group?"

He smiled. "Had to be something Mother would never find. My user name is Hedge. We can communicate there. I have sources throughout the known systems, sources I've cultivated. We can begin to plan what we can do after Mother's time ends. We can do this together."

Claribel wrapped her brother in a tight embrace. "Thank you, Thanan," she whispered in his ear. "Thank you for giving me some hope."

"Hope before fear."

Claribel recognized the phrase, from Palo's words. Hope before fear. Maybe she could feel hope again.

"Come, Lady Claribel," Adriana said. "We need to get you to your rooms before some of my fellow elite discover you missing."

A sudden fear gripped her. Was this all a test, orchestrated by the High Regent? Was she looking to trap Claribel into agreeing to this small rebellion to further justify her isolation?

No, Claribel would trust Thanan. Hope before fear.

"What is your part in this, Captain Nixa?" Claribel asked.

"My part?" The elite shook her head. "Just a soldier following orders, my lady, from the future High Regent. Seems like a solid career move."

Claribel turned back and hugged Thanan again. "Thank you, thank you. We can do this, can't we?"

He shrugged. "Who knows, but why not try? Mother raised us to be the most ruthless pair of siblings in the known systems. Might as well show her how well we learned all her silly lessons."

Claribel hugged him a third time and followed Adriana into the dark hallway toward her quarters.

claribel & caliban

PART 3

chapter 29

REVENGE

Ariel appeared in the control room, called by Sparo's command. He sat in complete darkness, the room's only light coming from Ariel's form. His eyes were closed, and his hands gripped his head as if he could pull the pain from behind his eyes. His face held its nearly constant grimace.

"How is the starjumper coming?" He spoke without opening his eyes, as if even Ariel's dim light wounded him.

"Not well," they responded. "The new engine will not work; it's unstable and is as likely to explode as it is to starjump. We need to find another way off Vesta II." Ariel had pieced together a new engine using plans from the jumpnet and materials found in the facility. It had always been a long shot.

"There is no other way." His voice hovered above a whisper, as if even the sound of his voice hurt his head. "My mind can barely pierce this cloud, and your race's ability to travel among stars has left you completely ignorant of starjump physics. We will live here, abandoned forever."

"There may be another way."

Sparo squinted at Ariel. "What?"

"The High Regent's daughter is to be married to the King of Nooteezia. The High Regent and her household will be traveling for the event. Your brother Balith will also be there."

Sparo's eyes opened farther at the mention of his brother's name, but they drooped just as quickly. "That would only be helpful if they were holding the wedding here." He choked out a brief laugh.

"What if they starjumped through Vesta instead of Fortuna?"

Sparo looked at them, his eyes dim. "That is something, but why would they jump through here? That would be unusual."

"We could ask Lazlo for help. Perhaps he could convince them to come through Vesta, an adventure through a lifeless system."

They'd accessed the jumpnet more than a year before, but despite Ariel's urging, Sparo refused to use it. Each time they'd mentioned it, he'd flown into a paranoid rage that somehow Balith would discover Sparo's survival and destroy him and Miram. He allowed Ariel to access the jumpnet, and he hungrily absorbed the information they shared. But despite a doorway opened to the universe beyond, he refused to use it. His madness continued to grow, and Ariel feared they'd be caught in it forever.

But instead of raging, he shook his head, the motion small and controlled. "Lazlo has abandoned us. Maybe he had a change of heart and hopes we're dead. Maybe alerting him to our survival will end what we have. It's lonely, but I prefer Miram know limited happiness here than meet the same fate as her mother."

His lack of rage was something, a small window of opportunity. But he'd also left more unspoken than said. He feared he was dying, though the medical scans showed nothing wrong with him. If he died, Miram would be alone, left with Caliban. Of course, Ariel would protect her, and maybe without the man's interference, Ariel could figure out how to free the tribe.

They pushed the morbid thought aside. They would not give in to the madness which seemed to infect this place.

"Regardless, what would we do even if we drew them here?" he continued. "We can't make them land, and my ship can't even break the atmosphere." Sparo bent over, putting his head between his knees.

"If they reached Vesta, I could pull them through the asteroid belt and to the planet. I could bring a starjumper to orbit, with drop ships and a way out of this system."

Sparo looked up, his eyes wider than Ariel had seen them in months. "You could do that so easily?"

"Easily? Maybe not. But I believe I could control the starjumper's systems. The Lanopians should not have security I can't penetrate, unless systems like Sycorax's have become commonplace. If it works, I could bring them to us."

"And I could have my revenge." Sparo looked into the darkness, exhaling deeply.

"Revenge?" Ariel's patience grew thin; they barely held their growing temper in check. "A way to escape. You could take one of their starjumpers and escape. Forget revenge; you and Miram could be free, find refuge on Camsarta or Scavart."

"No, we'll never be free, Balith and his friends will never let us be free."

"I know you know how to free me," Ariel continued. "You've unlocked most of Sycorax's secrets. You block your mind, you've reinforced the pheromone shield around the jungle, you've accessed her files on Caliban and his brothers. You have unlocked so much."

"I have not unlocked all of her mysteries." But he did not deny knowing how to free the members.

"You promised me my freedom," they said. "I have helped you make a safe home. I've helped you prepare for revenge. I have done all you asked."

"I cannot free you now." He looked at Ariel, his eyelids fluttering. "Not until I have figured out how to destroy my brother and ensure my daughter's future, a future devoid of loneliness, devoid of Caliban." He turned to the console, and with a wave of his hand, the screens sprang to life. "But this is a fantasy; how do we get them to jump through Vesta instead of Fortuna?"

"Reach out to Lazlo. Ask him to come here. It's not strange to travel through Vesta, just uncommon."

"You are due for your lesson with Miram." He looked away from them, his eyes focused on his screens. They'd been dismissed, another opportunity for freedom lost beneath the weight of Sparo's lunacy.

No, this opportunity would not pass. If Ariel could somehow get the Lanopian starjumpers into the Vesta system, revenge would be too close for Sparo to ignore. But as he had pointed out, why would they come through this system?

Ariel's mind cleared; the key was Lazlo. They would tempt him to come through Vesta, leave a message he couldn't ignore. Yes, a message from Sycorax. He'd worked with the cursed woman, had known of this secret base. But since only Caliban, his brothers, Sparo, and Ariel knew of Sycorax's death, a message, even after all this time, would be plausible. Ariel had learned much about Lazlo from the jumpnet, the man who had seen fit to maroon Sparo and Miriam on this planet instead of watching them die. He was a scientist, curious to a fault. How could he resist the possibility that Sycorax was active again or that Sparo might be alive?

But could he convince the Lanopian wedding party to come through a rarely-used system? Perhaps, or perhaps not, but Ariel would try. Ariel moved their essence toward Miram. Some chance was better than none.

chapter 30

CLARIBEL'S NEW DAY

Hope before fear.

Claribel stood outside the Church of the Heavens, a frequent trip since her Ascension three years before. Her Ascension was a highly-guarded secret, only known to church leadership, her disapproving parents, and a few others. It would not be good for the High Regent's daughter to be viewed as a superstitious follower of a maligned religion. But Claribel was an exile in her own home, a fact unbeknownst to almost all Lanopians. The embarrassment it might bring would do little to alter Claribel's life path.

Adriana remained close at hand, and Claribel could count at least a half dozen uniformed security personnel circling close by. That did not include the plain-clothed security also hovering; despite the unprecedented peace on Lanopi, Adriana remained vigilant. And seeing the security brought to mind Claribel's first trip to this beautiful building nine years before with Ona, when she hadn't noticed they were being followed. She had been so innocent then, so ignorant.

Claribel hoped beyond reason to find Ona milling about the crowd. It had been that long since she had seen her former tutor, and despite searching the jumpnet, she'd never found any trace of her. Claribel had considered using Regency resources to find Ona, but that would have made the High Regent aware of the search and if Ona had wanted to disappear from the High Regent's shadow, well, Claribel could understand and honor that.

"I would like to see her again, too," Adriana whispered

Claribel sighed. Ona had been in her life so briefly but was the most influential star in an otherwise dim universe.

They circled the cathedral one more time, Claribel acting as if she was nothing more than the High Regent's daughter out for a stroll on a pleasant Iopan day. The streets, which a decade ago had been dirty and crime-infested, were clean and safe, and not just as a show for her. Father's efforts to educate the people had borne fruit, and Lanopi enjoyed the start of a gilded age. Claribel envied the smiling people milling around the square; they did not see the coming storm as she did.

"Shall we return to the palace, Lady Claribel?" Adriana did not look at her but scanned the crowd. "The farewell dinner is in less than two hours."

Claribel smiled. "Piera will have me ready in less than twenty minutes. She's had the clothes and paint picked out for months."

"I do not doubt your maid's efficiency." Even in banter, Adriana's voice held its formal tone. "I worry more about the High Regent's blood pressure."

Claribel reached up and reflexively tried to pull on one of her three braids, but her long hair was gone, cropped close. It was strange to be without it. She didn't miss her hair, but she missed the memory it often brought of Nanna; her grandmother had worn that style most of her life. Another star in her universe, snuffed out three years earlier, shortly after Claribel and Thanan had started their secret communications.

She had kept the braids to annoy the High Regent. The braided style had become outdated, and the High Regent had asked her to shorten her hair for years. But until the week before, Claribel had ignored her mother. Now with the wedding quickly approaching, she'd decided to adopt a more fashionable style befitting an iconic Lanopian. The braids, this walk, even the clothes she wore, were small rebellions against the High Regent's choking grasp. Sometimes all the little actions made Claribel feel like a petulant, rebellious toddler. But this was their game. Small, imperceptible punishments and shame from the High Regent, followed by equally subtle rebellion from Claribel. It tired her, but she had to make sure her mother knew at least one piece on the High Regent's board moved on its own.

Pride is a virus which infects the soul. The words of the Heavener prophet Palo came to her mind. She'd read the holy text of her new religion, *The Universe, the Whole and the Well of Souls,* too many times to count. She'd replaced the High Regent's maxims with more comforting words.

Palo would probably not approve of her games with the High Regent. The actions smelled too much like pride. But someone had to fight Rissa, even if it seemed like trying to erode a mountain with a cup of water.

"Let's go back," Claribel responded. "Maybe I can see Thanan before the dinner."

"Thanan will not be attending, Lady Claribel," Adriana said, her eyes finally meeting Claribel's. "He has been assigned as one of the Fivestar pilots on the *Marsil*. He will be preparing his ship for the journey to Nooteezia."

Another move by the High Regent to keep her children separated as much as possible. But it was a wasted effort; Thanan and Claribel knew how to communicate when they needed to.

"Then I see no reason to return so soon." She kept her voice even. "For my last free day on Lanopi, I would like to walk through the shopping district on my way home."

"That will likely make us late for the dinner." If Claribel hadn't known better, she thought she detected a little mirth in the old guard's voice.

"Well, unless the High Regent directly commands us to return, I would like to go shopping." The game continued. She wondered if Adriana or the countless others caught in the waves of her and her mother's rivalry tired of it. Affecting their lives irked her, but she could see no way around it. Each life affected another in its circle, and she hoped the good she spread was greater than the turbulence.

They walked from the square across four blocks and into the newly refurbished shopping district. All Lanopians knew Claribel, and they gave her a wide birth, formal nods greeting her constantly. She smiled back, her cheeks aching from the motion. That too was another rebellion; the High Regent greeted commoners with casual indifference, and so Claribel used a pleasant smile.

"May I ask a personal question?" Adriana asked.

"Yes?" Claribel furrowed her brow and hoped Adriana would not be the first to start the Nooteezian tradition of uncomfortable questions for the bride to be.

"Why go through with the marriage? There is no law saying the High Regent, or any parent, can arrange a marriage. You are free. Yet you choose to obey the High Regent in this." Left unsaid was Adriana's understanding of Claribel's many rebellions.

"Lanopi needs an alliance with Nooteezia." She stared into a shop window, her eyes passing over the colorful glassware. "King Khayr is a traditionalist."

"Some would say a barbarian."

She turned to Adriana and smiled. "Well, someone has taken your muzzle off today."

"The High Regent forgot to fasten it properly this morning."

Claribel looked around but didn't see a single security guard, uniformed or not, within view. Adriana had guaranteed a private conversation.

"Yes." She continued walking slowly. "Some would call Nooteezian culture barbaric, at least the customs he's embraced. But they have a strength. Lanopi needs their strength."

"So you sacrifice your own work, your own happiness, for the good of Lanopi?" Earnest intensity coated her voice, more emotion than Claribel had heard from the woman in years.

"My work is for Lanopi. And being on Nooteezia will not isolate me like the High Regent believes. She sees me as a token, a commodity to exchange. I see an opportunity, a way to shape the union between worlds to serve Lanopi more than it serves the High Regent." Ona's first lesson from years ago rang in Claribel's mind. Nooteezia held a central place in the future, a future most could not see. Claribel would now be a part of that in a way she could never have imagined, queen to the most important of the known systems.

Adriana remained silent as they walked slowly from the shopping district onto the central thoroughfare. The palace peeked above the scattered buildings, shining on top of its hill. Claribel knew she might never walk these streets again, and even if she did, it would be as a foreign queen, not as the heir apparent she'd been as a child, and not as the figurehead she was now.

Adriana's guards reappeared, mixing in with the crowd, but they kept their distance.

"Do you ever think about that day on the way back from Cosart?" Adriana asked.

Claribel did not want to admit, even to herself, about how much she thought of the attempt on her life nine years before. She found it haunting, and spent as little time on that memory as should could. But the near-death experience came unbidden to her mind often enough.

"Sometimes," Claribel lied, wondering why Adriana dug up this painful thought.

"I do not think it was what we believe it was. Someone powerful arranged it, not whose feet it landed at." Adriana stopped, her eyes still fixed on the palace. "There is a ruthlessness in Lanopi. I wish it would not follow you, but if you desire to carry on your work as a queen and be more than a figurehead, then that ruthlessness will follow you. I don't believe there's a safe haven from the High Regent's gaze in the known systems." She turned and gripped Claribel's hand. "Be careful, Lady Claribel."

And with that enigmatic warning, they walked together toward the palace.

chapter 31

THE WEDDING

ope before fear, Claribel repeated to herself. She tried to pull a good passage from Palo's words to calm herself, but Palo had likely never conceived of the spectacle of a Nooteezian wedding. Maybe the gods, the Whole, had never seen such a thing.

Claribel, soon-to-be queen of Nooteezia, sat on a large chair, four enormous men holding her above the assembled dignitaries. As a child she had dreamed of her wedding, a solemn affair in the Lanopian style. As she grew older, she fantasized about a Heavener wedding, specifically tailored to mock the High Regent. What she'd never imagined was being hoisted onto a chair and guided around the room as guests asked her questions about how she planned to pleasure her new husband, or if she'd ever had sexual encounters with multiple partners.

Some of the questions were innocuous, but most were meant to cause shame; that was the game, since her refusal to answer initiated another round of drinks. Claribel had studied Nooteezian culture in depth, paying particular attention to the wedding ceremony. But her academic research hardly prepared her for the actual exhibition, a spectacle she might have enjoyed had she been a spectator and not the focus.

Shame is a wasted emotion, Palo had written. *Either you should feel guilt and repent, or you should discard the mocking barbs of those who walk outside the path to ascension.*

Claribel took a deep breath. She was doing nothing wrong, so she need feel no guilt. Yet she couldn't banish the shame. Remembering Palo's words was easy; actually living the tenants was another thing entirely.

They were in the seventh and final day of the wedding ceremony. People, tables, food, and drink filled the Nooteezian royal hall. The tables were made of a rich dark wood, almost black in color. Bright white chairs surrounded each table. Red marble adorned the floor and walls. Most of the tables held guests dressed in the bright colors of Nooteezian high fashion.

The foreigners stuck out like the High Regent would have at a meeting of Heavner priestesses. The Lanopians seated at tables to her left dressed in browns and grays, the proper Lanopian attire for a wedding. The most important Lanopians were all here--senators, famous actors, musicians, all of the rich and noble. The only notable absences were Second Regent Oratt, who ran the government in the High Regent's absence, and Senator Mura Chani, who'd been too sick for starjump travel.

Next to the Lanopians sat the Coznarians, mostly women with skin as dark as the tables and hair a shade darker than that. All of them wore hats, wide-brimmed for the women, and narrow and more conical for the men. The Eslazans sat next to them, their skin light and hair the color of wheat. The Pastrackians stood out the most, dressed in all grays and blacks, matching the gray hair most of their people had since birth. The rest of the known systems were small and scatted, from Mantalo, Camsartra, Alandria, and a single ambassador from war-ravaged Regno.

Most of the foreigners watched the proceedings with curious eyes. The pre-wedding ritual might be strange for them, but it wasn't one of theirs being paraded around the room. Her fellow Lanopians wore their unease as clear as their fashion, crossed arms or persistent scowls marking their disapproval.

Claribel looked at the head table to her brother, father, and the High Regent. Thanan wore a grimace, not hiding his distaste for the entire affair. Claribel had hoped he'd maintain his composure and not give away their continuing affection for each other. They'd hid it from the High Regent for years, allies in secret only. But having his only sister bombarded with strange, inappropriate questions was too much for him.

Father's similar stare was not a surprise. He'd been very public in his disagreements lately with the High Regent, including Claribel's arranged marriage. He thought it barbaric to use love and marriage as a political tool. The High Regent dismissed his objections, noting that Claribel had agreed to the arrangement. But her father didn't need to be noble born or connected to know the truth: the word of the High Regent acted like compulsion, even if the laws said otherwise. Laws confining the power of the executive only worked if there was some other body to dispute the actions; no such body existed on Lanopi.

As they passed a new table, the Coznarian ambassador stood to ask a question. Coznarians could be as vulgar as the Nooteezians, so Claribel feared the worst.

"What was your favorite childhood game?" the woman asked in Coznarian, the most common tongue among the assembled crowd.

"I loved mouse catcher," Claribel replied in her heavily accented Coznarian. "My brother Thanan and I use to play it almost every day." She smiled at her brother, and for the first time in the ceremony, his lips curved upward. "One child is the cat, the other the mouse. We chased each other all over the palace and its grounds."

She looked up at her new husband. His expression held little. King Khayr was as stoic as his people were boisterous. As was the custom, they had not spoken since the ceremony began, had barely even made eye contact. This wedding existed as a political transaction, and the king, her soon-to-be husband, treated it as such.

They approached the next table, a mixture of dignitaries from across the known systems, worlds which were not closely aligned with Nooteezia or Lanopi. The representatives from Alandria, Camsartra, and Pastrack were lower level government representatives or nobility, important enough to demand respect, but low enough as to not signal too much affection for Nooteezia or Lanopi.

The Second of Drissa of Pastrack stood to ask the required question of his table. He was a sour looking fellow, with a sharply carved gray goatee. His clothing fit the austere nature common of Pastrackians, a tight-fitting gray suit, accented with a green sash and matching cufflinks. For the life of her, Claribel couldn't remember if the color signified house, rank, or nothing at all.

"Good morning, Lady Claribel," the man intoned in broken Coznarian. He smiled--a short, forced gesture. Claribel nodded at him. "My question, unlike most, is about your future, not these trifling questions about your past." He turned, facing the Nooteezian throne and King Khayr. "Are you, Claribel, daughter of the High Regent of Lanopi, truly prepared to join with a monstrous killer and betrayer of all trust?"

A collective gasp echoed through the chamber, followed by stunned silence. King Khayr's head raised instantly, and he moved his body to the end of his massive chair, his eyes bulging, the only hint of emotion he'd shown during the seven days.

Claribel looked back at the man, unsure of what to say. "Pardon me, Second of Drissa, but I believe you may have misspoken. I know Coznarian is not your first tongue."

He shook his head, a real smile creasing his greasy face. "I have spoken as well as I can in this ugly tongue." He then spoke in his native Pastrackian, a language Claribel had never studied. More gasps greeted his words, his new statement clearly as inflammatory as his last to the few who understood.

"Speak carefully." King Khayr stood. He spoke in Nooteezian and a man to his left quickly repeated the phrase in Coznarian. "This is my beloved, the future mother of our world. You stand outside of decorum." The crowd waited as the translator finished.

The Second of Drissa turned to address the crowd, his back to the king. "Decorum?" he continued in Coznarian. "Nothing about this absurd ceremony is decent. The White Daughter frowns on your marriage and condemns your entire blasphemous world."

The crowd erupted into murmurs. The White Daughter was a Pastrackian god, the god who blessed all unions of any kind. Her condemnation guaranteed eternal suffering in the next life. The Second of Drissa leveled as clear and powerful an insult as he could muster, even if the Nooteezians and the Lanopians did not hold to his gods.

King Khayr remained still for a moment. He stood a head taller than her brother, and his dark curly hair hung to his shoulders, held from his face by a golden crown. His dark skin contrasted with the bright yellow garment draped over his shoulders, his broad chest mostly bare. All eyes rested on the war-tested general, the man who fifteen years before had repelled a Camsartan invasion. Despite his war hardened resolve, no violence seemed imminent. Tension rose through the crowd, but Khayr did not share in it, his initial anger melting away, replaced by a smooth placidity.

"I will pardon this statement and will not ask for a retraction." His words flowed like a wide river, soft but filled with power, the translator quickly repeating them. "But I command you to leave this room now, and to be off our world within three hours. If not, I will be required by honor and justice to remove your head from your body."

The Second of Drissa did not flinch at Khayr's threat, but held the king's eyes with malice. "I will leave but not because some dog commands me. I leave to be sure your filth doesn't make me completely unworthy to petition the White Daughter evermore."

The man turned and marched out, his one servant trailing behind. The crowd collectively tracked their movements, like spectators at a horse race. Silence hung for several moments.

King Khayr sat, and the quiet din of conversation returned. Khayr met her gaze and smiled softly, his first gesture in her direction. She smiled and nodded, and then his eyes drifted away. The four servants carried her onward, and the remaining questions were bland and innocent.

Piera led Claribel into a private chamber to make final preparations for the final step, the sealing of their union.

Piera gasped as their entered the side room just as Thanan stepped from behind a large pillar.

"Come now, Piera, you'd think you'd never seen a man." Thanan flashed his widest smile.

"I didn't expect one in my lady's chambers, even her brother." A tight smile ruined Piera's scowl.

"Leave us," Claribel commanded. "Don't let anyone in, Lanopian or otherwise."

Piera bowed and closed the door behind her.

"You take an unnecessary risk coming here." Claribel wanted to glare at her brother, but she didn't have the heart to, not on the eve of her isolation.

"I wanted to give you a final opportunity to pull out of this. It would be politically complicated, but I'm sure . . ."

"Enough Thanan." Claribel breathed deeply, fighting back a rush of emotion. "I appreciate your concern, but pulling back now would destroy relations with Khayr, the only ally we seem to have."

Thanan sighed, a high whistle. "I know." He looked around the room, pacing. "But I wish there were another way. I thought we'd be in a better spot by now, that we'd have more control. But Mother still pulls us along on her strings."

"We act on our own, Thanan. I made this decision. Just because it's what the High Regent wants doesn't mean it's not right for Lanopi. War is coming; we both know it, the High Regent knows it. Lanopi needs Khayr and his armies."

Thanan stepped forward, gripping her hands tightly. "You deserve better than this marriage. At least the barbarian defended you against that Pastrackian bastard. I was ready to cut him down myself, diplomacy be damned."

Claribel smiled. "Always the loyal brother. I will be fine. I will find my place here, find a way to influence these people and ours, capture their imaginations so we might one day . . ." She trailed off. What would they do eventually? Revolution? Rebellion? They'd danced around it for nearly a decade. Vocalizing it made it feel real and all the more terrifying.

"You leave tomorrow then?" Claribel swiftly changed the topic.

Thanan dropped her hands. "Yes. Curiously, we're going through Vesta."

Claribel laughed. "Vesta?"

"Apparently Lazlo wants to visit. He explored the system a generation ago, more likely two generations ago. The way that old dog reminisces, you'd think he was two hundred years old."

Claribel hugged Thanan, wetting his shoulder with sudden tears. "Be careful Thanan. The High Regent has plans within plans."

Thanan pulled back, his smile replaced with cold determination. "She trained us, molded us. She might have her plans, but we'll see them coming."

She hugged him again, her tears flowing. She hoped he was right, but many had underestimated the High Regent or had thought themselves her better. Yet she still ruled Lanopi unchallenged. And now Claribel would be fighting her from two starjumps away, isolated from her only ally.

"Hope before fear," she whispered into his ear before he slipped out of the room.

Hours later, Claribel sat on her bed. The wedding ceremony was done, and the Lanopians would be leaving the system soon. Now she was alone, Piera the only connection to her life before. Her tears had dried. She hadn't checked the time in hours, but she knew sunrise approached. Her first night of isolation on the planet Nootee was about to end.

She had waited for hours, fearing the arrival of her new husband and king. Though she had been pleased with his defense at the comments of the Second of Drissa, his statement had been a political necessity. An insult could not be ignored, not when delivered so publicly, so boldly. Though he had finally smiled at her, he'd made no such gesture during the ceremony that tied them together. She had knelt for three long hours next to the man, barely understanding the intonations of the Nooteezian priest. They drank from the same cup, their union complete. She was his wife, and the alliance between Nooteezia and Lanopi solidified in blood, her figurative blood, and the bloodline she and Khayr would create.

But the bloodline would not begin that night.

She had assumed, as was customary in her reading of Nooteezian culture, that King Khayr would take her on the final night of the wedding ceremony. But he hadn't come. He'd either spent the night alone in his own chambers or with another woman.

The terror of waiting had slowly worn off, but apprehension for her situation grew and drove away any chance at rest.

Claribel laid down and sunk into the deep pillows. Daybreak would come soon, her first day as a queen. She would face it with dignity and at least a little sleep.

chapter 32

FROM THE STARS

azlo stood on the observation deck of the *Marsil* just off the bridge. Alazar stood beside him, gazing at the asteroid belt floating in the near distance. The debris was thick, and he could not see the greenish-blue of Vesta II beyond it. What did he think he'd see? He wasn't sure, but that strange encoded message from someone claiming to be Sycorax had been clear: get the *Marsil* and its companion ships into the Vesta system, or all his misdeeds would be revealed. His involvement in the Sycorax program and his help in getting Sparo out of his death sentence.

The first threat did not bother Lazlo. High Regent Rissa and others in her inner circle knew of the Sycorax program and Lazlo's involvement. But how did this mystery person know about Sparo? In the nine years since Sparo's exile, Lazlo had never heard from the man. He'd wanted to take a starjumper to Vesta II and find out, but he couldn't do so without raising suspicion. And since Sparo had never reached out to anyone, had never been heard from again, Lazlo had assumed the worst: that Sparo and his family had died by drifting too close to the star, been pulverized in the asteroid belt, or burned up in Vesta II's atmosphere. Did this threat mean Sparo had lived? Or had just the knowledge of what Lazlo had done survived?

"Is this where it all happened?" Alazar stepped up beside him, his gray beard long but well-trimmed.

"Sycorax?" Lazlo whispered the word. The message had made him jittery.

"Yes, the failed egotistical project of Rissa's father. How did you get through the asteroid belt? It's as thick as ash fish soup."

Before Lazlo could respond, the ship lurched and the artificial gravity failed for a split second, not enough to lift them off the floor, but enough to turn Lazlo's sensitive stomach.

"What was that?" Alazar asked, stepping back onto the bridge. Lazlo followed.

An alarm began to sound, and the crew on the bridge worked furiously.

"Engines at eighty-percent thrust and increasing, Captain," a young crew member explained.

"Who engaged the engines?" The captain, a portly fellow with long hair pulled behind his head, stepped behind him.

The crew exchanged glances.

"Answer me!" the captain bellowed.

"No one," a second crew member said. "They activated by themselves. We're headed straight for the asteroid belt."

Lazlo gasped. Toward the belt. He'd allowed whomever had sent him the message to guide them to their death. But as they approached the belt, many of the asteroids began to swirl unnaturally in a pattern Lazlo recognized. Someone was opening the asteroid belt and guiding them to the planet.

"By Ghosra's bosom, what is that?" the captain muttered.

"Someone is letting us through," Lazlo answered, dumbfounded.

"What about our companion ships?" the captain asked.

"Inter-ship comms and sensors are down," the first crew member answered, "but manual observation is reporting that all three battleships remain in their previous positions."

Someone was isolating them. It would take weeks to fly a ship around the belt, and navigating it was impossible, especially for a larger vessel like a battleship. And if the defense systems were still in place, Sycorax's artificial asteroids would fight against anyone who tried to come or go without the code.

"I believe we're on a course for the system's second planet," a crew member said.

Lazlo had always wondered if he would see Vesta II again, but he'd never imagined doing so like this, brought to it like a fish on a lure.

"Get them off the bridge," the captain said, pointing to Alazar and Lazlo. "And get them to their escape ships."

Lazlo instantly understood the captains meaning. The *Marsil* was not a landing ship--if they reached the planet's atmosphere, the ship would be torn apart.

"Come, Admiral Alazar," a guard said, grabbing the older man's elbow.

"We need to get you off the ship right now."

Lazlo followed Alazar off the bridge, cursing himself for bringing this upon them.

Thanan sat in his fivestar fighter still attached to the belly of the battleship *Alazar*. He repeatedly tried to reboot his system, but nothing changed the fact that he sat in his fighter without power or communications. Everything had gone dead. Panic had gripped him initially, but life support still functioned. But he could control nothing. Some crazy glitch, for sure, but he calmed his breathing and decided it was nothing more than that.

Until the asteroid belt started moving.

The asteroids whirled, opening a hole in the expansive barrier. They shouldn't do that. He'd studied this belt in his school days, and it was too thick for most starjumpers to maneuver through. It was a curiosity, but nothing more, the only interesting part about this lifeless system.

Through his viewport, he saw the *Marsil* moving toward the opening. What in the name of Palo were they doing? They shouldn't take a cruiser into that. If the asteroids started to close it would pulverize the Lanopian flagship and . . .

It wasn't a glitch. This was deliberate. The other two battleships did not move to intercept or accompany, and no fivestars followed either. Inexplicably, someone had parted an asteroid belt and was flying the *Marsil* through it.

Thanan tried power and comms again but was greeted by empty clicks. He still couldn't fly or get orders. He unhooked his belt and floated behind his seat. His fighter lacked the artificial gravity of the battleship, so doing what he wanted to do would be difficult and dangerous. He grabbed the manual release for his fighter and tried to twist it, but he couldn't get proper leverage. He'd never heard of anyone using the release from this side. So he braced his legs against the wall and pushed with all of his might.

A clang and a sudden jolt let him know he'd succeed. He flipped himself back into his seat and strapped in. The force of the disconnection had him spinning away from the battleship. He took a deep breath as he reached for the power button. If the ship didn't start up now, this could be the most stupidly courageous thing he'd ever done.

The electronics sprang to life, and he initiated engine start. The familiar hum of his plasma drive came next.

"Thank Chimra," Thanan muttered aloud.

Comms also seemed to function, but he wasn't receiving, only broadcasting.

"This is Lieutenant Thanan," he said. "I am in pursuit of the *Marsil*. Please respond with instructions. What's going on, command?"

But no voice came, and the comms unit indicated no connection.

"Cruiser *Marsil*," he said. "This is Lieutenant Thanan. It appears you may be in distress. Please respond." Again, silence.

Thanan grabbed the stick and rotated the ship until he could see the *Marsil*. Half of the massive ship looked to already be in the hole in the belt.

He initiated full thrust and made for the *Marsil*. He looked back at the *Alazar* and the other two companion ships. They remained still, their gray hulls lit by the Vesta star but not with the lights you'd usually see from the outside. Whatever had disrupted the *Alazar* had afflicted the other ships as well. He didn't see any other fivestars. His detachment defied protocol, and his fellow fivestar pilots remained in position awaiting instructions which were not coming. Thanan couldn't decide if defying the protocols had been heroic or idiotic.

His fivestar reached the tail of the *Marsil* as it continued into the tunnel through the belt. Checking his charts, his computer calculated their trajectory: Vesta II, the planet just beyond the belt.

Thanan considered flying around the ship to one of the open observation decks to see if he could make visual contact with anyone inside. But he hesitated. Had there been a mutiny? Why was the *Marsil* operational while the battleships remained inoperable? He tried to come up with an explanation, but nothing made sense. Who could hack the closed systems of a cruiser and three battleships? An attack like this was an incredibly massive undertaking, and, until this moment, Thanan would have thought impossible. Who would be so bold? And how did they even pull it off?

Thanan matched the cruiser's speed and remained hidden from view. He might be the only hope for the *Marsil* and whatever greeted them on the other side. If there had been a mutiny, he couldn't give away his presence, not yet, not until he figured out more of what was going on.

Two hours later they left the belt, and Vesta II revealed itself as a green and blue sphere growing larger in his view. Thanan checked his rearview screen and saw the impossible movements of the asteroids behind them, inexplicably closing together as they had opened. He thought he saw thrust tales, as if some of the asteroids had propulsion systems. As improbable as that seemed, it made more sense than the asteroids moving of their own accord.

The *Marsil* accelerated after the belt closed behind them, its course true for the planet. Thanan matched the cruiser's speed and checked his sensors for the gravitational pull of the fast-approaching planet. Was the devious plan nothing more than slamming the *Marsil* into the planet? If the perpetrators had wanted to destroy it, they could have just forced it into the asteroid belt; it would have destroyed the cruiser just as easily as a planet would. Why bring it safely through the belt then?

Warning lights blinked as Vesta II's gravity took a stronger hold. Then a proximity alarm sounded, and the fivestar course corrected suddenly. An escape raft shot away from the *Marsil*, and only the fivestar's automated safety system kept the two ships from colliding.

But the change in trajectory had created its own problem. Now his fivestar was caught in the planet's gravity. Thanan reversed the engine, but the only response was a violent shaking; Vesta II's gravity had him, and he turned off the engines to avoid the two opposing forces ripping his fivestar apart. His viewport burned with the fire of re-entry, and he hoped the hull's integrity would hold long enough to get him to the planet's surface. He couldn't see the *Marsil* or the escape raft which had forced this terrible course. He hoped the *Marsil* and its crew fared better than he did.

I'm sorry, Claribel, he thought. Surviving an unplanned landing on an unfamiliar planet was not likely, but he pushed aside the morbid thoughts trying to crush his consciousness. *Hope before fear*, he told himself. He gripped the controls and prepared to land.

chapter 33

STARS FALLING

aliban crawled through the underbrush, his eyes trained on Miram. He knew he'd be in trouble if Sparo caught him following her, but Sparo watched little these days. He spent all of his time in Mother's room, sitting in the dark, complaining about his head pains. The silly old man hadn't been outside his room in days. Stupid Sparo hadn't spoken to Caliban or sweet Miram in at least as long, sending the fairy to do his bidding.

Miram stopped on a low, open hill, the grass pulling flat before she laid down. She pulled out her pad thing and began drawing. Miram drew everything, giving silly names to plants, animals, even to the streams and hills. She called the forest Eliel, and she called the jungle Witch Jungle. The gray plains to the south she'd named Desolation. Strange, funny names, but Caliban liked them. Miram was so smart.

Caliban crouched behind a bush, watching her. She wore Mother's old clothes, her small frame a good match in some ways but not in others. Miram was skin, bones, and little else; Mother had had a more womanly shape.

But Caliban cared little for shape. What was shape to him? Miram was so beautiful, but he pushed the thought away as quickly as it sneaked into his mind. Sparo couldn't read Caliban's thoughts, or at least he didn't think so, but he still needed to be careful. A gut-full of pain would come, maybe worse, if Sparo caught Caliban thinking that way.

Caliban had tried thinking of Miram like one of his brothers, but it hadn't worked. She wasn't a lizard man, and she wasn't like Mother. Miram was something different, something special. She might wear Mother's clothes, but she was nothing like Mother. Mother had been constantly angry, and Miram was never angry, though often sad. Mother talked, commanded, and berated. Miram spoke infrequently, as comfortable with silence as she was with conversation. And when she spoke, she spoke without commands or wrath. She sounded nothing like Mother, and nothing like idiot Sparo.

"I know you're there," Miram said. "You can come out. I hacked Father's security system. His birds can't see me now."

Caliban looked around, trying to find Sparo's birds. Miram said some birds had eyes watching for Sparo. Caliban saw several perched in a tree on the opposite side of the clearing. Could they really see for Sparo? If Caliban stepped onto the grassy hill, would Sparo punish him?

"Come on, Caliban, come out." Miram looked at him, her smile bright.

Caliban stepped out and lumbered up the slight hill. He watched the birds, their magic eyes following him. Did other animals work for Sparo, too?

He sat down near Miram, but more than an arm's length away in case Sparo did see them.

"What you draw?" Caliban asked.

"The sleeping grass." She held up her magic pad, and it was a painting of the grass, lying flat beneath a bare human foot. "The sleeping grass is one of my favorite discoveries."

They sat in silence for some time. The silence was pleasant and peaceful, not like that which often hung between Caliban and Sparo. Anger, hatred, and pain hid inside that silence.

"What should I draw next?"

Caliban looked around. Not Sparo's watching birds. Not the trees--Miram drew them often. Caliban's sharp eyes could not see any other animals; most of the animals in the forest knew to avoid Caliban and his stomach.

"Maybe something in the jungle," she replied to herself.

Caliban shook his head. "Jungle dangerous. Sparo very mad if Miram go there. Sparo hurt Caliban for letting it happen."

"But you can protect me, right?" She looked over at him, her blue eyes bright.

He shook his head. "Not for sure. Bad things there. Too many for Caliban to fight at once."

She glanced at her pad and drew lazily across the screen. "Maybe Ariel would take us. Ariel could protect us. Anyway, I think I've found a way to protect myself. I'm cleverer than everyone thinks."

Yes, the fairy could do it. But she wouldn't. The fairy did what Sparo wanted, and Sparo didn't want his girl in the Witch's Jungle. Acid spiders, lizard cats, and plants filled with poison. No, Miram was too delicate for the jungle. Even Caliban would die there. But Miram was clever, cleverer than anyone. If anyone could find a way to be safe in the jungle, she could.

Silence again. If she was upset by Caliban's refusal, she didn't act like it. She never got mad at him even if he did something she didn't like. She just smiled and moved to her next thought.

"Oh Caliban, look! What on Lanopi could that be? A meteor?" She pointed to the sky, her eyes as wide as he had ever seen.

Caliban followed her pointing finger. Two fiery stars streaked across the green cloudless sky. Did stars fall? He had never seen one land. Ariel and Sparo said stars were big, bigger than this whole world. But that made no sense. Stars were tiny little things, hanging like twinkling balls scattered across a black floor. How could something so small be so big?

The tips of the fiery trails grew bigger. "Spaceships?"

Miram's eyes grew even wider. "Spaceships? Starjumpers? What on Lanopi would they be doing here? Could there be people? Men? Oh my, I'm not ready to meet people."

Caliban had never seen her act this way, words pouring out of her mouth like they often did with other humans.

"Falling too fast," Caliban said. "Getting too big too soon."

"Crashing?"

He nodded.

"Oh, our first visitors can't die! They must not die. Maybe they have friends who could rescue us? I hope Father lets them help us."

Miram finished her drawing and laid back on the sleeping grass. "People. I wonder if any of them will be young men." She closed her eyes and smiled.

Caliban did not like what she said. He didn't know why, but her words made him anxious. He looked down at her soft face, at her small lips. He wanted to kiss her, but he knew he shouldn't. Even if Sparo's magic birds weren't watching, Sparo would know; he always knew.

Miram sat up, and Caliban leaned back to avoid them knocking heads. He hadn't realized how close he'd gotten. Miram hadn't seemed to notice.

"You need to hide." Miram looked behind them and then back at him. "Father's coming."

Caliban sprang to his feet, down the hill and into the forest, waiting for Sparo, hoping he wouldn't be too angry.

chapter 34

VESTA

In the three days since the wedding, Claribel had only seen her new husband in public settings. She spent her days touring the royal palace with her servants, walking through the dusty streets of Nootee City with her honor guard, or strolling through the vast royal gardens. Exotic sights greeted her each day, and the Nooteese people treated her with love and reverence, excited to share their culture with their new queen. All of Nooteezia seemed to adore her, with the possible exception of her new husband.

The day after the wedding, she'd watched King Khayr hold court. The scene had seemed lifted from an ancient story. On Lanopi, judges or senators might here pleas for mercy or justice, but on Nooteezia King Khayr acted as jury and judge, adjudicating the most vital matters of his people. He didn't hear all cases, but the High Court of Judges would refer some of the most delicate matters directly to the king. Hundreds of nobles and other dignitaries watched Khayr hold court. Claribel sat with the crowd, a hundred feet from Khayr. The spacious room could hold an audience as big as a thousand, though only several hundred watched that day. The hall opened to the sky; judgement would wait if foul weather came.

The acoustics were terrible with the open roof, and to make matters worse, Claribel was forced to sit among the Nootezian noblewomen who chatted constantly throughout the proceedings. The men were seated closer and spoke occasionally. She bristled at this preferential treatment. She'd studied Nooteezia's sexist culture, but living within it was an entirely different matter.

The only other time she saw her new husband was at dinner, which was always a group event. All of the king's closest advisors and their wives joined them each afternoon. Khayr and Claribel sat at opposite ends of a long table. They exchanged no words, only a few smiles.

As she readied herself for the day, Claribel had to suppress her growing frustration. She spent her days entirely isolated from the politics which had been the reason for her union with the foreign king. She knew nothing of the dealings at court or of the happenings outside of Nooteezia. She might as well have been staying on one of Nooteezia's two moons.

"My lady." Piera entered Claribel's inner chamber, flanked by a Nooteezian servant named Danda. The young Nooteese always seemed anxious, but this time her posture was more rigid than usual. She stood taller than Piera or Claribel.

"Something has happened to the Marsil," Danda said, her eyes on everything but Claribel. The girl was nervous.

Claribel's stomach clenched. "What happened to it?"

"I don't know any details," the girl answered. "Chief Nozrel would like to brief you and the king together."

Claribel wanted to push for more, but it was clear Danda had nothing, and one worried look from Piera indicated she knew nothing more.

"Then let's go find the king," Claribel said.

They walked together until they found one of the king's attendants who told them he was on the east balcony. Claribel walked briskly with the two servants trailing behind. When they reached the balcony, two guardsmen stood watch, long spears crossed across their broad chests.

"I'm here to see the king," Claribel said.

"I'm sorry, my queen," one of the guards replied, "but the king asked not to be disturbed."

"Did he specifically forbid his queen?"

The tall man looked unsure and glanced at the other guard, who returned his quizzical gaze. "No, my queen, he did not, but he's in a meeting and he asked . . ."

Claribel walked around him and down the hallway toward the balcony. Her two shocked servants and the two guards stared, but no one moved to stop her or said a word. And no one followed.

As Claribel approached, she could hear two voices speaking in Coznarian, one a woman's, and the other the deep baritone of her new husband. She stopped before stepping onto the balcony.

"I grow tired of waiting," her husband said. His accent was quite good; Claribel hadn't realized he spoke the foreign language so well. "My enemies grow restless, and Lanopi will surely ask for support soon, as soon as the wedding has sunk in and our alliance is sure. You promised me an army, and all I get is vague progress updates."

"You fear Pastrack and Alandria?" The woman spoke in unaccented Coznarian, her voice high and soft.

"Yes, and Mantalo. They ruled here once, and they would only need to take Fortuna to be on our doorstep again. And I also have rebels and the Tygens in my own system to worry about."

"Patience, King Khayr," the woman soothed. "It will all be ready soon. Alandria and Pastrack will have worries of their own, and Mantalo will cower at your new army."

"Do not patronize me. I have paid you richly, emptied my coffers. You will deliver, or there will be consequences."

The king's admonition brought silence, and Claribel strained to hear if anything else was said. Then she recognized small sounds, lips pressed together, the subtle smack of kissing. Claribel stepped around the corner and onto the balcony.

The king and the woman were locked in an embrace. The woman wore only tight, skimpy underclothes, her cloak lying at her feet. The king's back was to Claribel. The woman pulled away upon seeing the queen. Khayr turned and his eyes widened.

"My queen," he stammered in Coznarian. "What are you doing here? I was . . ."

"I don't require an explanation, my lord." Claribel tried not to fidget. She did not love this man and knew he would bed other women. Why should this bother her so much?

"Of course." He bowed slightly. "What can I do for you?"

"First, you can dismiss the whore." Claribel knew the woman was not a prostitute, but she would pretend that she'd fallen for the ruse. Even if they'd been discussing some strange political arrangement, she'd caught them kissing, which was definitely whore-like.

Khayr nodded to the woman. Her features were flawless, her skin smooth and white. Her figure was full in the right places, mocking Claribel's thinness. The woman bowed to the king, and then to the queen. A sick smile painted her face as she hurried around the corner, not replacing her robe until she could be seen by the guards and servants.

"Chief Nozrel is asking for our presence for a briefing," she said. "Something has happened to the *Marsil*."

"What happened?"

"I don't know. I was called to a briefing, and that was it."

The king nodded. "Nozrel will want to brief us separately."

"Why?"

"Because you're a woman," he said as if the statement wasn't sexist and idiotic.

"I am not accustomed to not being involved," she replied. "On Lanopi, women are considered equals to men, have been for a millennia. If something has happened to my family, then I will find out the same time you do."

The king nodded and smiled. "Of course, my queen. We shall go find Nozrel and hear it together." He extended his arm in the Coznarian fashion, and Claribel took it. For the first time since the wedding, the king and queen walked through the palace, arm in arm.

King Khayr and Claribel sat in a small conference room outside Intelligence Chief Nozrel's office deep in the palace. The spacious room held a large, oblong table and a dozen richly decorated chairs. One wall contained a half dozen screens, all dark. Chief Nozrel stood at the front, flanked by two analysts.

Nozrel was short and had a pointed face, giving him a rodent-like appearance. The diminutive man did not hold back his age like his master did. Nozrel's hair rivaled snow in its whiteness, and the lines at the corners of his eyes and his small nose gave him a constant squint or scowl. His skin was lighter than Khayr's and most of the Noteese Claribel had met, closer to her own bronze tone.

"We've just received news from Vesta," Nozrel began in nearly flawless Coznarian. "The *Marsil* and its companion ships reached the starjump point, and then before they jumped to Lanopi the story gets very strange." Nozrel laid out the details of the *Marsil* flying through an asteroid belt toward an uninhabited planet, Vesta II, the asteroid belt parting to let them through. All communication had been lost, and the three remaining ships did not know the status of the *Marsil* or its crew. Claribel's heart sank when Nozrel explained the only other ship to pass through the asteroid belt had been the fivestar fighter flown by her brother.

"This is impossible," Khayr said after Nozrel finished. "How could an asteroid belt part?"

"There are too many oddities to count," Nozrel replied. "Why have they lost communications? Why were the three battleships' systems temporarily disabled so they couldn't follow the cruiser through the belt? How did they get through it? I cannot answer any of the important questions, not yet."

"And the High Regent and all the dignitaries are on that ship?" Khayr asked.

"Actually no." Nozrel frowned. "It gets even stranger. Right before departure from the starjump base, High Regent Rissa changed her plans and hired another starjumper to fly through Fortuna instead."

"So the High Regent has reached Lanopi?" Claribel asked.

Nozrel shook his head. "As I said, the oddities continue. The starjumper she hired reached Fortuna, but she wasn't on it. The ship arrived with six of her elite guard who said they'd been sent as a decoy."

Claribel sat back in her chair. The High Regent was nowhere to be found, and most of the Lanopian aristocracy was trapped inside an asteroid belt that moved of its own accord.

"I need to speak with Second Regent Oratt," Claribel said. "I need to understand what's going on."

Nozrel stared at her, his eyes hard. "You cannot simply reach out to the Second Regent."

Claribel began to object, but stopped herself. Of course she couldn't. Their conversation would be official state communication, despite the fact that she'd known Oratt as long as she could talk.

"Let's reach out to him together," Khayr suggested. "We should commit resources to whatever rescue attempt they're contemplating."

Claribel nodded.

"What is being done to find the High Regent?" Khayr asked. "If she wasn't on the *Marsil* or that other starjumper, where is she?"

"Already underway, your majesty," Nozrel replied. "Only two people from the Lanopian wedding delegation didn't leave the planet. We found an immigration official who has admitted to being bribed to keep a man and a woman behind. He was paid twice his annual salary. We're trying to track that couple down. It's possible the High Regent stayed behind. She may have known what might happen in Vesta."

"She remained with only one other person?" Claribel asked. "That doesn't seem like the High Regent at all. And I can't imagine her elite agreeing to leave her with a single escort."

"A few hours ago I would have thought the same thing," Nozrel said. "But it seems as if these events sit outside the normal patterns. Your mother wasn't on the register of the *Marsil*, but was on the register of a ship she wasn't on, unless her own elite dumped her during the starjump between here and Fortuna."

"Show some decorum, Chief," Khayr chided, his eyes turning to Claribel.

His reaction surprised her, but then she shook her head. "It is all right, King Khayr. The Chief is only speaking of possibilities. Even if it's my family, we need to be honest about what might have happened." She left unsaid that while she'd feel a host of emotions if the High Regent died, grief would likely not be one of them.

The king nodded. "Then we should call the Second Regent and see how we can help."

chapter 35

PUNISHMENT AND WARNING

aliban crouched behind a tree, his heart pounding, his eyes scanning the brush for Sparo. He looked toward the sky, but the trees blocked his view.

How did Miram know Sparo was coming? Did she have magic of her own? Of course she did. She was Sparo's daughter; she probably had his magic just like she had his eyes.

"Hello, Father." Miram spoke before Caliban could see Sparo. The tall man walked from a clearing opposite Caliban with the fairy trailing behind him. "What brings you out on this sunny day?"

"The falling stars." Sparo's voice was soft and strained.

"Your mean the starjumpers."

Sparo sat next to Miram, laying his staff and its glowing ball across his lap. "Technically, they are not starjumpers. One's an escape ship, and the other is a fivestar fighter."

"How did they get to Vesta if they weren't starjumpers?" Miram did not look at her father but kept her attention on her sketch, her fingers moving smoothly across the pad.

"There's a disabled starjumper in orbit. The two ships launched from that."

"So you pulled them down. You brought them."

Sparo sat erect, his eyes wider than Caliban had seen them in some time. "What makes you think that?"

"Traveling through Vesta is rare," Miram replied. "And getting through the asteroid belt is nearly impossible. So if a ship orbits our little planet, than I assume you and Ariel had something to do with it."

"I'm not a god, Miram," Sparo said. "I can't pull ships from space."

Miram looked up, her eyes on the fairy. "But she's close to one. You could with her help."

Sparo closed his eyes, his mouth stretched in frustration. "How much do you know?"

"Practically everything." She smiled as she continued sketching. "I've learned so much about Sycorax's system. You really should encrypt your files, Father. Well, I'd break that eventually, too, but it would take longer."

Sparo laughed. When was the last time stupid Sparo had laughed? "My bright little star," he praised. "I always underestimate you."

"Yes you do." She held the pad up to her father. "What do you think?"

"One of your best."

Miram frowned. "You always say that. It doesn't mean much if you always say it." She looked at the sky. "You mentioned two ships, but I count three."

"Three?" Sparo glared upward, covering his eyes with his hand. "Where's the third?"

She turned behind them, pointing to the low horizon. "One falls there, toward Desolation."

He stood and scanned the horizon, his back to Caliban. As he did almost every day, Caliban thought about creeping up on the old man and smashing his head like he might one of the buzzy bugs. But he held still. He couldn't do that in front of Miram. But maybe if one day Miram wasn't watching . . .

Sparo turned toward the fairy. "Find out who's on that third ship. You were supposed to control all of this." Anger coated his voice, like it usually did right before he sent the pain into Caliban.

"Despite what Miram says, I'm not an all-powerful god," Ariel replied. "I could not anticipate everything."

Sparo sighed. "I know. I'm sorry. Search the *Marsil's* log and find out who else joined us." The fairy disappeared.

"What of the other two ships, Father?"

He sat down next to his daughter. "One of them holds my brother Balith and my old friend Lazlo, among others."

"You're going to kill your brother." She looked over at her father, her eyes wide and curious.

Sparo would not meet her gaze. "Balith framed us, killed your mother." His face boiled with anger, and Caliban retreated at the sight.

"It wasn't a criticism. He deserves death." Miram returned to her sketch. "And the fivestar fighter?"

"An accident but an interesting one. It's flown by the High Regent's son, Thanan."

"A young man." Miram smiled brightly. "I was hoping for not just old men." She looked at her father. "No offense."

They sat for some time, Miram sketching, Sparo watching her.

"Ariel and I will meet Balith and Lazlo," he said to break the silence. "Would you like to greet Thanan?"

She dropped the pad into her lap. "You'd let me do that? But he's a fivestar pilot, which means he's a soldier. Won't he just shoot me?"

Sparo laughed and laid back on the grass. She laid down next to him. "No, my star. He won't do anything of the kind. Ariel already disabled all his weapons. Thanan did not deserve getting stranded here; he has no part in my little game. Find him and bring him home. We should ensure his safety."

She hugged her father and jumped to her feet. She tucked her pad into a pocket. "What an adventure! I'll meet my first man." She glanced down at Sparo. "No offense."

The old man stood, smiling like Caliban had rarely seen. "Have fun. The coordinates of his landing site are on your device."

Miram reached up as far as she could and kissed the hair on Sparo's chin. Without a word, she turned and sprinted into the forest to Caliban's right. Sparo stood silently for some time, his eyes following her into the woods.

"You can come out, Caliban."

Caliban flinched at his name and considered running deeper into the forest, maybe following her. But he knew it was useless. Sparo had spared Caliban from pain for many moons, but Sparo was up again which only meant more suffering.

Caliban slowly crawled up the hill toward stupid Sparo and then crouched at his feet. Sparo's happy face was gone, replaced by his usual scowl, his eyes squinting and his mouth tight.

"I've told you not to follow her, not to be with her when I or Ariel are not there. Yet, here I find you with her. Explain yourself."

"Caliban only want to protect Miram . . ." At the mention of her name, pain erupted in Caliban's belly like a thousand tiny explosions. It radiated into his chest and hips, and he cried out. He pounded the ground with his fists.

As quickly as it came, the sharp pain stopped.

"I do not want you to even speak her name in my presence," Sparo growled, "you filthy beast. She is not yours."

"She not yours either," Caliban whispered and then flinched, waiting for another punishment.

"Not for much longer, no. But Miram is special, and she'll always need her father."

Sweet Miram did not need stupid Sparo, but Caliban could not say that, would not say it. Miram was smarter than Sparo, nicer than Sparo, prettier than Sparo. What did a woman like that need of a mean, dumb father? Miram was even smarter than Mother. Someday sweet Miram would be in charge, and Caliban would not suffer like this anymore. At least he hoped that would be true.

"I searched the starjumper's records for the third ship." Ariel hovered above Caliban, her small purple feet inches above his head. "Phana, the High Regent's chief of staff, is in the ship and another man named Trinc. They ejected an escape ship before I disabled them. I'm not sure how."

"Why wasn't the chief of staff traveling with the High Regent?"

"I can't say. The High Regent's ship should be to Lanopi by now."

Sparo's eyes closed, and he leaned heavily on his staff. "She discovered our message to Lazlo."

"Impossible. It was encoded beyond human programming ability."

"And yet she changed plans at the last minute and chartered another starjumper." He opened his eyes a little and stared at the fairy. "No matter. We got what we wanted--Balith is here."

"What of Phana and Trinc?"

Sparo turned to Caliban. "We'll see if this one can follow orders. Caliban, I want you to find the two humans who came down in the other ship, close to the middle of the plains north of here. Follow them."

"Can Caliban kill them?" He flinched as Sparo clutched his staff, but no more pain followed.

"No. Follow. Don't talk with them, don't do anything but follow. If they get close to the facility, come and let myself or Ariel know."

"Yes, master."

Caliban would look for the stupid humans, but he'd do whatever he wanted when he found them.

Ariel watched as Caliban fled in the direction of the gray plains, hobbling as he did using one of his arms as a third leg.

"He will try and kill you some day," they said.

Sparo nodded. "We'll be away from this place soon and Caliban will be nothing but a memory."

"You would leave him behind?"

Sparo considered it for a few moments, taking a deep breath. "Yes. I would leave him. He survived without us before. Caliban is a wild creature and deserves a wild life. It's the only choice."

"But you tell him all the time that he has many choices and he chooses poorly. Does that logic not apply to the great Sparo?"

Ariel expected an angry reply, but Sparo merely shrugged.

"Do you mock me?" His voice sounded tired.

"Will you hurt me like him if I do? Will you abandon me to fate? Am I no more to you than he?"

Sparo turned and faced Ariel. "You are something very important to me. You are my only friend, and certainly my only confidant."

Ariel's face twitched, but they controlled it. They'd become too human. Sparo had never called them a friend. A sudden thrill and a biting anger surfaced at the same moment. Was that possible? It must be, because that's how they felt.

"A friend would let me and my tribe go free." Part of Ariel regretted the words as soon as they formed, but only a part.

Sparo frowned, and his body slumped. "Soon." The word came out slow and long. "Double check the system and make sure we don't have any more ships we've missed. Once we're sure of that, we'll follow the rest of the plan. Get into my brother's head and see who helped him betray me. Then we'll decide who lives and who dies."

Ariel began to dissipate.

"Wait."

Ariel reformed at Sparo's command.

"Do you believe that I think of you as a friend?"

"Yes, I believe that. But I also believe you really don't know what being a friend means." Ariel dissipated and flew high above the forest, leaving Sparo standing alone.

chapter 36

BEHIND THE BELT

he screen went blank, the face of Oratt disappearing into nothingness. Their conversation had revealed little Claribel didn't already know.

Lanopi had communications with the three battleships in Vesta and was sending a cruiser and two smaller starjumpers to be used as rescue ships if necessary. The Second Regent had accepted Khayr's offer of help, and a Nooteezian battleship would join the growing fleet; Coznar and Alandria were also sending ships.

But Claribel wasn't sure what good that would do. The *Marsil* had disappeared behind the asteroid belt. Because of the belt's size, it would take several weeks for a ship to fly around it--there were holes and breaks but nothing close to the starjump point. If the *Marsil* and its crew were in mortal danger, the rescue mission would be too late.

The other option was to blast through the asteroid belt. Because of the belt's denseness, this was a risky maneuver, but Oratt said the Lanopian Navy was mapping out a plan.

Despite the massive political issues swirling around the *Marsil's* disappearance, Claribel's mind spent most of its worry on her brother. The Lanopian battleships had seen him eject and fly with the *Marsil* into the belt, but they knew nothing else. Whatever fate had awaited the starjumper likely held her brother as well.

Second Regent Oratt had seemed especially shaken by the disappearance of the High Regent. Publicly, the Lanopian government was claiming Rissa had been on the *Marsil* and was part of the missing crew. But Oratt knew nothing of her whereabouts. The elite guards who'd starjumped to Fortuna claimed not to know about her location, only that she instructed them to have their departure act as a decoy.

The known systems rallied to Lanopi. Even Pastrack and Scavart had sent messages praising High Regent Rissa and imploring their gods for her safe return. But Claribel had to imagine their rivals reveled in the chaos this bizarre situation had caused. And she certainly could not rule out that Pastrack and Scavart might have had a hand in this strange affair.

"Why would they jump through Vesta?" Khayr asked. Only he, Claribel, and Nozrel sat in the conference room.

"My brother said Lazlo, the High Regent's science advisor, wanted to see the system," she answered.

"Find everything you can on this man Lazlo," Khayr said to Nozrel. "If he was in bed with our enemies, we need to find the connection and trace it."

Nozrel nodded and left the room.

Khayr turned to Claribel. "You didn't mention that bit about Lazlo to Oratt."

"Something is going on here," she said, "something extremely strange, and I feel like the High Regent must be at its heart. She changes ships at the last minute, before a mishap like this? I know that woman. She does nothing impulsively. If she didn't get on the *Marsil* then she had a reason not to. If we find that reason, we unravel all of this."

Ariel observed the ships hanging outside the asteroid belt. Three Lanopian battleships were now accompanied by similar ships from Nooteezia, Alandria, and Coznar; humanity was uniting, at least some of humanity, behind the strange disappearance of the *Marsil* in a remote and ignored system.

And they weren't content to wait. A small drone had launched from one of the Lanopian battleships and flew toward the belt at high speed. The ship was small, smaller than a fivestar. As the drone entered the belt, Ariel entered its systems and considered dismantling it, shutting it off and turning it into debris. No, they would send another and another--the flagship of the Lanopian Navy was on the other side of the belt, and these humans would not rest until they figured out what happened. They needed something more dramatic to deter further exploration. Ariel couldn't watch these humans and complete Sparo's plan at the same time.

They took control of the asteroid belt system again, another brilliant piece of work by Sycorax. Most of the asteroids were rock, just as they should be. But throughout the belt, Sycorax's team had created a system of drones which looked and acted like asteroids until they were activated.

Ariel activated one of the asteroid drones, shooting it toward the small Lanopian scout ship. Its sensors anticipated the impact and enacted evasive maneuvers, but the asteroid drone was faster. The asteroid drone struck the Lanopian ship at high speed, ending in a bright display of sparks and mangled metal.

Ariel returned to Vesta II, content that their little display would discourage the humans sitting outside the belt, at least until Sparo finished with Balith.

It was late in the day, nearly midnight on Nooteezia, when Claribel was summoned to Nozrel's security area and into another briefing room.

She sat next to King Khayr, one wall of the room a screen. Nozrel stood before them, flanked by a young man that he introduced as an analyst named Abdel. Abdel was short and looked like he hadn't slept in a day or two, his hair ruffled and his eyes heavy.

"We've found something," Nozrel said, nodding to Abdel.

The young man swallowed hard before speaking. He touched his pad, and text appeared on the wall behind him. "We intercepted a message sent a few days ago. It came through an encrypted channel directly to Lazlo's official jumpnet access code."

Claribel directed her eyes to the screen.

Dear Lazlo,

It has been much too long. Please meet me in the usual place. We have so much to discuss. Bring your entire party--it will be more fun that way. If not, I'll let everyone know everything, including what you hid there.

Sycorax

"Sycorax," King Khayr said aloud, his voice soft and deep. He clearly recognized the word or name Sycorax.

"Who or what is Sycorax?" Claribel asked.

Nozrel glanced at Khayr before he replied. "Sycorax is a secret organization that builds weapons and other things for any system with enough money to pay it."

Claribel had never heard of the organization.

"We'll have our analysts dig deeper," Khayr assured her with a brief touch on her arm, the gesture full of a patronization she didn't care for.

"Yes," Nozrel said. "Abdel and his team are looking into that group and what connection they might have had with Lazlo. But Sycorax is very secretive, and I can't imagine they would use their name in such a sloppy manner."

Khayr simply nodded.

"There is other news." Nozrel touched his pad and threw an image on the screen. It showed a small ship flying away from a battleship toward an immense wall of asteroids. Shortly after it entered the belt, an asteroid came to life, zipped toward the small ship, and obliterated it.

"According to the Lanopian Navy," Nozrel continued, "they plan another drone penetration for tomorrow or the next day. One of the three battleships is also working its way around the asteroid belt, but that will take approximately 96 standard days."

"Could they set up a starjump point beyond the asteroid belt?" Claribel asked, wishing she'd paid more attention during her starjump physics lessons; Thanan had always been the one who'd loved that subject. She closed her eyes, pushing away the cold chill that crept up her spine.

"Possibly" Nozrel replied. "But they'd need to get to the other side to even see if there's a starjump spot over there. And as we just witnessed, someone or something does not want that."

"So all we can do is wait?"

Khayr placed his hand on her shoulder. "We're looking into other alternatives, but yes, we must wait."

Claribel closed her eyes, fighting back tears which stubbornly tried to break her defenses. Life had been lonely, and her clandestine conversations with Thanan over the past few years had helped her feel like she had an ally, even if they couldn't publicly act that way. And now her one and only friend in the universe was stuck behind an asteroid belt with no immediate way to help him.

Hope before fear, she repeated in her mind, more a prayer to the gods of the Whole than for herself. She believed, she wanted to believe. And she hoped the Whole would watch over Thanan and keep him safe until the Lanopians or the Nooteezians could find him.

chapter 37

MINDS

riel hung in the air around their forcefully invited guests. Their small escape ship had crashed in what Miram called the Witch Jungle, carving a small landing zone among the tall vine trees. Despite the bright sun, the thick canopy held the jungle in eternal twilight and thickened the air with moisture.

Two guards descended the ramp from the ship, weapons drawn and eyes moving. Both wore oxygen masks, afraid the atmosphere would be toxic. That should be the least of their fears.

"I told you this place is completely safe," an old man said from the top of the ramp. "We don't need rebreathers or any environmental aid." The voice belonged to Lazlo, Sparo's savior. He looked frail, nearing the end of his human existence.

Alazar and Balith stood behind him. Ariel paid particular attention to Sparo's brother, watching him for some form of treachery. They had heard about his evil nature from Sparo for so long that they expected him to do something despicable at any moment. But he just hung behind the others, his eyes wary.

The lead guard glanced at Lazlo, removing her mask. "How do you know so much about this planet? According to everything I've read, there is no life in this system. How does a living planet stay secret for so long?"

"It's classified," Lazlo responded.

"So you've said." The guard tossed her breathing device into the ship, and the other guard followed.

The female guard was dressed in a one piece, silver and maroon outfit, the Lanopian flag of five stars over her left breast. The male guard wore a different uniform, adorned in the colors and symbols of Sparo's family, blue with the family's crest above his left breast.

"What do you recommend, Captain?" Alazar spoke, his voice strained.

The guard's eyes scanned the trees. "I'd recommend we stay in the ship. Despite Lazlo's assurances, we know little of this planet and its dangers."

"I agree with Captain Adriana," Balith said from inside the ship, his deep voice echoing through the trees.

"I'd like to look around," Lazlo replied. "It's been many years, but I've been here before. As heavily armed as these two are, we should be fine."

Ariel took notice of their weaponry. Both guards held plasma pistols at the ready, and each had shock sticks holstered at their hips. Adriana also had a concussion pistol hanging from her other hip.

Lazlo's eagerness surprised Ariel. Wasn't he aware of what this jungle held, the terrors Sycorax had populated it with?

He and Alazar slowly descended the ramp, but Balith remained behind, his eyes tentative and his posture stiff. "I'd rather stay here and wait."

"Wait for what?" Alazar spit. "Our communications are down."

"Surely they'll send someone to rescue us." Balith's voice quivered. "And they're more likely to find us if we stay with the crashed ship."

"Maybe," Alazar replied. "But we have no idea what happened to the *Marsil* and if anyone can get through that blasted asteroid belt. I'm going to assume we'll be here for a while before Lanopi figures out how to reach us. Seeing as this planet is supposed to be a dead one, they're going to think us dead as well. The captain will keep us safe."

Balith paused, eyeing the High Regent's husband. "Well Nic and I will stay here while you explore." Balith pointed to the male guard.

"Absolutely not," the female guard stated.

"He's my guard," Balith said, his voice rising.

"He's assigned to you, Senator, but he's part of the military structure and falls under my command." She slapped Nic on the shoulder.

The second guard startled. Nic was by far the youngest member of the small party. He was nearly half a foot taller than Adriana but with a lean muscularity different from her stockiness.

"Captain of the High Regent's guard and yet not chosen to accompany the High Regent home." Balith stroked his belly absentmindedly. "Seems like your authority isn't what you think it is."

"Enough," Alazar snapped. "You can stay behind Balith, but we're moving."

"You have no authority either, Admiral Alazar." Balith spoke his title with clear disdain. "I'm a senator; I should be the one leading us."

Alazar walked quickly up the ramp, facing the larger man, his hand hanging menacingly above his own pistol. "We are marooned on a strange planet. This is now a Lanopian Space Navy incident, and as you so astutely pointed out, I hold the rank of admiral. So you and your man will follow."

Balith's face twitched with anger, but he simply nodded to Nic and followed Alazar down the ramp.

"Lead the way, Captain," Alazar said when they were ready to depart.

Evenly-spaced trees dominated the jungle, reaching a hundred feet above their heads. Thick, ropey vines hung from the top like tentacles, waving slightly with a humid breeze. Dead leaves and brush littered the jungle floor, squishing under their feet as they walked away from their ship.

The buzz of insects vibrated around them, some of the bulbous flies which were native to the planet flitting about their heads. Other insects crawled, flew, and slithered nearby, all creations of Sycorax, all designed to kill, maim, or paralyze. Ariel held them and the larger predators at bay with a pheromone shield similar to the one confining all of these abominations to the jungle.

The group stalked between the trees, Adriana leading the way, her pistol drawn and her muscles tense. Alazar and Lazlo followed close behind, matching the guard's rigid posture. Balith lingered farther behind them, followed by Nic, the younger guard's diligence mirroring Adriana's.

Ariel moved some of their essence toward Balith, slowly creeping into his mind. Human memories were not linear like of a member's, but random and filled with holes. A scent and sound from one moment, but no image. A distinct image, but the reality warped by time. Human memories existed as a twisted, complicated maze.

Ariel pulled several memories from the chaos. First, the day Sparo replaced their father, Senator Donn, after his death. Balith's memory dripped with bitterness. Sparo was everything a senator should not be: he lacked ambition and drive, and he'd trained as a scientist, not a politician. Balith had prepared, had believed he'd convince their father and mother of the folly of following tradition and installing their eldest as senator. But at the old man's death, the decree came, naming Sparo as Donn's preferred candidate, with their mother endorsing her eldest son publicly. His parents had betrayed Balith, given his rightful place to his idiot brother.

Ariel shifted to another day, Balith drunk and seething at Sparo's wedding. Balith lusted after the beautiful and intelligent Eliel, the daughter of another senator. Even Sparo's marriage trumped Balith's. More alcohol fueled his rage as he imagined sleeping with Eliel, not his homely wife of convenience.

Forcing their way further into his mind, Ariel uncovered the memory Sparo wanted, a memory Balith rarely visited, a tattered remembrance of days before Sparo's exile.

A man approached Balith as he sat in a small park, a prearranged meeting. The High Regent's daughter was almost killed, and someone needed to be blamed. Balith had, since his brother's election to the Senate, connected himself to the underbelly of Lanopi, and he suggested to the man that Sparo take the fall. It would be believable because of Sparo's sympathy toward the Onala Liberators. The idiot had written a paper in college stating that many of the Liberators' gripes about the High Regency and the transfer of political offices were rooted in truth.

Balith stood now in Sparo's house, Sparo and his wife gone for the day. Known to the staff, Balith easily entered with another, a hacker who'd been hired to help them. The hacker, a beautiful young woman, worked diligently to place all the required evidence on Sparo's computer making the information seem natively created.

A final memory, Balith sitting in the Onali Hall of Democracy, his election complete as Senator of Onal.

Ariel pulled away. They despised the human mind, filled with pettiness and duplicity. Balith's mind reminded her of Sycorax, bathed in cruelty and selfishness. How had humanity survived with such self-serving members?

Next Ariel entered into Lalzo's mind, hoping for a less despicable environment. His memories were less chaotic and flowed together in a clearer narrative.

Lazlo entered the exile ship and changed its destination, confirming the message he had left for Sparo on the ship's computer. Lazlo's heart ached when he thought back on little, innocent Miram running playfully in front of her parents. He wished he'd done more, had been courageous instead of a coward. But his guilt had faded over time, and he'd assumed Sparo and his family dead.

Another memory came, connected to his emotions. Years after Sparo's exile, Lazlo sat in conference with Alazar. The High Regent's husband wept, admitting to Lazlo that he had suggested to the High Regent they blame Sparo for their daughter's near assassination. Without acting directly, they had manipulated the bitter and ambitious Balith, knowing he'd believe he'd devised the plan all on his own, providing deniability if anyone ever uncovered their plot.

Alazar begged Lazlo for forgiveness, but Lazlo's heart only held disgust. How could Alazar doom an innocent man, woman, and child to certain death in space? But Lazlo pretended to forgive him, and convinced Alazar to atone for his mistake by making one of Sparo's dreams a reality: promote education and the arts, to make Lanopi great again by enriching the minds of the young.

Ariel pulled back from Lazlo's mind. Alazar and the High Regent had known, had been part of the plot to frame and exile Sparo. Over the years, he had focused his anger on Balith, believing him the mastermind of Sparo's downfall. If Ariel shared the truth of these memories with Sparo, his rage would grow and envelop the leader of a planet. His thirst for revenge would be almost impossible to sate.

Ariel hesitated before entering Alazar's mind. Did they really want to know how deep this conspiracy ran? What if they discovered dozens who'd participated? Sparo's vengeance would never end, a self-destructive spiral sinking the man and likely his daughter. And Ariel and their tribe might never pull free of his retribution's gravity.

So they would lie to Sparo, say they probed Alazar's memories. They'd keep the story tight: the villains were Balith, Alazar, and the High Regent. Ariel didn't know, and didn't want to know, the reason why the High Regent wanted to blame the blameless for her daughter's near death. If Sparo wanted to dig into that, he'd have to do it on his own. Ariel had done their part and wanted no more of this.

They hung in the air above their doomed guests, wondering how much blood Sparo's wrath would leave at their feet. Was their tribe's freedom worth this price, worth being complicit in the misguided revenge of a warped human mind?

Ariel floated slowly back toward the facility, hoping that the deal they'd made to ensure their freedom didn't strip away what made them a member of the Whole.

chapter 38

FRIENDS

Nothingness filled Desolation, and that's all Caliban had found-- nothing. He hated this place, hated the gray fatties and pointy- nosed wolves. But most of all, he hated Sparo for sending him to a dumb place looking for even dumber people.

Stupid gray rock dominated the landscape, broken up by thorny bushes. Caliban hated those bushes. If he got one of their pricklies in his skin, it was very hard to get out. He'd chased a rabbit into a patch of it once, and returned home with hundreds of them poking into him. Stupid Sparo made him remove each one by himself, even though the old human had Mother's magic that would have made it easy.

Foul Sparo! Caliban wanted to rip his stupid head from his stupid body and then toss it to a lizard cat and watch it tear the stupid flesh from his stupid bones! Mother had been cruel; Sparo was cruel. Caliban hated masters. Caliban had killed Mother, made her pay. Now he dreamed of killing Sparo, spent most of his waking hours imagining the hundreds of ways strong Caliban could kill weak Sparo. Mother and Sparo had magic, but what were they without their magic? Weak, silly, soft humans.

But these were dreams. This wasn't like the situation with Mother. If Caliban killed Sparo, Miram would hate Caliban forever. Couldn't Miram see they'd be happier without Sparo watching them every day? Was Miram stupid like other humans, blind to what would make them happy? No, Miram was smart. But whatever goodness she saw in her father was something Caliban could not see.

But what if Sparo died by accident? What if Caliban made it seem like an accident? Maybe there was hope to free Caliban and Miram from a master's rope. He bared his sharp teeth in a feral grin.

A flash of movement over the next hill caught his eye. A space person, maybe? Perhaps, one of his blue brothers? Or maybe he'd imagined the movement, now gone from his vision.

He crawled on all fours and peaked over the rocky ridge. But it wasn't a person. It was an old land whale, or at least that's what stupid Sparo called them. Caliban called them gray fatties. The gray fatties were huge, taller than Sparo with a long body supported by eight thick legs. They had a big fat tail and smooth skin. They blended in with the gray rock and plants, so sometimes, even though they were big and fat, they seemed to disappear.

The gray fatty did not move. It lay there, its eyes closed. It looked dead. Maybe dead for a long time. It was hard to tell with gray fatties. When they died, their tough skin could last for moons upon moons. The pointy-nosed wolves would eat their insides, but they did not eat the skin; even Caliban would not eat the skin.

Gray fatties feared Caliban, so he didn't need to worry about them. If the gray fatty wasn't dead, it would run. Maybe he could catch it then; eating gray fatties was gross, but chasing them was fun. But if the gray fatty was dead, what had he seen move?

He took a deep breath, trying to smell whatever crossed his vision, but he stopped his inhalation when a foul stench assaulted his nose. Yes, this gray fatty had been here for some time. He stepped out over the ridge, confident he'd imagined something moving; the fatty had not been moving. He circled the beast until he found where the wolves had entered it--they had ripped a hole into the fatty near the base of its neck. Caliban stepped over its legs to get a better look at the hole. The hole came to Caliban's waist, or about the height of a pointy-nosed wolf. The wolves could tear the skin of the fatties with their hundreds of sharp teeth, but they only chewed through what they needed to get to the meat.

Caliban's head snapped back as he heard a sound behind him, something brushing up against the bushes on the other side of the fatty. A pointy-nosed wolf, back to finish its meal? Caliban stuck his head into the fatty: there wasn't any meat left, just the animal's massive ribs. But again the sound came. Maybe another fatty? But what if it was the wolves? Caliban might be able to fight one or two, but he couldn't fight a pack, and the wolves liked traveling in numbers. So he stepped inside the fatty to hide.

Footsteps echoed around the creature. Caliban's heart raced, though he snickered at the thought of his heart beating as he stood where the fatty's heart had been. Slime covered the walls, floor, and ceiling of his gray fatty hiding place. Caliban would need to wash when he got home. It smelled worse inside the fatty, so he plugged his nose with his fingers; it didn't help much.

The footsteps continued around the fatty. But they weren't wolf footsteps. It sounded like a person. Did one of the space people survive? Had Sparo come to check on him? It wasn't Ariel, because the purple fairy didn't make footsteps. And it wasn't Miram, because Sparo forbade her to come to Desolation. He backed farther into the emptied guts of the fatty. The only light came from the hole the wolves had made. He was trapped.

"Even the animals are ugly." A human voice, and it spoke Sparo's language. "Go check it out, she says. Find out if it's dangerous, she says. But it's nothing more than a dead . . . slug . . . thing. What a waste."

The voice belonged to a man; it wasn't high and sweet like Miram's, but it wasn't like Sparo's either. Caliban crept slowly toward the light. No man could match Caliban, especially a man without Sparo's magic. Caliban was strong and fast. He would kill the space man quickly.

Caliban stopped halfway when he heard more noise. He stepped backward. Maybe the noisy man had attracted wolves. Stupid, noisy humans. He would stay here; the wolves could have the sloppy-talker.

"Crap," the man said.

The light darkened at the hole, and the man crawled in. The darkness hid the man's features. Caliban walked slowly toward him. The silly space man had ruined Caliban's hiding place. He would kill the man before the wolves arrived and give the man to them. Maybe they would let Caliban live if he gave them a gift. Everyone loved gifts.

Footsteps echoed outside again. Still not wolves. Caliban was confused. How many space people were there? And why was one space man scared of another space man?

"Dead," said another voice. This voice was not like the first. It sounded more like a woman's, higher but not sweet like Miram's. It was like her voice combined with the howl of a pointy-nosed wolf. Caliban snickered at the thought of a wolf with Miram's head trying to talk to him. "Trinc! Are you here?"

Before the man could reply, Caliban jumped and grabbed him around the neck, but they both slipped on the slimy insides of the gray fatty. Caliban lost his grip and struggled to maintain his balance. He reached again and gripped the man's throat, but his hands slipped, and the man kicked Caliban in the stomach. Caliban growled. The man stood, and Caliban swung his legs, knocking the sloppy-talker onto his back and splashing goo around. Caliban jumped and landed on top of the man, pinning him.

"Help!" the man cried.

Caliban put a knee on his throat, cutting off his voice. He'd crush the little man soon.

A shadow blocked the sun, and a tall woman stood in silhouette holding some kind of rod. Caliban stood and stepped toward the second human, growling.

A flash of light exploded from the woman's hand and hit Caliban's chest. He fell back, gripping the burning wound. It stung and surprised him, but it didn't hurt too much; he didn't have weak human flesh.

The man stumbled away and pulled out his own weapon, pointing it at Caliban. "What in the name of Chimra is that thing? It's humanoid."

"I told you," the woman said, "Vesta holds many secrets."

Caliban crouched, ready to pounce on them, but the woman pulled out another weapon and fired. Caliban flinched, but it missed him by several feet, blowing another hole in the side of the gray fatty.

"Careful, now," the woman said. "No need to get yourself killed." She tilted her head. "What are you?"

"I Caliban."

"That's your name? Caliban?"

He nodded.

"What are you?"

"A lizard man."

"He speaks Lanopian," the goo-covered man said.

"Do you speak any other languages?" the woman asked, this time in Mother's tongue.

"Yes. Caliban speak Mother's tongue."

"What did he say?" the man asked in Sparo's language.

"He speaks Coznarian, which makes sense."

"How does any of this makes sense? We're marooned on a planet that's not supposed to be inhabitable, and you're telling me this makes sense."

"I don't have to tell you everything. And I'm not going to discuss it in front of this one." The woman pointed with her gun toward Caliban, but he did not flinch. The two space people backed slowly out of the gray fatty.

"Come out, Caliban," the woman prodded. "I won't hurt you if you don't try and hurt us."

Caliban knew he couldn't trust humans, but what other choice did he have? Stay in the rotting gray fatty forever? He slowly crossed to the big hole and stepped out onto the sand.

He could see them clearly now. The man was tall, as tall as Sparo, but stronger looking and younger. His skin was dark, not light like Sparo's or Mother's. The tall, sloppy man tried in vain to wipe the gray fatty goo from his brown pants, but it clung stubbornly.

The woman was tall, though a hand or so shorter than the man. She had short hair, shorter than the man's, not long like Miram's. She wore clothes which were tighter like some of Mother's friends had, emphasizing that she was a woman. She had large breasts; Mother's man friends would have talked about the size of those. Her skin was dark like the man's. She held both weapons and kept them pointed at Caliban. He cringed.

"What do we do with you?" she asked.

"Kill it. He's a liability." The man tried to fling some goo from his hands, but it jiggled without moving.

"Please don't kill me," Caliban pleaded. "I mean no harm. My master sent me here to find you."

"How do you speak our language?" the woman asked.

"My master taught me the language."

"Who is your master?" The woman stepped closer, the weapon still pointed at Caliban. "Are there other people on this planet?"

"Yes. My master and his daughter. And I think other space people like you."

"So we're not alone." The woman glanced at the sky. "Others got stranded here as well."

"We need food and water." The man faced the woman. "We don't have much left."

"My name is Phana," the woman said, "and this is Trinc. Can you help us find food and water?"

"Yes." Caliban inched closer but stopped when the woman pointed her weapons forcefully. "Please, no more of your magic. I know where there is a lot of food. We can avoid my master, we can avoid the other space people. Plenty of food. Plenty of water. Space people will like."

The woman wrinkled her face. No wonder she had those lines coming from her eyes. "I don't know if we can trust this thing."

Caliban imagined smashing her face with a rock.

"You know more than you're telling," the man said to her, his eyes not leaving Caliban. "I can't properly protect you if I don't know what's going on."

The woman ignored the goo-covered man. "Take us to water and food. But if I think, for even a second, you're trying to betray us, I will kill you."

"This way." Caliban stood slowly and started walking toward Mother's facility. He didn't know if he liked Phana and Trinc; he didn't want new masters. But with the weapons they held, they might become Sparo's accident.

chapter 39

CONVERSATIONS

Unlike her last conversation with Oratt, Second Regent of Lanopi, this one would be formal. Claribel sat in the official state visit room of the Nooteezian palace, dressed in a bright yellow gown that was accented with a red sash and a necklace of sparkling blue jewels. She dressed in the Nooteezian style. Claribel had seen the High Regent engage in these conversations, and now it was Claribel's turn. But instead of representing Lanopi, this would be her first public act as Queen Claribel of Nooteezia.

The state visit room mirrored the prominent architecture of Nooteezia. Claribel sat in a high-backed chair, and behind her, spiraled columns rose to a thirty-foot ceiling. These columns copied the style of Nooteezia's most famous landmark, the palace entrance. Such majesty should help one feel royal, but the towering columns just made her feel small.

King Khayr stood next to her, dressed as he had been for their wedding: a rich burgundy tunic held together with brilliant gold ropes. As usual, his left breast was mostly visible, highlighting his chiseled body and reinforcing his image as the warrior king. Claribel had to admit the effect was quite stunning, the deep burgundy against his dark skin and darker hair, his muscled arms and full chest emphasizing his physicality. He looked like someone out of a legend, as if the demigod Cootmo had been plucked from the lines of a story.

Claribel hoped their appearance had an effect upon the Second Regent and on all the citizens who turned to the jumpnet to watch. But the High Regent's fifteenth maxim wounded Claribel's hope: *Hope is a strategy best reserved for the desperate and foolish.* Claribel hoped she was neither.

Nozrel stood nearby, his face compacted into its usual grimace. The man had been pleasant enough the past few days, but he didn't seem to trust her, and she didn't trust him. But Khayr genuinely respected his opinion, and that would have to do for now.

"I know you don't like Nozrel," the king said softly in Claribel's direction, as if reading her thoughts. "But despite some of his silly prejudices, the man runs a brilliant intelligence operation."

Claribel chided herself for allowing her feelings to be so readable. "I will value his opinion because you do."

Khayr smiled broadly.

"Is something funny?" She hoped her annoyance at his boyish smile did not come through as clearly as her dislike for Nozrel had.

"I believe I'm beginning to understand you a little more."

She couldn't help but smile. His grin was infectious, even if she wasn't sure what he was talking about.

Moments later, a large screen sprang to life in front of them. Oratt, Second Regent of Lanopi, sat on the left dressed in his gray uniform accented with the green colors of his family's house.

Next to him sat Senator Mura Chani of Aneis, president of the Lanopian Senate. By Lanopian law, she was now the second in line behind the Second Regent. Mura dressed differently than any other senator. The ruling body of Lanopi was filled with gray suits, the colors and style of traditional Lanopian rule. But Mura Chani eschewed such tradition. Before her election as senator, she had owned the largest clothing designer and manufacturer on Lanopi. She had been, in her younger years, an icon of fashion, sexuality, and culture. She dressed as such, in a gown of dark brown, cut low to reveal much of her breasts. Her arms were also bare.

Despite being more than three decades Claribel's senior, Claribel could not completely dispel feeling physically inferior to the woman. Mura embodied Lanopian feminine beauty: full features, perfect dark skin, long curly hair, and a symmetrical face. Claribel became suddenly aware of her square nose, flat chest and skinny legs.

Checking to make sure the sound had not been activated yet, Claribel turned to Khayr. "Mura is a dangerous woman. We must tread lightly with her. Though I like Oratt, it's possible he's being manipulated. Mura is no one's stooge."

"Our agents could never agree as to whether Senator Mura was an ally or enemy to your mother." Khayr spoke to her side, his mouth hidden from view of the screen.

Claribel leaned close to him and whispered, "Because I don't think even the High Regent has figured out if the woman's ambitions end with her current position."

Khayr nodded slightly, and they turned to face the two Lanopian leaders. Moments later, a green light indicated the audio was now connected.

"Greetings Oratt, Second Regent of Lanopi, and Senator Mura Chani of Aneis, President of the Lanopian Senate." Khayr spoke heavily accented Coznarian, but the Nooteezian accent only seemed to reinforce his image as a warrior king, not diminish it. Claribel wondered how the people of Lanopi would view her new husband. "I appreciate your acceptance of this formal communication."

"Greetings, King Khayr." Mura spoke, her voice like the flow of a wide river, powerful and beautiful. Claribel noted she had spoken first, not the Second Regent. "And greetings to our own Claribel." The Senator smiled brightly. "The queenship of Nooteezia seems to sit well with you."

Claribel smiled and nodded, impressed by Mura's ability to compliment and insult with one simple phrase.

"I am a man of few words," Khayr continued, "so I suggest we proceed with the matter at hand."

Oratt and Mura nodded.

"We know your people must feel a great deal of fear with thirteen of your senators and the family of the High Regent lost in the Vesta system. On behalf of the Nooteezian people, we'd like to offer any assistance we can."

Oratt looked at Mura, who nodded. "We appreciate your concern and would expect nothing else of our closest ally." Her words were perfectly crafted to say almost nothing.

"Though the Lanopian Space Navy is formidable," Khayr continued, "the Nooteese Space Corps has experience blasting through asteroid belts; we could help you clear a path to the planet and rescue your people."

Mura's smile didn't reach her eyes. "We appreciate your offer. We are currently considering options but have not decided how to proceed. This bizarre affair makes it difficult to decide what to do. Based on the drone attempt, any efforts must be marked by the shadow of the danger from that strange asteroid belt."

"What of the High Regent?" Claribel asked. "We've read rumors across the jumpnet that she did not jump with the *Marsil*." The jumpnet swirled with these rumors; she left unsaid the official records she had at her disposal.

Mura's smile disappeared. "Your concern for your mother is certainly appreciated. We believe her to be with the *Marsil*, trapped with the others."

Claribel considered Mura's statement. They believed, or did they know something the Nooteezian intelligence force had missed? Or maybe Mura and the Second Regent were playing coy for the cameras, trying to reveal little?

Claribel looked at her new husband. He was not as accomplished or practiced in state craft, but his face mirrored the passivity of Mura's well-honed, no-tell countenance.

"Please let us know what we can do during this trying time," Khayr said, his smile pleasant. "My marriage to Queen Claribel," he looked over at her and grabbed her hand, "is not our people's only connection. We are bound by word and deed, and the Nooteezian people stand ready to assist at a moment's notice."

"Thank you." Senator Mura's short response indicated an end to the conversation and not the friendliest end.

Moments later, smiles exchanged, the image disappeared.

"They have no idea where the High Regent is," Khayr said.

"Maybe," Claribel responded, not as sure in her opinion as the king was in his. "They know something we don't for sure."

Khayr frowned. "It will take them weeks to circumvent the belt. They've sent one drone and no other attempt. If I were trapped behind that belt, I believe my people would turn those asteroids to dust to find me. Senator Mura Chani seems content to let events play out. Is it possible she's is making a play for the High Regency?"

"I cannot say. She is ambitious, but the High Regent's hold on the people is firm. The economy is humming, safety is high, and our alliance makes interstellar war seem unlikely, at least in the short term. Even if the necessary twenty senators called for a vote, the people would re-elect Rissa by a wide margin. It would never reach a head-to-head election. And with much of the senate on the *Marsil*, they need senatorial elections before they could even do that. If the High Regent is missing for a long time or found to be dead, it could take years to figure out who leads next, and they could be bloody years." Claribel stifled a shudder as she considered the possibility of the first Lanopian civil conflict in nearly a century.

"Yes, but how long would the High Regent need to be gone or dead before Mura made her play?" The king reached out and grabbed her hand again. "I'm sorry. I don't mean to theorize politics around the life and safety of your dear mother."

Claribel smiled. Khayr might indeed prove to be as ruthless in politics as he was on the battlefield. "I was raised by High Regent Rissa to think first of the state. Even as queen of Nooteezia, I still have Lanopi's interests in my heart." And she didn't say that no one had ever called Rissa 'dear,' least of all Claribel.

"We must dig deeper," he said.

"Even though our ally implied they have everything under control?" She tried to keep her tone light and not accusatory; they needed to dig and find the answers before the Lanopians did.

"Though I respect the Second Regent and the senator as the current leadership of Lanopi, our alliance was based on conversations and negotiations with High Regent Rissa. This danger, whatever it is, could threaten this alliance. There are several hundred people on that ship who need our help. If we can figure out how to help them, we should."

"Then let's get to work."

chapter 40

THOUGHTS

Sparo sat in his dark room, his eyes and face struggling to remain conscious. Ariel's hope that his proximity to his ultimate vengeance would cure him seemed a foolish notion now.

They had shared the memories of Lazlo and Alazar with Sparo, and he'd sat in silence for fifteen long minutes. With his mind shielded from them, they could not tell if he contemplated his revenge or if his mind was clouded by pain and grief; maybe it was both.

"All the way to the High Regent," Sparo finally said, closing his eyes. "Balith likely did not even initiate it, only took advantage. All this time I thought Balith to be the primary villain of my tale, but High Regent Rissa is the villain."

"The memories only implicated Alazar . . ."

"The High Regent's husband is a puppet. If he was part, so was she."

Ariel's spirits sank. This vengeance plot was not going to end today. Sparo would need Ariel, possibly for years. Killing Balith would be easy. Bringing down the High Regent of Lanopi would not, especially since she'd avoided their best chance to get her.

And even if they found a way to exact revenge on the High Regent, such a massive political action could have a cascading effect across the human known systems. Sparo's revenge could become a comet which disrupted all of humanity. And Ariel, Five, would be in the middle of it all.

Sparo struggled to open his eyes, as if great weights held them shut. "Have we discovered Rissa's location?"

"No," Ariel said. "Rumors fill the jumpnet that she's missing. She wasn't listed on the *Marsil*, but I haven't been able to confirm anything beyond that."

"Find her!" Sparo's sudden shout echoed through the small room.

If Ariel had been truly human, they would have flinched.

"That bitch is responsible for all of this, I know that now." He spoke quietly, but the intense anger remained. "She must be found and punished."

"As you say, master."

He looked up again, his eyes wider. "What of our other prey?"

"Miram has reached Thanan, son of Rissa and Alazar. They have met each other, and she's bringing him here."

"Good." Sparo smiled, but it carried no human happiness. "Thanan is a pawn now. Maybe revenge will take a different turn." He closed his eyes and wiped his face with his hands, though the gesture did nothing to erase his exhaustion. "Miram is beautiful. Maybe she can seduce him. Maybe Alazar and Rissa can die knowing their seed mixes with mine."

Ariel kept their face even, but could not fight the feeling of disgust welling within them. Would Sparo use his own daughter, a girl he professed to love, to twist his knife of wrath? Miram was still so young, more girl than woman. Ariel had believed Sparo to be a good man driven to darkness by forces beyond his control. Now they worried the darkness had eaten his very soul, leaving nothing behind.

They wanted to object to this new facet of his plan, to defend Miram, to keep her out of this ugliness. Yes, Caliban had nearly raped the girl, but his heart held no malice and his mind held little understanding. Sparo knew better, yet he acted even worse.

Ariel also wanted to tell Sparo it wasn't likely to work. Though soft-hearted Miram might fall in love with the first man besides her father she'd ever truly met, Thanan was the son of Rissa, trained in state craft like most human children might be trained in sports, art, or music. He was unlikely to be trapped by a guileless girl years younger than him.

But Ariel made no objections. This part of his plan would naturally fail; they'd only intervene if they needed to. They wouldn't let Miram fall through this wretched hole her father dug.

"What of Caliban?" Sparo asked.

"I have not been out to Desolation to check on him. Should I?"

Sparo waved his hand and shook his head slowly. "No, it's not worth our time. He'll report anything of note. Despite the High Regent's part, I will not harm her staff or any other Lanopians."

Ariel wondered why this did not apply to his own daughter or Rissa's son.

"And what of Balith and Alazar?"

"Proceed as planned. Let's put on a little show for Balith and Alazar, put the fear of the gods into them. But first, let's go fetch Miram and her new friend. I can't have a trained soldier interfering in what we need to do. After that, Balith and Alazar will get theirs." His eyes opened wide, the scent of revenge reviving him. "They will die, but first we'll let them know whose web they've fallen into."

As the sun approached the horizon, Caliban led the space people toward the river cliff. He did not spend much of his time in this part of Desolation, and landmarks were few in this wasted space. But once they had the river cliff in sight, they could travel north to the east entrance, a door Miram and Sparo rarely used.

Caliban limped in front of the two space people, glancing back occasionally. Phana gripped her magic weapon, and the other one hung at her hip. The man, Trinc, walked beside her, his eyes always scanning the flat, boring plain, his weapon also at the ready. Caliban wanted to reassure the man that nothing followed them, but Caliban couldn't be sure of that.

"Who is your master?" Phana said.

Caliban wasn't sure he should say. Sparo had never said it was a secret, but who would Caliban have told? A tree? An acid spider? A rock? But these were space people, and maybe Sparo didn't want them to know.

But stupid Sparo wasn't here to give commands, and Sparo the idiot hadn't ever instructed Caliban not to tell.

"His name Sparo," he replied.

Phana stepped in front of Caliban, bringing him to a halt. Her weapon was lowered, and he considered jumping her and taking the magic from her hands; then Caliban would be in charge. But no, he would not act like Mother; he would treat friends like friends until the moment they were not friends.

"Sparo." Phana whispered the word, barely audible even to Caliban's ears. "Sparo." She looked over to Trinc but was met only with an unknowing glance.

"Sparo," she repeated. "The former senator of Onal."

Trinc's eyes lit with recognition. "The one who disappeared?"

"Yes," she said. "The official records say he and his family were lost due to a starjump accident while on vacation, but there's more to the story than that."

Trinc whistled. "Is it even possible the man ended up here?"

Phana turned back to Caliban. "And his wife Eliel?"

Caliban shook his head. "No wife. Just Sparo and Miram. And Ariel the fairy."

"Fairy?" Trinc said. "What do you mean by fairy?"

"Fairy helps Sparo do things, watches over Caliban. Fairy floats around doing magic things."

"He probably means an AI or something," Phana replied, waving her hand. "The daughter lived but not the wife." Phana rubbed her chin with her freehand. "If Sparo lives, then it might explain all this."

"How?" Trinc asked.

"Senator Balith took his place, and he's also responsible, in a way, for his disappearance. Sparo brought the Marsil here to get revenge on his brother. The motive is clear, but the method seems impossible. How could a man stranded on a remote planet pull all this off? He had to have help."

"Are we even sure what this green man is telling us is true? He's talking about faries and magic."

"He thinks my gun is magic," she responded. "You must think of things in his context. Caliban: how does Sparo control the fairy?"

"With his staff and its magic ball. It also hurts Caliban, makes Caliban's insides churn and boil."

"Computers," Phana mumbled. "Sparo was an accomplished scientist. Artificial intelligence, nanobots. All of this is explainable."

"How?" Trinc asked. "The man's marooned on a livable but primitive world. How would he access engineering of this magnitude?"

"He found something here." Phana looked into the distance. "He found something which had been lost, and he's mastered it. What an idiot. He's found the power of gods, and instead of using it to free himself or gain power, he chases revenge."

"He found Mother's place," Caliban added.

"Mother?" Trinc questioned. "I thought you said the mother wasn't here?"

"Not Miram mother, my mother. She live here many moons before mean Sparo. Mother had many friends, big building. Mother made me."

"Who's your mother?" Phana asked.

"Her friends called her Sycorax."

Phana's eyes widened, as if she might have recognized Mother's name, but her face returned to normal very quickly. Maybe she hadn't.

"We should keep moving." Caliban looked around the darkening landscape. "Dark soon. We sleep by the river cliff."

Phana nodded, and Caliban continued leading them.

As the sun fell below the horizon, they made camp several feet from the cliff. Caliban convinced them to not build a fire; fire brought out the curious, pointy-nosed wolves who were more active at night anyway. And who needed fire? The summer night was plenty warm, especially on the wind-blasted plains.

Caliban lay on his back, watching the stars. Would he ever get to see the stars? Sparo said he and Miram fell from the stars, and Mother's friends had often spoken about traveling among the stars. But Caliban had only seen Vesta II, and not very much of that. What was Lanopi like or Coznar? He'd heard others tell, but hearing about and seeing were totally different. If he described the stars to someone, it would be nothing like laying here and watching them.

"Do you like your master?" Phana asked, breaking the still silence.

"Caliban no like any master."

"Would you like to be free of your master? Come to Lanopi with Trinc and me?"

Had the woman been reading his mind? Did she have magic like Ariel the fairy?

"Caliban would like to leave here, see other places. But Sparo has dark magic over Caliban, can hurt Caliban so bad." He stifled a growl; humans didn't like it when he growled.

"What if Trinc and I helped you get free of Sparo? This world has riches, and they could be ours. We would free you, Caliban, free you of your mean master."

Caliban thought about it. He had been free once, and it had been wonderful. These space people could help him be free again, he could use them to be responsible for Sparo's death. Then he could be with Miram, even if that meant killing these space people to avenge Miram's father; humans loved vengeance.

"Yes. Caliban would like that very much."

He closed his eyes then, hoping for a little sleep, but opened them when he heard a sound in the distance, someone or something trying to quietly walk toward them. Caliban closed his eyes and focused only on the sounds. Several footsteps, several creatures. He even heard the belly growl of a hungry pointy-nosed wolf.

"We're not alone," Caliban whispered to his companions.

chapter 41

CLARIBEL AND KHAYR

Claribel sat at her console in the jumpnet analytics room, rubbing her eyes. Hours of searching by the entire team, and little had been found. Rumors about Vesta peppered the jumpnet, but mostly stories told by old starjumpers of ghosts haunting the system, of spirits possessing those who traveled there. Pure rubbish, but the strange disappearance of the *Marsil* had rekindled the tall tales.

She'd asked Abdel, the young security analyst who worked for Nozrel, to look into the finances of Second Regent Oratt and Senator Mura. The Nooteezian analyst had reported that everything seemed in order. Oratt was a life-long politician, the former senator from Illiopa. His holdings were small and unchanged. Mura was extremely wealthy, one of the richest people on Lanopi. But there had been no recent changes to that wealth. If foreign agents controlled them, it was not by visible financial means.

Claribel exhaled in frustration. Years of training to cut through political mysteries like this, and yet she found nothing. She had been taught to anticipate the moves of her enemy before they even knew what they were going to do, but she couldn't puzzle out any of this. She felt they were missing a huge piece of what was going on.

"Queen Claribel."

She looked up to see Abdel standing before her, a small pad in his hand.

"Yes."

"I think I've found something." He threw a file from his pad to hers. "That message Lazlo received came from the Vesta system."

"From Vesta?" Nozrel stepped up behind Claribel. "That doesn't make sense, unless it was sent from a starjumper. Are you sure someone didn't leave you a false trail?"

If Abdel was intimidated by his boss, it did not show. He looked at Nozrel like the smartest student in class might look at another student who wasn't following at the same pace. "You can have my work double-checked, sir, but I traced it a dozen times; that message to Lazlo came from Vesta."

Claribel read the message. Without the unexplained stop in Vesta, this message would have made little sense or would have been analyzed in a much different context. But the implication was clear: bring someone to Vesta.

"The High Regent found this message," Claribel stated.

"That's a large jump, my queen," Nozrel said.

"No." She shook her head, her eyes fixed on Lazlo's message. "The High Regent is the most careful and calculating person in the known systems. She figured this out; that's why she didn't get on the ship."

Abdel nodded, his eyes lit with excitement. "That's what I thought, too! It's impossible to know who else might have found the message. It's encrypted, but I'm sure she has talented analysts."

Claribel smiled at the implication that Abdel thought of himself as a talented analyst.

Nozrel leaned in closer, as if proximity to the cryptic message might help him better believe it. "I'll admit, it is a plausible theory, though I'd caution against jumping too far into this ocean before we explore others."

"Abdel," Claribel said, "can you get a list of known associates for Lazlo? We're really looking for rebels, criminals, anyone who might want to do harm to the High Regent, my father, or . . ." Claribel paused, looking to the message again. "Or anyone on that ship. That's a pretty large net, but that's where we have to start."

Abdel glanced at Nozrel. The gray-haired advisor seemed annoyed at Claribel's order but nodded slightly.

After the two men walked away, she continued her search, focusing on Vesta rumors. Was the location part of the plot or just a convenient place to ambush someone? No, it had to be part of it all.

She'd found an entire board on the jumpnet dedicated to conspiracies swirling around Vesta. One thread spoke of how Alandria actually controlled the system and had a space navy shipyard off Vesta III. Another user claimed to have firsthand knowledge of a Camsartran plot using Vesta to find new jump points into all the known systems and beyond. Each theory seemed more convoluted and less plausible than the last.

As Claribel considered moving on, one of the rumors caught her attention. The user's name was SycoraxSurivor, and he was only active on this thread, no other posts on the board. He or she claimed to have spent time on Vesta II working for a woman named Sycorax creating weapons for the Lanopian government decades ago. She had been ready to discard the rumor, but the username contained the same name which had been in the message.

But before she closed the thread, she read the last message from SycoraxSurvivor:

TEXT: I realize you all think me mad, or worse, a liar. But I know. Go see Vesta II for yourself. On the largest continent you will find a research facility rivaling anything among the powers of the known systems. It would be hard to verify my story but not impossible. Reach beyond the belt of Vesta to find it.

This message had been posted three years ago, and nothing on this thread had been posted since. Whomever SycoraxSurvivor was, he'd gone quiet.

Claribel continued, searching for the term Sycorax; the word was completely foreign. Was it a name, a place, an acronym? She found scattered references to the word, but nothing tying it to the Vesta system, Lanopi, or Lazlo. Then she came across a single reference on a Camsartran board. The board discussed current events, mainly around Camsartran politics. One thread simply said: *Sycorax sleeps with Nooteezia now.* The responses to the thread were only questions, none of which the author had responded to. The username was #Fundam3ntalTr&th, and this was the only post they'd ever wrote or contributed to.

An unwanted memory emerged, of Khayr embracing that Coznarian whore. It had only been three days ago, but the events of the past few days had stretched time.

Of course, the woman hadn't really been a whore; she'd been an agent or emissary, someone with whom the king was discussing hiring a mercenary army of some sort, or possibly advanced weaponry. Claribel could not erase the memory of the fair-skinned, small Coznarian woman.

Something clicked in her mind. SycoraxSurvivor's post had talked about a military research facility beyond Vesta's belt, and King Khayr had been talking with that woman about something similar. Could they be connected?

Claribel sent a message to Abdel, and he was by her side within seconds. "Yes, your majesty?"

"How hard would it be to look at security footage of the palace from three days ago?"

"You've found something."

She shook her head. "Probably nothing, but it's worth a shot."

"What would I be looking for?"

Claribel glanced around, making sure no one was close enough to hear her whisper. Nozrel was on the other side of the room. "I want to get a good look at a woman who met with the king three days ago on the east balcony."

Abdel's face went pale. "Your majesty, I really don't think this type of thing is appropriate for me to search for . . ."

Claribel flushed, suddenly uncertain of a request which had seemed so reasonable moments before. "No, it's not like that. I overheard them talking and wanted to know more about her business."

Abdel gave her an incredulous look.

"No, not that kind of business," she said.

Abdel stole a glance at Nozrel. "That makes it more precarious. You're asking me to spy on my king. Nozrel has five analysts in a separate room monitoring the rest of us, checking for duplicity. I can't help you, my lady. Sorry."

Abdel scurried away, his usual boldness gone.

Claribel wasn't sure what embarrassed her more, that her request seemed jealous and petty, or that Abdel thought he knew exactly what the Conzarian woman had been doing with her husband.

As she tried to calm herself and refocus, the doors opened and Khayr entered. He wore his formal military uniform, golden embroidery on his shoulders adorned a form-fitting cream coat and indicated his preeminent rank. The rest of the uniform was white, as bright as sunlit snow. A large gold belt wrapped loosely around his waist, holding a large ceremonial sword on his left hip. The entire outfit emphasized his intimidating physicality.

Every analyst had turned to look at him. Their faces, even Abdel's, lit with admiration, not like the fearful respect shown the High Regent on Lanopi. These men loved King Khayr, and their eager glances looked more like adoring fans or religious acolytes than fearful subjects. Everything Khayr built underneath his throne was nearly the opposite of what the High Regent had built beneath hers.

He surveyed the room and walked briskly toward her. Claribel smoothed her dress and hoped her embarrassment from moments before would not show.

"Good morning, my queen." His deep voice rang through the room.

"Good day, King Khayr."

"Nozrel says we have had a bit of a breakthrough."

The mousy man sidled up to Khayr at the mention of his name. Nozrel's face held none of the adoration her analysts had when looking on their king. His semi-permanent scowl had been replaced by a cool, blank facade. Claribel needed to watch that man closely.

"Update please," the king said.

"One of our analysts traced the strange message to Lazlo to the Vesta system," Nozrel said. "Not sure what that means, but we're digging further. We've discovered nothing else about the High Regent's whereabouts."

Claribel walked up to the two men and stood beside her husband. "What does the word Sycorax mean to you?"

For a moment, she thought the king's breath caught and his eyes widened. But the nervousness disappeared so quickly that Claribel wasn't sure she'd seen it at all.

"Only that it was in that strange message to the Lanopian science advisor."

Her new husband might be a skilled liar, but she'd been trained by the High Regent and could taste a lie when fed one.

"The search continues with Lazlo's known associates," Nozrel said, as if Claribel had not spoken of Sycorax. "We are close to finding a motive and hopefully an accomplice."

"This was an elaborate plan," the king said, "perpetuated by someone with great resources and skill." The king paused, his eyes distant.

"Likely done by an enemy of Lanopi," Nozrel added.

"Likely," Khayr said. "But we need to walk carefully here. The known systems rest on an uneasy peace; I'd rather not tip it over until we're ready."

The king turned to Claribel and smiled. "You and I have not had much time together since the wedding. Would you like to walk with me?"

Claribel looked back at her screen, eager to continue her search. Then she surveyed the team of dedicated analysts. She had duties beyond here, and they called to her. "Of course, my king."

• • •

The king and queen walked through the palace gardens, their pace slow and deliberate. Claribel held Khayr's arm, his lean muscles flexing beneath his military uniform. He presented a striking figure, almost like a hero from an old tale, strong in battle, both political and physical, yet kind and gentle. But Claribel had been raised to be wary of such people; she had seen the persona the High Regent showed in public and the vicious person behind the mask. It would be many years before she could know the real Khayr.

The palace gardens matched anything Claribel had seen on Lanopi. Paths meandered through collections of bushes, trees, and flowers. The gardens smelled like a stand selling perfumes on the streets of Iopa, dozens of scents blending together in strong but pleasant aroma. The air, so often dry on Nootee, hung heavier with the humidity which must be necessary to keep such a stunning display vibrantly alive.

The famed, tiny insect-birds flitted about between the bright flowers, their wings resembling a dragonfly, but their bodies like a tiny lizard with a twitching tale, its mouth curving into a dark beak. Some Lanopians spent a small fortune importing the birds as pets. Khayr kept hundreds of the native creatures in this private garden.

The most striking element of the gardens were the dancing flowers, a native plant of Nooteezia. The straight green stems ended in a bulb of brilliant color: bright red, soft blue, or perfect white, matching the colors of the Nooteezian flag. But the flowers were not known for their beauty, but for the unique relationship they shared with music. A soft, peppy song played through the gardens, guitars and strings, and the flowers swayed with the music in what looked like a choreographed routine. The insect-birds floated among the flowers, entering the dance. When the music shifted to another song, the flowers changed their motion, flowing from roots to petals to a slower, softer tune.

Claribel concentrated on their beauty, trying to still her mind. The passion she felt when she remembered the woman on the balcony confounded her. Her and Khayr's union was a political one, not some girlish story plucked from page or screen. She had assumed Khayr would take other women, and that she would likely find her passion somewhere else as well; that was the way of marital alliances.

They walked in silence, Claribel waiting because he'd made the invitation. Khayr wanted to say something, but she was content to let him take his time.

"We are planning a rescue mission to Vesta." His voice hovered softly above the music filling the gardens. That wasn't what she thought he might say.

"A rescue mission? How? Why?"

"We have a new technology which will allow us to jump into the Vesta system beyond the asteroid belt."

Claribel tried to keep her face even; such technology would be a massive tactical advantage. Starjumping was limited to discovered access points in each system. Most systems only had one, and satellites were needed on both ends to safely facilitate the jump. Blind starjumps, as they we called, without a known access point or satellite link, were extremely dangerous and, therefore, extremely rare.

"How would you do that safely?"

"We have a new starjumper, a military secret. It uses its own computations, does not depend on starjump satellites to connect to its destination. Our mathematicians and starjump engineers have been working on it for two decades. We can jump farther and faster than any other starjumpers in the known systems. Speed isn't particularly necessary in this situation, but since Vesta has only the one starjump point, we can change the situation by jumping beyond the belt."

Claribel whistled softly. A fleet of ships not bound by the current paradigm of starjump physics. Typically only three ships could move at a time using predetermined access points. But if a fleet could move wherever it wanted without these restrictions, this would change everything. Right now, controlling the starjump satellites meant controlling entrance into a system.

"Farther? Like how far?"

"Two starjumps in one."

Claribel stopped, and Khayr did as well. That meant the Nooteezians could jump directly to Lanopi or Mantalo, avoiding Vesta or Fortuna. They could also reach Regno without going through rival Eslaza. The political, military, and trade implications of such technology were massive.

"I won't bore you with the particulars," Khayr continued, "most of which I don't understand myself. I'm a sheep herder and a warrior, not a scientist. But we have three small, working starjumpers with this capability, and seven more under construction."

"Fully armed?" she asked.

"Yes. Photon bombs, plasma cannons, and nuclear weapons. When complete, we could starjump into Eslaza undetected and lay waste to their planet before their navy even mobilized against us."

The High Regent had chosen her ally well. Had Rissa known about this advantage?

"Was the woman with you on the balcony involved in the construction of these starjumpers?" Claribel asked, thinking back on the words they'd spoken before kissing.

Khayr blushed, and then continued their slow walk, pulling Claribel beside him. "No, that is a different project." He didn't share more, and she decided to not push that topic, not yet.

They walked for several minutes as Claribel digested his revelation. The king had used Eslaza as his example, but the same could be said of Lanopi. Once completed, he could send these new ships to her home world and decimate it. Apart from the massive Camsartran navy, this innovation gave Nooteezia military superiority to every other system, a secret weapon hatching countless possibilities. Even the threat of this technology would shift the balance of power across the known systems to Nooteezia.

"Do you know why I follow our ancient religion?" Khayr asked, breaking the silence. She shook her head and he continued: "As I fought to expel our Camsartran masters all those years ago, I had abandoned the religion of my mother as foolishness. I indulged every passion, and as the hero of my people, women were more than willing to give me what I wanted." He blushed again.

Claribel blushed with him. "Your majesty, this really isn't . . ."

"Please," he said. "This must be said. After the Camsartans were expelled, I turned to uniting my people. But my lasciviousness had poisoned us. Though I only took what was offered, I did not realize the coercion that went on without my express knowledge. These women gave themselves to me, often under threat of . . ." Khayr looked to the ground, a slow growl in his throat.

"And it had spread to all my leaders," he continued. "The old ways of treating women with high respect had been replaced by seeing them merely as objects. When I finally stepped back and opened my eyes, I was disgusted by me and by my people. We had freed ourselves from bondage but in so doing had taken on a lustful, invisible master."

They walked past a few more beds of dancing flowers before Khayr finished. "It's then that I looked back to my mother's teaching. I adored her when she lived, but I had dishonored her in death. So I reconverted to the ancient religion, and under my influence, the ways of Nathree became the predominant belief system once again on our world. Our savior and prophet was a woman, and yet we treated them as little more than cattle."

Khayr stopped and stepped in front of Claribel, folding her small hands into his. Under his intense glare, she almost turned her head. The form of the woman from the balcony appeared in her mind: fair skin, wide hips, full figure. Claribel looked like a teenage boy in comparison.

But despite her fear, she held his eyes.

"I should not have been with that woman. I covenanted long ago to discipline myself. But we needed a reason to meet, and she convinced me that it would keep up appearances in case anyone caught us from a distance."

"It certainly convinced me," she said, looking away from his eyes for a moment.

Khayr frowned. "And it was wrong. I believe she hoped to manipulate me with it. But never again. Tonight I would like us to dine, together. We can grow to know each other as people usually do before marriage. I know I must earn your trust and respect, but through the love of Nathree, I hope to gain it."

Claribel did not know how to respond. She had not expected this, an attempt at romance. She had not wanted this. It would be cleaner and safer to keep their union as a purely plutonic alliance. But even as the thought crossed her mind, she could hear the taint of Rissa's philosophies on it. The one hundred and seventy-fifth maxim played in her mind: *Romance should be reserved for poets, actors, and fools. This attachment will be used by your enemies and will make you blind to reality.*

But Claribel would not be her mother. And she could certainly understand a religious awakening. She wanted to share with him, her own conversion, the light she'd found for her own soul through the words of Palo. But not yet.

"I would love that. Tonight?"

"Yes. It would have to be. I leave with the starjumper in the morning."

She dropped his hands. "You're leading the expedition to Vesta? But you're the king. You can't run around the known systems like a soldier."

"A king is not greater than his lowest soldier. There is great risk in this, and I must carry it as surely as they do."

"But you must let your people bear the burdens, let your people play their part."

He smiled, and Claribel chastised herself for letting it soften her heart. "I appreciate and will always welcome your counsel, but I shall lead my men into Vesta. Hopefully all we'll find is a stranded starjumper and a grateful crew."

Claribel smiled, but she knew that this would not be resolved that cleanly. Whatever was happening beyond that asteroid belt was bigger than they knew.

chapter 42

MIRAM AND THANAN

riel floated through the trees, their form stretched to near invisibility. The sun burned hot. They could sense the temperature, but it made little difference to them; they were as comfortable in the cold of deep space as they were near the surface of a burning star. But Miram and Thanan felt it, sweat beading on their foreheads.

The young son of the High Regent stood almost a foot taller than the diminutive Miram. He walked wearily, his eyes constantly scanning the forest for danger from this alien world. He dressed in his gray military uniform, though it was burned and tattered from his crash landing. Equal parts caution and anger lit his face.

Miram tried conversing with him, but he said little. She looked so small and young next to him. Sparo's vision of romance blossoming between his daughter and the High Regent's son seemed even more ridiculous now as Ariel watched them interact. Thanan wasn't interacting with the teenage girl in a flirtatious manner; his tone was cautious and formal.

As was often the case, Miram seemed oblivious. Nine years on Vesta II had warped her personality. She only interacted with a distracted and distant father, a socially inept genetic super soldier, and an alien being whose most earnest desire was to leave. It came as no surprise that Miram was awkward in her first non-father human interaction.

"I love trees, bugs, and animals," Miram blurted as they walked. "I draw them a lot."

Thanan smiled, like he was addressing a small child. "I like nature, too."

She beamed at him, as if his minor confirmation of a mutual interest was a strong point of relation. Miram's expectations, like her father's, were likely to be dashed against the sharp rocks of reality.

The pair made their way through the forest and crested the hill near the northern entrance to the facility. At the top of the hill, Thanan stopped suddenly, eyeing a figure standing near the door: Sparo.

"Who's that?" Thanan asked.

Miram stopped several feet in front of the young space pilot, her body leaning toward her father. "That's my father. We should go meet him."

Thanan's eyes held worry, and his feet did not move.

Miram stepped back toward him and reached to take his hand. Thanan began to flinch before he relaxed and allowed her to hold his hand.

"My father is a good man. Let's go meet him."

Thanan sucked in a deep breath, and then gave in as she tugged him down the grassy hill.

With the sun burning fiercely overhead, sweat covered Sparo's face. He wore his flowing white robes, a garment of his own creation. His eyes were bright, as alert as they'd been in years. He leaned slightly on his staff, the ball on top of it swirling with a cloudy blue. His appearance looked like images of a mighty wizard from ancient human stories. And as tall and strong as Thanan was, Sparo stood taller and wider still.

"Introduce me to your new friend." Sparo's voice held no warmth or welcome.

"His name is Thanan. He's a space pilot." Miram still held stubbornly to Thanan's reluctant hand. "Can he stay with us, Father?"

"Things have changed since I sent you to look for him," Sparo responded.

"You are Sparo," Thanan said, "former senator of Onal."

Sparo spared a quick, dangerous smile. "You know who we are."

"Yes. I was young, but my mother told us about your betrayal." He pulled his hand away from Miram's. "You tried to kill my sister."

Miram's eyes widened. "You tried to kill a little girl?"

Sparo's gaze held Thanan, and he did not respond to his daughter's question.

"Now you will have your revenge," Thanan continued. "I'm just glad my sister is safely out of your grasp."

"You are a foolish young man," Sparo replied. "How dare you come to my home and accuse me of anything. You know nothing except the despicable lies your parents have nursed you on since you were born."

Thanan's face and fists clenched in anger, but he said nothing.

"This is my world," Sparo continued, waving his hands in a large gesture. "You are my guest."

"Guest or prisoner?" Thanan asked.

Sparo's dangerous smile returned, this time bigger, and it stayed on his bearded face. "Both. I will do you no harm, but I can't have you interfering with what I must do."

Thanan charged Sparo, but Ariel quickly entered the young man's mind and put him to sleep. Thanan collapsed at Sparo's feet as Ariel appeared next to their master in their human form.

"Well done, Ariel."

Ariel looked at Thanan's slumped body and said nothing.

"Father!" Miram squealed. "What have you done to my friend?"

"Things have changed, Miram. He's a part of this now, and I didn't know that when I sent you to fetch him." Sparo's dangerous expression fled before a wave of exhaustion. He rubbed his temples. "So much betrayal. So much . . ."

"He didn't betray you." She stepped forward and kneeled next to Thanan. "He was a boy then." She gently touched Thanan's head. "He's so beautiful, so interesting. A man."

Sparo's self-satisfied grin returned. Ariel did not like the light burning in his eyes. Its darkness, which used to only shadow Balith, now hovered over the young man and Sparo's own daughter. Their essence flickered, wishing they did not have to play a part in this human depravity.

"I will not harm him," he said. "He is a prisoner only until I complete what I need to do. He is our guest."

"I wonder what he looks like underneath his uniform." Miram stroked his hair.

Ariel waited for a rebuke from Sparo at Miram's forward language, but he said nothing. If it had not been clear to Ariel before, it was clear now: Sparo would spark whatever flame he deemed necessary, and he did not care who it burned.

"Go inside, Miram." Sparo stepped beside her. "I'm sorry we made your friend sleep, but he'll be awake soon. I'll make sure you have time alone with him."

Miram stood and kissed the hair on her father's chin. "I forgive you." She looked back at Thanan and then walked toward the facility.

As soon as the door closed behind her, Sparo leaned more heavily on his staff and his face slumped, the gravity of his exhaustion overcoming his forced alertness.

"Involving the young man and Miram is not necessary," Ariel said, hoping beyond reason that Sparo might finally see the level of his folly.

Sparo closed his eyes against the midday sun. Sweat dripped on either side of his eyes and down his nose. "This is how it must be. These choices are not mine; this life was forced upon me. But I will see it through."

Ariel wanted to scream that fate had nothing to do with any of this. But reason had fled Sparo's mind and there was little hope of restoring it today.

"What next?" they asked.

Sparo considered the question for several moments before responding. Ariel clung to the silence, afraid of his next step.

"We put Thanan safely away," he finally said, "and then we show my brother and Alazar the same measure of mercy they extended to my sweet Eliel."

chapter 43

THE NIGHT AFTER

laribel forced herself awake on her third attempt. Piera patiently watched from a chair, reading something on her pad. Claribel's Nooteezian servant Danda was notably absent.

"You were up late," Piera said casually, not looking up from her pad.

Claribel groaned. She'd had too much Nooteezian wine the night before, and her aching head and clouded mind confirmed it.

The night had been lovely. Khayr had treated her to dinner in his suite, just the two of them talking. Khayr spoke of his mother and her influence on his reign. Claribel remained guarded about her family, sharing only part of the distance she felt with her mother. The king seemed to be opening up, forging a true relationship. But she had guarded her feelings, not completely open to sharing the deepest parts of her.

But then the wine had kicked in. The High Regent looked down on alcohol consumption, particularly in political meetings, and Claribel knew that, despite the soft lamp light, the wine, and the privacy, the dinner had been a political meeting.

Her tongue had loosened, mostly about her mother. Memories were fuzzy, but she remembered calling her mother names and crying about her missing brother.

She groaned again. The next memories were fuzzier still, and embarrassing. She was mostly sure she'd spent several minutes extolling the king's fine figure and had even walked clumsily around the table to give him a kiss. He'd called for Piera and Danda, and they'd carried her back to her chambers. She remembered nothing else.

Had she been manipulated? No, the wine on Nooteezia was known for being stronger than on Lanopi. She had been careless, acting more the child than the adult.

"Bring me the strongest coffee you can find," Claribel told Piera, resting her heavy head back on the pillow. "And whatever Nooteezians take, eat, or drink for a hangover."

After the coffee and some tasty meat-filled biscuits, she began to feel herself again. She ate hungrily trying to avoid Piera's amused expression.

"You're not my mother," Claribel chastened. "I can take care of myself."

"Really?" Piera laughed lightly. "So Danda and I didn't carry you away from the king's suite as you went on and on about how much you wanted to see him naked?"

Claribel flinched. "When did I say that?"

"You shouted it, but luckily we were away from the king and in a back hallway between your room and his. Danda and I had a good laugh, but no one else heard."

Claribel sighed. "Danda has probably shared that with the entire staff."

Piera shook her head, stealing a little biscuit from Claribel's plate and stuffing into her mouth. "Danda is a quiet one and not just around us. She doesn't interact much with the other servants."

"Where is she?"

"Exercising." Piera eyed another piece of biscuit but held still. "The girl gets up early every morning and exercises for two hours. No wonder she looks like she could crush most men."

It was true; Danda was nearly as muscular as Khayr. The thought made Claribel blush, as she recalled an attempt from last night at a poem spoken in Lanopian praising the king's thighs. She sincerely hoped that Khayr was not pretending to not understand her native tongue.

Danda joined them an hour later after Piera had readied Claribel. It was mid-morning, and Khayr and his expedition had left orbit to prepare the blind starjump to Vesta. They might already be there. The two servants followed her to the intelligence center to get an update on the king's progress.

Nozrel stood in the waiting area, surrounded by whispering analysts. He looked up as she entered and moved toward her. His eyes flicked to the servants but then back to Claribel.

"Good morning, Queen Claribel." He bowed slightly. "Your servants have not been cleared; I'd ask that they wait outside."

Claribel nodded at her attendants. They backed into the hall. She turned to Nozrel. "Any updates?"

The man squirmed as if spies might spontaneously spring from the wall of his own intelligence center. "We should speak in private."

He led her to an adjacent room, a small glass enclosure with a door to the waiting area. "I'm sorry for the precautions," Nozrel said, closing the door behind him.

"My maidservant Piera is trustworthy, and I assume your staff vetted Danda."

"I'm not really worried about your servants." He stared out at the lobby.

Who could he be worried about? What was the man hiding even from his own people?

"Against my better judgement," he continued, "the king led a team on one of our Bizretrir."

"Bizretrir?"

"It's the name of a small rodent in Boort. Devious little creatures who burrow through almost anything." He coated his words with admiration. "I believe the king told you of the ships yesterday and their . . . unique capabilities."

Claribel nodded. She noticed a visible change in the man's countenance. He usually emitted nervous energy like Khayr projected confidence. But today he was different. His darting eyes and twitching fingers suggested a manic energy, a battle lust.

"It will be a few more minutes before we know if the ships made it to Vesta safely. But the Bizretrir were tested extensively, and we're confident they will succeed." Nozrel's expression indicated that wasn't his only concern.

"Good. I would like to return to the intelligence center and continue my investigation."

She stood to leave, but Nozrel lightly grabbed her arm. Claribel almost flinched at the touch.

"Stop looking into anything unrelated to the task at hand," he said, his eyes fiercer than before. "I will ensure the safety of Nooteezia by all means at my disposal."

She focused, forcing her growing anger down. She would use it later, but she had to remain clear-headed now. She pulled her arm away in a soft, fluid motion.

"I am queen of Nooteezia. What goal could I have that threatens the safety of this world?"

"The king and I disagree on much," he replied. "For example, I think leading the expedition to Vesta is dangerous and foolish. He is my king, and I will carry out his instructions. But where vagaries exist, I will do what needs to be done."

So many possible implications coated his threat that it was hard to unravel his potential intent. Clearly he'd disapproved of the marriage and her involvement in this investigation. Was it sexism? Distrust because she was a foreigner? Or did Nozrel carry his own agenda outside even Khayr's knowledge, a dangerous and sly rival like Senator Mura Chani was to the High Regent?

"If you could specify what you'd like me not to research, it would make this easier. Clearly you're monitoring my activities."

"Sycorax," he said. "Stop looking into Sycorax."

Sycorax. So she had stumbled onto something important, something hidden from view. Nozrel's normal skittishness returned for a moment before being absorbed into his manic energy. He hid something, but from whom? Just Claribel, or from Khayr as well?

"You are probably right." She smoothed her face into placidity. "I'll return to my room. Please send me an update about the king when we have one."

Nozrel's brow furrowed in confusion. He hadn't expected her to back down so easily. Good. She needed to keep him guessing.

"As you wish, Queen Claribel. As the king stated, you are always welcome here."

"Yes." She smiled, forcing as genuine a smile as she could muster. "Your hospitality is noted."

She walked into the hall. Piera and Danda hurried to catch her.

When they were halfway to her chambers, Claribel stopped and faced Danda.

"You are released from your duties for the day," she said. It was likely Danda was a plant, placed close to Claribel to monitor the new queen. She couldn't risk the woman's possible duplicity.

"But I . . ."

Claribel glared, and the taller woman shrunk into a bow.

"As you say, my lady." She gave one more glance, and then hurried away.

Claribel marched toward her rooms, Piera struggling to keep pace. She left Piera in the sitting room, saying she wanted some time alone. Once inside, she brought out the pad Thanan had altered all those years ago. She hadn't tried to use it during her short time on Nooteezia, but she needed it now. She would use its secure connection and dig to the bottom of the Sycorax puzzle. This was all connected, and she needed to find out how these pieces fit together.

Once she got onto the jumpnet, she went to an obscure board for entertainment news, finding a thread about the Fortunan singer Bith. She found username 66Dix8889. Good; he was on net. She sent him a direct message: *Call me sexy. Unusual channel.* She pressed send and then went to another board, a Mantaloan sight for fishing. She clicked on its voice chat app. Moments later, her pad blinked indicating an incoming transmission.

"Are we secure?" a male voice asked.

"As secure as I can be," she replied.

"I guess I should call you your highness or something like that."

Claribel smiled. Fon was one of her oldest contacts. She'd connected with him when she was only thirteen. He'd been a source for her grandfather but had been turned aside by Rissa after she took over grandfather's intelligence network. They'd struck up a relationship a bit more than she had with other sources, and she enjoyed his advice and perspective.

"Not necessary. We only have a few minutes. I can't be sure how long this will be secure."

"Then how can I help? I assume this is about the disappearance of the ship."

"Yes. Have you heard anything?"

"Very little, which is strange." He paused. "There are rumors the High Regent has disappeared and wasn't on the starjumper bound for Vesta."

Claribel knew how the game worked. She needed to give him something in exchange for what she was shortly going to ask. "I can tell you she wasn't registered on the *Marsil* and she chartered a starjumper to Fortuna but the ship arrived there without her."

Fon whistled. She'd never met the man, but she'd seen a picture from grandfather's archives. He'd be nearly seventy years old, with wispy white hair on his otherwise bald head.

"So it's true. Where did that slippery jump fish go?"

Claribel treated the question as rhetorical. "I've been digging around and looking into something that might be related, and I was hoping you could help. What can you tell me about Sycorax?"

Fon remained silent for several moments. Claribel glanced to make sure they hadn't lost their connection.

"Stay away from this one, dear," he finally said. "You don't want to shine light on that dark corner of the galaxy."

She leaned back in her chair. Fon had never been nervous or hesitant to discuss anything. What made Sycorax so dangerous?

"There are references to Sycorax in regards to Vesta," she continued, "and I think it may have a connection here on Nooteezia as well. Everyone seems to want to dissuade me."

"You should listen." His voice grew softer, like he was afraid someone might be listening. "I'll give you what I know, but I won't be responsible for what happens next. And you can't contact me again for a year. If you agree to that, I'll talk."

Claribel felt her stomach drop. What made a man like Fon that scared? His entire life hung on the edge of danger, and yet the mention of Sycorax had sent him into a near panic. But she had to know.

"Agreed."

Fon sighed. "All right." He paused. "Your grandfather hired Sycorax to help him create an army a generation ago."

"Is Sycorax a person or an organization?"

"Both, I think, but no one knows for sure. I connected Marsil to a broker who dealt with Sycorax. They had a secret facility on Vesta II developing weapons for Lanopi."

So it was connected. She needed more, but these strange pieces were fitting together.

"Marsil spent billions on this," Fon continued, "but it never turned into anything."

"What happened to Vesta II?" she asked.

"I don't know. Lazlo, the science advisor, led the project. I heard he shut it down thirty years ago."

Lazlo. So he had been involved. Maybe Sycorax, or some part of it, still existed on Vesta II and that was who he'd been contacting.

"Why are you so nervous about this?" she asked. "Sounds like an arms deal gone wrong."

"Not an arms deal, dear," he said. "A genetically engineered army."

Holy heaven above. Claribel had read rumors of this kind of thing, but genetic creation of new life was highly regulated, limited by the Genetic Accords signed more than a century before by all the systems except Regno. Though the Heavener religion had not played a significant role in the Genetic Accords, Palo had been explicitly clear that genetic manipulation disqualified one for happiness in the Well of Souls. Claribel shared that moral view on the subject; creating life, especially for one's own gain.

"You get involved in a lot of illegal things. Why does this make you nervous? What about Sycorax makes you so worried?"

"Remember that broker I mentioned?" he asked. "He died days after Lazlo's trip to Vesta II. Every other broker I've known who's dealt with Sycorax directly is dead. Assassins arrive in the night, throats cut or heads missing . . ." His voice trailed off.

"But what about Nooteezia?"

"Rumors swirl that your new husband might be working with Sycorax. He's been seen with a young Coznarian woman."

Claribel was glad Fon couldn't see her blush. "So?"

"Marsil's contact with Sycorax was a young Coznarian woman."

"But that's decades apart."

"I'm not saying it's the same woman, dear, I'm just saying it's the same method of contact. Your husband might be trying to build an army just like your grandfather was."

Khayr had called his involvement with the woman *another project*. That had been quite an understatement.

"I urge you to drop this." Fon's voice was tense, strained like he had a knife to his throat. "Sycorax is dangerous. They kill without mercy, they operate outside any law or treaty. And they play all sides. They've taken money and worked for half the known systems in the previous few decades. And despite that duplicity, they seem to continue to operate freely."

"I'm sorry if I've put you in any danger."

"Good luck, dear. May the stars watch over you."

"No, wait . . ." The connection ended, terminated by Fon.

Claribel set the pad down. She needed to think. Should she tell Khayr what she'd discovered about his plans and the connection to Vesta and Lanopi? It was possible he already knew. Maybe she should reach out to Lanopi and share what she'd learned with Oratt?

Though she felt sure of what she'd learned, she wasn't sure she had enough to convince the Second Regent of anything, and now that she'd connected Sycorax to Khayr, she couldn't be sure the Nooteese weren't more connected to this than she'd believed.

Claribel took a deep breath and closed her eyes. She would find peace in meditation, think through what she wanted to do. Her next step might be the most important one of her life.

chapter 44

A NEW PURPOSE

he night had been tense, no sleeping. Caliban tried to let them sleep, said he could stay awake. But Phana and Trinc clung to their weapons.

After listening intently hours before, Caliban was certain they were hunted by four creatures. Two were pointy-nosed wolves, which he'd told his companions. Since he'd also said the pointy-nosed meanies hunted in packs, Phana and Trinc assumed all four creatures were meanies. But two of them were much worse.

His blue lizard brothers. They were here, one hundred yards away. Certainly they knew it was Caliban, but they had not approached from their hiding place over the hill. Were they still mad at Caliban for killing Balthazar and throwing Mother off the cliff? And there were two wolves as well, their heartbeats near the brothers. Did the wolves follow his brothers? Were they pets? Friends?

"Why aren't they getting closer?" Trinc asked.

Caliban ignored him, focusing on the heartbeats pulsing above the hill. The pointy-nosed wolves were anxious; they could smell the stinky humans and wanted meat. Even with his limp, Caliban could outrun the weak humans, leaving a kill for each of the wolves. If his brothers released their pets, Caliban would run.

"Great," Trinc said. "We're being hunted by alien dogs and our guide's become mute."

"Silence." Phana walked up behind Caliban. "We should keep moving. Maybe they're afraid to attack us."

"Maybe." Caliban kept his eyes on the hill. The wolves' hearts beat faster. "Phana right; we should keep moving."

They walked briskly along the ridge, approaching the eastern entrance Caliban had used on Mother's last day. On Balthazar's last day. He hoped approaching it again did not make this his last day.

His brothers and the wolves followed slowly, not closing the distance. They stayed far enough behind to remain hidden. Nothing about this made sense. Caliban had not seen his brothers since that day. If they had survived, why hadn't they shown themselves before? And how did they become friends with pointy-nosed wolves? Caliban shook his head, trying to shake the troublesome thoughts free.

After coming over a small ridge, they could see the facility a few miles in the distance, the shining silver dimmed by time and gray dust. But it still looked out of place on the gray plains, like a shiny scaled fish on soft ground.

"By Chimra, what is that?" Trinc asked.

"A confirmation," Phana said.

Caliban understood all of her words, but little of her meaning.

"You can get us in there?"

"Yes, but we won't make it. They're getting closer now. They know Mother's place means safety for us."

Phana looked behind them, and Caliban turned. On the next ridge by the cliff stood his brothers with their pets.

Trinc pointed his magic gun at Caliban. "You slippery little devil. You fed us into a trap."

Despite Trinc's magic gun, Caliban did not flinch. He would flinch before no one. He had killed Balthazar when no one else could. He had killed Mother when no one else could. And he would lead these two humans or his brothers to kill Sparo.

"I said only two meanies," he said. "The other two not Caliban's friends. Caliban has only one friend, and she prettier than them."

Phana motioned with her arm, and Trinc lowered his gun. "Are they going to hurt us?"

Caliban shrugged.

"Great." Trinc eyed Caliban and his hand twitched. "We're being led by an idiot."

"Caliban not idiot," he said. "Caliban just not talk if Caliban not have something to say. Not like humans, who talk to hear their own squeaks."

Trinc glared at Caliban but said nothing.

"Could you talk with them? Find out what they want?" Phana looked at Caliban, her eyes soft, not like Trinc's nasty glare or Sparo's demeaning look. And her eyes weren't like Mother's knowing look, or Miram's kind eyes. Phana was different than other humans, though Caliban didn't know if that was good or bad.

"Caliban can talk with them." But he didn't want to. He wanted to run and hide, but it was too late for that.

He limped across the plain between the hills. His brothers watched him, their eyes holding the fear he'd last seen. As he grew closer, he could hear their breathing, rapid and nervous. Were they still scared of Caliban? Would they do what Caliban said? Even though they'd obeyed him all those years ago when he'd told them to run away, Caliban couldn't imagine a world where anyone listened to anything he said.

"Caliban. You're alive." The brother on the left spoke in Mother's language.

"As are you, brothers." It felt strange to speak in Mother's tongue again. He also hoped they thought of him as a brother, even if they never had before. But before there had been many blue lizard men, and now there were only two, and Caliban.

"Brothers?" the second one spat. "You left us to die."

Caliban stood as tall as he could. "You left Caliban first, mocked Caliban. Why would Caliban treat you well? I didn't kill you like I did Balthazar and Mother. That was nice."

The second one glared, a darker look than Trinc's moments before. But the first lizard man seemed worried, not angry.

"Why did you come here?" Caliban asked.

"We saw the human ships fall from space," the first one said. "We saw the other humans, the man and the girl, land years ago. We left you alone, but we tire of living off the land, trying to survive. It is time for us to come home, time for us to return to what Sycorax left behind."

Sycorax. That's what everyone else called Mother. Why didn't the blue lizard men call her their mother?

"I found two space people. My new master found more, I think."

"Who's your new master?" the first one asked.

Sparo would not be happy about all these visitors and probably wouldn't want more lizard men. But maybe he would. They could be more servants to work under his bad magic. The blue lizard men had been cruel to Caliban, but they didn't deserve to serve under Sparo's mean hand; no one deserved that.

"The other man you saw land all those moons ago," Caliban said. "But he's mean, meaner than Mother. Sparo thinks we are animals. You not want to work for Sparo."

"What about these humans?" The first one looked behind Caliban at Phana and Trinc standing on the opposite hill. "What do they want?"

"What do any humans want?" he answered. "Control. Food. Servants. Slaves." Saying the words made him angry. If Sparo had been there, despite the worst pain, he would have killed him. Caliban hated Sparo.

"Can we trust them?"

Caliban wasn't entirely sure what hope sounded like, but maybe the first one spoke with hope.

"No." Caliban looked back at Phana, and then to his brothers. "But we can use them. They help us kill Sparo, and then we find real freedom."

"Freedom?" The second one said. "We already have freedom." The pointy-nosed wolf at his side growled. "I want food. I want comfort. Freedom is for humans, not for us."

Caliban did not like the second lizard man.

"Maybe we can have it all," the first one said. "Caliban, my name is Dax, and this is Stacra."

"What happened to the other?" Caliban asked.

They exchanged a glance.

"He died years ago," the second one, Stacra, mummured. "We're not even sure why. Got sick one day, dead the next."

"We don't want to live out here anymore," Dax said. "We don't want to live on these plains, hunting like animals for our next meal. We want to go home. Can you help us get home?"

Caliban looked at the next hill and thought of Mother's building. It had been his home most of his life, but it did not feel like home today. Could Phana help him make it a nice home, a welcoming home? Or would he simply trade mean masters? The only difference might be Phana was nicer to look at with breasts and womanly form, but Mother had been pretty, and pretty women could be as cruel as ugly men. Would anything be different?

Maybe not. But could it grow worse? Probably not.

"Caliban can try to help."

"Good," Dax said, licking his lips. "Let's meet these humans."

The second brother, Stacra, pulled out a small white thing and popped it into his mouth. He handed one to the first, who did the same.

"What that?" Caliban asked.

"You don't have to take these?" Stacra questioned.

Caliban shook his head.

"The zinc deficiency was only in the later generations," Dax said.

"Lucky bastard."

Bastard. That's what Balthazar had called them, the name he'd given himself and Caliban. It felt good to be a bastard again. Mother's three children walked across the empty plain with the two wolves stalking beside their masters.

"How did you get pet pointy-nosed meanies?" Caliban asked.

"We killed their parents for food," Stacra said. "We raised them as pups. They help us hunt and keep us from being lonely."

"They are friends?"

"The only friends we've ever had besides each other," Stacra replied. His answer made Caliban lonely and sad.

As they approached Phana and Trinc, the two humans gripped their guns but kept them lowered. Maybe if they killed the humans, Caliban's brothers could use the magic guns. He had never learned to use guns, but the blue lizard men had. If Phana did not help them, maybe her magic weapons would be enough to beat Sparo.

"Stop there please," Phana said in Sparo's tongue.

The brothers stopped and looked unknowingly at Caliban. Of course. They didn't speak this language. And they probably still thought they were smarter than Caliban, especially mean looking Stacra.

"They no speak like that," Caliban said.

Phana switch to Mother's language. "Stop there please." Did all humans speak both languages? "Are you friend or foe?"

"That depends," Dax replied. "What is your intention?"

"To treat you as you deserve to be treated." Phana's voice remained calm despite facing three lizard men and two pointy-nosed wolves. She was brave like Mother. "You are wonders, created to fight and kill. I will give you that chance."

"You'd make us slaves," Stacra spat.

"No. I would employ you like I would human soldiers. But I'd pay you more, treat you even better. You're even more valuable than human soldiers. You are better, stronger. But you need purpose. I can give you that."

Caliban looked to his brothers. Their shoulders slumped, and their eyes widened with yearning. Phana's words were like human sweetbread covered in sticky honey, delicious, leaving him wanting more with each bite.

"What purpose?" Dax asked.

Phana put her gun away at her hip. "First, we rid this world of Caliban's master and take its discoveries and wonders as our own."

Caliban's heart beat faster, and he leaned forward. Sweet, sticky words.

"Then we set our eyes on other worlds," she continued, "getting you three where you can do what you were meant to do: kill. You'd be my knives, cutting out whatever stood in our way. And you'd live like kings, better than all but a few humans. Every lust and desire fulfilled as long as you stayed loyal to me."

Phana walked closer, and even the pointy-nosed wolves seemed pacified, their thick tails still for the first time. The tall woman stood above a crouched Caliban.

"You, Caliban, have been abused, cast aside as nothing more than a servant, a pet. Your masters thought you dumb. They did not see your loyalty or your strength. I see it, Caliban. No more mean magic, no more cruel masters. No more misery."

Caliban felt warm inside, excited by the sweetbread words. Her promises seemed pulled from his mind. Did she have greater magic than Mother or Sparo? Could she read minds like the fairy?

"And you chaps have been abandoned," she said, pointing to the brothers, "cast aside like scraps at a dinner table. But do you know how many humans would have survived this many years on this unforgiving rock? None. You are stronger than any humans in the known systems. You are nearly gods."

His brothers seemed to grow taller with Phana's words, their eyes glowing brightly.

Caliban looked at Trinc. He seemed unaffected, watching Caliban, his brothers, and the wolves like a rabbit would a hungry predator.

Caliban looked back at Phana. Her eyes burned with passion like nothing he'd seen before. He lusted for her, for her power and strength. He loved her like Mother and like Miram at the same time. Just because humans had lied to him, hurt him, didn't mean all humans would. Miram hadn't. Jules hadn't. Maybe Phana wasn't like Mother, wasn't like Sparo. Caliban would hope, at least for now.

"First, we take back what's yours from Caliban's terrible master. We rip him to shreds after he's taught us the secrets of this place. Will you follow me? Will you?"

"Yes." All three brothers spoke the words together, quiet and strong.

Phana smiled wickedly, and it sent another wave of heat through Caliban's chest. "Show us the way, Caliban."

chapter 45

A WARNING

Hours had passed since Claribel's conversation with Fon, and she remained in meditation. Nozrel had sent word that Khayr and his ships had reached the Vesta system beyond the asteroid belt, but the jumping point was hours from Vesta II's orbit, and they were searching for the *Marsil* and Thanan's fivestar. They hadn't found either yet.

All the training she'd received at the hands of Rissa, and she felt completely unprepared for the tangled universe she'd found. Genetically manufactured armies. Starjumpers which defied all everyone knew about starjump travel. And she'd been married off to a king who was layered beyond what outside intelligence reports said of the man. She sunk deeper into meditation to keep growing worries from overwhelming her.

A thud came from her sitting room, and Claribel's eyes snapped open. It sounded like a piece of furniture falling. But the door was closed, and she sat in darkness, so opening her eyes revealed nothing.

The next sound was more distinct: like someone stubbing their toe. The second sound brought Claribel to complete awareness, her meditative state destroyed. Piera had never been clumsy.

Her double doors burst open, the light from the sitting room flooding her bed chamber. A tall man stood there, appearing as a silhouette. Claribel could not make out his features, but she was sure she did not know the man.

"Who are you?" The words came out weak and choked. She knew she should scream for help, but the exclamation remained trapped in her throat.

The man made no sound, but slowly walked toward her bed. She could see his face now, half of it lit by the light behind him. His skin was pale, too pale for a Nooteezian, and his hair was bright blond. In his right hand he held a small object that glowed purple in the shadow of his body. A surgical blade. He carried a plasma surgical blade. Only then did Claribel notice his clothing: the light green suit of a medical student. She'd seen a group of them earlier that day touring the palace. Despite his obvious intent, his eyes held no malice. They were calm, like pools of rain water. His face wore the expression of a man going about his daily tasks, not a man about to murder a queen.

Before Claribel could summon a scream, another figure entered the room, flying at the assassin. The newcomer kicked the assassin in the hip, sending him sprawling. The newcomer stood, her face clear in the light: Danda.

"Stay calm," Danda said through heavy breaths. "Help is coming."

The assassin regained his feet quickly and came at Danda. He rained a series of vicious blows on her, and she blocked or avoided each one. Their movements were so fast that Claribel had trouble discerning what was happening. After his initial attacks, he paused, and they circled each other like lions. The assassin attacked again, this time even faster and more ferociously. Danda dodged his first two strikes, but then he landed a hit to her face, his blade cutting her cheek. Danda screamed.

The assassin kicked her in the stomach, flinging her into the wall, her head striking in a hollow thump. She collapsed to the floor, her neck bent unnaturally. The kick had been beyond human power. He'd discarded the tall, solid servant like a child might a doll. He was bionic or something else. Claribel had never seen such power.

The assassin turned, his breaths even and rapid. He jumped from the floor onto her bed. Claribel backed against the headboard, looking for a way out or a way to defend herself. But her only weapons were pillows, and the assassin stood between her and any chance at an escape.

"In the bedroom!" someone shouted from the sitting room.

The assassin turned his head to the noise but quickly faced her again. He jumped, angling his blade for her neck. Claribel finally summoned the will to scream.

A loud pop filled the air and the assassin's chest exploded in blood. The gore landed on her legs, and the assassin's hand went limp, the surgical blade barely missing her chest. He landed on her, and she screamed again and pushed against him. As she twisted, she fell off the bed, the assassin's body still on top of her. The assassin looked up at her, his eyes impossibly clinging to life. Another pistol shot rang out, and the assassin slumped, his eyes still open but focused on nothing.

A soldier appeared at her side, lifting her to her feet. She turned to see Nozrel standing there, a pistol outstretched, smoke drifting from its barrel.

"Get medics for the two girls," Nozrel barked in Nooteezian. "I want ten guards outside these chambers. And get a cleaning crew in here now. Full alert. Wake everyone up. He might not be alone. And arrest every med student." Several soldiers surrounded the intelligence chief, and two peeled off to carry out his orders.

"Take her to my sitting room," he said to the guard who was propping Claribel up. "She's in shock. Get a physician in to see her as well. Ten soldiers here, ten more guarding her."

"Come, my queen," the soldier the words barely registering in her fractured mind.

She took a step, but her knees buckled. The soldier caught her and lifted her effortlessly into the air. Claribel refused to look back at the assassin but spared a glance for Danda; she still lay slumped unnaturally against the wall.

"Close your eyes, my queen," the soldier said.

She obeyed.

A few minutes later, the soldier set her in a chair, and she finally opened her eyes. The room was not furnished as opulently as hers. The large soldier stood next to her, erect and alert. Claribel could see the feet of more soldiers outside the door. She heard shouts ringing through the halls. The assassination attempt awoke the sleeping palace.

Claribel's thoughts swam, incoherent and wild. Shock. Nozrel had said she was in shock. It was likely true, but it felt strange to admit to that state while still in it. She took deep breaths to calm herself, but she could not force her mind into a peaceful state. The calm she'd held just before the assassin arrived completely eluded her.

"You're excused."

Claribel opened her eyes to see Nozrel standing in front of her.

"Are you all right, my queen?" Nozrel's eyes held their usual intensity, softened only a little by the circumstances.

"I'm not physically harmed, if that's what you mean."

"No. I know that," he said, his voice gentling a little. "Is your mind well enough to discuss what happened?"

She raged at his coldness, but she suppressed it. She would not let her dislike for Nozrel cloud her judgement. She knew it was important to discuss these events quickly afterward before the memories were warped by time.

So she related everything, though she admittedly had seen little.

"Where's Piera?" she asked as she finished her account.

Nozrel's eyes darted to the floor and then back to her face. "The assassin pierced her skull with his blade. She's in surgery."

Nozrel's sparse details fed her fears, and her emotions bubbled over. She curled into the oversized chair and sobbed. She didn't notice Nozrel leave.

chapter 46

THE GOOD IN HUMANS

Ariel placed the four humans in the middle of the Witch's Jungle, a pheromone shield of their own design protecting them. But even with the shield, they could feel creatures circling, smelling something foreign in their tight ecosystem, something worth coming out for.

Alazar, Balith, and their two guards lay on the ground, unconscious. Ariel did not envy the terror which would fill them soon. Sparo's plan called for theatrics Ariel found disgusting. But they would play their part.

Ariel pushed them awake. The female guard, Adriana, jumped to her feet and reached for her weapons--but Ariel had done away with those, leaving both guards only their short swords, which would help cut through the jungle but do very little against the nightmares they would soon face.

"Where are we?" Alazar muttered, propping himself up.

"Where's Lazlo?" Balith asked.

"What do you last remember?" Adriana asked.

"I'm not even sure," Alazar said.

Ariel took their human form before them, floating a few feet above the ground.

Alazar gasped and fell. Balith stepped back but kept his feet. The two guards put themselves between their masters and Ariel, raising their swords.

"By Feezrith, this is not possible." Alazar's eyes filled with tears.

"It's a trick," Balith said. "It must be a trick."

"What do you see?" Ariel made their voice large, echoing through the trees like a fierce wind. Their hair moved as if blown by a mad wind, but the air in the jungle was still.

"You know this thing?" Adriana asked, not taking her eyes off Ariel.

"It's Eliel, wife of Sparo, come back to haunt us . . ." Alazar's voice shook wildly.

"I am not Eliel, as her spirit has passed to the Well." The statement was true, even if they would interpret it differently than the truth. In all their years before finding Vesta II, Ariel had never lied or twisted the truth. Now they did it daily. "But as the god of this world, I seek vengeance on those who sent Eliel, Sparo, and Miram to their undeserving death."

Balith smiled. How could the man smile in the face of this? "So Sparo lives." He turned away from Ariel and addressed the trees. "Do you lie in wait for us brother? Come out and face me like the man you never were."

"Silence," Ariel bellowed. Wind swirled around them, and dark clouds roiled above, punctuated with sharp lightning strikes. Alazar and the two guards look dumbfounded at the tempest roiling above, and even Balith looked concerned if not scared.

One of Sparo's mechanical birds lurked nearby; he watched, his mind twisted by grief and rage.

"I am of the Whole," Ariel continued over the raging storm, "from a religion your people discarded centuries before. But believe it now, weak human criminals, because I am your judge."

"Criminals?" Balith questioned. "What are we accused of?" He tried to stand erect, but the powerful wind kept him hunched against its fury.

"You sent Sparo and his wife and his daughter to a cold death in space because of your sins. Admit it before me: Sparo was innocent, and you were the guilty parties."

"I admit it." Alazar crawled to his knees. "Please forgive me, Eliel, for what I did. I've tried to atone, I've tried . . ." His words disappeared into sobs.

"Shut up, you old fool," Balith snapped. "Sparo's recording this. It's some kind of trick. I won't admit to anything under duress so my brother can throw it onto the jumpnet to clear his sullied name." He turned again to the trees. "I'm not sure how you and your family survived, but I won't help clear a traitor!"

Ariel did not respond. This wasn't going according to Sparo's script. Sparo had assumed everyone would cower and ask forgiveness, and then he would have them killed. He wanted video of their confessions so his return to Lanopi would be safe for him and Miram, even though most Lanopians knew nothing of his forced exile.

But Balith had seen through it and would not play Sparo's game. Ariel waited for instructions.

"You are ever so intelligent." Sparo's voice echoed through the clearing, emanating from a bird perched on a tree. "My loving and wonderful brother."

Balith grinned again. "Show yourself Sparo. Does Eliel approve of all of this?"

"Eliel is dead."

Ariel recognized the cold fury in Sparo's voice. They had not expected him to show any mercy, but Balith flippantly reminding Sparo of his dead wife would bring a quick resolution.

"She died in space before we got here. You robbed me of my life, my wife, of everything."

"I'm so sorry, Sparo," Alazar pleaded. "Please know I've tried to make up for it. Had I known you were alive . . ."

"Had you known I was alive, your wife would have had soldiers sent here to kill me. No, Alazar, you don't get to escape this with an apology. You and Balith will pay."

"You brought this on yourself, brother." Balith continued to stand tall, though his voice lacked some of the bravado from before. "You mismanaged Onal, you ignored your duties, and you were disloyal to the High Regent. Eliel's death, your exile, these are your sins to carry, not ours. We did what had to be done."

Sparo's laugh filled the jungle, a dark sound matching the thunder. "Do you actually believe your own lies, Balith? Do you think I really need penitence from you or the High Regent? I'm not looking for a confession. I don't need your reticence. This is about revenge, about pain and agony. Like you did to my family, I dispense judgement in secret, and I pronounce your sentence: a gruesome death."

Though the script had been changed, Ariel knew what they had to do. They pulled their essence from the grove and found an acid spider walking around the pheromone shield, its heightened senses driving it into a frenzy. Ariel entered its small brain, and pushed it through the shield. This would be enough. The creature craved blood, and its programming made humans its sweetest prey. Sycorax had designed it for one purpose: the brutal and painful destruction of humans.

Ariel positioned themself back in the grove but did not take form. The acid spider scurried into the grove but stopped, assessing its prey. The creature stood two times the height of a man, its four long legs ending in sharp points digging into the ground. Its legs bent downward from their peak, supporting a cylindrical body. Hanging below its abdomen was its sack-like mouth, a clear membrane filled with the bile it used to disable and digest its prey. Its tongue, which could stretch twenty feet from its mouth, dangled in front.

The two guards shifted to stand between the creature and their masters, their short blades looking like toothpicks compared to the acid spider.

Nic, the younger guard, stepped forward, rushing the creature. He approached its nearest leg and chopped. But the acid spider's legs were hard and nearly impenetrable. Nic's swing did nothing more than knock the sword from his hand.

The acid spider's tongue flicked from its mouth and wrapped around Nic's waist. He screamed as the creature's acidic saliva melted his tunic and then his skin. Adriana stepped up, but before she reached her companion, the spider pulled Nic into its membranous mouth.

This was the sick genius of Sycorax's design. The clear membrane showed the others how painful their ends would be. Nic flayed against his doom, but the acid ate at everything now, his skin, his eyes, his hair quickly gone. His horrific screams were muffled by the membrane, but audible enough to provide verbal confirmation to the visual horror.

"Feezrith, Chimra, and Diede," Balith muttered. "This is not my brother. He couldn't do this." The younger brother had finally fallen to the ground, his confidence melted by his guard's digestion.

"He is what we made him to be." Alazar stood now, his tears gone.

"Run, Alazar," Adriana said. "Run."

"No. There's no escape. I'm sorry you had to be pulled into this, Captain."

"I'm not giving up yet, my lord." The woman stepped forward and picked up Nic's sword, securing it in her belt. The acid spider paid her no mind, content to finish digesting its first meal; it would take the creature several minutes to fully break down an adult human body. And with its speed and tracking ability, it would have no problem finding them when it was done.

Adriana climbed a nearby vine tree, scaling it to a level above the height of spider. At least one of its future prey was not content to act like subservient food.

"What are you going to do against that thing?" Balith muttered.

Adriana ignored Balith's inquiry. Leaning away from the tree on a large vine, she held out her sword. Kicking off the tree, she swung toward the acid spider, landing roughly on its abdomen. The creature flinched, but barely, like how a human might react to a fly. Climbing along to its cephalothorax, Adriana raised her sword and plunged it into one of the spider's eyes.

The creature danced with pain and began shaking its body to dislodge Alazar's guard. But the woman wrapped her legs around it and held to the sword still lodged in its eye. She extracted the other sword and stuck it into the membrane below her. The spider bucked again, almost tossing her aside. But Adriana held on, pulling the sword along the bottom of the abdomen, cutting the membrane loose from the spider's body.

Acid spilled to the jungle floor burning the grass and ground. Nic's partially digested body landed with a thud.

Leaving one sword in its eye, Adriana sat up on it like she was riding a horse. Raising the sword high above her head in a two-handed grip, she stabbed the spider in the abdomen repeatedly. The creature roiled and bucked, but could not shake her free. After a seventh stab, Adriana finally lost her balance and tumbled to the ground, landing roughly on her shoulder. Her two weapons remained lodged in the spider. Acid burns covered her right arm, and little spots of exposed skin dotted where drops of acid had melted her uniform. She raised herself with her left arm, her injured right arm dangling.

The acid spider stepped away from the humans, stumbling into the jungle. But it only made it a few steps before it collapsed. It twitched with its last energy of life.

Alazar rushed to Adriana's side. "Are you all right Captain?"

Adriana waved him away. "Don't touch me. I still have acid all over me."

Ariel let some of their essence into the woman, probing her mind. Loyalty. Love. The woman protected Alazar, performing her duty even under seemingly impossible circumstances. A human mind clear of the hate and anguish she knew from Sparo, a human mind with compassion and nobility.

The woman, Adriana, did not deserve to die. She had not hurt Sparo, had nothing to do with his betrayal on Lanopi. Neither had Nic. Ariel wept inside, ashamed of their complicity in this barbarism. What had they become? What had they let themself be? They were not Ariel, not some toy of human creation. They were a member of the Whole, a race of peaceful explorers. They could not be a part of this. Member Five could not be a part of this.

"Finish this." Sparo's words echoed in Five's consciousness.

But Five did not respond. They reached into the mechanical bird, disabling its energy system. It fell with a crash.

"What is happening there, Ariel?"

They were not Ariel. They were not his slave. Five put the survivors to sleep and carried them to the facility.

chapter 47

ALLIES AND ENEMIES

Claribel sat in her temporary chambers with her pad, trying to do some research, but she couldn't stay focused for more than a few seconds. She'd slept little that night, her dreams haunted by the nearly unstoppable assassin who'd almost finished the job other assassins had failed at nine years ago. Was Claribel destined to die that way? How had she twice avoided assassination? But others had not been so fortunate. Soldiers in the support ships had died during the first attempt. This time several guards had died, and Piera and Danda had narrowly avoided death. How many people would lose their lives protecting her?

She set the pad on the table and leaned back in her chair. Piera had survived surgery and was recovering but still unconscious. Danda would also survive, though it was difficult for Claribel to clear the unnaturally slumped body from her mind. The incognito guard had a concussion and a broken vertebra at the top of her neck, serious injuries, but not life threatening or even altering.

Part of her mind screamed at her, that as much as she tried to control everything, to remain independent of Rissa's dominant hand, the truth was that she was helpless. Helpless to hold back the tide of the political forces shaping the known systems. The High Regent held a piece of her fate. Whomever wanted her dead, Sycorax or Pastrack or someone else, held a piece. Khayr, her husband and king, held another piece. Whatever tiny shard Claribel controlled . . .

No, those thoughts were poison. She'd known her whole life that doing the right thing could lead to her own end. By the Heavens, even doing the wrong thing would be dangerous. Being in a position of power and authority made her a figurative and literal target. And twice enemies had taken aim, and twice they'd failed. She would continue to live and work and strive to make whomever had tried to kill her regret not finishing the job. She would not crawl into a pit of hopelessness and wallow in it.

Hope before fear. But as she repeated the phrase in her mind, the rest of the passage came unbidden. *Fear becomes whatever you want it to be. Fear is not real, even in the face of certain death. And like darkness, fear flees before hope. But do you have the courage to hold hope's fierce light before the darkness? Or would you stumble in fear because it makes it easier to do nothing?*

She re-focused on who might have tried to kill her. There were possibilities, but her mind had not landed on anything solid. Her mother? Seemed too far-fetched and didn't seem to benefit Lanopi or Rissa's own power. Pastrack? After that public rebuff at the wedding, seemed too obvious. Perhaps the mysterious Sycorax? Much more likely. A chill ran through her when she remembered the fear Fon had expressed in their brief call.

But she didn't really know, and by Palo's white hair, she didn't even really know who'd try to kill her nine years ago. The official story was the Onala Liberators, which had been literally true, but the unofficial farce about Senator Sparo and his family made the whole thing so strange. Who benefited the most from the attempt, successful or not? The Liberators had been crushed after that, executed and imprisoned by the dozens. If anything, it had consolidated Rissa's power during a time when . . .

Claribel dropped her pad into her lap, a vibrant and depressing realization slamming her mind and dissipating all other thoughts. How had she not seen this before? It seemed so clear now, the sun's light cresting a darkened horizon. The High Regent's power had been enhanced by that assassination attempt. Rissa gained much more from the failed event than any separatist group would have had it worked. Only Claribel's death would have been more galvanizing to Lanopi.

What were Rissa's maxims all about? Power, strength, leadership. These were the guiding principles of everything the High Regent did. Two came to Claribel's mind now, brightly interwoven.

Five: Family will be your closest allies, but not because of love. Love can blind you. Family is a great ally because you know more about them than often they do themselves.

Eighty-eight: Theatrics are needed to unite the common. They rally around death, symbols, and enemies. Put on a show and they will follow.

Claribel's own mother had manipulated the Liberators somehow, had orchestrated that first assassination attempt.

The High Regent had used theatrics to unite. Claribel had been the cherished daughter, followed by the press and beloved by her people. Lanopians had united after the attempt on her life; they had come together in hatred of the Onala Liberators. Though Sparo and his wife had been privately convicted as ringleaders, there had been many public trials, and also some riots in which citizens dragged suspected Liberators into a public square and collectively beat them to death. Dozens had been killed, and hundreds more were assaulted and jailed. In the years since, Lanopi stood behind its High Regent. The exile of Sparo and Eliel finally made sense: a trial would have allowed Sparo's allies to put together a defense, possibly exposing the truth. But the rumored exile would send fear through the ruling elite that crossing High Regent Rissa meant a cold, unforgiving death.

Nausea replaced the stark realization. How could her own mother order her death? Despite Claribel's dislike and distrust of Rissa, she'd always held to a supposed truth that her mother loved her, even if Rissa's love for power had twisted it. But could she love someone and then have them killed to ensure her political future? No definition of love fit those circumstances.

Claribel's nausea melted before a hot anger. Mother had been behind her first flirtation with death. She reconsidered whether the High Regent might be involved in this one, whether striking soon after the wedding might help her in some way. But she dismissed it again. No, this wasn't Rissa. Another maxim came to mind: *Only use desperate measures in time of great desperation. Be efficient in getting the job done, not wasteful.* This attempt had been desperate and sloppy. If Rissa had tried, it would have been invisible.

Claribel scooped up her pad and stormed from the room, letting her anger fuel her. Her own mother had tried to kill her. She would not stand idly by as people like her mother carved the future of the known systems. She would play her part. Maybe it would end in her death, or maybe she'd fail. But she knew the righteous path, the peaceful, human path, the path Palo would want her to take. Even if she walked it alone, she would keep walking.

She stepped through the doors of her new rooms, a small crowd gathered in her new sitting room, ten heavily armed guards and two servants.

"Take me to the intelligence room," she said to the older, plumper servant.

The woman nodded and led her from the room. The other servant and two guards remained behind. Their entourage entered the intelligence room, and Nozrel stood there waiting for her.

"Welcome back, Queen Claribel. How can I help you?" The man smiled more pleasantly than she'd ever seen.

"We need to talk, Nozrel."

"Of course." He shot a glance at the guards, and everyone stepped back. "Follow me."

They entered the main area, every terminal occupied by an analyst.

"Any word from my husband?"

"Yes." Nozrel motioned to a solar system map projected on the far wall. Vesta. A green dot approached the system's second planet. "Yes, they are in orbit around Vesta II. They have found the *Marsil*; it's in orbit around Vesta II as well, and they are approaching it."

"Have we reached out to Lanopi to let them know?"

"Not yet. The king decided to wait until we understand what we've found."

"What about my assassin?"

Nozrel looked at her, not caught off guard by the rapid subject change. "A genetic creation. He'd been accepted as a medical student two years ago from Eslaza, imbedded into our society. The students were on a tour of the palace's medical facilities when he broke off from the group and came to you." He turned toward her, his eyes heavy from a sleepless night. "I suspect Sycorax was behind this. Your investigation into that organization triggered a reaction."

Claribel wanted to chastise the man for implicating her in her own near demise, but she let it go. If Sycorax had been behind the assassination attempt, then she'd unwittingly moved like an insect to a flame.

"Nooteezia has been employing Sycorax." Claribel made her words into a statement, though she couldn't be sure it was true without Nozrel's confirmation.

He regarded her for a moment, then nodded. "Yes. Another thing I disagreed with the king on. Sycorax is dangerous, and they play all sides. Surely your contact on Coznar mentioned that."

He taunted her with his knowledge of her private conversation, but she wouldn't be drawn in by his muscle flexing.

"There's so little information that can be deemed reliable about Sycorax," she said. "I'm not sure what to believe."

"This is certain." Nozrel's eyes squinted with fury. "Once the king learns of this treachery, that woman and her entire organization are going to wish she'd never had any dealings with Nooteezia."

"I didn't realize you cared for my well-being." Claribel tried a taunt of her own.

He shrugged. "I am warming to your presence." He smiled in what might have been the most genuine expression she'd seen on his wrinkled face.

"So what is next?" she asked.

"The king is going to infiltrate the ship or planet depending on what communications he receives from whomever he finds and what sensor data can assess. The situation remains extremely fluid."

"I believe the High Regent of Lanopi knew something bad was going to happen," Claribel added. "Something caused her to change her plans, and either she was behind this catastrophe or see saw it coming. I only wish I knew how she was connected to all of this . . ."

"Your mother is one of the most talented strategists in the know systems." He wrung his hands, his eyes lost in thought. "She avoided the fate of the *Marsil*, but where did she go?"

"What about the Lanopian couple?"

"My men are still searching the mountainside for them. It's taking time, but we'll find them. Maybe the High Regent feared for her life and hid herself on Nooteczia."

Claribel sighed. *What are you up to, Rissa?*

chapter 48

FIVE'S STAND

ember Five floated in Sparo's room, their light seemingly paler against the bright lights. Sparo had not used the lights in this room for years, complaining about the glare's effect on his headaches. Now the lights burned bright, clearly showing the anger on the man's face.

"You disobeyed me." His voice quieted with each word. "You allowed Alazar and my brother to live."

"They are still yours to be had." They waved toward two images floating near his head, the two men unconscious in separate empty rooms. "You can do with them as you wish."

"I wished you to kill them!" His words exploded from his mouth, and his rage pulled him to his feet like he might strike them or worse. But he held still, his fists white as he dug his fingers into his palms.

"The Whole are peaceful," they said, their voice steady and even. "We do not kill other sentient lifeforms. The death of the guard Nic will haunt me forever and is a stain against the Whole and my tribe."

"I don't give a damn about your Whole!" Sparo's forehead twitched. "I want my revenge. I want justice. I want a life of hope and joy for Miram. And nothing will stand in my way, not your Whole, not you, not anyone!"

"I will help find a life for you and Miram, but I am done with your human revenge games," they replied. "I should have never taken part, and I will take part no longer."

Sparo collapsed in his chair, the anger replaced by an exhausted sadness. "I am sorry, Ariel."

They did not correct the name, though they refused to think of themselves by that moniker any longer.

"My promises are as untrue as the villains I hunt. I should be a better man than this. Balith is a liar, but he was right about one thing: my Eliel would be ashamed by what I've become."

His body seemed to re-inflate with hardened anger, not the rage from moments before. "But Eliel is dead, and I will do it myself." He turned to the screens. "Please check in on my daughter and the other prisoner. Make sure that goes according to plan." He fixed his eyes on his brother. "I will take care of this. Please go watch Miram until I have further need of you."

Five watched Thanan split logs in the hot sun. He worked diligently, despite the injustice of his imprisonment. Miram watched from the edge of the glade drawing on her pad.

By Sparo's request years ago, Five had stayed outside of Miram's mind, and they were glad. Miram had been raised in a difficult situation, and she didn't need a member bouncing around in her brain. But Five really wanted to know what was going on inside the young woman's head, to see how she viewed these swirling events.

"What your father is doing is wrong." Thanan sat down on the ground and drank heavily from water Miram had brought him. His metal bracelet, a device provided by Sparo, rattled against the metal water bottle. The bracelet made it possible for Sparo to cause Thanan extreme pain or render him unconscious.

Miram looked up, raised her eyebrows, and then focused on her drawing while speaking. "Wrong? Any more wrong than your father and mother sending us to die in space?"

"I'm not defending my parents." He took another deep drink. "Diede knows I don't always agree with what my parents do. But if it was unjust, it was done with Lanopi's interests at heart. Your father has only revenge; that's not the same."

Miram set her pad down and walked toward Thanan, stopping two feet away from him. "You know nothing. You were raised eating platinum and pooping silver. I was raised with a weird father, a deformed experiment, and a captured deity. What could you possible understand about any of this?"

Thanan sighed and looked at the ground. "You're right; I don't know what you've been through. I can't imagine the isolation you've felt. But killing my father, destabilizing a world, keeping me as a hostage, none of that changes your past. It likely makes your future even worse. Your father will become a galactic fugitive and villain."

Miram turned away, a cold anger not unlike her father's stretched across her face. She sat down and picked up her pad.

Thanan took two steps toward her, like he might say something more. But when he saw her face, he shook his head and returned to work.

Five was not an expert in human romance, but this didn't look like a blossoming love story. Every piece of Sparo's plan hung precariously over a dangerous cliff.

chapter 49

GROWING DANGER

Claribel sat at a terminal, scouring the jumpnet for clues, anything which would help them discover the High Regent's whereabouts. Nozrel's agents combed a mountainside where the mysterious Lanopian couple were supposedly hiking, and Nozrel believed they'd find those two Lanopians and some answers within the hour. While it might reveal Rissa or a clue to her plans or whereabouts, it seemed just as likely that two wealthy Lanopians stayed behind for an adventurous vacation.

So baring Mother being holed up with one of her boy toys on a Nooteezian vacation, something bigger played out here. Claribel felt certain Rissa had discovered the message to Lazlo, but what would she have done? She would have taken the offensive, but Claribel couldn't see any evidence of that. The High Regent's machinations twisted and entangled so much, it was nearly impossible to unravel it all and find the truth.

Claribel leaned back in her chair and tried to wipe the exhaustion from her tired eyes. She knew she wasn't thinking straight, that her mind was still rattled from limited rest and stress. But she did not want to return to bed and find terrors haunting her dream.

"Good afternoon, Queen Claribel." Nozrel approached behind her and stopped, his arms behind his back in a formal stance. "Please follow me. We have more news."

Claribel followed him out of the analyst's room and down a narrow hallway.

"Welcome to my office," Nozrel said as he led her into a room at the end of the hall.

His office surprised Claribel. Art from around the known systems covered the walls of the spacious room. She recognized most of it, prints of obscure paintings by well-known artists. *Regno Triple Moon Night* by Scarvatian DusDus Hilier. *Desert Hawk Finds Prey* by the Lanopian painter Falo Hunda. *And Spirits Die a Second Death* by Eslazan artist Drivia Doorsa who'd been trained by Falo Hunda. All the works were a realistic, photographic style with supernatural elements mixed in: spirits leaking from the Regno moons, a ghost escaping the rat underneath a hawk's talons, and a haunting scene of the spirits of young children watching the aftermath of their own deaths. The third painting was one of Claribel's favorites.

"You like art?" Nozrel asked.

"Very much." Her gaze lingered on her favorite. She identified with the loneliness and helplessness oozing from the dark, muted tones.

"You enjoy Drivia?"

Claribel nodded and looked back at Nozrel, trying to banish the familiar melancholy that piece laid on her soul.

"We should get you with the palace art master," he said, his eyes soft and aglow. But within a moment, the tenderness fled before his intense tenacity.

"You said you had updates?"

He nodded. "King Khayr boarded the *Marsil*. No casualties, but the ship is disabled; only life support is working. The starjumper's computers are unresponsive, and neither their technicians nor ours can seem to fix them."

"Sabotage of some kind?"

"Perhaps." He paused and sat behind a small desk, motioning for Claribel to take a chair opposite him. She smiled but remained standing. She might have misjudged him, and he might have misjudged her, but they were not friends.

"You haven't mentioned the High Regent or my family."

"That's because they're not on the ship. The captain confirmed that Rissa did not board the *Marsil*, but your father and a few others left in a life ship when it appeared the starjumper was going to meet a fiery end in Vesta II's atmosphere. Your brother's fivestar also crash landed on the planet."

Claribel closed her eyes, calming herself with a deep breath. They were alive. She had to assume they were still alive. She had to. Thanan could not be gone, not like this.

"What's next?"

"The king and an extraction team are headed for the surface. They've located a sizable facility on the planet's central continent. An old base of some kind."

"A base? On Vesta II? Is it Sycorax?" *The Sycorax facility.*

Nozrel arched an eyebrow. "Maybe. We won't know until the extraction team tells us. They're going to land in a jungle northwest of the facility."

An unknown inhabitable planet. How had it slipped through all of the known systems? Sycorax. A dark organization shading each central star. How long had it existed? And did its tendrils cover the entirety of the known systems?

"But if this was all a trap from Lazlo's unknown accomplice," Claribel added, "the king and his men are entering the dragon's lair."

"Yes. They are prepared."

"What of Lazlo?" she asked. "Was he apprehended?"

"No," he replied with a shake of his head. "He was among those who fled to the planet."

Claribel took the seat Nozrel had offered earlier, her head spinning with exhaustion and consternation.

"I fear the king doesn't recognize just how great the danger may be," the intelligence chief continued. "If that is indeed a Sycorax facility, if they have a weapon powerful enough to control a starjumper and an asteroid field, then who can say what Sycorax is capable of, what surprises might greet them on the surface? And since Sycorax specializes in creating genetically-engineered soldiers, the king and his men, even as trained and dedicated as they may be, could be outmatched."

Claribel leaned forward, trying to parse Nozrel's precise language. She'd noticed how each word escaped slowly, deliberately. The man wasted nothing. This small statement was layered with meaning and implications. Political games were ingrained in him like only one other person she'd ever known: Rissa. As an ally, Claribel knew he'd be invaluable. As an enemy? Well, she'd worry about that another day.

"You're asking me to approve something," she said, guessing at his intentions.

He smiled. "Yes. I would like to send two more Bizretrirs into Vesta to assist, but I have no military authority. The ranking military officer is General Cardono. He's an old man, very traditional. He sees me as the pesticide used to kill unwanted vermin but dangerous in my own right."

"At least he's a good judge of character." Claribel meant it as a friendly jab, but Nozrel seemed to ignore it.

"There's only one person remaining on Nooteezia who could overrule the general. The acting agent of Nathree."

Claribel had studied the term. King Khayr held power, officially, as the agent of their god, Nathree. If he was unavailable to make decisions, then another could be raised to temporarily fulfill his stead.

"But I thought Cardono would be the acting agent," Claribel said. "I remember reading that the line of succession falls on military authority."

"You've studied our law well," he replied. "But much of it is open to interpretation. I would interpret it differently now that the king has married."

She smiled. "You want me to claim the title of acting agent of Nathree."

Nozrel nodded. "Yes, and then you could authorize my proposed mission. Cardono is no fan of mine, but like most of our people, I believe he's very fond of you and would bow to your claim. I've had Abdel put together a justification with scriptural verification that you should be the acting agent. The king is busting into a stinger's nest, and he's going to need more help. Sycorax could have any numbers of devious surprises awaiting them, if indeed, this is connected to Sycorax."

"Something is happening here, Nozrel," she replied, "something revolving around Sycorax, High Regent Rissa, Lazlo, and whomever Lazlo is working with. The stability and future of the known systems sits on our decisions."

She expected Nozrel to disagree with her assessment, proclaim it as nothing more than an overreaction. But he only nodded. "Then lets make sure we make the right decisions."

chapter 50

ONLY EVIL MASTERS

Caliban's stomach churned as they approached the east door. Sparo would be so mad. And his magic was powerful, maybe even powerful enough to stop Phana's magic, three lizard men, and two pointy-nosed wolves. And if Sparo did stop them, he would kill Caliban.

No. Magic did not always win. Surprises won. Balthazar surprising Mother's friends. Mother surprising Balthazar. And then Caliban surprising Mother. Caliban had to make sure he was on the right side of the surprise.

"Any chance your master is watching us?" Phana asked.

He stopped short of the door. "Maybe. Sparo has silly birds that watch you, and Mother's place has eyes everywhere. But Sparo is sloppy and old; he won't notice us coming."

Phana nodded as he put his hand on the identity pad, and the door slipped open.

Caliban looked over at the sweet-talking Phana. Now that she trusted him, her stance was casual, comfortable. He could kill her before she did anything, and his brothers would follow suit and kill Trinc. A step inside meant betraying Sparo and possibly losing Miram. But Sparo was a mean, stupid master, and Miram wasn't his anyway. Good changes would come, or maybe his death would come; either seemed better than living out life under Sparo's hands.

They stepped inside an empty hallway. Phana and Trinc moved slowly, their muscles tense, their magic weapons raised. Caliban's brothers also looked fierce, and their wolves growled at the narrow hallway.

"Follow Caliban."

He moved a little faster, and the others matched his pace. The hallways seemed more silent than usual, like they had the days after he'd killed Mother, his days of triumphant silence.

"What was this place?" Trinc asked.

"A wonder," Phana answered. "A starjump away, hidden from everyone. Brilliant, really. Terraform a planet behind an asteroid field-- no reason for anyone to look beyond what they think they know."

"Mother," Caliban said, his tone hushed. He still worried about saying her name, like speaking it might bring her back to life. "Mother made all of this. Mother was very smart."

He stopped and the others did too, their bodies going rigid.

"The door ahead is Sparo's room," Caliban said. "He'll be there, and maybe the fairy Ariel."

Phana turned to him. "You said Sparo controls you by pain in your belly. How does Sparo control his fairy?"

Caliban shrugged. "Sparo never tells Caliban nothing. But I think it's his ball on his staff. It's how he sends pain to Caliban, and it's how he controls the fairy. Maybe."

"Ball on a staff?" Trinc threw his hands into the air. "I'm not going to be shocked if there's nothing but a skeleton beyond that door. We've seen very little that proves him right."

"Trust that I know what you don't," Phana replied. "There's a lot to gain here." She turned back to Caliban's brothers. "Keep the wolves at bay, but when I say, let them loose. I want to talk with Sparo first, find out what he knows and controls. But I'd rather have *him* dead than us."

His brothers nodded, and their wolves growled to match Phana's intensity.

"Let's go inside," she whispered to Caliban. "It's your time now."

He reached up and touched the pad.

The room wasn't dark like usual, and Ariel was nowhere in sight. Sparo had his back to the door, watching his floating screens.

"Don't bother me now Miram; I'm almost done." Sparo's voice was strong, stronger than it had been in some time.

Caliban cringed. "It is Caliban."

Phana poked his back and they all stepped inside.

Sparo turned, his eyes widening at the site of the newcomers. Then he laughed. The laugh filled the room, echoing against the walls, his large voice filling every inch. Caliban cringed again. It was rarely good news when Sparo laughed.

"And here I thought you'd not come at all," Sparo said, his eyes on Phana. "Very clever; take yourself off the ship log, but remain onboard.

Very clever, indeed. You must have seen the message to Lazlo."

Sparo knew Phana? The woman hadn't mentioned that.

"Not as much of a surprise as finding the long-dead Sparo very much alive." Phana smiled, then looked at the three screens floating behind Sparo; each held an image of an older human man. "I see you caught your prey. Your plan seems to be working. I assume this whole play was written to get revenge on your brother."

Sparo's eyes narrowed. "Revenge on all who wronged me. Your husband already admitted his involvement. And I can't imagine your lapdog operated without his wife's knowledge."

"Indeed. Alazar is excellent at execution but terrible with strategy." Phana glanced at one of the screens. "When I intercepted the message to Lazlo, I thought maybe he was working with a foreign agent. Finding you and finding this facility was a better outcome than I'd imagined. I made my ruse so Lazlo would feel free to do what he needed. I thought I'd made a mistake until I found Caliban." She smiled down at him.

Sparo studied his staff, then his gaze hardened on Phana. Then he cast his eyes on Caliban. "You helped them, helped my enemies."

"I didn't know they were your enemies," Caliban mumbled. "Caliban only brought space people like Sparo said to do."

Sparo's hand twitched, like he might grab the staff, but his hand remained in place.

No. Mean Sparo would not hurt Caliban ever again. Mean Sparo would die. It did not matter who Phana was or what she knew. Caliban would be free of dumb masters, free forever.

He reached for his staff. But Caliban moved faster, jumping to the old meanie's staff and pulling it away before Sparo could do anything. Sparo's hands were empty, his stupid magic gone.

"Ariel!" Sparo called to the air. "Come to me Ariel! Come!"

No. He would not call the fairy, he would not call down pain on Caliban. Caliban raised the staff high above his head and smashed it to the ground. The ball shattered, liquid oozing onto the metal floor, pooling amidst glass shards.

Sparo gasped. "No Caliban! What have you done?"

"Caliban not Sparo's friend," Caliban hissed. "Caliban only friend is Caliban."

Five hovered outside of Balith's room, ready to release Sparo's brother on his command. Sparo would no longer share his plan with them, but he had promised Five that they would not participate in killing. If something went wrong they would protect Miram.

"Ariel!" Sparo's panicked voice rang in their head. "Come to me Ariel! Come!"

As Five began to move toward Sparo's room, a familiar sensation pulled at them: the tribe's prison, calling them back to it. *No. Not now!* Sparo's game was nearly complete; there was hope their tribe would finally be free. What was happening to Sparo? Who called them to their prison now?

Everything faded, and their presence and power waned. To anyone watching, Five would be growing fainter. But no one watched. They dropped into darkness alone.

"Where's your daughter, Sparo?" Phana asked. "This creature said she lives."

"Rot with Feezrith, Rissa." Sparo's eyes burned as though he hoped they could hurt her. Phana did not flinch, but Caliban felt fear growing inside him even though Sparo's magic ball lay in pieces.

"What is Rissa?" Dax asked.

"It's my name," Phana, whose name was Rissa, said. "I'm the High Regent of Lanopi, the leader of a whole world."

Caliban did not understand. What was a High Regent? If she was something special, why had she landed on Mother's world almost alone? None of this made sense to Caliban.

Rissa turned to Sparo. "And where's my son?"

Sparo stayed silent.

"Fine." She turned to Trinc. "Take him."

Trinc grabbed the back of Sparo's neck, tossing the older man roughly to the floor. Sparo groaned, and rolled onto his back.

Rissa sat in Sparo's chair, in Mother's chair. "Show me Miram."

A fourth screen appeared, and Miram sat in the middle, her face in her pad as usual. Another spaceman stood near her, splitting wood.

"Shut down protocol . . ." Sparo's words ended when Trinc brought his gun down on the old man's head.

Rissa pointed to the screen with Miram and the shirtless man.

"Where is this?"

"Outside," Caliban said. "West entrance."

Rissa turned to his brothers. "Go bring me those two."

Both his brothers smiled wickedly as they left the room.

"What will happen to Miram?" Caliban asked.

"Sparo's daughter?" Rissa sat in Sparo's chair, rubbing its arms. "Do you like her? She can be yours."

"Mine?"

"Yours, Caliban. For whatever you want to do with her."

"Miram not mine, not yours."

Rissa swiveled toward him. "Everything is mine, Caliban, including her. This world and all it holds are mine now." She motioned to Sparo's unconscious body. "Take him to one of the rooms. You'll never be his slave again."

Her tone, her voice, her authority. Rissa sounded like Mother, so in charge, so bossy, so mean. Caliban had helped her, helped her take Miram. The bad people who'd sent Miram and Sparo to him now controlled Miram's fate. Caliban did not understand humans very well, but he knew they did not forgive. Miram would never have the life she deserved, never know the life Sparo had wanted for her. And it was Caliban's fault; Caliban was stupid, silly. He had a new master now, Rissa, the High Regent, and she would be the same as the others.

Caliban pulled Sparo over his shoulder and dragged him toward an empty room.

chapter 51

RISSA REVEALED

ozrel briefed the colonel who would be leading the additional ships into the Vesta system. King Khayr and his assault team were less than an hour away from landing on Vesta II; her new husband had listened patiently to Claribel's plea to wait for reinforcements, but his counter-argument had been strong: without knowing what was happening on the surface, the hours spent waiting might mean the death of whomever had survived crash landing on the planet. They all agreed that someone sinister pulled all these strings, and Khayr wasn't going to wait. Claribel hoped the reinforcements wouldn't be too late; they might get there a day after Khayr's assault.

As Nozrel continued his briefing, the young analyst Abdel entered the room. Nozrel paused, and Abdel whispered in the older man's ear. Nozrel's eyes widened, and he looked back at the group.

"Everyone clear the room, except for the queen."

The six men, including Abdel and the space navy colonel, left the briefing area, leaving Claribel alone with the intelligence chief.

"My men located the Lanopian couple," Nozrel said. "It was Rissa's chief of staff, Phana, and an actor by the name of Trinc."

The color drained from Claribel's face. She'd studied the list of passengers on the *Marsil*. "Weren't they on the *Marsil*?"

Nozrel held up his pad, the two names highlighted on the screen. "Yes, they were supposed to be."

"The High Regent is on the *Marsil*." Claribel took a deep breath and considered the revelation for a moment before continuing. "She intercepted the message to Lazlo and decided to stay on the ship. But why go incognito? What did she believe would happen?"

"She wanted Lazlo to reveal himself or whatever he was involved with," Nozrel replied. "A dangerous ploy, sending most of her elite away."

He pulled back his pad and touched it three times. "Only seventeen of the High Regent's eighteen elite are accounted for. I'm guessing she's got one with her."

Claribel nodded. "And she's on the *Marsil* and no one knows she's there."

Nozrel turned to his pad, touched it several times, and the wall behind him erupted into life. A middle-aged man with a goatee filled the big screen.

"Captain Durus," Nozrel said. "Has the king descended to the planet?"

"Yes, sir," the man replied. "Just moments ago."

"Are you on the *Marsil*?" the intelligence chief asked.

"Yes. And curiously, the ship just came back to life. Whatever twisted its systems is gone."

"Excellent news. Have you accounted for all passengers on the *Marsil*?"

"Yes, sir. The High Regent's husband, a man named Lazlo, a man named Balith, and two guards left on an escape ship. We've also realized the High Regent's chief of staff and another man may have launched an escape ship. We found a second pod missing and two dead guards stashed in a utility shaft near the missing escape ship. No one discovered this before because of all the chaos."

"Thank you, captain."

The screen went blank.

"She's on the planet," Claribel said after a few moments of silence, and then they were quiet as they considered the implications that the High Regent of Lanopi was stranded on Vesta II with the others.

"Judging by her hasty departure," Nozrel said, "it appears that staying on the *Marsil* did not work out how the High Regent had anticipated."

Claribel nodded. The High Regent was on the planet, as were Claribel's father and brother. Her new husband led a strike team to the surface to find out what was going on and safely extract everyone. She could not shake the feeling that the next few days, possibly the next few hours, would shape the future of the known systems. Something monumental transpired in that forgotten system, and billions of people would feel the ripples emanating from Vesta II.

"I need to be at Vesta II," Claribel said.

Nozrel regarded her, his eyes wide. "Out of the question. This is enough of a mess with the king stranded on a planet with Sycorax and your mother."

"But Khayr is not a diplomatic strategist," she objected. "He is perfect for a fight but not to match the High Regent and whatever web she weaves. You can be sure she's going to frame events to best suit her agenda, regardless of how surprised she's been by what happened."

"The High Regent is our ally," he asserted. "And for all we know, she's dead or living inside her escape ship on the planet. Or they could have skipped off the atmosphere and are floating in open space around the planet. Most likely, she's dead or sitting around."

"No, most likely she is in the middle of this," Claribel replied, "and the king shouldn't face her alone." She could feel the heat gathering inside her, anger directed at her mother. She had to push the emotions aside. This wasn't about a failed assassination attempt from years before, or her mother's manipulation of Claribel's life. This was about the future and not letting that foul woman bend circumstances to her will.

"Fine, we'll send an experienced diplomat, someone familiar with the High Regent . . ."

"No. We will send me. I was trained by the High Regent for times just like this. I should go."

Nozrel regarded her again. His eyes held none of the dismissive disdain he'd shown in their first interactions. They might have even held a little respect.

"All right, but may I request that you stay in orbit until the planet is secured?"

She nodded and smiled. "Now that the *Marsil* is operational, the known systems will soon know about your new starjumpers. I hope we did not reveal them in vain."

Nozrel shrugged. "They were bound to be discovered at some point. If we save the Lanopian aristocracy and stop whatever Sycorax is doing, it will have been worth it."

Caliban cowered against the wall of Mother's room, Sparo's room, now Rissa's room. The man, Trinc, worked on the computers trying to connect with something called the jumpnet, but so far they had gained little control over Mother's facility. Good. These meanies deserved control of Mother's magic least of all.

Caliban was still needed, even if for now he was forgotten. Phana--Rissa--stood next to the shirtless man who'd been with Miram.

"We need to interrogate Sparo," the shirtless one said. "He's the only one who knows how all this works."

"I understand that, son," Rissa said. "But he's unconscious now. And we can't trust him. He may give us a protocol that locks us out completely. We'll crack this eventually. Once we make contact with the *Marsil* we'll have a team down here to unlock these secrets." Rissa's attention returned to Trinc's efforts.

"What of Father? Why is he still in a cell?"

"Your father is being punished." Rissa's voice rang cold. "He admitted involvement in framing Sparo with the help of Balith. If true, those are dangerous allegations which could undermine my rule."

"So you're going to kill him."

Rissa turned to her son. "I will assess and do whatever is necessary to ensure the safety and security of Lanopi. You should understand that as well as anyone."

"And what of the girl?" The son looked over at the screen with her image. "What will you do with her?"

"She's disposable." Rissa turned toward the screens. "Don't go soft on me now, Thanan. Mercy and compassion are not for those who lead."

"I'm going to go find my shirt," he replied and left the room. Rissa did not turn to watch him go.

Caliban limped out after the man and matched his quick pace.

"What will happen to Miram?" Caliban asked.

Thanan pursed his lips and exhaled deeply. "I don't know. Mother will probably kill her."

"I had a mother once."

Thanan shot Caliban a skeptical glance.

"It is true. My mother built this place."

"What happened to your mother?"

"Caliban killed her."

Caliban's words stopped Thanan like he'd almost run into a wall. Caliban stopped, looking up at the shirtless man.

"Are you the only one who can open doors?" Thanan asked. What a strange question.

"Caliban not know. Maybe. Sparo could, and Miram. Your mother not know all the magic yet."

"No, she doesn't. Can you take me to Miram's room?"

Jealousy burned inside Caliban, and for a moment, he thought of choking the life out of the shirtless man. He knew that a lack of clothes and love were somehow connected, but Caliban didn't understand how.

"What you do with Miram?"

"Set her free, gain some leverage with Mother." He lifted his face toward the ceiling. "Sorry, Claribel. I can't be my mother's puppet any longer. I can't watch her kill these people, including our father."

"Is Claribel your god?" Caliban asked. He knew some humans believed in a big magic person they called a god.

Thanan laughed. "Not exactly; she's my sister."

Caliban shrugged. Humans were weird. "Follow Caliban."

They sprinted until they reached Miram's room. Despite being a weak human, Thanan kept the pace well.

"Once we let Miram go," Caliban said, "your mother and my brothers will come for us."

Thanan nodded, but he put his hand on his hip. He had one of the magic guns. "Is there anywhere safe to take her?"

"To her forest, but your mother and her friends are between here and there."

"Where's the nearest exit?"

"Jungle door. Very dangerous. Jungle will kill sweet Miram."

Caliban heard something as he stopped, feet moving in the distance. One of his brothers coming with a meanie wolf. There was no more time to talk.

He reached up and released the door. Light from the hallway illuminated Miram's dark room. She was curled in the corner, her body as small as it could be.

"Come, Miram," Caliban whispered. "Time to go."

Miram looked up, but then away. "They could have only gotten Father with your help. You betrayed us."

Her words struck Caliban hard, and he shrank into himself. Sweet Miram was right: he had betrayed them, and Miram would die because of his pettiness.

"We need to go, Miram," Thanan pleaded. "My mother, the High Regent, she's going to kill everyone. If you and Caliban escape, we gain leverage. She doesn't know how to operate the computer system. But you and Caliban do."

Miram sat up. "Better than that. I can shut the whole thing down, or bring Ariel back to help us."

"Then come. Quickly. This is our only shot."

Footsteps grew closer between them and Mother's room. The jungle exit was their only escape.

Caliban stepped inside the room and picked Miram up, slinging her over his shoulder. "Sorry, Miram. Caliban do what need done."

He raced down the hall, but his limp was much slower with a person on his shoulder, and his brother and wolf could run fast.

"We not reach the door before my brother and his meanie get us," Caliban panted.

Thanan stopped. "Keep going. I'll hold them back."

"No!" Miram cried. "They'll kill you."

"Go, Caliban," Thanan ordered.

Caliban nodded and turned the corner toward the jungle door. Shots from the magic gun rang out, and a pointy-nosed wolf howled.

He placed his hand on the pad, and the door slid open. With Miram screaming and hitting his back, calling for her father and Thanan, Caliban ran into the jungle.

After several feet, he set her on her feet, expecting her to run back to Mother's place. But Miram gripped his hand.

"Let's go," she said, her sad eyes staring over his shoulder.

Caliban sprinted through the jungle, holding Miram's hand. He extended his senses outward; he could smell jungle cats some distance away. The stench of the ugly giant acid spiders mixed with the lizard cats. Caliban heard the leathery wings of the killer birds hovering near the jungle's canopy. Each smell and sound held terror and death. Miram seemed unaffected by the sounds, glancing about as if they were walking through her woods instead of Mother's deadly jungle.

"We not safe here," Caliban said, hoping to strike the proper fear within her.

She shook her head. "I am safe, Caliban. I've been preparing for this day."

Caliban shook his head, and he stopped by a tall vine tree. "We should climb to be safer."

"No, Caliban, climbing would do nothing here." Miram took small steps, like she was walking through her forest to observe and draw. "The lizard cats can climb, the acid spiders tongues could reach us, and the killer eagles could pick us off like fruit out of a tree."

Caliban shuddered. She was right; they would be dead soon. Their smell would attract all the terrors.

But nothing came closer. If anything, the sounds and smells drifted away. Why would Mother's hungry pets leave them alone? Caliban looked at Miram. She stood confidently, examining the closest tree, and then watching an insect flit away from them.

"Magic," Caliban sputtered.

She nodded. "Yes. Father uses nanobots to hurt you, but I figured out how to make them help me. Once inside the jungle, my nanobots were activated. Pheromones leak from my every pore. Nothing in the Witch's Jungle will bother us."

Caliban was confused. Nanobots? Pheromones? These words were long and strange, tumbling in his brain like pebbles down a cliff.

Miram put her hand on his shoulder. "I use magic, Caliban. The magic is inside me, and your mother's horrors won't bother us."

Caliban felt warmth shoot from her gentle touch. This was just how he'd hoped, Miram and Caliban together, alone and happy. Her magic would keep them safe, and not even foul Rissa or his stupid brothers would dare bother them in the jungle.

Shouts interrupted Caliban's pleasant feelings, echoing from deeper in the jungle. Popping sounds came next, which sounded like guns or rocks striking rocks. Jungle cats roared.

"More spacemen," Caliban said.

"How far?" Miram asked.

"Not sure. Half a mile, maybe less. They die."

"Help them, Caliban."

He hesitated. He didn't have Miram's magic inside him; the magic inside him ripped him apart, it didn't protect him from jungle meanies. And Caliban did not want to help humans; whenever he helped humans, things got worse.

"Please, Caliban," she pleaded. "I will follow, but you can move so much faster. Please help them." Tears filled her eyes as more screams filled the air.

Why did Miram care about spacemen she'd never met? Kind, good Miram. Yes, he would help the new spacemen if he could. He could be good like Miram, good for Miram.

He climbed the nearest tree, scaling dozens of feet into the air. He gripped one of the thick vines, tugging on it to make sure it was strong. He'd seen Balthazar do this when he and some brothers had saved

Caliban from lizard cats. If Balthazar and the brothers could do it, so could Caliban.

He swung for the next tree, reaching it easily. He grabbed another vine and pulled. Soon he didn't touch or swing for the trees, but moved vine to vine like he'd seen Balthazar do.

The human screams grew louder, and Caliban stopped in a tree on the edge of a small clearing. Ten lizard cats surrounded eight humans. Two jungle cats lay dead near four humans. One of the men fired his gun, and a flash of blue struck one of the cats but ended in sparks and nothing else. The tough, thick hide of the cat protected it. Mother made only strong, hard things.

A man shouted in a language which sounded like dogs barking. The man stood in the middle of the others, a long sword in one hand. He was the biggest man with muscles which reminded Caliban of Balthazar. He had a presence like Balthazar; the other men clearly followed him. The man said something else, and all the men dropped their guns and pulled out short swords. One man responded, and then their leader growled viciously. The men tensed, ready to fight to their death. And they would die; ten lizard cats would shred ten men, even strong ones with swords.

Caliban leaped from his hiding place, sailing through the air and landing on one of the cats. He quickly twisted the cats head, snapping its neck. After only a moment, he jumped back into the air. Lizard cats attacked in twos, and his feet just cleared the claws of two leaping cats who didn't like Caliban killing one of their friends. He flipped and landed with his hands on their throats. One slashed him across the chest, but he ignored the burning wound. With his large left hand, he snapped another neck, and then he slammed the one who'd slashed him to the ground, placing his foot at the base of its throat. He pulled with both hands, yanking its skull free. He tossed it away and growled. Mother only made terrible things, and Caliban was the most terrible of all.

Three dead cats beneath him, and the remaining five pulled away. The men looked at him, eyes wide, swords outstretched.

Miram ran into the clearing, and the cats howled, dashing into the jungle.

One of the men stepped toward Caliban, his sword raised. Caliban did not flinch; he didn't fear a man and his tiny little knife.

"Stop." The largest man impeded the attacker with his arm outstretched.

Miram came to Caliban's side, looking down at the carnage below his feet. "Well done, Caliban."

He bent down into his usual hunch and purred as she stroked his neck.

"Who are you?" the largest man said in Mother's language.

"I am Miram. Who are you?"

"King Khayr of Nooteezia."

Miram giggled. "I'm supposed to believe the king of Nooteezia came into our jungle? That seems unlikely."

The man smiled. "Unlikely as it may seem, I assure you I am the king and I am here."

"What is the king of Nooteezia doing on my world?"

"Looking for some lost Lanopians."

Miram laughed again. "You've found a bunch of lost Lanopians, some in the stars, and some here."

"Who are you? How did you come here? Were you on the *Marsil*?"

"I don't know what a *Marsil* is. I'm the daughter of the exiled Lanopian Sparo, and we've been here for a long time, most of my life." She bowed deeply and looked back up at the strong king. "Welcome to Vesta II, King of Nooteezia."

chapter 52

PLANS UNDONE

here were dozens of humans now, all following the large man who called himself a king. More had arrived shortly after Caliban and Miram had rescued them.

The king and his men listened as Miram explained what was happened inside Mother's place. With Miram's encouragement, Caliban shared a few details, but shame burned within him when he thought of how he'd helped the woman Rissa. Why had he been stupid enough to trust a human like her? She was like Mother, like Sparo.

But this king didn't seem like either of them. He listened to Caliban speak and met Caliban's eyes without fear or hate. Were kings better than other humans? Smarter? Kinder? Caliban could not say, as this was the first king he'd met.

"I need to get inside that place before Rissa kills anyone," King Khayr said after Miram and Caliban finished the explanation.

"I can get you inside," Caliban said.

Miram knelt next to Caliban and patted his shoulder. "This is your chance to redeem yourself. Prove to me, prove to them," she pointed at the king, "that you can be trusted."

He nodded vigorously. "I can be trusted. Caliban not stupid anymore. Caliban only listen to Miram and the fighter king. Caliban not trust anyone else."

He led them through the rest of the jungle and to the door to Mother's place. The king man led his people, strong soldiers who carried big guns and swords. Miram stood with some of the soldiers in the back, out of view of the door. She would be safe from mean Rissa or anyone else.

The king mumbled to his soldiers in his language, and Caliban hunched in front, waiting for the order to open the door. Even if Rissa had Sparo's magic, she wouldn't be able to stop the king and his men.

The king looked at Caliban, his eyes holding none of the disgust humans usually carried. Was it respect? How would Caliban know? He was so used to disgust, disappointment, and rage, he didn't know what anything else looked like.

"Let us in," the king said in Mother's language.

Caliban nodded and touched the hand pad. The door swooshed open, and he stood to the side. The soldiers rushed in; their leaders had memorized Miram's instructions on how to get to Mother's room, so they didn't need Caliban to guide them any farther.

Caliban stepped inside after the last soldier, and the door slid shut behind him. The king and his men had a mission to stop Rissa; Caliban had his own mission, given to him by sweet Miram: find Sparo and make sure he lived.

Limping down an empty hallway, Caliban thought of the future. Miram assured him he'd have no more masters, that he'd be free. As much as he loved Miram, and as clever and beautiful as she was, she was only a girl, too young to make such promises. Certainly Sparo would kill Caliban or at least hurt him badly; Sparo did not forgive easily. He'd spent thousands of moons plotting to kill a brother who'd betrayed him.

But still Caliban walked toward Sparo's room. Miram worried that her father would be killed by the terrible Rissa lady the moment she saw the king and his men. So Caliban limped to the room to save Sparo, even though Sparo might kill him once he got there. He had broken Sparo's magic ball, but he knew better than to think Sparo helpless. The old man always had tricks.

Caliban slowed as he rounded a corner. He heard nothing but the neverending swish of air through the facility and the buzz of electricity. No one had come for Sparo.

Caliban placed his hand on the pad, but nothing happened. He did it again, and the pad beeped angrily.

"It's not going to let you in."

Caliban wheeled to face his brother Stacra, the mean one, with his pointy-nosed wolf at his side. The beast's stomach growled, empty and unfed, and Stacra's heartbeat increased, ready to fight. Somehow he hadn't heard their approach.

"I've been sent to kill the man behind that door, your old master," his brother said. "What are you here to do, Caliban?"

"Protect him," Caliban replied.

Confusion covered Stacra's stupid, blue face. "Why? You wanted out from under the old man, and now you protect him? Are you truly that stupid?"

"Caliban not stupid."

Stacra laughed. "Yes, you are stupid. Do you even know the differences between my brothers and your flawed carcass?"

"Blue brothers uglier, dumber." Caliban smiled at his quick response.

"No, Caliban." Stacra slowly shook his head. "We have real human minds stolen from humans. You have nothing. You were a failure, a blank screen that failed to become anything useful."

The blue brothers had the minds of humans? Did they get human brains? Caliban did not understand, and he felt stupid. Why did so many know what Caliban did not?

"Yes, now you realize how dumb you are," Stacra said. "Sycorax let you live, and Balthazar saw you as a brother. Dax is still polluted by the sympathy others showed you. I am not. You're an older version, a prototype, and it's time we erased you."

With a click of his tongue, Stacra's wolf charged Caliban, knocking him onto his back. It sunk its teeth deep into his left shoulder and then raked its front claws across his belly.

Caliban felt the searing pain, but it did not distract him like Stacra's biting words had. It did not matter if the blue brothers had human brains, which was weird and gross. They were not his brothers, not really. Caliban was different, Caliban was alone. And Caliban was Mother's best.

He balled his right fist and struck the wolf three times in the ribs. On the third strike, they cracked like thunder. The wolf whimpered and released Caliban's shoulder.

He pulled his legs into his chest and put his feet on the wolf's belly. With a firm kick, he sent the wolf flying at its master. Stacra tumbled underneath the creature's weight.

Ignoring the pain and blood, Caliban came to his feet, ready for Stacra's attack. The blue brother pushed the wolf off him, standing over his fallen pet. The wolf whimpered.

Stacra glared at Caliban. "You will die for hurting him."

Caliban said nothing.

Stacra stepped forward and unleashed a series of vicious blows. Caliban blocked most of them, but his left arm was slow to respond to his thoughts, and his mind became fuzzier with the loss of blood. Stacra had been created to fight and kill, and he was good at it.

But Stacra was sloppy. He hadn't fought as much as Caliban had, hadn't fought alone like Caliban had. After Stacra connected with Caliban's ailing shoulder, Caliban leaned against the wall, looking weak and wounded. Everyone saw him this way: crippled and useless.

Stacra's heartbeat raced, the thrill of his near victory filling him. He raised both hands above his head, a kill shot to be rained down on Caliban's skull.

Caliban bolted upright, grabbing Stacra's chin with his powerful left hand, the jaw cracking in his grip. Before a stunned Stacra could respond, he launched the top of his head against the blue lizard man's throat. Another satisfying crack and Stacra slumped to the floor. To be sure, Caliban lifted Stacra's head in both hands and slammed it five times against the unforgiving metal floor. Stacra's breath was gone, and his heartbeat faded. His brains and blood painted the floor.

Caliban stepped over to the wounded wolf, tears growing in his eyes. He didn't know why he was crying; he'd never cried before. This wounded pet was more like him than the blue brothers. Caliban had been a pet all his life, yoked to stupid masters. Stacra had acted like he loved the wolf, but the stupid blue lizard man had to have known his pet wouldn't survive against Caliban. Even crippled, he was strong. Stacra had seen him kill Balthazar and Mother.

Caliban patted the wolf's head as its breathing slowed and its heart marched toward death. "Caliban sorry. Wolf not deserve death, wolf not understand. People use us, let us suffer."

He curled against the dying wolf and cried.

The Bizretrir ship had come out of its starjump inside the asteroid belt in Vesta a few hours before. Claribel's stomach was just now calming after the travel. She hated starjumping. At least this time she hadn't rejected the contents of her stomach.

The starjumper was approaching orbit around Vesta II. When they'd arrived in the system, the captain had contacted King Khayr's men, but they hadn't heard from the king himself; he led a group of soldiers on a raid of the Sycorax base. Claribel hoped against hope they'd find Thanan alive and well. She also felt a twinge of guilt when she hoped they might find the High Regent dead. Rissa's death would make things easier, elevating Thanan to a powerful position and ushering in a new era for Lanopi. But she wouldn't allow her emotions to drag her that low; in bringing down the High Regent, Claribel would not become her mother.

"Incoming message from King Khayr." A stiff voice rang in her small room. The starjump captain had given her his quarters and a bit of privacy. The screen in front of her revealed her husband's face. He looked as handsome and strong as ever, though he had a bandage on his left cheek.

"Welcome to Vesta, Queen Claribel." He smiled slightly, and Claribel had to resist returning his warmth like an enraptured school girl.

"Good to see you well, King Khayr. What's going on down there?"

"We took the facility with the help of a girl named Miram and one of Sycorax's discarded creations. We have the High Regent in custody, and your brother is being attended by our medical staff. He was hurt helping Miram escape your mother."

Claribel let out a deep breath. Thanan was alive. As she basked in the good news, the name Miram tickled her consciousness. "Miram? I didn't hear anyone but that name listed on the *Marsil's* manifest."

"She wouldn't be on that. Her father is also here, a man named Sparo. He was a senator on your world a decade ago."

Claribel let out a deep breath. Senator Sparo and his daughter had survived? How? Their starjumper had disappeared exactly according to Rissa's plan; nothing had been heard from them in nearly ten years.

"The message to Lazlo was from Sparo," Claribel concluded.

"Yes," Khayr responded. "Sparo orchestrated this using Sycorax technology. He and his daughter have been stranded here. They recently got jumpnet capability, but Sparo opted for revenge instead of a rescue."

Sparo, the exiled senator, the falsely accused terrorist. "What of Sparo's wife, Eliel?"

Khayr shook his head. "I didn't know of the wife; only Sparo and his daughter are here."

"And what of the High Regent?" Claribel asked. "How is she reacting to all this?"

"She's under guard, and she's not happy about it," Khayr said, his eyebrows raised. "She's threatening to end our alliance and even intimated that Nooteezia and Lanopi could be headed for war. She demands to see me, but so far, I've kept my distance per your instructions."

"You arrested her?" Claribel couldn't keep the shock from her voice.

"Not officially. I'm just not letting her connect with her ship or people, and I've isolated her from the other Lanopians."

Khayr's forced isolation sounded a lot like an arrest, but Claribel decided not to argue semantics. This is why she'd come, to avoid a diplomatic mess like this. Now she'd have to figure out how to fix it.

"It was the right choice," the king continued. "She had ordered the death of Sparo and his daughter, and she was threatening your brother after he helped Miram and Caliban escape."

Even a few days ago, hearing that Rissa had threatened Thanan would have been shocking. Now that news just formed a consistent pattern with the High Regent's past behavior.

"Who's Caliban?" she asked.

"He's a prototype Sycorax created. He's survived all these years since Lazlo shut down the Lanopian program. He'd been living with Sparo and Miram."

Claribel nodded, considering. A vestige of the Sycorax program remained, and they could not let the High Regent have the technology those mercenaries left behind, especially if Rissa was serious about dissolving the alliance with Nooteezia. Mother would use this to her supreme advantage unless they stopped her.

"We don't have any real grounds for holding her against her will," Claribel said. "This could very well mean war, diplomatic or otherwise."

The king did not flinch at Claribel's mild chastisement. "We did what we thought we must. We have evidence of her misdeeds. The man Sparo initiated a security protocol after Rissa entered the building, and all of the High Regent's conversations were recorded. Sparo is helping my men splice it together right now. So far, we have your mother ordering Sparo's death and threatening to kill Thanan and your father. She also spoke of violating several treaties, namely by aggressively taking this neutral system as part of Lanopi. We had grounds and reason to be careful."

Claribel paused. The recordings were significant. Rissa was usually more careful than that, but she hadn't been in complete control of her environment. And Claribel had to stop thinking of the High Regent as infallible; even the great Rissa, daughter of Marsil, made mistakes.

"That gives us leverage," Claribel replied, "but I'm still not sure what we do with that information."

"Wouldn't the Lanopian courts be interested in plots of murder and plans to break intergalactic treaties?"

"Possibly, but the High Regent controls the courts as tightly as she controls everything else on my home world. I think they'd find technicalities to dismiss most if not all of the charges, assuming they even decided to hear the case. And I'm sure Rissa's lawyers would find a reason to get everything dismissed."

Silence slipped between them. Khayr's decision had been a rash one, a military decision made in the moment with mostly short-term considerations. But maybe, just maybe, this was the crack Claribel and Thanan had been searching for to remove Rissa from power. It was a decade or two sooner than they'd thought possible, but these revelations, combined with the first assassination attempt--if Claribel could connect the High Regent to that--might be enough to turn sentiment among the people, especially the aristocracy she needed to maintain control of. This could be their moment.

"We are where we are," Claribel finally said. "Let's see how we can use this. I'm coming to the planet. Keep Rissa isolated; I'll be the first one to talk with her."

"As you wish, Queen Claribel."

chapter 53

QUEEN CLARIBEL

laribel stepped off the landing ship and onto the gray sand of the planet's surface. Soldiers flanked her, their eyes scanning a barren, rocky plain. From this vantage point, Vesta II looked lifeless, but she knew better. To the north lay the jungle Khayr and his men had landed in, a place teeming with monstrous, artificial life. Gray deserts covered most of this continent, but besides the jungle, there were some wooded areas to the north and a massive mountain range beyond that, visible in the distance. The topography on this small planet was remarkably varied, and Khayr's scientists were eager to explore the new world.

Six soldiers led Claribel toward the large silver building that gleamed in the sunlight. Based on their scans of the planet, this was the only manmade structure on Vesta II. But it was not the small outpost one might expect on a nearly virgin world. It was nearly as large as the Regency Palace on Lanopi. The outside walls were a reflective silver, smooth and rounded. It looked like a fashionable private starjumper that had landed on the planet's surface.

As they entered the facility, activity buzzed around Claribel. Soldiers searched for unfound dangers, and scientists scurried about looking to unlock untold secrets. How had this world remained hidden from the known systems? How had Sycorax remained hidden? Lazlo had told Khayr's men that the facility had been abandoned by Lanopi after a revolt by some of the genetically engineered soldiers. Lazlo's team had been unable to unlock most of the facility's secrets. Would the Nooteese have better luck?

The soldiers led her into a large room where they found Khayr surrounded by several of his officers. He dismissed the soldiers shortly after she entered the room, leaving them alone.

King Khayr smiled at her, and she returned the gesture. Despite the bandage on his face, he looked beautiful. Her heart beat faster. She knew she shouldn't let her feelings drift this way; this was a distraction she couldn't afford. But her feelings moved as they willed, and despite her reservations, she let them.

Section break?

Khayr dressed in a burgundy uniform with high black boots and a form-fitting tunic. It was then she noticed that the small bandage on his face wasn't his only wound; he also had his arm in a sling.

"Don't be concerned," Khayr said. "My wounds are minor; others were not so lucky."

Claribel doubted luck had much to do with it. "I think, as your queen, it is my right to be concerned when you're injured."

He smiled again, and her heart thundered. She'd been a fool that night in his chambers, fueled by wine and battered emotions. But his gravity held her again, and she couldn't blame alcohol this time.

"Kings should not rush into battle."

"Maybe not. But I only know one way to do this. I've never been an administrator, Claribel; I'm a warrior. It's all I really know. Becoming king was an accident."

She took a deep breath. He wasn't like the politicians she'd known her entire life, scheming men and women grasping for whatever power their greedy hands could hold. She'd also met leaders from throughout the known systems and been impressed by very few. Nooteezia's king was an aberration. More of a schemer than he'd admit, but with an underlying purity she'd never seen. He was the sort of leader Ona had been coaching Claribel to become.

"You are going to meet with your mother." The king stood and stepped toward her.

"Yes."

"Would you like me to join you in the discussion? I know I don't need to warn you about her, but if you feel a team approach would be best. . ."

Claribel waved her hand. "This I need to do alone. The High Regent is a fierce opponent, but for the first time in my life, I have the upper hand."

"Whatever path we take, we need to be thorough and swift. As my people are fond of saying, 'You can kill a condar bear by cutting its head off, but it's safer to cut off its legs as well.'"

Claribel smiled. "My mother is much more dangerous than a condar bear, though just as cantankerous. The plan is to weaken her, to lessen her grip on Lanopi. I believe we have the information to force her into giving up some power, maybe to resign."

The king took her hands in his. His dark eyes held hers, all the aloofness from their wedding ceremony replaced by tenderness. "You are the diplomatic warrior, so I will defer to your judgement. But if you need me, I will be close by. Thanan will be as well."

She wanted to see her brother before she confronted the High Regent, but he'd try and talk her out of this, saying they should wait or do it together. But Claribel needed to do this alone. She hoped that was sound strategy and not misplaced emotion.

She stepped closer to him, their bodies touching. His eyes held more than tenderness; he looked at her with respect, and that intensified her attraction. He was handsome, kind, and strong--a hero more likely to be found in an old-fashioned story than in flesh and blood. Their union had been nothing more than a political alliance. Could or should it be more than that? Could the warrior king love the skinny politician?

She reached up and touched his face, and he smiled again. Then she leaned forward, bringing her lips to his. At first, he did not kiss her back, and for the briefest moment, she considered pulling back, shame rising that she'd been too forward, assumed too much.

But his unwounded had reached for her hip, pulling her close. She placed her other hand on his chest and fell into the kiss.

The door slid open and Claribel stepped into the small room where the High Regent waited. The leader of Lanopi stood against the far wall, dressed in Phana's uniform.

"I like the outfit," Claribel quipped.

Rissa glared. "You act rashly, Claribel. You bring our nations to the brink of war, for what? So you can play queen? You're still the silly little girl I pushed away from leadership. You've proven my intuition."

Claribel smiled; she was immune to the High Regent's acerbic barbs. "We are not at the brink of war, High Regent."

"I will decide that."

Claribel paced the room, clutching her pad to her chest. Per her direction, the room had been emptied. No chairs, no windows, no distractions.

"No, Mother, you will not."

Rissa bristled but did not respond.

"And I will tell you why."

Claribel stopped pacing and held out her pad. With a tap, an image appeared above of it of her father prostrate on the jungle floor. They watched his confession of unfairly condemning Sparo, Eliel, and the girl to a death in space.

Mother's face remained flat. "I had nothing to do with that. If Alazar committed treason, I was not involved. You'll find nothing to connect it to me. All the judges will see is a desperate old man trying to save his hide from a deranged exile."

"Oh, Mother, I won't use judges. *Those who rule with you are not treated as commoners, they are treated more like dogs. When loyal, reward them openly and lavishly. When treacherous, punish them severely and privately.* I'd give this to Senator Mura Chani. I'm sure she could come up with a creative use for the information."

Claribel had hit a nerve, breaking Rissa's placidity if only for a brief moment. "Oh, Claribel, you're still playing children's games."

"I'm not done."

Another wave and different image played. This was Rissa, dressed as Phana, and her elite guard Cruz trying to board an escape ship. Two guards stepped into their way, holding out their hands to stop them. Cruz attacked one, knocking him down in an instant. The other soldier reached for his gun, but the elite shot him in the chest with a plasma bolt. The first soldier stood back up and received a plasma bolt to the face.

"The High Regent of Lanopi," Claribel said, "stepping over the mangled bodies of loyal soldiers, fleeing like a bird before a powerful storm. This one could find its way to the jumpnet, giving the tabloids and your opponents fodder for years. The dedicated servant of Lanopi revealed as a cruel coward."

The High Regent's face remained impassive, but her shoulders slumped slightly. Claribel was winning.

"And that's not even all of it," Claribel continued. "Sparo had every conversation in this place recorded, including your orders to have him killed by one of the Sycorax soldiers, and when you plotted with your elite guard to kill your husband and possibly your son." Claribel held the pad against her side and began pacing again. "By themselves, each of these acts could be attributed to duress, but together, well, I think it will be enough to unravel your entire regime."

Rissa grinned. "You are overplaying what you have."

Claribel stopped and held the pad out to her mother. "I am not. Listen to the other conversations. You admit to your part in the plot against Sparo in a circular way, and you disparage almost all of your allies. It's a beautiful series of rants. Listen."

Rissa looked at the pad but kept her hands at her side.

"Suit yourself." She tucked the pad against her side.

"What do you want, Claribel?"

"I want you to resign from the position of High Regent and name Thanan your chosen successor."

The High Regent's eyes held shock for a moment, but then she laughed. "You have to be joking, Claribel. And is Thanan with you on this? Have my two little protégés been conspiring behind my back?"

Claribel ignored the deflection. "You will resign, or I will dump this all over the jumpnet, and the Lanopian courts will have no choice but to open an investigation. As I said, Senator Mura Chani and other opponents will jump all over it. They've been looking for a weakness for decades, and this will give them a starjumper's chance of dumping you completely."

"I'll declare martial law," Rissa replied. "I'll shut down the courts and prepare for war."

"Then we'll kill you now."

Rissa's eyes grew wide. "You wouldn't dare." Her voice held more malice than anything Claribel had ever heard from her mother.

"If it is best for Lanopi and the known systems, we will do it." It was a bluff; Claribel could not order the death of Rissa, not without the courts behind her. But Rissa didn't need to know that.

"We? You and your new husband?" The High Regent dipped the last word in a sarcastic tone.

Claribel ignored another deflection. "And why should my ruthlessness surprise you? You trained me, raised me to be devoid of compassion. And, it could be called revenge, since you tried to have me killed almost ten years ago."

The High Regent's eyes lit with something for a brief second, maybe recognition, but she said nothing.

"I never really understood Senator Sparo's exile," Claribel continued.

"Why not put on a trial? You made many public examples in that purge of the Onala Liberators, but not of Sparo. But I understand better now why exiling Sparo was the best choice: Sparo wasn't guilty of anything, and a trial might have revealed Balith had planted everything. And that might lead back to you, since you planted the idea with Balith to frame his brother.

"But why Sparo? He was from Onal, but it was more than that. He wrote a paper at university calling for more frequent elections, a more transparent democracy. He was also anti-military spending. Removing him was removing a rival. He'd always been subtle in his opposition to you, but I found evidence of it in his writings and public commentary. And you had never been public in your disdain for him, but I know you, and after reading his beliefs, I knew he was just the type of rival you would despise: idealistic, democratic, and imminently popular. My failed assassination attempt was the perfect cover to bury one of your rivals in the vicious way you prefer. Would you like to finish this, or should I continue my version?"

The High Regent remained silent.

"So you ordered me killed, somehow manipulating the Liberators to do it. You'd already decided I wasn't fit to lead, so I could become a symbol of unity, a martyr against your enemies. But Adriana stopped my death. I'm sure you already knew what to do if I survived; your plans always have secondary options."

"You have no proof of these outlandish accusations," the High Regent finally replied. "No one will believe I ordered an assassination attempt on my daughter. None of this is true. It's the fantasy of a desperate girl who's bitter her mother decided she wasn't fit to lead."

"I'm sure you were thorough, Mother, but even the most silent of predators leaves a few marks. As the courts hammer you about the accusations we'll put forward, we'll find your connection to my close encounter with death."

"I will not step down," Rissa said. "I will fight these accusations in court, declare martial law in order to preserve the strength and stability of my people." She was making a political speech now, assuming the conversation was recorded. "You've learned nothing from me, Claribel, and you and Thanan clearly don't have it in you to be true leaders. You threaten me with death, but I don't believe you can do it. I think it's an empty threat, because if you wanted me dead, I'd be dead. No, you're still playing the game with compassion and hope. The game we play requires neither."

The High Regent had called Claribel's bluff.

"I learned many things from you," Claribel responded evenly. "But mostly I learned the kind of leader I did not want to be, the kind of person I could not be. You see this as weakness, trusting the system and the people to do the right thing. But how will the senators react to you sending one of them to his death? I think you overestimate your power. It may seem complete, but it still rests on the fear and respect of the aristocracy; I don't believe you will have either of those things anymore. Step down, or we will absolutely bury you under the weight of all your misdeeds."

Mother smiled again, her teeth showing with feral intensity. "You have leverage for now, but you will not have it forever. You've entered waters filled with predators you can neither understand nor truly fight. Chimra smiles on you today, but without her favor, you'll always be the same insecure little girl afraid to do what must be done."

Claribel stepped past Rissa and the door opened. "Goodbye, Mother," she said without looking back. The door closed behind her. She stopped, closed her eyes, and took a deep breath. She clutched her pad to her chest to keep her arms from shaking, but she couldn't slow her rapid pulse. She'd gone in believing she had the High Regent on the ropes, but Rissa's confident retorts had dented Claribel's conviction. Would all this come to naught? Would Rissa weather this solar flare like she'd deflected other crises in the past?

No, Claribel would have hope before fear. She'd trust the Lanopians to see through Rissa's web of lies now and find the rot underneath her veneer. Claribel breathed in deeply again, filling herself with more hope. No, the High Regent wouldn't escape this time. Even if Rissa resisted the change, Claribel chose to let hope drown out her fear.

chapter 54

CLARIBEL AND THANAN

the gray field south of the Sycorax complex held half a dozen jumpships, three with the distinctive obsidian of Nooteezia and three with the shiny silver of Lanopi. But the two groups did not mix, did not interact. What had recently been a celebrated alliance was now an icy coexistence.

Claribel stood on the invisible line between the two camps, the symbol of their once strong coalition. She hoped that the events of the past week wouldn't destroy that; it would only make Pastrack and Alandria stronger if Lanopi and Nooteezia abandoned each other. Officially, there was no rift yet. High Regent Rissa's imprisonment by the Nooteese was not public knowledge. So far, Rissa had praised Nooteezia for their bold rescue, saving her and her people from the deranged revenge attempt of marooned, presumed dead, senator. From the outside, it might have still appeared a strong connection.

Claribel hoped they'd crippled the High Regent enough with their threats of exposing her indiscretions on Vesta II, but more fuel had been added to Rissa's rage since Claribel's brief conversation with her mother.

First, King Khayr had granted asylum to Sparo, his daughter Miram, and Lazlo. Sparo had agreed to give up his revenge in exchange for asylum on Nooteezia. The High Regent had demanded he be turned over to her elite; Claribel was sure the former senator wouldn't live to make it back to Lanopi if they did that. King Khayr had remained firm. Sparo had agreed, but only if his daughter Miram got the best schooling Nooteezia had to offer.

The other sticking point was Vesta II. The Nooteese technicians were working on the facility and exploring the planet. Though they'd discovered little of Sycorax's secrets, the potential of reverse-engineering what had been accomplished on this planet forty years before was worth the effort.

The High Regent claimed Vesta II as the official discovery of Lanopi since the Marsil had been the first starjumper to officially arrive in orbit. King Khayr countered that since his people had rescued the Lanopians, the claim was theirs under Nooteese law. So for the moment, both Lanopi and Nooteezia had agreed to depart the planet together, leaving the Sycorax facility unoccupied. Their claims to Vesta II, and to the Vesta system, would now find their way into the known systems' courts. The courts were notoriously slow and politically charged--a verdict could take a decade or more after appeals were heard. The more likely scenario was either a compromise between the two planets or war. Claribel hoped they could reach a settlement which wouldn't end with her two worlds pitted against each other.

She took a deep breath. She couldn't solve everything, not here, not now. A compromise would be possible, but only if the High Regency changed hands. Claribel could not fathom a scenario in which Rissa gave up Vesta II. She hoped they had enough to disable the woman's power, and that Thanan could step in to fill the void.

Claribel looked up to see Thanan walking toward her, Lanopi's best hope for a brighter future. His tattered fivestar pilot uniform from the crash had been replaced with a brand new one. He looked the part of a future world leader, his chiseled frame filling his starched uniform. His eyes caught hers and they both smiled.

"I'm sorry we have to part like this," Thanan said as he reached her. "But at least we don't have to pretend indifference anymore."

"I kind of liked our clandestine sibling relationship," Claribel quipped. "Publicly being friends won't be nearly as much fun."

Thanan hugged her. She fell into his embrace, wishing they could truly work together now. But Thanan had the hard part of their plan; he returned to Lanopi with a woman who'd likely want him dead for betraying her, and to a world which could be torn apart by the struggle for power.

Thanan pulled back but held her hands. "Look at my little sister, all grown up, a queen and everything."

"And my older brother, ready to take on the High Regent."

A comfortable silence came then, and they enjoyed a moment of peace before the oncoming tempest.

"I should be going," Thanan finally said. "Good luck, Bel. Nooteezia doesn't know what it has in you yet, but they'll learn."

"And Lanopi doesn't realize the great leader waiting in the wings," she replied. "You are a good man, Thanan, better than Rissa, better than grandfather Marsil, better even than great-grandmother Junda. You'll be the best leader Lanopi has had in a millennia, and you'll do it with compassion and grace."

Thanan smiled and hugged her again. "I love you, Bel. Remember that. I'm not sure I can live up to the man you think I am, but I will try." He pulled away. "And I brought you a present."

Thanan waved his hand, and a woman approached from one of the Lanopian drop ships carrying a large bag. Adriana, formerly of the elite, and now a member of Father's guard detail. And the only other person on Lanopi who'd known of Claribel and Thanan's continuing friendship.

"Hello, Queen Claribel," Adriana said, bowing her head.

"Adriana would like to come to Nooteezia," Thanan said. "You could have another person you can trust there, someone to watch your back."

Claribel had told Thanan everything the day before, including Rissa's involvement in the first assassination attempt and the most recent attempt on Nooteezia.

"She will protect you, Bel."

"I will try," Adriana added.

"You saved me from certain death nine years ago," Claribel said. "I have no doubt you'll be as good as your word."

"Farewell, sister." Thanan stepped up and kissed Claribel lightly on the forehead. "Wish me luck in taking down our good, old mother."

Claribel forced a smile, but it barely came. She couldn't help but feel like the past week's events had forced Thanan into a battle he wasn't quite ready to win.

Thanan turned and walked back to his jumpship, and Claribel deeply hoped she'd see him again.

Hope before fear.

Thanan turned before entering the jumpship to watch his sister and Adriana walk north toward the Sycorax facility. His sister had grown into the best person Thanan knew, the leader Lanopi needed but would never have. Thanan had more respect for Bel than he could ever express, and that's why doing what he had to do to ensure Lanopi's future would be so hard; Bel would never forgive him for it.

But it had to be done. To most, Thanan seemed like a joker, the spoiled son of the High Regent. He was liked, but not respected, and that had been on purpose. Mother was never to know the threat he posed to her. And though it was a couple years ahead of the timeline, he had to act. If Rissa landed on Lanopi, she'd declare martial law and have Thanan and Alazar arrested. Despite Bel's hope, Thanan knew the courts would side with the High Regent, and she'd remain in power. Thanan likely faced execution, and Nooteezia and Lanopi would be pointed toward war. But Thanan could not let Lanopi walk down that dark path. So High Regent Rissa would never set foot on Lanopi again.

Thanan had been planning this for years, developing scenarios to kill his mother. Her death needed to look accidental or, if not, like the act of one of their enemies. Then Thanan would step forward to claim the High Regency and bring stability and peace. No one would oppose his claim as most political forces on Lanopi believed they could use Thanan as a puppet to bring forth their agenda; he'd cultivated that belief among the planet's powerbrokers. Even the ambitious Mura Chani would fall in line. Thanan could not wait to see all their faces when it became clear he wouldn't fall under anyone's control.

Killing Mother would be simpler now--no need to make it look like an accident. This entire incident would look like one of their enemies had done it, especially with Pastrack's outburst at the wedding. Thanan controlled half of Mother's elite, and her death had already been ordered. She'd die during the starjump, and Thanan would move to consolidate his power the moment the Marsil reached the Lanopi system.

Exquisite planning creates its own fate. One of Mother's precious maxims. Too bad the High Regent would die not realizing her death came at the hands of her most vicious and destructive creation: him.

Bel had shared with Thanan her theory about the assassination attempt from nine years before. Thanan had feigned surprise, but he'd known for years; it was the only explanation which fit the facts. Bel saw the good in the universe, the good in the souls of mankind. When news of Mother's death reached her, it was likely Bel would figure it out, not fooled by blame being placed at the feet of Pastrack or Alandria. Bel might see through Thanan's plot, and he only could hope she wouldn't hate him for stooping to Mother's level. But Thanan could see no other way. War with Pastrack and Alandria was inevitable anyway, and better that he lead it than Mother.

Thanan took one last look at Bel as she disappeared into the distant building. He turned and walked into the ship, ready to do what must be done.

chapter 55

CALIBAN AND FIVE

aliban licked the last of the sticky sugar from his fingers. Miram had brought him a tray full of sweetbread from the mean High Regent's spaceship. He'd eaten all of it, not able to control himself and save some for later. There might not be a later, so best to eat it all now.

But his stomach ached as he lay on the floor of Arena One. He had been in this room many times, ripping apart Mother's creations. But no one watched him now, and the room was empty except a layer of dust and the crumbs of the sweetbread.

Of course, someone might be watching. Mother and Sparo had had eyes everywhere watching everything. Did the big king man watch him? They'd let him roam these last few days, though the king's people were careful not to get to close to him. Their caution was good-- Caliban was strong and could easily kill any of them, especially if they didn't have guns.

He wasn't sure why he'd come to Arena One to eat the sweetbread. He'd wanted to take Miram to her woods and eat it there, but she'd had little time for him in the days since he'd saved Miram and helped the king. Was she spending her time with Thanan? The thought caused more churning in his stomach than even a tray full of sweetbread.

A door opened, and he immediately stood, rising to attention.

Queen Claribel entered. He'd seen her from a distance, the wife of the king and the daughter of the jerky Rissa. Her clothes were fancy, her long dress sparkling in the bright lights of the arena room. She was skinny, even skinnier than Miram, but taller, and her face was not as round as Miram's. She also wasn't pretty, not like Miram, not even like the stupid High Regent.

But her eyes. They reminded him of Sparo's before he'd started hating Caliban. They were strong and kind. Would Claribel turn on him like

Sparo had? Or could Caliban make better choices to keep her as a friend?

Behind her entered another person, a stocky, strong-looking woman with a gun strapped to her hip. No one trusted Caliban, not with a queen, not with anybody. And after betraying Mother and Sparo, Caliban doubted humans would ever trust him again.

"What is this place?" the queen asked.

"The arena." He spoke in Sparo's language. "This is where Caliban tested by Mother, where Caliban killed things."

Claribel frowned, her eyes sad. "I think we both had mothers who treated us poorly, who molded us for their own purposes." She looked toward the window walls as if she looked at someone else. Caliban followed her gaze, but there was no one there. "But we're under their dominion no longer. We're both free."

Free. Caliban wanted to believe the queen, whose voice sounded like the sweetest of sweetbreads. But he'd hoped before, and hope didn't last long, not for Caliban.

"The king's soldiers speak of your bravery and skill," she continued. "I've seen the video of you protecting Sparo, a mercy he didn't deserve from you."

Caliban flinched. Had she seen him cry like a wounded pup? Shame burned his chest.

"What do you want, Caliban?" the queen asked.

"Caliban not know what you mean."

"You are free now, Caliban. Sparo is no longer your master. You may remain here or come with us to Nooteezia or, well, whatever else you desire."

Whatever he desired? Was he allowed to want something? Something about choosing made him nervous, made him sick, or maybe it was the sweetbread filling his stomach. "What is Nooteezia? Will Miram be there?"

Claribel smiled. "A nice place, a place to start over. And yes, Miram will be there."

"Why?" Caliban stepped closer. "Why would you let Caliban come? I am a monster, a killer. Caliban not human, Caliban not like the queen, not like Miram."

"First, because you are a sentient being. You have rights which have been consistently abused since you were born." Claribel frowned. "First the woman scientist, then Sparo, and then my mother. Manipulated and controlled. But you are not an animal, Caliban. You should choose your own fate."

Hope swelled in his chest. Could it be possible?

"Second, I need you. You know Sycorax better than anyone living. You can help me stop them."

"Them? Sycorax is Mother. Sycorax is a woman."

Confusion filled the queen's face. "It's an organization, a group."

Caliban shook his head. "No. Sycorax is Mother's name. She controlled it all. Mean, cruel Mother. But I threw her off a cliff. Sycorax will bother no one no more."

Claribel pulled a pad from her dress and an image appeared above it. At first, Caliban only saw the king, standing with a small woman. "This picture was taken a few weeks ago. Who is this woman? Did she work with your mother?"

"No!" he shouted, jumping back against the window wall. "That is Mother! It can't be Mother. Mother is dead! This must be an old picture. Please tell me it's old!" Caliban crouched against the wall, trying to distance himself from the image.

The queen's eyes widened. "This is the same woman who created you?"

"Yes!" Caliban cried. "Mother lives. Oh no. Mother will find Caliban, Mother will kill Caliban!"

The queen put the pad away and stepped closer to him, placing her hand on his quivering shoulder. "That's not possible, Caliban. You told Sparo you killed her thirty years ago. And this is a picture of a young woman, someone maybe a few years older than me. Maybe this woman just looks like the woman you called Sycorax."

Caliban shook, fear gripping him. "Mother has strong magic. Mother more powerful than a king or a queen. Mother more powerful than death." Caliban crouched smaller, wondering if Mother watched him still, if Mother's eyes would always follow him.

The queen stepped away, her eyes focused in the distance. "Alive. Unbelievable. Sycorax is a person." The queen faced Caliban. "Will you help me find her?"

Caliban tried to stop shaking. "No. Caliban will hide where Mother can't find him. Caliban not want to find Mother."

"I will protect you as best as I can." The queen stepped closer and put a hand on his shoulder again, and somehow the gesture calmed him, as if some of her strength seeped into him. "You just need to answer some questions. I will keep you away from that foul witch. But I must find her, must stop her before she destroys everything. She's the most dangerous person in the known systems, a virus that needs to be eradicated."

Now Caliban could see Rissa's face in her daughter. It held a similar intensity, a boiling heat. But it lacked something: the meanness behind the power. Like Miram was like Sparo but different, like Caliban was like Mother but different, the queen was the same and different than the meanie High Regent. Maybe Claribel could face Mother. Caliban had chosen the opposite side of Mother all those moons ago. Mother did not forgive; he'd only be safe if someone ended her. But how could she stop a person that even death could not stop?

"Caliban will come to this Nootee place with the sweetbread queen. Caliban knows how bad Mother is, knows what she can do. Caliban will help."

Claribel smiled. "Thank you Caliban. You are braver than most, purer than most. I hope we can become friends."

Caliban kept his feelings buried, but a small sliver of hope shined through. A friend. Caliban wanted to believe he could have one. He nodded to the queen and flashed his best, tooth-filled smile. To his surprise, she smiled back, no disgust in her eyes. The small sliver of hope burned even brighter.

Member Five watched the river carve its way through the deep ravine. They could, with their acute senses, tell that the water had cut a meter deeper since they first saw this ravine as the prisoner of Sycorax. It had been many human years since, but the Whole did not feel time the same way humans did. Members lived for human millennia before they faded. Five had lived for more than two hundred human years. But since their imprisonment, they'd felt time in human terms, and it had caged them as much as Sycorax's prison.

Miram had learned how to free them, and the surviving members of the tribe had taken to space, eager to leave this system behind. They waited for Five, their impatience pulsing through their bond. The fear of being trapped had changed them. Before this, Five had never felt impatience among their kind. But Sycorax's prison had filled the tribe with an emotion unknown to them. But imprisonment had transformed Five even more. They could have fled just as quickly, but they remained to help Miram restore order and to keep Sparo from hurting Caliban. And despite all he'd done, how unfaithful he'd been, Five still felt something for Sparo. Not love, especially not the romantic kind that tripped up humans so often. But they felt something.

Freedom scared Five almost as much as enslavement. Since their release, they had felt the presence of the others in the tribe. The sensation was both familiar and alien. Five could feel them searching their presence, gingerly touching Five's new self. They said Five felt too human, not like a member of the Whole.

Even worse than that, the tribe felt foreign. They were emotionless, passionless. Five loved, hated, felt emotions on a level the Whole found primitive. Would this new consciousness, this Ariel persona, fade over time as they reintegrated with the tribe, or had they been forever changed into something that betrayed their own race?

"Good morning, Ariel, or should I call you by a different name?" Sparo's voice rang deep and rich, a perfect complement to the sound of the rushing water echoing through the ravine.

"Ariel is as good as any," Five replied.

Sparo stood beside them and looked into the ravine, his deep brown eyes contemplating its power. Humans used water, the earth, and now the stars, as sources of power. Would one such as this be able to resist using the Whole in a similar way? Would Sparo find more of their kind to enslave, even if their tribe flew free? No, Five would destroy Sycorax's technology before they left. Humans could not be trusted with it; they would use the Whole if they could, trap their kind again. That could not be allowed.

"This is an historic spot," Sparo intoned. "Somewhere along this ridge, Caliban threw Sycroax to her death."

"Killed his first master and betrayed his second one," Five said. "I think the woman Claribel is unwise to take him along. I feel for Caliban, but he is a mercurial creature created only to maim and destroy. Civil life will never suit him."

Sparo nodded. "I agree, but he is no longer my charge. And had I treated Caliban more kindly, he would have dismissed the High Regent's manipulation. Both Sycorax and I fed his rage by starving him of what he wants more than anything: human affection. Born in a lab, born of a womb, or born in the universe's expanse, all creatures need to feel like they belong.

"But Caliban is not the only one I've treated poorly." Sparo turned to Five. "You have been a friend, a loyal companion, and I've held you too tightly. You belong with your kind, Ariel, not confined to a human form, used in a human way. I have destroyed the files in the computer related to how to capture and hold a member of the Whole. Your race will be free."

"What do the others think I am?"

Sparo turned back to the ravine. "I've asked them not to pry. Miram tells everyone you are an artificial intelligence created by Sycorax. Regardless, I've destroyed the files."

Was Five ready to rejoin the greater universe, to leave this cursed planet behind? Were they ready to join the tribe and be part of the Whole again? A shot of fear rumbled through their soul, followed by shame at feeling afraid. Five shouldn't really feel or recognize these emotions, but they did. The Whole felt no fear, because they believed they had nothing to fear. And shame existed for weaker races. If that was true, if they felt something they shouldn't feel, what did that make them? And didn't the Whole have reason to fear humanity now?

"I should have freed you from the start," Sparo continued. "But I was selfish. I needed help to create a life here, and I couldn't see past my revenge. Truth be told, during most moments, I still want to find Balith and choke the life from him. But I have to let go. For Miram's sake, I need to let go."

They existed together for several minutes, watching the water rush by, listening to the call of a distant wolf. Though Vesta II held some beauty, Five would not miss this place and vowed to never return.

Sparo looked down at the river. "I know you likely do not feel the same, but I will miss you Ariel. I gave you my wife's appearance, hoping that it would give me comfort, hoping that in some small way you could replace her. Nothing can replace her, but I found an unexpected friend and companion. I wish you great fortune in your unfathomable future."

Nervousness pulsed through Five, fears swirling inside. Why couldn't they let go? Why would they want to continue to feel so human?

Five stretched out their being, keeping part of it there with Sparo. The universe and its expanse came to Five's senses, and the collective consciousness of their tribe. The other members of the tribe stretched throughout the system, their voices calling to Five, urging, their collective eagerness overwhelming them. At least one of the emotions coursing through the bond felt familiar: the thrill of exploration. The tribe had found its purpose again.

"Goodbye, Sparo." Five wanted to say more but held back. They needed to act of the Whole again and stop flirting with the trappings of humanity.

"Goodbye, Ariel." Tears ran down the man's clean cheeks, and they could see the sadness that often overwhelmed Sparo when he thought of his wife. Could he love Ariel like that? Did they mean nearly as much to him as his wife and daughter? Five had never considered that possibility. "Will I ever see you again?"

The tribe tugged, pushing toward the freedom of space. "I do not think so. The Whole never explores the same place twice, and all your known systems, save one, have been explored; we explored Lanopi and Nooteezia millennia ago. We will be reaching out beyond any stars you can see from one of your systems."

Sparo's eyes filled with more tears and his mouth twitched. Five felt like consoling him but resisted the urge.

"I did and still do consider you a friend," Five finally managed. "I also wish you good fortune in your new life. I wish you happiness."

Five could stand no more. They released the human-like form for the last time and launched into space. If a member could cry, Five would have. Sadness gripped them, trying to pull them back to the planet, another goodbye, a better parting. But the tribe chastised them for these human trappings, so Five buried their sadness deep, beyond the tribe. They had never held anything back before, never hidden anything from the tribe. Had this always been possible, an unknown ability buried by lack of use?

The tribe flew through open space, accelerating, the celestial winds of the Whole blowing through the universe, waiting for instructions on where to go, on what they would next see.

With instructions received, they moved away from Vesta. They moved faster than light, using the same starjumps humans used, only a million times more efficiently. Freedom drove them, and Five relished the power and liberty. The tribe was free. Five was free. Even if they'd changed forever, they were free.

• • •